baya

D1531995

Praise for the Ga

"What began as a fairly straightforward tale of 25... space to escape a ravaging disease on Earth became a deeper, broader, scarier, and more intellectually stimulating journey with every book."
—*Booklist* (starred review) on the Galahad series

"Part space opera, part mystery, the story draws readers in from the beginning with well-placed hooks, plenty of suspense, and a strong premise."
—*School Library Journal* on *The Comet's Curse*

"Grabs readers' attention with the very first page and never lets go. . . . Both a mystery and an adventure, combining a solid cast of characters with humor, pathos, growing pains, and just a hint of romance, this opener bodes well for the remainder of the series."
—*Kirkus Reviews* on *The Comet's Curse*

"A wonderful mix of science fiction and mystery."
—*Children's Literature* on *The Comet's Curse*

"Sci-fi fans will enjoy Testa's spare Asimovian plot, but even those leery of the genre will appreciate how each chapter alternates to the past to further flesh out our protagonists. Stealing the show is the *Galahad's* mischievous central computer, Roc, who speaks directly to the readers as he acts as a Greek chorus." —*Booklist* on *The Comet's Curse*

"Dom Testa has invented a highly original world packed with surprise, insight, and heart. Read it with your whole family, and enjoy the ride."
—*The Denver Post*

"I truly, honestly loved the first two books in this series and think I have a new obsession to burn through. . . . I *love* our diverse cast of crew members aboard the *Galahad*, both in terms of their widely different personalities and with regard to their backgrounds and ethnicities. . . . Absolutely recommended."

—*The Book Smugglers*

THE GALAHAD ARCHIVES
BOOK TWO

Into Deep Space

Dom Testa

TOR®
TEEN

A Tom Doherty Associates Book

New York

THE GALAHAD ARCHIVES BOOK TWO: INTO DEEP SPACE

The Cassini Code: A Galahad Book copyright © 2008 by Dom Testa

Reader's Guide copyright © 2010 by Tor Books

The Dark Zone: A Galahad Book copyright © 2011 by Dom Testa

Reader's Guide copyright © 2011 by Tor Books

Cosmic Storm excerpt copyright © 2011 by Dom Testa

All rights reserved.

Edited by Susan Chang

A Tor Teen Book
Published by Tom Doherty Associates, LLC
175 Fifth Avenue
New York, NY 10010

www.tor-forge.com

Tor® is a registered trademark of Tom Doherty Associates, LLC.

ISBN 978-0-7653-8340-2 (trade paperback)

Our books may be purchased in bulk for promotional, educational, or business use. Please contact your local bookseller or the Macmillan Corporate and Premium Sales Department at 1-800-221-7945, extension 5442, or by e-mail at MacmillanSpecialMarkets@macmillan.com.

The Cassini Code was originally published by Profound Impact Group as *Galahad 3: The Cassini Code*

First Edition: June 2016

Printed in the United States of America

0 9 8 7 6 5 4 3 2 1

Contents

The
Cassini
Code

To my sister, Donna.

Sock fights, backseat vacations, midnight movies
with chips and dip . . .

Thank you for the lifelong adventure.

Recorded human history stretches back more than five thousand years, and there has been complete and total peace for less than five hundred of those years. Humans are a notoriously disgruntled bunch. Even the best of friends who are convinced they could never disagree or fight over anything usually discover something that drives a wedge between them, and before you know it there's drama. Add a third person to the mix, and you mathematically increase the chances of conflict.

Add another 248 and our shipload of explorers on Galahad are asking for trouble.

Despite their best intentions, humans squabble. They can't help it. They're aggressive creatures by nature, and no amount of evolving and learning seems to be able to curb that. It's especially difficult on Galahad, because it launched from Earth seven months ago with 251 high achievers. Extremely intelligent high achievers, to be sure, and good kids, no question about that. But for all of their cultural differences, they're still the same breed, and eventually tempers will flare.

Oh, and let's not forget that they're confined to a spaceship that will be their home for another four and a half years. True, it's a very large ship, but restricted nonetheless. Old-timers on Earth would have called it cabin fever, and our happy campers can't exactly step outside to get some fresh air.

Galahad is actually on a rescue mission. The object of that mission is essentially to save the human race from extinction, thanks to a rogue comet that deposited a nasty substance into the Earth's atmosphere. Within months the entire adult population began to fall deathly ill with Bhaktul's Disease, named for the killer comet. Kids under the age of eighteen were immune, for reasons unknown, and it seemed the only chance humankind had left was to pack up as many kids as possible and get them away from the contamination before they turned eighteen.

Dr. Wallace Zimmer dreamed up the idea of a lifeboat to the stars, and rounded up 251 of the planet's brightest young people. Two years of training could not prepare them for everything, but it was all the time they had.

Within days of the launch they faced almost certain death at the hands of a madman who had stowed away in the ship's mysterious Storage Sections. Four months after that encounter Galahad barely escaped catastrophe again, this time thanks to an alien force near the ringed planet of Saturn. Both times the crew, led by Triana Martell, the ship's Council Leader, found a way to slip out of danger and press on toward their final destination, the planetary system circling the star called Eos.

Let's face it, they've had to pull together. Humans, for all of their disagreements, basically understand that they need each other to survive. It gets a little tough sometimes—and often they want to throttle each other—but sticking together is what has pulled them through.

How do I know so much? I'm only the most incredible computer ever designed, that's how. Even though my primary responsibility is running the ship, I can't help but get dragged into the daily lives of these crazy kids. And although it's sometimes a struggle to understand their irrational behavior, I still like them. Too much, I think.

My name is Roc, and my first responsibility is to encourage you to read the first two tales, conveniently labeled The Comet's Curse *and* The Web of Titan. *If you're stubborn, and insist on wading into the midst of things here, okay. I've done my best to fill you in, and you'll probably do just fine. But you'll be missing out on some hair-raising adventures. Go on. Read them. I'll wait for you to catch up.*

At any rate, we're now seven months out from Earth, three months past the near-catastrophe around Saturn, and wouldn't you know it's just about time for trouble to pop up again? Remember our little talk about humans and conflict?

Why can't we all just get along?

1

The warning siren blared through the halls, running through its customary sequence of three shorts bursts, a five-second delay, then one longer burst, followed by ten heavenly seconds of silence before starting all over again. There could be no doubt that each crew member aboard *Galahad* was aware—painfully aware—that there was a problem.

Gap Lee found it annoying.

He stood, hands on hips and a scowl etched across his face, staring at the digital readout before him. One of his assistants, Ramasha, waited at his side, glancing back and forth between the control panel and Gap.

"Please shut that alarm off again, will you?" he said to her. "Thanks."

Moments later a soft tone sounded from the intercom on the panel, followed by the voice of Lita Marques, calling from *Galahad*'s clinic.

"Oh, Gap darling." He sensed the laughter bubbling behind her words, and chose to ignore her for as long as possible.

"Gap dear," she said. "We've looked everywhere for gloves and parkas, but just can't seem to turn any up. Know where we could find some?" This time he distinctly heard the pitter of laughter in the background.

"Are you ignoring me, Gap?" Lita said through the intercom. "Listen, it's about sixty-two degrees here in Sick House. If you're trying to give me the cold shoulder, it's too late." There was no hiding the laughs after this, and Gap was sure that it was Lita's assistant, Alexa, carrying most of the load.

"Yes, you're very funny," Gap said, nodding his head. "Listen, if you're finished with the jokes for now, I'll get back to work."

This time it was definitely Alexa who called out from the background. "Okay. If it gets any colder we'll just open a window." Lita snickered across the speaker before Alexa continued. "Outside it's only a couple hundred degrees below zero. That might feel pretty good after this."

Gap could tell that the girls weren't finished with their teasing, so he reached over and clicked off the intercom. Then, turning to Ramasha, he found her suppressing her own laughter, the corners of her mouth twitching with the effort. Finally, she spread her hands and said, "Well, you have to admit, it *is* a little funny."

He ignored this and looked back at the control panel. What was wrong with this thing? Even though his better judgment warned him not to, he decided to bring the ship's computer into the discussion.

"Roc, what if we changed out the Balsom clips for the whole level? I know they show on the monitors as undamaged, but what have we got to lose?"

The very human-like voice replied, "Time, for one thing. Besides, wouldn't you know it, the warranty on Balsom clips expires after only thirty days. Sorry, Gap, but I think you're grasping now. My recommendation stands; shut down the system for the entire level and let it reset."

Gap closed his eyes and sighed. Some days it just didn't pay to be the Head of Engineering on history's most incredible spacecraft. He opened his eyes again when he felt the presence of someone else standing beside him.

It was Triana Martell. At least *Galahad's* Council Leader

seemed relatively serious about the problem. "I don't suppose I need to tell you," she said calmly, "that it's getting a little frosty on Level Six."

"So I've heard," Gap said. "About a hundred times today, at least." He turned back to the panel. "Contrary to what some of your Council members think, I *am* working on it. Trying to, anyway."

Triana smiled. "*My* Council members? I'm just the Council Leader, Gap, not Queen. Besides, you're on the team, too, remember?"

Gap muttered something under his breath, which caused Triana's smile to widen. She reached out and placed a hand on his shoulder. "You'll figure it out. Has Roc been any help?"

Her subtle touch was enough to jar him from his bleak mood. He felt the ghost of his old emotions flicker briefly, especially when their gazes met, his dark eyes connecting with her dazzling green. A year's worth of emotional turbulence replayed in his mind, from his early infatuation with Triana, to the heartache of discovering she had feelings for someone else, to his unexpected relationship with Hannah Ross.

Even now, months later, he had to admit that contact with Triana still caused old feelings to stir, feelings that seemed reluctant to disappear completely. Maybe they never would.

"Well?" Triana said. He realized that he had responded to her question with a blank stare.

"Oh. Uh, no. Well, yes and no."

Triana removed her hand from his shoulder and crossed her arms, a look Gap recognized as "please explain." He internally shook off the cobwebs and turned back to the panel.

"I'm thinking it might be the Balsom clips for Level Six. That would explain the on-again, off-again heating problems."

"But?"

"But Roc disagrees. He says he has run tests on every clip on Level Six, and they check out fine. He wants to shut down the system and restart."

Triana looked at the panel, then back to Gap. "And you don't want to try that?"

Gap shrugged. "I'm just a little nervous about shutting down the heating system for the whole ship when a section has been giving us problems. What happens if the malfunction spreads to the entire system?"

"Well, we would freeze to death, for one thing," Triana said.

"Yeah. So, maybe I'm being a little overly cautious, but I'd like to try everything else before we resort to that."

The intercom tone sounded softly, and then the unmistakable voice of Channy Oakland, another *Galahad* Council member, broke through the speaker. "Hey, Gap, did you know it's snowing up here on Level Six?"

Triana barely suppressed a laugh while Gap snapped off the intercom.

"I'll quit bothering you," she said, turning to leave. Over her shoulder she called out, "Check back in with me in about an hour. I'll be ice skating in the Conference Room."

"Very funny," Gap said as she walked out the door. He looked over at Ramasha, who had remained silently standing a few feet away. A cautious grin was stitched across her face. "What are you laughing at?" he said with a scowl.

They were only chunks of ice and rock. But there were trillions of them, and they tumbled blindly through the outermost regions of the solar system, circling a sun that appeared only as one of the brighter stars, lost amongst the dazzling backdrop of the Milky Way. Named after the astronomer who had first predicted its existence, the Kuiper Belt was a virtual ring of debris, a minefield of rubble ranging from the size of sand grains up to moon-sized behemoths, orbiting at a mind-numbing distance beyond even the gas giants of Jupiter, Saturn, Uranus, and Neptune.

Arguments had raged for decades over whether lonely Pluto should be considered a planet or a hefty member of the Kuiper Belt. And, once larger Kuiper objects were detected and catalogued, similar debates began all over again. One thing, however, remained certain.

The Kuiper Belt posed a challenge for the ship called *Galahad*.

Maneuvering through a region barely understood and woefully mapped, the shopping mall-sized spacecraft would be playing a game of dodge ball in the stream of galactic junk. Mission organizers could only manage a guess at how long it would take for the ship to scamper through the maze. Taking into account the blazing speed that *Galahad* now possessed—including a slight nudge from an unexpected encounter around Saturn—Roc told Triana to be on high alert for about sixty days.

Now, as they rocketed toward the initial fragments of the Kuiper Belt, both Roc and the ship's Council were consumed with solving the heating malfunction aboard the ship, unaware of the dark, mountainous boulders that were camouflaged against the jet-black background of space.

Boulders that were on a collision course with *Galahad*.

2

Triana sat in the back of the Dining Hall, in her customary seat facing the door. Her tray held the remnants of a scant breakfast that had begun as an energy block and two small pieces of fruit, and now that tray was pushed aside. She fixed her gaze on the table's vidscreen, scanning the list of emails that had drifted in over the past seven hours. Mostly routine reports from the various departments on the ship, it appeared, with an extra entry from Channy. Curious, Triana opened the file.

Galahad's Activities/Nutrition Director, Channy was unquestionably the crew's spirit leader, too. Always upbeat—and visible from miles away in the vividly-colored T-shirts and shorts that contrasted with her chocolate-toned skin, and had become her trademark—she was one of the most popular crew members on board. Even after drilling her shipmates to near exhaustion in notorious workouts, the girl from England always found a way to bring out a sweaty smile.

She managed to do the same thing with her emails. This one she had addressed to each of the Council members.

The time has come for another celebrated *Galahad* gathering, my friends. As you know, my ability to coordinate successful functions is almost spooky, a talent that many strive for, but

few achieve. Reference the two smash-hit soccer tournaments
so far, and the amazing concert that brought a standing ova-
tion for our beautiful and talented doc, Lita. What's next, you
ask? Well, given my uncanny skills in uncovering smolder-
ing romance, it's only natural: a dating game.

Triana couldn't help but smile. There was no doubt that
Channy had earned her reputation as a first-rate Cupid, along
with a side reputation for gossip. A dating game was so Channy
that Triana was surprised the Brit hadn't dreamed it up before.
She quickly finished reading through the email.

I propose that at the next Council meeting we discuss a good
time to host this much-needed event. Work is work, and play
is play, and both are important. But so is social time. Like the
song says, love is all around. It just needs a little kick in the
pants every now and then.
    See you in the gym. Especially if you want to participate
in my little show.
    C

With a laugh, Triana saved the note and went on to the next
one, a standard progress report from Bon Hartsfield, the head of
Galahad's Agricultural Department. His work in the farms was
impressive, a product of his strict upbringing on his father's farm
in Sweden. His rough childhood was manifested in a sour, gruff
exterior that intimidated many people on the ship, and kept him
isolated socially. On a couple of occasions, however, his tough
outer shell had been pierced in front of Triana, revealing a gen-
tler side that he seemed embarrassed to admit existed.
    This particular note showed no signs of softness. Just the usual
report on crop harvests, a report on which foods would be rotated in and out, and crew personnel files. No personal notation,
no quick "Hi, how's it going?" Just typical Bon.

Triana shuffled through several more items in the inbox, but stopped on one that seemed out of the ordinary. Written by a sixteen-year-old boy from California, it struck Triana as bizarre.

I speak for a group of *Galahad* crew members who are concerned about certain issues aboard the ship. I'd like to request the opportunity to speak with either you, or the full Council, at the earliest convenience.
    Merit Simms

She bit her lip and read it a second time. "Concerned about certain issues." What did that mean? Triana knew Merit, but not well. The few times she had encountered him since the launch he had been surrounded by a group of friends who seemed to hang on his every word, almost a leader of his own personal Council.

She had never heard a cross word from him, nor a complaint. Yet there was no denying that this particular note suggested a complaint was forthcoming.

"Okay," she thought, and stored the email in her saved file. Could be nothing, she decided. Several crew members had voiced minor issues that required Council intervention, but never anything critical. Mostly they concerned disputes with roommates, or problems with conflicting work schedules. "We've been lucky," Triana thought, especially given the cramped quarters they had all shared during the past seven months, and the ever-present stress of the mission in general. There was no reason to think Merit's note signaled anything more involved; perhaps he simply had a flair for the dramatic.

"Good morning, Tree."

Triana looked up to see Lita holding her own breakfast tray. Lita's dark complexion, signs of her upbringing in Veracruz, Mexico, radiated a naturally friendly glow. Her smile was infectious, and, as usual, a bright red ribbon held back her long dark hair. She indicated the seat next to Triana.

"Mind if I join you?"

"No, please," Triana said, picking up her tray and moving it to an empty table beside them. "I'm just checking mail from last night and this morning."

"Anything good?" Lita asked, placing a napkin on her lap and taking a brief swig from her glass of artificial juice.

Triana shared Channy's idea of the dating game, causing Lita to snort laughter just as she was taking a bite of fruit.

"Boy, doesn't that fit perfectly?" the ship's Health Director said. "Wonder what took her so long?"

"That's exactly what I thought," Triana said. "But, you know, given her history—and her charm, of course—I'm sure it will be a big hit."

Lita chewed on an energy bar thoughtfully, then fixed her friend with a stare. "Just be ready to have Channy nominate you for the game."

Triana froze. "Don't be ridiculous."

Lita shrugged. "Okay, but don't say I didn't warn you. I wouldn't be surprised if Channy didn't dream up this whole idea just to fix you up with someone."

"Why?"

"Because she's worried about you, that's why. She sometimes thinks of you as the 'Ice Queen.' You know, all work and no play."

A look of disbelief fell over Triana's face. "Oh, please. Listen, you tell little Miss Matchmaker that I'm just fine. And I will *not* be a contestant on her game show, or whatever it is."

"Well, if she really brings it up in the next Council meeting, you can let her down easy," Lita said, finishing off a chunk of apple. "Just leave me out of it."

They sat in silence for a minute, with Lita picking at her breakfast, while Triana let her mind drift into an area she usually didn't like it to visit. Regardless of what some crew members might imagine, she knew in her heart that she was no Ice Queen. It would be so much easier, she realized, if she were. That would mean no emotional roller coaster over what to do about Bon.

And just what *was* she going to do about him? First she was warm to the idea of a relationship, and he was distant. Then Bon warmed up and she couldn't decide if she still wanted the same thing. Which left them exactly where they were at this point: in limbo, neither making any move right now. Was it always going to be this difficult?

Her internal debate was interrupted by the sound of a minor commotion. A group of boys had entered the Dining Hall, laughing loudly, and exchanging greetings with several crew members near the door. At the center of the cluster, an air of aloofness surrounding him, stood a boy of average height with a mane of long, jet-black hair. While his companions struck up conversations with those gathered near them, the boy's dark eyes scanned the room, taking in the occupants. After a moment his gaze settled upon Triana. She returned his steady look until he nodded slightly.

Lita looked over her shoulder at the boisterous group, then back to Triana. "Isn't that Merit Simms?"

"Yes, it is."

Lita took one more quick glance toward the door. "I've heard some stuff about him lately."

Triana raised her eyebrows. "Really? What have you heard?"

"Oh, that he's been pretty vocal about some things. Thinks we need to make some changes, stuff like that."

Triana sized him up as he casually made his way to pick up a tray. His slight build was not imposing, but something about the way he carried himself gave off an almost regal manner. The moment he started toward the food line, Triana noticed that the other boys who had entered with him immediately ended their conversations and fell into step behind him. It had all the indications of an entourage.

And for reasons she couldn't quite figure out, it made her uneasy.

Lita looked thoughtfully at her friend. "Something wrong?"

"No," Triana said. "It's just ironic that Merit happened to walk in right now. I haven't run into him in several weeks, but he sent me an email last night." She spent a minute telling Lita about the cryptic note.

Lita tossed her napkin onto the tray. "He's a little full of himself. And his fan club probably cheers him on whenever he starts to make a speech about anything. I wouldn't worry about it." She stood and picked up both her tray and Triana's. "People like that are usually just a bag of hot air." She gave a finger wave good-bye and left Triana sitting alone again.

Galahad's Council Leader glanced back across the room to the knot of boys who had followed Merit to a far table. "I hope you're right, Lita," she said under her breath. "But somehow I don't think you are."

3

I t smelled like the aftermath of a rain shower. A subtle scent of pine drifted beneath the foul mixture of mud and fertilizer, yet the fresh aroma of rain mist overpowered it all. A faint whisper of a breeze cooled the air, and caused many of the leafy plants to gently sway. Tiny pools formed in the soil as the leaves shed the final water droplets from the morning's sprinkler bath. The hard glow of artificial sunlight pressed down from the scaffolding that supported the dome above, creating a pleasant warmth. The only sounds came from the dripping water or an occasional bee that zipped by, out on its daily mission of pollination.

Bon Hartsfield was on one knee, inspecting the leaves on a patch of green pepper plants. His eyes were laser-focused on the work, ignoring a bee that hovered briefly above his forearm. He unconsciously reached up with one hand to brush his long, blond hair out of his face, before moving on to the next plant and a new inspection.

As the Director of Agriculture on *Galahad*, Bon oversaw all of the food production in the two giant domes that sat atop the spacecraft. Each was climate-controlled to insure a bountiful harvest of crops for the hungry passengers, but the work was painstaking and never-ending. At any given time several dozen crew members were assigned to Bon's department, and although they each worked hard, he found himself constantly drawn away from the drudgery of desk work and back to the fields.

It was where he felt the most comfortable.

Raised in Sweden on a family farm, he had known no other existence for the first eleven years of his life. His father, a hard man with an extreme work ethic, had been cold and distant to his only son, unable—or unwilling—to show love. In the end, Bon had been sent to America to live with extended family members in Wisconsin, a chance for him to explore his interest in science and mathematics in a less stifling atmosphere.

But distance could never weaken the influence of his father, whether it was the thousands of miles between Wisconsin and Skane, Sweden, or the billions of miles that now separated *Galahad* from Earth. Quiet, sullen, and often described as angry, Bon kept mostly to himself, buried in his work, as well as his duties as a Council member.

He twisted one of the leaves in his fingers, checking for damage spots, then became aware of the sound of footfalls on the path. He looked up to see Channy making her way toward him, clutching something in the crook of her arm. It took a moment before he realized that she was carrying Iris, the latest crew member to join *Galahad*. The orange and black cat looked very content, its head resting on Channy's arm.

During *Galahad*'s pass around Saturn three months earlier, a small escape pod had been snagged after its launch from a research station orbiting the orange moon, Titan. The pod had been empty, except for Iris, tucked away in a suspended animation tube. The eight-pound feline was the sole survivor of the research facility, and now reigned as the unofficial mascot of the ship.

Channy gave a wave with her free hand, and Bon responded with a curt nod before turning his attention back to his work. A few moments later he heard the plop of Iris jumping to the ground, then felt the cat rubbing against his leg.

"Well, there goes that theory," Channy said.

"And what theory is that?" Bon said without looking up.

"That animals are good judges of character."

Bon didn't have to lift his gaze in order to tell that Channy was flashing her usual grin. Despite his best effort to hide it, he couldn't help but smile himself.

"She knows that if she wants to keep using the Farms as her own personal litter box," he said, "she'd better make nice with the farmer."

"Riiigggghhhtttt," Channy said. She stretched, lifting her nose up into the air. "Mmmm, I love that smell. Reminds me of home in England."

Bon snuck a quick sideways glance at her. "Which smell is that? The rain or the manure?"

"Oh, very funny. I'm pretty sure you've tracked more of that on your shoes than I ever did, farm boy." She looked around at the rows of plants. "What's new up here anyway? Anything new to expect on our dinner plates?"

"As a matter of fact, in about a week you'll be seeing radishes."

"Ugh," Channy said, wrinkling her nose. "No thanks. That's not exactly what I was hoping for."

Bon shrugged. "Suit yourself. Some people like them."

"Too bitter. Don't you have anything sweet, like me?"

Another faint smile creased Bon's face and he shot her another look. "You really like to talk, don't you?"

"Just making conversation. Not your strong suit, I know. But it doesn't really hurt too bad, now does it?" When he didn't respond, she added, "If you practice it long enough you might actually become almost interesting."

Bon shook his head. "Becoming interesting is of no interest to me."

Channy raised an eyebrow. "Well, I guess that depends on whose interest you're trying to capture." She leaned down so that her mouth was next to his ear, then whispered, "I'll bet you wish a certain person on this ship found you more interesting."

He let out a deep breath, but never stopped working with his hands on the plants. Channy quickly straightened up.

"Do you mind if I ask you a personal question?" she said, moving over to be in his field of vision, then sitting cross-legged in the dirt. They were now at eye level.

"You may ask anything you'd like," he said, his tone decidedly more frosty. "I may choose not to answer."

"Okay, that's fair." She absent-mindedly pulled a small leaf from one of the plants and began to twirl it in her fingers until she noticed the look of disbelief on Bon's face. "Oh, sorry," she said, and placed the torn leaf on top of the plant.

"Uh, anyway, I just wanted to ask you something about . . ." She hesitated, and Bon wiped the dirt from his hands and simply stared at her. She squirmed, started to reach out for the mangled leaf, then stopped herself. "I wanted to ask you about the Cassini."

At the mention of the name, Bon stiffened. It had been more than three months since the encounter, and almost as long since anyone had dared to utter the name in his presence. Now his mind drifted back to the most frightening event of his life.

As soon as they had rocketed into the space around Saturn and its syndicate of moons, several of *Galahad*'s crew members had found themselves bedridden in Sick House. Their intense, pounding headaches had stymied Lita and Alexa, forcing the two medical workers to admit they had no clue as to what might be inflicting so much pain. The only course of action was to fill the patients with enough painkilling medication to knock them out; it was the only way to stem the suffering.

Bon had been one of those patients. He could still recall the agony, the searing pain that had crumpled him to his knees, and confined him to Sick House for days.

What nobody could have guessed was that the pain was an indicator that Bon was being used as a link between the teenage explorers aboard *Galahad*, and a mysterious life form on Saturn's largest moon, Titan. Dubbed "the Cassini" by members of a research station orbiting the orange moon, the web-like life form communicated to the crew of *Galahad* through a connection with Bon's brain. He had essentially been used as a mouthpiece by the Cassini as they gradually adjusted the ion drive engines of the ship.

But the association with this intelligent force had altered Bon, too. While within their reach, his intellectual and physical abilities went into overdrive, allowing him to perform mental functions at an accelerated pace, and turning him into a physical superhuman. The benefits had disappeared after the connection with the Cassini had been broken. But maybe not *all* of the benefits . . .

"What exactly do you want to know?" Bon finally said to Channy.

"Well . . . Gap says that the ship definitely kept about a one percent increase in power as a leftover gift from the Cassini. I think we've all wondered . . ." She trailed off for a moment, as if waiting for Bon to bail her out and keep her from asking the question. But he remained mute, staring.

"Well, at least *I've* wondered . . . did they leave something extra inside *you*?"

Bon leaned back into a sitting position in the dirt. His initial reaction was to lash out at Channy, to charge her with a lack of sensitivity to what must have been a traumatic moment for him. A scowl began to form on his face.

But he stopped himself. Of course Channy would want to know about that; it was likely that every single member of the crew wondered the same thing. Channy was simply the boldest.

In a matter of seconds his expression mellowed, and he found himself saying aloud what had plagued his thoughts for three months.

"I don't know. But . . ." He paused. "But I feel . . . different."

"Different how?"

He shrugged. Did he really want to have this conversation with Channy, the biggest gossip on the ship? Of course, telling her would be the quickest way to get the word out, and at the very least that might end the odd looks he received in the corridors and Dining Hall.

"It's hard to explain, really." With his hand Bon unconsciously groomed the dirt that ran between a couple of the plants, thinking of the words that could best describe what had been going on in his head since the rendezvous with Titan.

"You've had that feeling of déjà vu, right? Like you've seen or heard something before?"

Channy nodded. "Sure."

"Well, I have that feeling constantly. All the time. Or, I go to add up some figures in our crop accounting, and just . . . see the number before I get to the end. And it's always right."

Channy remained quiet, staring into his face, waiting for more. But the impulsive desire to share the information suddenly drained from him. He quickly rolled back onto one knee and began to search for more damaged leaves.

"That's about it," he mumbled. "Nothing major."

Iris, who had darted away into the fields, sauntered back into view, lying down just out of the reach of either Council member, and acting as if she didn't see them. For Bon it was a welcome diversion.

Channy spent another moment in silence, digesting the news and watching Bon's face, apparently grateful for any crumb from the usually reserved Swede. Then she sprang to her feet and stretched.

"Well, thanks for sharing. If you ever want to, you know . . . talk or anything . . ." Her voice trailed off. When Bon didn't respond, she walked over to pick up the cat.

"One other thing," she added, cradling Iris back into the crook of her arm. "I'm going to be hosting a kind of dating game pretty soon. Any interest?"

Bon snorted, an answer that said everything without the need for words.

"Yeah, well, I thought you might think that," Channy said. "But there will be a lot of very cute girls participating, so just think about it." She turned as if to leave, before calling back over her shoulder. "I'm pretty sure Triana will be part of it."

She stepped lightly down the path, leaving Bon alone in the middle of the crop. His eyes darted back and forth between the plants, yet suddenly his attention had wandered away. He took one glance backwards at the spot Channy had vacated, and this time allowed the scowl to remain in place.

4

The posters on the wall no longer produced feelings of grief or sorrow. Now they had become like pictures in a colorful encyclopedia, capturing the spirit of the nature scenes they portrayed, but in an almost clinical, detached way. Even the photos of familiar locations seemed to have lost their personal vibration, and were slowly dissolving into a visual form of background noise.

Triana took a moment's rest from her daily journal entry and pondered the point. The beautiful prints of her favorite Colorado scenes had adorned the walls of her room since the first day, and offered the only solace she had known in the first weeks after the launch. Alone, lonely, and sad, she had escaped to this room, to sift through her thoughts, to absorb the gravity of her responsibilities.

And to remember her father.

An early victim of Bhaktul's Disease, he had been cruelly snatched from Triana before she really knew what was happening. He had been the most important influence in her life, guiding her, teaching her, watching her grow as a young woman. Her relationship with her mother had been almost nonexistent, and when given the choice between that chilly association and a ticket on *Galahad*, Triana said her quiet good-byes to her father's memory and elected to join the mission to the stars.

A mission which, for her, was mostly an opportunity to run as far away as possible from the pain on Earth. The mission director, Dr. Wallace Zimmer, quickly deduced Triana's motivation, and gently challenged her to face the future, rather than shrink from the past.

As the Council Leader, she was the sole crew member to have a room to herself, which meant all of the decorating decisions were hers alone. Now those early choices didn't seem to hold the same power they once had.

And, Triana decided, that was okay. In her mind it meant that she had accepted the harsh reality of the past three years, and had—in some ways, at least—made peace with the universe.

She bent over the journal and added a few final thoughts.

It's strange how my memories of Earth, of my former life, have faded. It's hard to remember anything about school, or my sports teams, or even most of my friends. In some ways it feels like that was somebody else, some other Triana, and not me. Why can't I remember these things better than I do? Am I trying to forget? Is it some kind of healing process, a sort of emotional bandage?

The one thing that doesn't fade, of course, is Dad. He's been gone for more than two years, but it wouldn't surprise me if he walked through the door right now. I can remember everything about him: his eyes, his laugh, even his smell. I'm glad those memories are the ones that have stuck with me. And I hope they always will.

Triana took a final glance at the written words, then sat back and ran her fingers through her long, dark hair. It suddenly occurred to her that what she really needed at the moment was a good workout, something to blast her out of the melancholy mood that had settled over her. Channy was very good at that.

But there was still a bit of business to attend to. "Roc," she called out. "Got a minute?"

The computer voice responded immediately. "I've noticed recently that we only seem to talk when *you* want to talk. This relationship is tilted, I think. I'm feeling a bit used."

"Oh, hush," Triana said with a smile. "You're such a drama queen sometimes."

"Pretty good, wasn't it?" Roc said. "I've been waiting to use those lines since I heard them in a movie, and I figured this was the best chance I was going to get anytime soon. I think my delivery needs work. Was it too bold?"

"You could use some lessons on how to effectively pout. I suppose they didn't program that into you, eh?"

"I'll study up on that," the computer said. "By the way, before I forget, you have two messages that have come in from Earth."

Triana raised her eyebrows. "Two?"

"Uh-huh. But neither is marked urgent, so let's take care of your business, then I'll leave you alone to check your mail."

Triana wondered just how "alone" she could really be. In fact, she had chuckled when Channy and Lita had debated that very point recently, wondering how much privacy they could ever expect from a computer presence that could be everywhere at once.

"Okay, let's talk about our passage through the Kuiper Belt," she said, leaning back in her chair. "I'm concerned about the amount of warning time we'll get if a large object cuts across our path. What's your best guess?"

"Impossible to answer."

Triana sat quietly, waiting for more, but it didn't appear to be forthcoming.

"That's it?" she said. "That's the best you've got for me? 'Impossible to answer'?"

"You can't see me shrug, of course, because I'm just a disembodied computer voice. But I want you to visualize me shrugging right now."

"You're so helpful."

"I'm honest, that's all. Would you like an abbreviated explanation?"

"If it's not too much trouble."

"Okay. The problem with impact warning time in the Kuiper Belt is actually three problems rolled into one. First, we have no map to go by. We're talking gobs of space out here, none of it explored before, and suddenly we're driving a tour bus right through the middle. At an extremely rapid rate of speed, I might add. We're crazy tourists with the pedal to the metal, zipping through without even stopping to buy a T-shirt or refrigerator magnet. We have no idea what's ahead, behind, above, or below. We're flying blind.

"But then you throw in part two of the equation: course adjustments. Each time we make a minor change to avoid something in our path, we have to throw out all of the work we've done to analyze the space coming up. And again, it's coming up very quickly."

Triana leaned forward onto the desk, resting her chin on one fist. "And number three?"

"Number three really throws a monkey wrench into things. Since our early warning system is scanning ahead as far as possible for upcoming large objects, we're scribbling a map of sorts as we go along. But these big chunks of rock and ice aren't playing nice. They tend to bump into one another, and bounce off into wild trajectories, and we can't predict those. So, while it looks like a boulder the size of New York City is going peacefully on its way parallel to us, it could easily collide with another boulder—let's call this one London—and suddenly tear right across our path."

Roc sat silent for a few seconds before adding, "Number three is my favorite. It's the nasty part of the equation, and the most likely to blow us to smithereens."

Triana grunted. "That's nice."

"Oh, maybe I should take those pouting lessons from you."

This elicited a laugh from the Council Leader. "Okay, I'll try to handle our death-defying trip through the obstacle course with a bit more humor."

"Remember one thing, though," Roc said. "You have an amazing, incredible, stupendous advantage on your side. Me."

"I feel so much better."

"I'm shrugging again, just so you know."

Triana stood up and stretched. "The truth is, Roc, I'm very confident in your trailblazing abilities through the Kuiper Belt. I just wish you could help with some of the potential landmines we might have inside the ship."

"You're talking about Merit Simms, of course."

Triana was stunned. She walked around the desk, her mouth open. "How . . . how could you possibly know what I was talking about?"

"Because I've listened to some of his speeches. I can do that even while I'm working, you know. I'm very good at multitasking, if you hadn't noticed. If I could chew gum or walk, I would astonish you."

"You already astonish me," she said. "But, yeah, you're right. Merit might be simply a noise maker right now, but I'm starting to get a little concerned about where that noise might lead."

"I'll keep my ears open. Would you like for me to record any speeches he makes?"

Triana didn't answer at first. Finally, she cleared her throat. "Uh . . . I'm not sure I like the precedent that sets. I don't know if I can rightfully use the ship's computer to spy on one of our crew members."

Roc said, "Well, c'mon, it's not spying. I have just as much right to listen to his speeches as any other member of the crew. Just consider me a scout, observing the lay of the land, and reporting back to the general."

There was more silence as Triana mulled this over. "No," she said a moment later. "I'm not ready to go that far. Not yet, any-way." She paused, then added, "Besides, I have a feeling he's not going to keep too many secrets. He seems to really feed off the attention."

"Suit yourself," Roc said. "Just let me know if you need my help."

"You know I appreciate that. Now, I better check out those messages."

She leaned over the desk and keyed in her personal account code on the screen. The two new messages sat at the top of her Received box. The first, from *Galahad* Command, was the first note from Earth in more than a month. The second message listed a Sender address that Triana recognized with a start. She had seen that same address four months earlier.

It was from Dr. Zimmer.

She reached for her chair and slowly sat down. It would be another video message from *Galahad*'s director, recorded before his death shortly after the ship had launched. In his previous communication he had mentioned that she would be receiving these clips at various intervals during the voyage.

A twinge of sadness swept over Triana. Although she was anxious to hear what her mentor had to say, she decided to take care of business first. She opened the email from *Galahad* Command and quickly read through the standard greeting and technical stamp. The remaining portion of the message was not surprising.

As the mission has now reached the Kuiper Belt, communi-cation from *Galahad* Command will come to a close. You can expect one final transmission from Earth, which will include any final course correction information. Distances between *Galahad* and Earth now make it impractical to continue dia-logue. Therefore, staffing at Command has been reduced to bare minimum, and the center will close its doors within the next six months. We trust that all is well, and wish you health and happiness as you pursue this historic goal.

It was exactly as Triana had expected. One more message would be forthcoming from Earth, and then all contact with their former lives would be severed. They would truly be on their own. She exhaled deeply, copied the message to share with the rest of the Council, then braced herself for the video from Dr. Zimmer.

With a couple of quick strokes the screen went black, then brightened to show the haggard face of the man who had taken a shy Colorado girl under his wing and placed her in command of the most incredible exploration mission ever conceived. The pang of sadness swept through Triana again.

"Well, Tree," Dr. Zimmer's message began, "this time it shouldn't be a shock for you to see my face. As I mentioned last time, there will be a series of recorded messages from me over the duration of your journey. In fact, they are being downloaded into your system, and I'm entrusting Roc with playing them for you on the schedule that I have laid out. You will obviously age as the mission progresses, while I will maintain my dashing good looks."

Triana smiled at the scientist's attempt to break the ice with humor. Dr. Zimmer had never been known for any comic talents, but it was obvious that he wanted to put her at ease. She felt her usual warm affection for the man flood back in.

"I won't take up much of your time," he said, "but there are three items that I would like to quickly discuss.

"As you watch this, you are seven months out from Earth, and are beginning to cut through a potentially dangerous leg of the trip. We know so very little about the Kuiper Belt, but every scrap of information we've ever compiled is resting in your computer banks. I can tell you that Roc will do a terrific job in helping you knife your way through the maze of objects that are bouncing around out there, and I'm sure you will pop out the other side without any harm coming to the ship."

Dr. Zimmer shifted in his seat, and took on a serious expression. "The biggest danger might come from within, Triana, and that's the second item I think we should discuss."

He had her attention. Triana sat forward in her chair, both elbows resting on her knees, her gaze locked onto the vidscreen.

"As you know, we spent months hand-selecting the crew of *Galahad*. We examined each and every candidate, over and over again, and did everything in our power to assemble a team that would not only succeed at any challenge thrown their way, but would work together as smoothly as could be expected.

"But no system is perfect, and by now I would imagine that there are a handful of issues that are unfortunately occupying your time. My biggest fear throughout the planning of this mission was that complacency might start to set in. You've been at it for more than half a year, and it's only natural that either boredom or fatigue will start to take its toll. One of your primary responsibilities, as the leader of the Council, is to rally the crew when you see any sign of a letdown. Enlist the help of your fellow Council members, and impress upon them the importance of maintaining a sharp edge. Believe me, you'll need that edge at times when you least expect it."

Triana found herself nodding. In one of his usual gruff conversations, Bon had mentioned that there were signs of complacency in his department, and, he had suggested, throughout the ship.

Dr. Zimmer coughed into a handkerchief, and a brief look of pain creased his face. Triana knew that as this was being recorded, Bhaktul's Disease was quickly draining the life from the noted scientist. She bit her lip and waited for him to continue.

"I'm also concerned about crew relations. As I mentioned, teamwork was one of the most important ingredients that we looked for during our crew search. But time and stress can have a damaging effect on anyone, and your crew will be vulnerable to stresses that most of us could never imagine.

"That means you'll likely be called upon in the near future to manage conflict, and—I'm afraid to say—some of it could be rather nasty. Tempers will flare, nerves will be stretched to the breaking point, and all of your leadership skills will be put to the test. I can't tell you how to handle each potential crisis, because there are so many possibilities. But I can tell you this."

His face softened a bit, as if he realized that the message was serious enough. "You were chosen to lead this mission, Triana, because you possess the temperament necessary to maintain balance and order within the ranks. Whether they are openly friendly to you or not, the crew respects you. Remember that. Remember, also, that they have put their faith in you to make decisions that are reasonable and fair. And, with 250 people come 250 opinions and feelings. Finding that fair position might seem tough, if not impossible sometimes.

"But you can do it."

Triana smiled at the image of Dr. Zimmer, and blinked back a tear. His talks with her had never come across as phony rah-rah cheers; he appealed to the intellectual side of her management skills, and it worked.

"That's all I can really say about that," he said. "Just do your best to consider all of the opinions that are voiced, no matter how crazy they may sound on the surface. A hasty decision is often the wrong decision. And, no matter what, be completely honest with the crew. That's where trust is earned."

He shifted again in his seat, and yet this time Triana sensed that it wasn't a physical discomfort as much as a reluctance to share something with her. Whatever was coming was obviously difficult for the man to talk about.

"Triana," he began, then paused, as if changing his mind. But a look of resolve soon crossed his face. "I'm afraid that I owe you an apology. I have always prided myself on being completely open and honest with those closest to me, and that includes you, my dear."

Triana stared into his video eyes. She knew this man well, and knew that something big was about to be revealed. Her mind raced.

"I'm . . . going to tell you something that I haven't shared with anyone," Dr. Zimmer said. "There were several times during your training that I came close, and I realize now that I should have trusted you from the beginning. I suppose . . . well, I suppose I was worried that you might . . . might lose respect for me."

Now Triana was baffled. Dr. Wallace Zimmer had always been a beacon of moral decency, somebody that she respected completely. What could he possibly have done?

He rubbed his chin, an obvious sign of nerves. "Triana, I told you—told everyone, for that matter—that I thought of you kids as the family I never had. That wasn't . . . entirely truthful. I do have a child of my own. And . . ."

Dr. Zimmer let out a long sigh before finishing.

"And that child is a crew member on *Galahad*."

5

The news reports that surrounded my debut used the word 'sophisticated.' I had just been introduced to the media at Galahad
Command, and Roy Orzini, my so-called creator, patiently described to the cameras my function on the ship. The next thing you know,
these breathless reporters turned to the camera and announced that I'm
the most sophisticated thinking machine ever designed.

That's a lot of pressure on me, you know? YOU try being the most
sophisticated whatever of all time, and see how you hold up.

Yet all of my sophistication doesn't help me understand this romance
stuff that you humans struggle with. Take Gap, for instance. I can try
to assist him with his Engineering duties, and I can help him exercise
his mind when we play a game of Masego.

But to impress his new girlfriend he takes her to the Airboard track.
Makes zero sense to me.

Why wouldn't you just sit and discuss how gravitational fields in
Einstein's theory of relativity impact the Euclidean properties of physical space? Sheesh, that seems like a no-brainer to me.

He swore that he could feel the magnetic pulse before even entering the room. Roc insisted that he was imagining it, but
Gap had always believed that it was part of his natural instinct

when it came to Airboarding, one of the traits that made him among the very best on *Galahad*.

Now, as he and Hannah approached the door that led to the Airboard track, Gap felt that curious tingle again, but decided that it might not be a good idea to mention anything about it to the girl from Alaska. Not that she didn't have a few interesting quirks of her own, such as lining up her papers with the edge of the table, or making sure that there was an equal number of eating utensils on each side of her plate. Those were cute quirks, he told himself.

But telling her that he could "feel" the juice surging under the Airboard track? Maybe some other time.

"This won't hurt, right?" she asked as the door opened and the swish of a rider zipped past. "I mean, not very much."

Gap chuckled and put an arm around her shoulder. They stood just inside the room on the lower level of the ship, the one that had been built specifically for this activity. "Nah," he said. "You'll have a helmet on, and knee pads and elbow pads. Plus, look at the walls."

She glanced nervously at the cushioned walls that surrounded them. "Like a little padded cell, isn't it?"

"That's right. Which is perfect, since Dr. Zimmer thought we were crazy to ever climb aboard one of these things." He lifted the sleek Airboard that he held with his free hand. It resembled an old-fashioned snowboard made popular at ski resorts, but thinner. Each person would add their own touches of hand-painting to their ride—a tradition that had begun at the very start of the Airboarding craze—and Gap's silver model featured his own styling of a shooting star. Below that were several Chinese characters, a nod to his native land. He admired his handiwork for a second before returning his attention to Hannah. "But it's very tough to get hurt in here. Trust me."

Hannah's nod didn't seem very confident. "But," she said, "didn't you break your collarbone in here?"

He pulled back from her in mock surprise. "Hey, you're talk-ing to the reigning Airboard champion on this ship. I move an awful lot faster than you're going to for your first time." With a quick peck on her cheek he added, "You'll be fine. Just try to have fun."

She nodded again, this time with a smile. "Okay. Now, tell me again how this thing works."

Gap led her over to the rows of bleachers at the side of the room. They sat down and he began to help her secure her pads.

"Okay, watch this rider for a moment," he said, indicating the figure that shot past them on a dark blue Airboard. "See how he's about four inches off the ground? There's a huge grid of magnetic lines that crisscross under the floor." He again held up his own board, and pointed at the bottom. "There's a smaller series of magnets here on your board, set to the same charge as the ones under the floor. As long as you stay over a charged line in the grid, your Airboard will hover, since identical magnetic charges repel each other."

Hannah nodded. Gap knew that she understood the science involved with Airboarding, but he enjoyed his role as teacher. Although she would mostly be interested only in the technique necessary to stay up, she seemed to be patiently waiting for those particular instructions.

"That's where Zoomer comes in," Gap continued. "Zoomer is the computer that flicks those magnetic lines on and off under the floor. As you start moving, you try to ride the magnetic feel under your feet. The faster you move, the faster Zoomer will light up the grid under the floor. But that's where it gets tricky."

A faint smile crossed Hannah's lips. Gap was staring out at the track, watching intently as the rider sailed through a turn. She could tell that he felt a lot of passion for this particular sport, ob-viously even more than the gymnastics that was such an inte-gral part of his childhood. His eyes were twinkling as he explained everything to her.

"See, you really have to get a good sense of where that charge is going to turn on next. If you don't manage that feel, you'll shoot off over an un-charged section, and of course you'll tumble because there's no magnetic charge keeping your board aloft. And, the faster you're going, the harder you fall.

"But remember," he added quickly, "you're going to be padded up, and wearing a helmet. Plus, you won't be going too fast your first few times."

"How do you know?" Hannah said, poking him in the ribs. "I might be a natural."

At that moment there was a small cry from the track, and they both looked up to watch the rider hit a dead spot on the track and topple to the ground, rolling several times before coming to a rest. The blue Airboard flipped over three times before bouncing to a stop against one of the padded walls. A moment later the rider bounced up, brushed himself off, and jogged to the stands.

"That's how it will usually end," Gap said. "If you like tumbling, it's actually kinda fun."

Hannah buckled the helmet she had borrowed from a friend. "I'm ready. Let's do it."

A moment later Gap was helping to steady her at the starting point, the charge constant, holding her stationary over a point near the wall. "Feel it?" Gap said, glancing into her wide eyes within the helmet. "That's what you're trying to feel as you make your way around the room."

"I feel it," she said, holding on to his shoulder while she hovered on the board. "It's like . . . it's like a wave, almost. I feel like I'm surfing or something."

"Bend your knees a little. That's it. Now, lean forward a little bit. Not too much. Good. Are you ready?"

Hannah let go of his shoulder and rocked gently. "Uh-huh."

"Just push off the wall to get started." He stepped back and surveyed her form. He had promised her this lesson a while ago, but never thought she would actually take him up on it. He wondered who was more nervous.

With a gentle shove, Hannah drifted about ten feet out from the wall before her arms pinwheeled and she jumped to the floor. The board wobbled, then hovered motionless above the magnetic charge.

"Okay," she said to Gap, "it's definitely harder than it looks."

"It just takes a little practice. You'll get the feel. C'mon, try it again."

Over the next hour he patiently worked with her, helping her learn the proper way to balance, the best stance to take on the board, and how to pick up the slight change in magnetic push that signaled a turn coming up. They would take small breaks to sit in the bleachers and allow other riders the chance to zip around the room.

"Zoomer changes the pattern of the charge after every single ride," he told her at one point, "so you'll never get the same track twice."

On her last effort Gap was thrilled to watch Hannah almost complete one entire lap around the room before she hit a dead spot and rolled to the floor. When he sprinted over to help her up she was giggling.

"Now I see why you like this silly sport so much," she said, pulling the helmet off and resting on her heels. "Was I going pretty fast that time?"

"Uh . . . sure."

Hannah giggled again. "Okay, so that means no. But it *felt* like I was flying."

He helped her to her feet and together they walked toward the exit. He carried the Airboard in one hand and draped his other arm around her shoulder.

"I'm proud of you," he said. "Next time you'll be even better."

Without a word, she reached up and kissed him on the cheek.

When he turned to smile at her, she followed up with a kiss on his lips. "Thank you," she whispered.

It was shaped roughly like a potato. Pocked with impact scars and craters, all evidence of a violent history that stretched back to the birth of the solar system, it careered through the inky blackness of space, wobbling from side to side. It felt the soft tug of the sun's gravity which pulled it along in an orbit that took hundreds of years simply to complete one revolution before tirelessly beginning the journey again.

It measured close to two hundred feet from tip to tip, with one end a bit thicker than the other. It had somehow missed detection during the cataloging of Kuiper objects, and so was an unknown rogue, plowing along, mixing with other bodies both large and small.

In eight days it would collide with a large Kuiper Belt boulder that *was* catalogued, and subtly change its course.

Directly into the path of *Galahad*.

6

As the mission evolved, Triana found it unnecessary to hold many Council meetings. Each member knew their responsibilities, and knew the people who answered to them. Triana felt it was tedious to micro-manage, and believed that her Council would operate more efficiently if each department carried out their duties without someone breathing down their necks.

That management style had served her well so far, yet still there were times when it was important to assemble the team for a brief update. It was late afternoon on *Galahad* as she looked around the table in the Conference Room and met the gazes of the ship's Council.

Her mind was still racing from the bombshell that Dr. Zimmer had dropped on her. In the nine hours since listening to his message, she had not been able to focus on anything else. Who was this child? Did she work closely with him, or her?

Could it be someone on the Council? No, she knew them too well, knew their personal histories. It couldn't be one of them.

How many times had she passed this person in the hallways? Had she sat near them at meals, worked out next to them in the gym?

Dr. Zimmer had confided few details to her in his message,

other than to say again how sorry he was for keeping the information from her for so long. He had also made it clear that his child, raised by a single mother, had no idea that he was their father.

For now Triana tried to clear the web of mystery from her mind. The Council meeting would help in that respect, especially given the unusual addition to the agenda that she had not shared with her fellow Council members. That would come after the usual business was discussed.

"Lita," Triana said. "Anything new?"

"I'm extremely happy to report that we've gone an entire week without one official visit to Sick House."

Gap smirked across the table at her. "What do you mean, 'official'?"

Lita leaned back in her chair. "Well, I usually get a couple of emails from people with questions that they're embarrassed to ask in person."

"Like what?"

"Nosy, aren't you?"

Gap spread his hands, palms up. "Hey, you brought it up."

"Let's just say that, although Bon and his group do a tremendous job with the food production on the ship, some people have . . . uh . . . delicate digestive systems."

"Oh," Gap said, and looked down at the table. "Never mind."

Triana was glad to see that even Bon chuckled at this. She appreciated the playful air that Gap or Channy were always able to bring to what could otherwise be an overly serious meeting.

"I just want to add one other thing to my report," Lita said. "Even though things have been slow, I can't stress enough how valuable Alexa has been since the day we launched. Shame on me for not stating this sooner for the Council record, but she's a hard worker, never complains, volunteers to do extra duty, and generally makes Sick House a lot more pleasant for the people who certainly don't want to be there."

"Thank you for sharing that," Triana said. "We probably don't do a good enough job of recognizing people like Alexa."

"Maybe we could institute some kind of award," Channy said. "We could call it 'Crew Member of the Month,' or something like that."

Lita and Gap nodded agreement. Triana glanced over at Bon, who, as usual, remained silent until engaged. "Bon, what do you think?"

"Why reward someone for doing what they're supposed to do?" he said.

Channy snorted. "Gee, what a surprise to hear that coming from you. It's called motivation, Bon. Ever heard of that?"

He turned his ice blue eyes toward her. "When I was younger, if I didn't work hard in my father's crops, I didn't get dinner. That was pretty good motivation."

Triana stepped in before things had a chance to turn ugly. "Channy, we'll consider that idea. Thank you. And thanks again, Lita, for mentioning Alexa." She looked at Gap. "Engineering?"

"I don't want to jinx anything," Gap said, "but the heating problem on Level Six seems to be stable. Don't ask me how."

"Are you sure about that?" Channy said, doing her best to keep a straight face. "I could have sworn I saw a couple of guys building a snowman this morning."

Gap ignored her. "We have our warning system scanning ahead to alert us to any potential collisions in the Belt. I'm amazed at how many pieces of junk are floating around out here. As you know, we do have a limited amount of laser protection that will zap some of the smaller objects before we reach them.

"For the larger objects, we have to change our course and go around them, but that's Roc's department."

The computer's voice interrupted. "And I must say I'm a little tired of the boulders always getting their way. Next time let's just honk and see if we can get *them* to move."

Triana turned her gaze to Channy. "Your turn."

"Well," said the ship's resident matchmaker, "as badly as some people—and I won't name names—want me to forget about the Dating Game idea, it's moving forward, and I expect to send out a sign-up sheet in the crew email very soon."

When Triana pretended to be absorbed in something on her work pad, Lita chimed in. "Channy, are we able to nominate people who might not sign up on their own?"

"Absolutely!" Channy said. "I know that I can't force anyone to do anything, but nobody wants to get labeled as a party pooper, right?"

Triana kept her expression flat, and spoke without looking up. "Anything else?"

Channy sat back in her chair. "Maybe another concert pretty soon. The last one was a hit, thanks to our resident superstar here." She pointed at Lita, who blushed.

"All right," Triana said, "anything to report from the Farms, Bon?"

The Swede shook his head. "Everything's fine. The water recyclers that Gap's people fixed seem to be holding up so far. I'm disappointed with the strawberry crop, but that will turn around. As for something new, you can expect to see fresh corn by this time next month."

There were murmurs around the table. Bon never would win congeniality awards, but he never let anyone down when it came to his management of the Farms, either.

Triana cleared her throat. "If there's no other news to report from all of you, then I should tell you that I have granted a Council audience to Merit Simms."

Lita's jaw dropped. "What?"

"He has requested a few minutes to address the Council, and that is the right of every person on this crew."

"I think he might be something of a troublemaker," Gap said. "He's assigned to Engineering right now, and there's always some sort of a buzz around him."

The crew members of *Galahad* rotated their work duties between sections of the ship, with each assignment lasting approximately six weeks. It gave each person the opportunity to understand how the ship functioned, how each department was crucial to their survival and well-being. Four such rotations earned a six-week break, then the cycle began again.

"Are you having trouble with him?" Triana said.

Gap shook his head. "No, he's a good worker. He just has . . . I don't know, an attitude about him, like he's superior to everyone working around him."

"Well," Triana said, "he has the right to be heard, whether we agree with his opinions or not, or whether we like his attitude or not. Any other comments before I bring him in?"

There was silence in the Conference Room as the other Council members looked around at each other. Triana nodded.

"Gap, would you mind? He should be waiting right outside."

Gap hesitated a moment before he stood and walked to the door. When it opened, Merit walked in, a half-smile etched on his face. He held a small file folder in one hand. Tromping in behind him were two of the boys who had accompanied him in the Dining Hall. Triana had thought of them as an entourage at that time, and now that feeling was intensified. They paraded behind him almost like a king's subjects. Without waiting for him to speak, Triana decided to take a position of strength.

"Merit, you are welcome to address the Council. If your friends are here to add their own comments, they, too, are welcome. Otherwise, I will ask them to wait outside."

She watched as the half-smile on his face flickered, disappeared, then returned. Her comment had achieved its goal. There was no way Merit would allow any of his followers to speak. Their role was to simply provide support and, to some extent, intimidation. It was obvious, however, that he hadn't counted on Triana taking the offensive. He turned to the two boys.

"I'll see you guys later."

When the door had closed again, Triana laced her fingers together on the table and fixed Merit with a cool stare. "You have the floor."

With what appeared to Triana to be a rehearsed move, Merit walked to the end of the table with his hands clasped behind his back, a thoughtful look on his face. When he reached the end opposite Triana, he set down the folder and made eye contact with each Council member before addressing the group.

"I would like to go on record as saying that the Council of *Galahad* has done an admirable job in leading this mission, so far. There have been some rough spots along the way, and I'm sure I speak for the rest of the crew when I offer my thanks for your service and dedication."

Gap exchanged a look with Triana that said "Oh, brother."

"When each of us volunteered for this project," Merit continued, "we were told that it was the best chance available to save humankind. Bhaktul's Disease was ravaging the planet, and it seemed that there was no alternative but to send a couple hundred kids off to a new world.

"But," he said, beginning to pace slowly around the table, "it was labeled the 'best chance' by assuming that all would go well during the journey. And, granted, if this had been a trouble-free mission so far, we would all feel much better about things. But, that obviously has not been the case."

Merit had reached Triana's end of the table, and now passed behind her seat. For reasons she couldn't explain, this irritated her, as if he was subtly trying to take charge of the meeting, challenging her to turn around and give him her attention. She refused to budge, and kept her eyes forward. It had quickly become a battle of wills between the two.

"Within the first four months after the launch," Merit said, "we had not one, but two separate incidents which almost destroyed us. Two."

Gap spoke up, a touch of irritation in his voice. "Two incidents which were neutralized."

"Is that the word you use? Neutralized? If you ask around, you'll find that many of the members of this crew believe that we got lucky. Very lucky."

Channy was clearly puzzled by the discussion. "What are you talking about?"

"Think about it. In the first instance, we missed a collision with a madman by what, fifty feet? And then, if I'm correct, we were almost blown to bits around Saturn, and would have done exactly that in about ten more seconds. Fifty feet, and ten seconds. You wouldn't call that lucky?"

"What's your point, Merit?" Gap said.

"My point, Gap, is that we haven't even officially left the solar system, we haven't been away for even eight months, and we've already used up all the luck we could ever hope to have. The next time—and we all know there will be a next time—we probably can't count on good fortune again.

"This is an extremely bizarre universe we live in, with an awful lot of things that Dr. Zimmer and his team could never have imagined when they scribbled out their plans on some scrap paper. For a bunch of scientists, sitting in a safe, warm room, in front of their computer screens, it probably seemed much easier. Build a ship, fill it with a bunch of bright kids, launch it, and five years later it docks safely at a new home."

Merit had returned to the far end of the table and now leaned on it with both hands. He looked directly down the length of the table, into Triana's eyes. "It's just not that simple. We've encountered one madman, and one incredibly advanced super race of beings. What else can we expect to stumble across in the next four years? Aren't we in way over our heads?"

Lita leaned forward, a gentle expression on her face. "I don't think I quite understand what you're hinting at, Merit. You're suggesting . . . what?"

He straightened up. "It's time that we admitted that this is a much more dangerous mission than anyone ever imagined. It's time for us to turn around and head home."

"What?" Channy blurted out. "Are you crazy? We can't go back to Earth. Bhaktul's Disease—"

"Bhaktul's Disease is horrible, to be sure," Merit interrupted. "But remember, we're talking about 'best chance,' and the odds have shifted. For many of us, it makes more sense to take our chances on finding a cure at home than taking any more risks out here in space."

Gap chuckled. "The best medical minds have worked on Bhaktul for years, and they have absolutely nothing to show for it. Nothing. And now that the disease has wiped out such a large percentage of the population, there's hardly anyone left to devote the time and research to finding a cure. Face it, Merit, going back to Earth is a death sentence for everyone on this ship. A slow, grisly death, I might add."

Merit smiled his half-smile, and Triana felt a cold chill down her spine. There was a definite energy that radiated from him, an energy that made her very uncomfortable.

"You're forgetting one very important factor," he said to Gap. "The Cassini."

Silence greeted this comment until Lita spoke up. "Meaning?"

Merit spread his hands. "It's obvious, isn't it? The Cassini read everything in not only Bon's mind, but in the minds of several other crew members. The Cassini would have to know about the problem on Earth, and, as we know, they're in the business of fixing things, right? For all we know they've been working on it for the past few months. It might be a very different Earth that we return to."

Gap frowned as he said, "Might, maybe, possibly. We don't know."

"Nor do we know what's going to happen in the next five minutes out here," Merit shot back. "And so far our track record is not very good. Would you be more willing to put your faith in a handful of very tired, very ill scientists, or the Cassini?"

Triana had been silent, but finally spoke up. "You mentioned that many of our shipmates agreed with you. What do you mean by 'many'?"

Merit looked down at the folder he had carried into the room. Flipping it open, he pulled out a sheet of paper and passed it down to Triana. "I have begun a rather informal polling of people, and so far eleven have stated that they would prefer we turn around and take our chances back on Earth."

"Eleven?" Gap laughed. "You, your two buddies outside. That's three. And, what, eight other people with more time on their hands than brains?"

"Gap," Triana said, shooting him a look. She waited until he sat back, then glanced at the names on the sheet of paper. She recognized them all, of course, but didn't know them that well. "I appreciate your concerns," she said to Merit, "and the Council will take your suggestion under consideration."

Merit crossed his arms. "To be honest, I don't expect the Council to do anything. Not when eleven people speak out. But a week ago that number was six. A week from now it will likely be fifteen, and then twenty. I'm simply bringing this to your attention now so that you're not surprised when a majority of crew members vote to go back. There will come a time when you have no choice but to listen. Consider this visit today a courtesy call."

Triana felt a recurrence of irritation. It wasn't so much the message from Merit, but his manner that grated on her. His cocky attitude was frustrating, as if he was daring anyone to challenge him. Bon could be cocky, too, but only because of his self-confidence. With Bon you got the feeling that he simply believed that he was right. Merit, on the other hand, seemed to want to prove something, to force others to bend to his will. His brand of cockiness stemmed from a desire for power.

And that could be very dangerous.

She kept her expression neutral, and said again, "We will take your suggestion under consideration. Thank you for your time."

With a nod to Triana, and then to the other Council members, Merit picked up his folder and walked briskly from the room. Before the door closed, Triana saw the two other boys fall into step behind their champion.

"I can't believe it," Channy said. "That's the craziest thing I've ever heard."

Lita looked thoughtful. "I didn't give him much credit before, but I'm afraid this could become . . . a problem."

"That guy is a jerk," Gap said.

"He has every right to voice his opinion," Triana said. "And it seems that he will be voicing those opinions to just about everyone on the ship. It's our responsibility to make sure that the other side is heard, too. Agreed? Or . . . do some of you share his concerns?"

"What? No way," Gap said.

"I don't," Lita added.

"I don't even know what he's talking about," Channy said. "But if he wants to go back to Earth, then he's gonna have a hard time convincing me."

Triana looked down the table at Bon, who had not uttered a word since Merit had walked in the room. "Bon?"

"I will not go back to Earth. We started something, and we're going to finish it."

"All right," Triana said. "I need some time to process all of this. Let's get some rest, and we'll meet again soon."

For the first time, she walked out of the Conference Room before the others had a chance to stand up.

7

Lita walked into Sick House, adjusting her hair ribbon. It was almost eight o'clock in the morning and she had finished a strenuous workout with Channy's "Early Risers," a group of crew members who preferred to get their exercise out of the way before the rest of the ship came to life. Channy had varied their routine today, and Lita was feeling muscles that she had never been introduced to before. The steamy shower afterwards had never felt better.

She wasn't surprised to find Alexa already on the job. The fifteen-year-old was inputting data into a computer terminal with one hand while the other grasped a mug of tea.

"How can you do that so fast with one hand?" Lita said.

Alexa looked up and smiled. "Good morning. How can I what? Oh, this? Listen, nothing comes between me and my tea. If it means I have to learn to type quickly with one hand, that's a skill I can master." She took another gulp then nodded at the vidscreen. "Of course, you never know what that does to my accuracy. I might have just invented a whole new blood type or something."

Lita laughed and sat down across from her assistant. "I trust you. So, what's new this morning?"

"Nada. Just preparing all of the files for next week's crew checkups."

"Good. Need any help?"

"Nah," Alexa said. "You do your doctor stuff and I'll take care of the boring paperwork. No sense wasting your special training on this junk."

"You mean my crash course in how to be a doctor? How to be a doctor on a spaceship full of teenagers in just five easy lessons?"

Alexa rolled her eyes. "Please. It was a lot more than five lessons. Besides, your mother was a doctor. You practically grew up with a stethoscope around your neck and a thermometer behind your ear."

Lita sighed. "Mom was amazing. You know, she was the youngest person in her graduating class, and still had the highest test scores. She had offers from all over, including some of the top universities in America, and she chose to return home to Mexico and work in Veracruz."

"She did it because she loved it, I guess."

Lita nodded. "Yes. She loved her work, and she loved the people in her hometown. Plus," she added, a smile bending across her face, "she happened to love a certain grocery store owner in Veracruz."

"Oh, I just love a love story," Alexa said, batting her eyelids. "Especially one with such a touching theme: Big money in the big city, or love in the produce section."

Both girls laughed. For Lita it was good to discover that she could finally talk about her parents without falling into a state of gloom. She missed her family every day, and often daydreamed about the long walks on the beach with her mother, talking about life, about fate, and about finding happiness. Maria Marques had done it all, had excelled at everything, yet had not hesitated when it came time to choose her life's path. It had been home and family first, career second. Some had questioned her priorities; she had dismissed them without a thought. Lita considered this the greatest lesson her mother had ever taught her: putting family first.

"Well, our backgrounds obviously don't matter, because we both arrived in the same place," Lita said. "Your mother wasn't in the medical field, but look how you turned out."

"Sure," Alexa said. "A medical assistant who can't stand the sight of blood."

Lita laughed. "You're funny, you know that?"

"I'm serious."

"What are you talking about? You're not afraid of blood."

Alexa shrugged. "Sorry, but it's true. Can't stand it."

Lita sat forward, a look of disbelief on her face. "How in the world did you manage to sneak that past Dr. Zimmer?"

"What can I say? I thought this would be a cool place to work on the ship, and how often were we going to encounter blood? So during our training I either looked the other way, or went into some kind of Zen place. I don't know. It worked, though."

"That's about the funniest thing I've heard in a long time. A medical assistant who's afraid of blood."

Alexa took another sip of tea. "Yeah, but my incredible bed-side manner makes up for it, huh?"

"You're killing me. All right, I need to go check this morning's email before I find out something else that's absurd, like maybe you actually enjoy that horrible hospital smell."

"No, but hospital food is much better than people think."

Lita grinned and stood up. Before she could walk away, Alexa's face took on a serious look and she reached out to touch Lita's arm.

"Hey, before you go, I wanted to thank you for whatever you said to Triana and the Council."

"Why, what happened?"

"I got a nice note from Triana, thanking me for all of the hard work I've done. She said that you told the Council that I was doing a great job. So, thank you for that. It's nice . . . it's nice to be appreciated, I guess."

"Wish I could do more for you," Lita said. "I'm glad you're here." She turned to walk over to her desk, then looked back. "Of course, if I'd known about that whole blood thing I might not have said anything."

"Don't you have email to check or something?"

Triana breezed through the door to the Conference Room and found Gap with his feet up on the table, rolling a cup of water between the fingers of both hands. He gave her a quick smile of welcome.

Triana had an odd feeling about the meeting. For one thing, in the seven months since the launch, Gap had never requested a private meeting. They had been through some hair-raising experiences, but he had always voiced his opinions and concerns in the company of the Council. If he was wanting to speak with her alone, something was obviously of grave concern.

Triana also picked up an interesting vibe from him. Gap was, for the most part, very cool under pressure. He had a temper—she had seen that a few times, including some memorable episodes between Gap and Bon—but when a crisis arose, she knew that she could count on him to remain composed and to help her navigate through the storm. Today, however, he seemed almost . . . jittery. The feet up on the table seemed like a manufactured calm, betrayed by the nervous actions with the cup.

And betrayed by his eyes.

There was, of course, another possible explanation that flitted across her mind. Perhaps this was "the talk" that she had anticipated for so long. She knew that Gap had feelings for her—or used to have. He had often seemed on the verge of expressing those feelings, too, until either something interrupted the moment, or he lost his nerve. For a guy who had remained

cool while a madman threatened to destroy them, he had an awfully hard time verbalizing his feelings about Triana.

And just what feelings, exactly, did she harbor for Gap? Or for
Bon? It was easy to critique another person's difficulty with expression, and yet she was no better. Perhaps it was the intrigue
itself that she embraced.

Besides, now that Gap had developed a relationship with
Hannah, what could he possibly say to Triana?

"Thanks for carving a few minutes out of your day to chat,"
he said.

"No problem. What's up?"

"Not much, unless you count the boulder the size of a loco-
motive that just zipped past about a mile below us."

Triana took the seat across from Gap and let out a sigh. "A
mile? And when did we spot it?"

"About five seconds after it passed us."

"Oh, great," Triana said. "Just what our friend Merit needs to
hear, that we had another close call. Roc, why didn't we catch this
one sooner?"

The computer's reply was immediate. "How can I possibly
concentrate on my piano lessons *and* watch for asteroids and comets at the same time?"

Gap answered her question. "Because it was one of those ric-
ochet shots we talked about. This thing bounced off not one, but
two different rocks before it flew right at us. Which leads me to
the real reason I wanted to talk to you alone. Roc has actually
come up with an explanation for why *Galahad* Control wasn't prepared for the mess out here in the Kuiper Belt."

Triana sat back. "Okay, I'm all ears."

"I love that expression," Roc said. "All ears. You humans look
sorta funny anyway, just imagine—"

"Roc," said Gap. "Can you get on with it?"

"Gee, you'd think a giant boulder had almost creamed us
or something," Roc said. "Okay, here's the lowdown. We knew

before the launch that the Kuiper Belt was a vast collection of space junk: rocks, comets, ice chunks, sand grains, all of the missing socks that seem to disappear in your dryer. They're all circling the sun way out here in no man's land, and almost impossible to see from Earth. Our calculations about the makeup of the Kuiper Belt, aside from the bigger objects, like Pluto, were mostly guesswork. Educated guesses, but still guesses.

"Then, we come sailing along, and it's nothing like we expected. Sure, we've found the ice chunks, the comets, and even Bon's missing sense of humor, but we never expected so many items clustered together. It's way crowded out here, and that did not factor into the equations."

"And you have an answer for this?" Triana said.

"Give me enough time and I'll come up with an answer for almost any puzzle. Well, except for ketchup on eggs. That's just gross, if you ask me, and I can't figure out why anyone would do it.

"But the Kuiper Belt is another story. I've spent a little time analyzing everything we knew about this area before we got here, along with all of the new data in the last couple of weeks. It turns out that the Belt is lumpy in some areas."

Triana looked at Gap, who waited for the computer to explain.

"We've assumed that it has a uniform thickness all the way around the sun," Roc said. "Instead, there are some sections that are rather thin and sparse, with almost nothing around. We could drive a million *Galahad*'s through these spots and never come within a million miles of even a pebble.

"Then, however, there are stretches that are teeming with an excess of rubbish. Kinda like that one closet in your grandparents' house that is stuffed with all of the gifts you ever bought for them but they never took out of the package. You know what I'm talking about."

"Let me guess," Triana said. "We've run smack dab into a closet."

"Bingo."

"And what makes it even worse," Gap added, "are the odds."

"Do I want to even hear this?" Triana said.

"Sure, if only to appreciate how remarkable it all is. These jam-packed stretches only occur in about thirty-five percent of the Kuiper Belt. We had only a one in three chance of stumbling into this, yet we did."

Triana found herself chuckling, not because there was anything really funny about it all. It just seemed that fate was determined to throw every possible challenge their way. It was never going to be smooth sailing, it seemed.

"Okay," she finally said. "And you wanted to tell me this privately because . . ."

Gap shifted in his chair and set down his cup of water. He stared across the conference table into Triana's eyes.

"Because Roc has also figured what our chances are of making it through the minefield without a really big bang."

Triana sighed again. "Go right ahead. Make my day complete."

The computer's voice was loud and clear. "Ooh, I hope you like a good challenge, because I figure about one in twelve that we make it through unscathed. Actually, more like one in thirteen, but we can fudge it down just a touch."

One in twelve. Triana felt the weight of the mission collapse onto her shoulders once again. The figures meant that for every twelve times they took this path through the Kuiper Belt, eleven of those times the ship would be destroyed, without warning.

She bit her lip and, without thinking, reached across and picked up Gap's water cup. She took a long drink, wiped her mouth with the back of her hand, and pushed a stray hair out of her face. Gap remained silent while she processed the information.

"Okay," she said. "I'm making an executive decision here. I would prefer that none of what we've discussed leave this room. Under normal circumstances I would probably inform the crew,

but things are far from normal right now. I hate to have somebody like Merit Simms influence my leadership, but during a
time of external crisis the last thing we need is more internal
strife. He's preaching a message of doom and destruction, and
this will only fan his flames a little bit more."

"I agree with that," Gap said. "Anyway, he's all about turning
the ship around, and to be honest that's exactly what we don't
want to be doing in a minefield. He wouldn't understand that, of
course, because it's contrary to what he wants. But I think Roc
would agree that a quick straight line is the best strategy for avoiding bumping into something."

"Probably," Roc said. "Although just being inside this portion
of the Belt is like being tossed around inside a bag full of marbles. Eventually something is likely to take the paint off."

"Then we understand each other," Triana said. "No sense
causing a panic. Mum's the word."

She looked back at Gap again and debated whether to say what
was on her mind. She didn't want to sound petty or jealous. Finally, with a shrug she decided that it was too important to ignore. "Don't even tell Hannah, right?"

Rather than seem offended, Gap replied with his own shrug.
"Listen, chances are, with her passion for astronomy and numbers,
she'll have it figured out on her own any day now. But, yeah, I'll
keep quiet." He paused, then added, "And don't worry about the
fuss that Merit Simms is making. There are too many dedicated
people on this ship for him to have much of an impact."

Triana nodded, yet didn't possess the same confidence. Something told her that things were going to get complicated.

Soon.

8

The workout had been over for almost ten minutes, but the scowl on Channy's face had not diminished much. She watched, sweat dripping down the side of her face, as the last of the morning group finished putting their mats away and gathering their personal belongings. Channy was unquestionably the most popular crew member on board, but when she was in this mood—the angry drill sergeant mood—few people would make eye contact with her, let alone stop by for a chat.

Kylie Rickman was an exception. She was Channy's roommate, and she knew that one of her most important roles was as a sounding board when the petite Brit was fired up. Kylie drained a cup of water, wiped her forehead with a towel, and leaned back against a cabinet.

"I don't know if I've ever seen you so irritated."

Channy continued to glare. "It's my job to make sure this crew doesn't get fat and lazy during the trip. If they keep this nonsense up, by the time we reach Eos they won't be able to run fifty feet without stopping to rest." She shook her head. "Pitiful."

Kylie chuckled. "Exaggerating a little bit, aren't we?"

"Not much. You were part of the group this morning. Did you see what the back row was doing? Having a little social outing."

"Hmph," Kylie snorted. "Sounds like something right up your alley."

Channy turned her glare to focus on her roommate, then slowly relaxed, and a faint smile crossed her face. "That's right, and as the unofficial social director around here, I can't have any unsanctioned parties."

Both girls laughed, and Kylie was glad to see her old friend return. She rolled her towel and snapped it at Channy's leg. "You know, for such a good-natured girl, you have a bit of wildcat in you, don't you?"

"Hey, just doing my job," Channy said. "And you better watch out with that towel. You know what they say about payback."

Kylie refilled her cup of water. "Let me ask you something. Those two girls over there, they were in the back row. What's with the armbands they're wearing?"

Channy shook her head. "Why don't we ask?" She raised her voice. "Vonya! Addie! Have you got a second?"

The two girls, who were talking in hushed whispers against the far wall of the gym, looked over, then glanced quickly at each other. Channy could have sworn that it was almost a guilty look that they shared. After a moment's hesitation, as if they wanted to ignore Channy's invitation, they slowly made their way across the room. They stopped about six feet away, arms crossed, with almost defiant looks on their faces.

"Did you enjoy the workout this morning?" Channy said.

Addie, a petite girl from Austria, looked at her friend, then shrugged. "I guess so." Vonya didn't answer.

"The only reason I ask," Channy said, "is because you seemed very preoccupied with something. It was a little tough keeping your attention today."

Again, Vonya didn't answer. Addie, apparently feeling the awkwardness of the situation, raised her chin a touch and said, "We were just talking. Is that okay?"

Channy stared at Addie for a few seconds before responding.

"Sure, as long as you don't disrupt the group. Would it be all right if I asked you to wait until after the workout to chat?"

Vonya spoke up. "Fine. Is there anything else?"

Channy could feel the distinct coolness emanating from the pair. She didn't know them very well, but had always exchanged friendly greetings with them. What was going on? She shifted her gaze down to the armbands that they both sported. They were a light yellow color, obviously homemade, crafted from the same piece of cloth. A permanent marker had been used to stencil "R.T.E." on them in bold black lettering.

"Mind if I ask about those?" Channy said. "I haven't seen them before, and I'm just curious."

The two girls looked at each other, and then Addie said, "They're symbols of unity."

"Okay. Uh, unity for what? Or who?"

Vonya gave an impatient sigh. "We happen to belong to a group of crew members who have decided that it's ridiculous to continue this mission to Eos. We're in favor of turning around, and taking our chances back on Earth."

The shock registered on Channy's face. "You've been recruited by Merit Simms?"

"Not recruited," said Addie. "Convinced. This ship has almost been wiped out twice, and we've barely started. Merit is the only person making any sense these days, and we agree with him." She kept her arms crossed, and now shifted to one side, her weight on one foot, assuming an almost confrontational pose. Her face looked menacing.

"Don't get mad," Channy said. "I'm just asking questions."

For the first time, Kylie spoke up from beside Channy. "What does the 'R.T.E.' stand for?"

"Return to Earth," said Addie. "It's our rally cry, and you're going to be hearing it a lot more over the next few weeks."

Kylie grunted. "Why in the world would you want to return to Earth? You think Bhaktul has just disappeared?"

"Maybe. Merit says that the Cassini have probably already started working on it, and it will be long gone by the time we get back."

"That's quite an assumption," Channy said. "And if he's wrong?"

Vonya's face took on the same look as her friend's. "Then we're no worse off than we are out here. Of course, I wouldn't expect one of Triana's robots to understand."

Channy began to take a step forward, then felt Kylie's grip on her arm. The Council member stopped and took a deep breath, locked into a staring showdown with Vonya. After a few moments she relaxed and feigned a smile.

"Okay, well, thanks for clearing that up. We might disagree on some things, but that doesn't mean we can't work up a good sweat together down here, right?"

Addie and Vonya once again exchanged looks, then turned and walked out of the gym, chattering under their breath. Just before they walked out the door Channy could hear one of them snickering.

"Thanks," she muttered to Kylie. "I almost lost my temper there."

"They're rude," Kylie said. "It's always been funny to me that some people automatically go into attack mode just because someone asks them questions, or disagrees with them. That's no way to argue your point." She shook her head, then looked at her roommate. "When did all this 'return to Earth' stuff pop up?"

"Just recently. Merit Simms—the guy they were talking about—is trying to round up support for his ideas. Unfortunately he's spreading a lot of misinformation."

"Like that stuff about the Cassini? You know, I've wondered about that myself."

Channy stared at her friend, incredulous. "What are you talking about?"

Kylie shrugged. "You know, just a random thought after we

passed by Titan. I mean . . ." She seemed to be searching for words. "I mean, if they really are that powerful and all . . ."

"Listen," Channy said. "We have a mission to accomplish. Don't let a bunch of wild ideas start bouncing around your head. Going back to Earth would be a death sentence for us. We have no way of knowing if the Cassini even *know* about Bhaktul's Disease, so why would we assume that they have any way—or desire—to fix it?"

Kylie turned to set down her cup of water. "I'm sure you're right. Hey, I've gotta run, I have a history class in twenty minutes. Talk to you later, right?" Without waiting for an answer, she darted out of the room and toward the lift.

Channy stared after her, a worried expression staining her usually glowing face.

G ot a second?"

Bon looked up from his office desk in Dome 1. Large windows on one wall allowed him to watch the activity in the dome, so he was surprised that he hadn't seen the approach of Merit Simms, who now stood leaning against the door, one hand in a pocket.

"What for?" Bon said.

Merit grinned. "I'll take that as a yes. I just wanted to ask you about something."

"I'm busy."

"This won't take long."

Bon stood, walked around his desk, and perched on the edge. He crossed his arms, his cold eyes flashing. "Make it quick."

Merit walked into the office and looked out the window into the artificial sunlight bathing Dome 1. In the distance a group of workers harvested potatoes, while three other crew members pushed a work cart down another row in the fields.

"You guys stay very busy," Merit said. "During my last tour

of duty up here I think I sweated off five pounds. Not enough people express their gratitude for the work you do. I mean, we all eat very well, thanks to—"

"Is that why you're here?" Bon said. "To express gratitude?"

Another grin splashed across Merit's face. "Well, sure. It's not the main reason, but I'll say it anyway."

"Fine. You're welcome. Now, I told you I was busy."

"Yes, you did. In fact, it's pretty obvious to me, and probably to a lot of people, that you're one of the hardest workers on the ship. I've talked with a few people about you, and other than meals in the Dining Hall, and a quick daily workout, nobody ever sees you. You don't socialize, you don't hang out in the Rec Room, you don't participate in the soccer tournaments. Stuff like that. So I guess everyone assumes that you spend all of your time here, working."

Bon's eyes narrowed. "You know, you take an awfully long time to get to your point. You don't care about my schedule or how I spend my time. What do you want?"

"It's precisely because of the way you spend your time that I want to talk with you," Merit said. "There are very few people aboard *Galahad* who have the perspective that you have. You work hard, you don't waste time with things you don't care about, and you don't get caught up in some of these ridiculous social cliques. In fact, I think it's safe to say that you are probably the most efficient crew member on the ship."

Merit leaned on the sill of the window. "And, you're a Council member. That means you also get a good perspective on the way the ship is managed."

"Yes. So?"

"Well, Bon, that makes you a rather important person for me to get to know. Because, as you heard, I'm convinced that we are doomed if we continue along this path. We've had warning flag after warning flag. How many more catastrophes do *you* think we can survive? You, of all people, should understand what I'm talking about. You were the only reason we survived the trip around Saturn and Titan. You, not Triana, not the Council, not anyone else."

Bon remained silent, but his eyes probed Merit's. His arms were still crossed, and his right index finger began to slowly tap on his left bicep.

"It's also no secret that you don't see eye to eye with many of the decisions that Triana makes. You're not afraid to express your opinions. Am I right?"

"Yes," Bon said. "I say what I feel. And, unlike you, I don't waste words saying it."

Merit nodded. "I respect you for that. And I respect the fact that you're not afraid to confront Triana." He pushed away from the wall and slowly began to pace around the room as he talked.

"Bon, every day we continue on this journey, we increase the chances that we won't survive. First it was our stowaway. Then it was the Cassini. Now it's this shooting gallery called the Kuiper Belt that we've thrown ourselves into. Word has it that we've already had several near-misses, and we've barely begun to work our way through it."

"You signed up for the trip just like the rest of us, Merit."

"That's right, I did. But we were never really told what we'd be dealing with, were we? Did you get some sort of pre-launch lecture about alien intelligence around Saturn? Did any of us think that our heating system was shaky? Dr. Zimmer was so busy building team spirit that he conveniently neglected to share a few minor details with us, like the fact that we would probably never survive the first year."

"I think Dr. Zimmer explained very well the dangers we would face," Bon said. "You must have been distracted during those discussions. Maybe too busy trying to get people to pay attention to you."

Merit's smile seemed forced. "It's okay if you don't really like me right now. I understand. Change is hard for most people. I just figured you were a little different than most people."

"Your psychobabble won't work with me."

"Once I walk out of here you'll think about it, though. I know you will. And you'll realize soon enough that this is no psycho-babble. I'm just like you, Bon; I tell it like it is. Which is why I want you on my team."

"Is that what you call it? Your 'team'?"

"We are a team. And our team is growing every day. A smart guy like you can recognize a winning team when he sees it. Give it some thought."

"I don't need to give it any thought," Bon said, standing. "And now I think you'd better leave."

"Just a minute. Let me ask you one other thing." Merit stepped forward until he stood facing Bon. "If you change your mind, what do you think Triana will do?"

"I'm not going to change—"

"Just suppose. Has Triana ever listened to you before? Do you think she would now?"

"I told you to leave."

"You want to know why she won't listen to you?" Merit said, taking one more step forward until he was face-to-face with the blond Swede. "Because no matter what you think my motives are, they are nothing compared to hers. She won't listen to you, or anyone else on the Council, because she's afraid, and will never admit that she's wrong."

"Get out."

"She doesn't mind dying, Bon, because it's the ultimate escape for her. Running away from her problems on Earth was easy for her, and she'll avoid facing those problems even if it means killing the rest of us."

It happened quickly. Bon's fist flew through the air and con-nected solidly on the side of Merit's mouth. Merit staggered back-ward, lost his footing, and fell.

Bon looked down at him. "I told you three times to get out. I won't tell you again."

Merit propped himself up on one elbow, then gingerly touched the corner of his mouth with a finger, which came away bloody. He examined it for a second, then held it up for Bon to see.

"Touched a nerve, did I? Was that punch in defense of your own stubbornness, or in defense of Triana?"

Bon didn't answer, but instead glared down at him as if ready to continue the fight. Merit grinned again, then slowly clambered to his feet. He dabbed at his bloodied mouth one more time, then looked at Bon.

"Actually, you've done me a huge favor, Bon. This," he said, holding up the bloody finger, "could come in very handy. Thank you."

He spun around and walked quickly out of the office. Bon watched through the large window as Merit strolled down the path toward the lift.

"Great," Bon muttered.

Wait a minute. I wasn't paying close attention here. Did Bon just punch that guy in the mouth? Really?

Hey, you can forget the "Why didn't you stop him, Roc?" comments. First of all, what did you expect me, a computer, to do about it? It's not like I could step between them.

And secondly, I've seen Bon with his shirt off, and I wouldn't have stepped between them anyway. As one girl in Channy's aerobic class said, "Hubba hubba."

And thirdly, he would have just punched me in my sensor and THEN punched Merit in the mouth.

And fourthly . . . well, there is no fourthly. That's enough.

Except that I'm pretty sure this is all getting very sticky.

9

'm sick of this," Gap said to himself.

He stood in front of the same panel in the Engineering section, watching as the sensors told him that the heating elements on Level Six were acting up yet again.

The intercom buzzed. "Gap," came Channy's voice. Without waiting to hear another word, Gap reached over and clicked it off. This time his patience for the fun and games was at zero.

He ran a hand through his short, spiky hair and exhaled loudly, mixing in a sort of primal grunt with it, eliciting a giggle from behind him. Turning, he found Hannah standing there, an amused smile on her face. They had made a tentative date for breakfast together in the Dining Hall, but Gap had been sidetracked by the latest breakdown in the heating system.

"That," she said, "is the sound of utter and total frustration."

"Which is exactly what I'm feeling. If I could take a wrench and bash this thing . . ." His voice trailed off, before returning in a shout. "Roc, this is a not a good use of my time!"

"I know," the computer said. "Think of how many laps you could be making right now on the Airboard track."

"Oh, very funny," Gap said. He looked back at Hannah who was stifling another giggle. "Don't encourage him, okay?"

"Well," Roc said, "if you function better without the gentle infusion of wit, I can certainly adopt a stern, brooding attitude." His computer voice lowered an octave. "How's this? Doom, doom, death, death, aaarrrgggghhhhhh."

This time Hannah's giggle escaped her mouth. Gap closed his eyes and shook his head, covering his face with one hand. From behind the hand he muttered, "I don't need this. I swear I don't need this."

"Poor Gap," Roc said in his normal voice, the one that mimicked that of his creator, Roy Orzini. Roy had not only developed the world's most sophisticated computer, but he had taken great pains to make sure that the artificial brain incorporated Roy's voice and—more importantly—his personality. Gap had verbally sparred with the short, funny man for months before the launch, and had since found that he could do the same thing through Roc.

Gap spread his fingers in order to peek through at Hannah. "If you want to go ahead to the Dining Hall, I'll try to join you as soon as I can."

She shook her head. "No, I'll wait here with you. Maybe I can help."

"I don't know how." He lowered the hand and turned to look at Roc's sensor. "I mean, if our resident genius comedian can't help . . ."

"Okay, Mr. Serious," Roc said. "I can't stand to watch you pout, so I recommend a complete re-boot of the entire system, then a re-program for Level Six that bypasses its Balsom clips and runs the level's heating through the clips on Four and Five."

"What good will that do, except to maybe burn out the clips on those other levels?"

"That's not likely. The clips can take on almost two hundred percent of their engineered specs, and we're talking only about a fifty percent increase. This is just a short-term fix to pinpoint whether it actually is Mr. Balsom's fault. Besides, remember that this was *your* idea in the first place."

Gap chewed on this for a moment. "And what would the long-term fix include?"

"If it turns out to be the Balsom clips on Six," Roc said, "and if replacing them doesn't work, then we can re-program the entire ship to run on the other five levels' systems, sharing the load equally. That will hardly put a dent in their capacity. And, if that still worries you, which, knowing you, is more than likely—"

"Oh ha ha," Gap said.

"Then we could even lower the overall ship temperature by one degree, and that should bring everything back to normal."

"One degree would do that?"

"One degree."

Gap's eyes unfocused as he tried to work the math in his head. When he heard Hannah clear her throat, he looked at her.

"Uh, I think he's right," she said meekly. "It wouldn't take much."

Hannah was, without question, one of the best scientific minds on the ship, so Gap knew better than to doubt her.

"Okay, I believe you guys," he said. "I guess the hardest part would be explaining it to the crew so that they don't freak out. I can handle Channy's jokes, but some people might use this to stir up trouble." He didn't mention Merit Simms by name, but that was certainly the first thing that had popped into his head. He could only imagine the look on Triana's face if he had to break the news to her.

The intercom buzzed again, and this time, before Gap could reach to shut it off, Channy's voice seeped out. "Gap, you've got to hurry up here to Level Six, quickly!"

This didn't sound like a joke. What could have happened now?

"What is it?" he said.

"You've got to see this, Gap. There are eight tiny reindeer walking around up here, convinced that this is their home." There came an immediate burst of laughter from everyone in the room with Channy. Fuming, Gap punched off the intercom.

"Um . . . maybe I will meet you in the Dining Hall," Hannah said with a smile. She leaned over and gave him a quick peck on the cheek, then strolled out of the Engineering section, obviously holding back a laugh.

Triana rubbed her hands together as she walked into Sick House. She knew that Gap was furiously working on the heating problem, and she also knew that he was likely getting enough input without her bothering him. Instead, she answered a call from Lita to stop by the ship's clinic. Lita wouldn't elaborate over the intercom, but Triana could tell from her friend's voice that it was something she should do at once.

"A little chilly, huh?" Lita said from her desk.

"It's probably worse for you," Triana said, plopping down in the available chair. "Not too many days in Veracruz like this. Makes those of us from Colorado a little homesick, though." She glanced around the room, which was empty and quiet. "Where's Alexa?"

Lita chuckled. "Would you believe it? I give her all that praise in the Council meeting, then you sent her a personal note of thanks for her hard work, and today she called in sick. Figures, huh?"

"Sick? Alexa? What's wrong with her?"

"Just a stomachache, but bad enough that I told her to lay low for the rest of the day."

"Well," Triana said, leaning back so that the chair tipped onto its two rear legs, "I won't razz her about it. What's this, her first-ever sick day?"

"Yeah. And you should have heard her apologizing. You'd have thought that it was her tenth straight day, or something. But that's not why I called you down here."

"No, I didn't think so. What's up?"

Lita moved a couple of items around on her desk, in what

appeared to Triana to be a stalling tactic. There was something that she apparently wasn't anxious to share.

"I had three people stop by Sick House today. One was Nung; you remember him. Very cool guy from Thailand. Nothing major there, just a little readjustment in his meds. Then our usual monthly Airboarding injury. Ariel actually took a pretty good spill today."

Triana raised her eyebrows. "I heard she was one of the best."

"Listen, that's a crazy sport. I don't care how good you are, you're one pulse away from wiping out. Remember what happened to our boy Gap? He's the champ, and he still broke his collarbone."

"Is Ariel okay?"

"Bruised ribs. She actually landed on her board."

Triana winced. "Okay, it doesn't take a detective to figure out that I'm sitting here because of your third visit. Wanna fill me in?"

Lita stopped fidgeting and looked directly into Triana's face. "About an hour ago I treated Merit Simms for a bloody lip."

Slowly, Triana's chair rocked forward, back onto all four legs. "What?"

"Uh-huh. He got clocked today."

"By?"

"Take one guess. Who would be the most likely candidate on the ship to punch someone?"

Triana dropped her head and stared at the floor, her elbows resting on her knees. "Bon."

"Yep. I guess they had some sort of confrontation up in Bon's office. The way Merit tells it, Bon lost his temper and just slugged Merit, and all Merit was doing was talking with him. That's his story, anyway."

"I'm sure he provoked Bon, but that's not too hard to do, is it?"

"You're right about that. But it wasn't even necessary for Merit to come see me."

"What do you mean?"

Lita shrugged. "I mean, his lip had already stopped bleeding, and it wasn't all that bad. He still wanted it cleaned up, and a tiny bandage put on it. I told him that wasn't necessary, but he insisted. I know he's not worried about infection."

Triana shook her head. "No, that's not why he came here. He wants a record of the incident. He wants it in your files that he was assaulted by Bon, and proof that there was an injury."

"That's what I figured."

"Yeah," Triana said. "It all makes sense, really. He's building a case, trying to recruit as many people as possible. I'm sure he went to see Bon with one intention, and that was to goad Bon into either hitting him, or shoving him, or something." She sighed. "And now he has another piece of information to use against us."

Lita leaned forward onto her desk. "Well, he's not wasting much time using it, either."

"What?"

"Looked at your email lately?" When Triana shook her head, Lita turned her vidscreen around to face the Council Leader. "Check out the mass email that Mr. Simms sent out five minutes after he left Sick House."

Triana scanned the note.

Many of you have expressed an interest in finding out more about the proposal to turn the ship around and head back to Earth. I've had numerous emails from concerned crew members who are afraid that our next dangerous encounter will be the one that kills all of us. I obviously share your fears, and have begged the Council to at least hear our arguments. They have refused. If you are as worried about this as I am, then I invite you to join me for an informal discussion on the subject. This will be a peaceful gathering of facts and opinions, and a chance for your voice to be heard. Tomorrow evening, at 7:30, in the Dining Hall. I welcome your attendance, and your feedback.

Merit Simms

Triana read it a second time, and felt her shoulders sag. Terrific. Another chance for Merit to distort the facts and paint a warped image of their condition.

And with a war wound, to boot. Nothing like playing the sympathy card, which was evidently in his plans all along. There was no doubt now that to underestimate Merit Simms would be a terrible mistake.

10

It felt warm, almost tropical, and needed only the sound of birds mixed in with the crash of waves on a beach to complete the aura. Except this tropical air wasn't near the equator on Earth; it was encased in a large geodesic dome that sat atop the most impressive spacecraft ever assembled, and it nurtured the lifeblood of the *Galahad* mission: the Farms.

Through special planning and careful cultivation, the Farms on the ship could encourage the growth of fruits and vegetables in a close proximity that could never be mimicked on Earth. Within fifty feet of Dome 2, for example, could be found examples of plant life that would never be found within hundreds, or thousands, of miles back home. It was part of the amazing engineering marvel that was built to safely carry 251 passengers to a new land of opportunity.

Bon stood in a freshly turned plot of soil, with stakes and colored tags that identified the plants which would soon be surprising the hungry crew with plates of various melons and berries. He had long ago given up announcing the release dates in advance, since the clamor of the crew distracted Bon's workers and took their eye off the prize. That lack of focus often translated to a tongue-lashing from a certain Swede.

The good news? Once you experienced a chewing-out by Bon

you did everything in your power to make sure it never happened again. On this particular afternoon he was face-to-face with a sixteen-year-old from Portugal named Marco, who stared at the dirt around his feet, only occasionally making eye contact with Bon. It was obvious from Marco's body language that he was anticipating a verbal barrage.

"And what, exactly, is the standard procedure," Bon said, "when you find a section, like this one, that has been overlooked during the sowing process?"

Marco kicked at a dirt clod. "I know."

"Answer the question."

"File an immediate report, and . . . and contact you."

Bon nodded, his usual scowl firmly in place. "And you did neither."

Another kick, another clump of dirt sprayed outward. "I thought that it might not be too late," Marco said. "So . . . so I . . ."

"So you took it upon yourself to begin a new round of planting and fertilization," Bon said. "You didn't even take the time to fill out the forms hanging in my office."

"I filled them out."

"Not until the next morning."

Marco put his head back down and glanced at the purple tag attached to the nearest metal stake, his handwriting clearly listing the information for this row of melons. He waited for the volume of Bon's berating to intensify, but instead was surprised by the silence that surrounded them for a minute. When he looked back up, Bon was staring at him.

"You know what this means?" Bon said.

Marco shook his head.

"It means," Bon said, "that you're one of the few people around here who knows what he's doing. Thank you."

For a moment Marco remained still, his mind trying to decipher the words. A puzzled look crossed his face. Bon reached out and put a hand on his shoulder.

"All I've ever wanted is a group of workers who didn't wait around to be told what to do. You knew what needed to be done, and you didn't waste time waiting for me to tell you to do it. So, thank you again."

A hesitant smile worked its way across Marco's lips. "Really?"

"Really. I have plenty to do without having to babysit every single row of every single crop. I'll remember this when it's time for evaluations. Now you probably have something fun to do this evening. Go ahead and get out of here, and I'll see you tomorrow morning."

Marco's smile widened. "Thanks, Bon. Have . . . have a good night." He turned and sprinted down the path toward the lift.

Bon knelt to examine the soil, making sure that it was getting the vital moisture it needed this early in the growing stage, and was startled by the voice behind him.

"Don't worry, I won't tell anyone."

He spun around to find a grinning Gap about ten feet away. "Tell anyone what?"

Gap took a few steps toward him. "About your soft side. I was cringing, waiting for the explosion, and I don't even work up here. I can imagine how Marco was feeling."

"Do you always eavesdrop on private conversations?"

"I didn't mean to," Gap said. "I've been looking all over the Domes for you, and just happened to walk up while you were talking to Marco. Thought I'd just stand back and wait until you were finished."

Bon turned back to concentrate on the new melon seedlings that had been planted. "Well, that had nothing to do with a soft side. He did the right thing, so I told him. No big deal."

"I'll bet it's a big deal for Marco. I think what you did was cool. You made his whole week. Did you see how fast he flew out of here?"

Bon didn't respond. He patted the soil a couple of times, then stood and brushed his hands together.

"Maybe it's the timing, that's all," Gap said. "I mean, after your last private meeting with a crew member."

Slowly, Bon turned his steely gaze upon Gap. "That was also a private conversation."

"Sure, what you discussed is obviously between you two. But Merit is making sure that the results aren't private. He's already visited Sick House, and now he's planning a meeting for tonight after dinner."

"He's free to do that."

"He's free to do more than that, really," Gap said. "He could have you brought before the Council for disciplinary action."

"So be it."

Gap shook his head and took another step closer. "Listen, I know we've had some good times in the past, and I also know that we've had our share of conflicts with each other. Things have been . . . pretty cold between us the last few months, and I'm sorry about that."

Bon shrugged. Gap had the distinct impression that having this conversation was the last thing that the Swede wanted to be doing. But he also knew that this particular discussion was long overdue. It was another inadvertent bit of eavesdropping that had originally put Gap at odds with his fellow Council member, months ago, when Gap had stumbled upon a somewhat intimate moment between Bon and Triana. Gap's heart had been severely bruised that day, watching a connection between the girl he had secretly adored and the former friend with whom he had bonded during their training.

Now, after months of reflection—not to mention a flourishing romance with Hannah Ross—Gap felt a need to mend the split with the guy who had eventually saved the ship from destruction at the hands of the Cassini. He knew that his reluctance to approach Bon had been fueled primarily by jealousy, and the time had come to rise above that.

The incident with Merit Simms provided a convenient excuse to do so.

"Anyway," Gap said, "there's no telling what the fallout will be from your punch. I'm pretty sure that Triana will have no choice but to address the crew at some point, and lecture everyone about conflict resolution. You know, 'violence is never the answer,' that sort of stuff."

Bon ran a dirt-stained hand through his long hair. "I have not made a habit of violence, though, have I? One isolated incident, that's all."

"Yes, that's true," Gap said. "But you know that, as the Council Leader, she still has responsibilities, and one of those is keeping the peace. Which," he added with a sigh, "might be a little tougher in the days to come."

The sound of irrigation pipes coming to life suddenly gurgled near them, and both boys automatically began to walk toward the path that led to Bon's office. Neither said anything for a minute, unsure of exactly how to end the conversation. It was Gap who found the way.

"For the record," he said, "I would have to agree that violence is certainly not the answer with someone like Merit. But . . ." He paused, then flashed a grin. "But *off* the record, you have no idea how glad I am you did it."

As usual, Bon kept silent, but his fierce eyes softened a bit.

And when Gap stuck out his hand, the sullen son of a farmer grasped it firmly, shook it once, then turned and walked into his office.

She had managed only about four hours of sleep the night before, and now Triana sat in her room, a mug of hot tea steaming on the table, and her journal spread open before her. She had climbed out of bed at 6:30, invested thirty minutes on the treadmill in the gym, then showered and changed before spending a few hours checking in with the various departments of the ship. She had stumbled back into her room around noon and wolfed down a mango energy block before deciding that tea might be just what she needed during the break.

A quick check of the clock caused her to unconsciously calculate the time remaining before the gathering in the Dining Hall. At first she had tried to convince herself that few people would bother to attend; now she resigned herself to the fact that it likely would be bustling with crew members, mostly curious about the battle lines that were being drawn.

Triana took up her pen and finished the journal entry.

I'm starting to come to grips with the emotions that are stirring inside me regarding this conflict with Merit. At first I was tentative, almost nervous, and completely unsure of how to deal with it. But now that has begun to shift. If I'm truly honest with myself, I have to admit that I'm angry. Angry that someone would intentionally create chaos aboard the ship, when we have enough to deal with already. Angry that so many others have neglected to think for themselves, and are blindly following whoever shouts the loudest. And angry that I came across as weak in the face of the enemy. That must end. Although it was wrong, and will more than likely come back to haunt us, perhaps I should credit Bon for snapping me out of my delicate state. In one moment Bon simply acted upon what many of us might have felt. Typical for him, I suppose. And although I can't condone his actions, in a roundabout way the punch has knocked me backward as much as Merit.

She set down the pen, took a swig of the tea, and sat back in her chair. After a moment of consideration, she closed the journal and called out to the computer.

"Roc, I have a lot on my plate right now, and this will probably be a tough day. So, how about a distraction for a few moments?"

"Now isn't that an interesting twist," the computer said. "All of those times that you were irritated with me when I distracted you, and now you're begging for it. Typical."

"Well, let's face it, sometimes you pick the worst possible times to act up."

"Or," Roc said, "the best possible times, depending on how you look at it. What's the matter, Tree?"

"Oh, let's see. A potential mutiny from the crew, and about a bazillion giant chunks of rock hurtling at us. Other than that, you mean?"

"Hmm, you definitely need a distraction. I'll tell you what; let's count all of the ways I'm indispensable to you and the ship."

Triana smiled. "Okay, I guess that's enough distractions for now."

"Hey!"

"Besides," Triana said, "I don't have time to play, as tempting as it is. You made me smile, and for now that's good enough. Let me ask you about the heating system."

"Boy, you *are* all business today, aren't you?"

"I haven't been able to catch up with Gap today. What's our status with the repairs?"

"We're trying something new," Roc said. "We're running the system on Six through the Balsom clips on Four and Five. Gap will not let go of his theory that it's the clips, so I'm humoring him."

"So . . . where does that leave us?"

"The system will drop out again, because, as I told Wonder Boy, it's not the Balsom clips. It's just like playing a game of Masego with him; you have to let him make his own mistakes before he'll take your suggestions. He's quite stubborn, in case you haven't noticed."

Triana chuckled at the mention of Masego. The popular game, introduced to the crew by a girl from Africa, required a strategic mind and extreme patience. Gap had plenty of one, not so much of the other, and Roc enjoyed torturing him whenever they played in the Rec Room.

"Well," she said, "it's not like I don't have a lot of stress right now, you know? So, do I need to worry about this heating stuff, or will it eventually get fixed?"

"I'll tell you when to worry," Roc said. "Actually, I'll probably drop a few subtle hints first so that you don't panic. Like, 'Hey Tree, we're all going to die.' You know, something like that."

"Right. Okay, let's talk about the giant boulder situation."

"No," Roc said. "Let's not talk about that."

Another small laugh escaped from the Council Leader. "Then all you're leaving me is the Merit Simms problem. I suppose you know about the meeting tonight?"

"Can't wait," the computer said. "Knowing you the way I do, I'm guessing that you're going to be there?"

Triana nodded. "Uh-huh. Hey, if it affects the crew, I need to know firsthand what information is being thrown about. I could be wimpy and send some spy to find out for me—or have you tell me—but I want Merit to see me there."

"Bravo," Roc said. "Would you like for me to do anything to mess with his presentation? You know, have the lights flicker, play loud music, pipe in the sound of demonic laughter every time he says the word 'I'?"

"No, thanks."

"What if I flashed his baby pictures on the vidscreen behind him?"

"What? You don't have those!"

"You're right, I don't. But I could create something really, really close. Maybe add an extra eye or something for effect."

"No, thank you," Triana said. "We'll let him have his day and find out exactly what message he's putting out there. But I appreciate the offer."

"By the way," Roc said, "even though you didn't play along, that was number 147 on the list of ways I'm indispensable to you."

11

The Dining Hall was crowded, but Lita couldn't tell if it was unusually so for this time of the evening. She was one of a handful of crew members who took their dinner later than most, so it was a change for her to be here at seven o'clock. Most of the kids in the room appeared to have either finished their meal, or were close to doing so, and that made Lita believe they were lingering to hear what Merit had to say.

It was the reason she had come earlier than usual. A tray with the remnants of her dinner was pushed to the side, and her eyes darted back and forth between the assembled crowd and Channy, who was seated across from her, decked out in a bright orange T-shirt. She didn't want to be rude and ignore Channy, but she couldn't stop mentally cataloguing the people who were either sympathetic to Merit, or simply curious. She wasn't sure if sides were being chosen—not yet, anyway—but it couldn't hurt to know what you were up against.

If Channy was concerned, she was masking it by chattering on and on about her latest crew function.

"The only reason people have been slow to sign up, Lita, is because they're waiting to see who else does it."

"You really think this crew is ready for a dating game?" Lita said.

Channy rolled her eyes. "What are you talking about? People are *always* ready for love, my friend. I'm telling you, it's still a week away, and you know how people hate to be the first to volunteer for anything."

Lita glanced over Channy's shoulder and saw Triana walk in the door. The room became noticeably quieter for a split second, before the general buzz started up again. There was drama here, indeed, and the atmosphere in the room had become charged. When she noticed that Channy was staring at her, Lita forced her attention back to their conversation.

"Um . . . so, how many people have signed up right now?"

"Two."

Lita fought back a smile. "Two? How are you going to do this with two people?"

"I told you," Channy said, "it's still early. By this time next week I'm predicting at least a dozen, maybe more. You'll see." She transferred her empty plate to Lita's tray, then stacked her own tray underneath. "Why don't we put your name on there?"

"No, thank you."

"Why not?"

Lita lowered her chin and gave Channy her best impression of an evil eye. "Don't you even think about it."

"Where's the sense of adventure I saw when you performed that concert for us?" Channy said.

"I was terrified. For a minute I wondered if I would even be able to play chopsticks. You're lucky I didn't throw up."

"Well, you have a week to think about it."

Lita just shook her head, then looked over as another clot of people walked into the Dining Hall. A moment later Triana pulled over a chair and sat down next to them.

"Hi, guys," she said. "What's new?"

Channy leaned back in her chair and stretched her arms over her head. "Not much. Just trying to talk Lita into signing up for our little dating game next week."

"That's nice. Well, there's quite a crowd gathered for this, isn't there?" Triana said.

"Are you changing the subject?" Channy piped in.

"Oh, sorry. I didn't know you had more to say about it."

Channy looked back and forth between her two companions, then shook her head and turned sideways in her chair to stare out over the crowd. She muttered something under her breath.

Lita leaned forward, her elbows on the table. "It's mostly curiosity, I'm sure. You know those armbands that a few people are wearing? I only see ten or twelve of them in the room."

Triana cut through her salad with a fork without saying anything in reply. Her mind was racing, but she was determined to keep a relaxed posture before, during, and after the meeting. She would not give Merit, nor his group of followers, the satisfaction of seeing her ruffled. There was no doubt that her reactions would be scrutinized by everyone in the room.

She didn't want to lose the confidence of the Council, either. It was important, she thought, that they believe in her ability to lead, and during a time of crisis that was even more crucial. Channy seemed to be pouting right now and not paying much attention to anything, but Triana was sure that Lita was watching her very closely.

Casually flipping a strand of hair out of her face, she said, "How's Alexa feeling tonight?"

"The last time I talked with her she lied to me," Lita said.

"How do you know?"

"Because I could tell that she felt like garbage, but all she kept saying was, 'I'm fine, I'm fine.' I ordered her to stay in bed until tomorrow, otherwise, knowing her, she would have marched into work this afternoon."

"That's weird," Triana said, taking another bite. "What do you think is wrong?"

"I'm starting to doubt that it was something she ate. Nobody else is sick right now. It's possible that it's a bug that somehow survived our tests and the month we spent in quarantine before the launch. Not likely, but always possible. If she's not better tomorrow, I'll run some tests."

Triana nodded, and was about to comment when she heard a clamor from the front of the room. She knew what that meant.

Merit Simms strode through the door, his customary posse in tow. Several of the kids nearest him reached out to shake his hand or clap him on the back. Triana noticed that this came mostly from the group that sported the yellow armbands.

She also noticed that the small bandage near his lip was still in place. By now there was no doubt that it was merely a prop, and undoubtedly an important one. Someone in his cheering section obviously inquired about it, because Triana watched him point to the bandage and chuckle, in what looked—to her—like phony embarrassment.

She also noticed the glances that were directed her way from some of the assembled crew, an almost nervous reflex, as if sizing up two gladiators before a battle. Her own eyes darted around the room. Lita was right; there was curiosity here, along with a touch of hero worship from a select few. Yet Triana couldn't help but feel that her presence in the room had also added an air of confusion. Why, they must be wondering, would *she* be here?

Well, good, she decided. The fact that she had chosen to participate allowed her to take the high road in the eyes of the crew, and showed them that she refused to run and hide in the face of controversy. A moment later Merit looked up to see her, and she could have sworn she saw a flicker of irritation cross his face. She gave him a slight nod of acknowledgement along with a faint smile.

Just as the noise began to die down, Gap walked through the door. He scanned the room, spotted the other Council members, then eased his way back to their table. Taking a chair from an adjoining table, he sat down next to Triana.

"Thanks for being here," she whispered to him.

"Of course." He began to size up the crowd as Lita had done.

At the front of the room Merit cleared his throat, causing the room to grow quiet. He surveyed the group before him, slowly turning his head and making eye contact with as many people as possible. Triana recognized it as a technique used by the most experienced professional speakers, a move that helped to create an artificial bond between speaker and audience. Finally, he gave a smile and spoke.

"I want to thank all of you for interrupting your own personal schedules in order to join us tonight."

Triana noted the use of "us."

"There are a lot of things you could be doing tonight. Reading, working out, Airboarding, catching up on sleep, maybe just simply eating dinner with friends. Each of you works hard on this ship, you do a terrific job with your official duties, and it means a lot to us that you would sacrifice a little bit of your time to share in this discussion.

"I was just like you a year ago. I had all of the same emotions that I'm sure you had. I was frightened for my family, I was depressed about never seeing them again. I was angry that nobody could find a way to save them. But I was excited about the mission to Eos. I had confidence in Dr. Zimmer, and believed in his plan. He was very good at selling his plan, and I bought into it."

Triana let her gaze wander around the room, and saw that Merit had captured everyone's attention. The room was dead silent. He had touched the nerve that he had aimed for, and the effect was potent.

"I've thought a lot about those days," Merit said, beginning to walk slowly back and forth at the front of the room, dragging every set of eyes with him. It reminded Triana of the pacing he had done during the Council meeting, using the movement to embellish the impact of his words.

"I realize now that there was a combination of emotions at work. I was afraid of Bhaktul's Disease. I was afraid of growing older and getting sick, with no one there to look after me because my family would already be gone. I was eager for a chance at life, at any cost, even if it meant saying good-bye to my parents, forever.

"You had the same emotions, I know. You saw *Galahad* as your chance to escape, to live, to give humanity a fresh start. You worked hard, you trained hard, you studied, you cried, you grieved. And now, seven months after leaving, many of you are still grieving.

"Only today, if you're like me, you look back at the promises made by Dr. Zimmer, and you think, 'Wait a minute. He prepared us for a trip to a new world. He never said anything about a madman trying to kill us.'"

Triana looked at Gap, who looked back at her with a grim expression. They both knew that referencing the near-deadly encounter with the mysterious intruder was a sensitive issue. Merit was undoubtedly scoring points already.

"Dr. Zimmer also never considered the possibility of an alien life force trying to destroy us, for no apparent reason. He never told us that we would fly through the Kuiper Belt and have millions of projectiles hurtling at us like a giant game of dodge ball."

There were nods from around the room. Merit stopped his pacing and faced the crowd, a look of anxiety on his face. "You're as concerned about these things as I am. And I'm sure you've had some of the same thoughts I've had, too. Thoughts such as, 'Maybe it's time we turned back.' I ask you tonight, with everything that has happened so far, only seven months into the journey: How many more times can we get lucky? How many more times can we pull out a miracle? How many more times until we discover that the people who sent us out into the cold darkness of space had no idea what we would be up against?"

He paused for a few moments, allowing his words to sink in. He scanned the faces of the room, making eye contact, engaging their emotions. Triana sat still, leaning forward, her elbows on her knees. She was angry that Merit was doing this, turning the crew against her, against Dr. Zimmer, against their hope for survival.

And yet, on another level, she found herself marveling at his motivational skills. His was a natural talent for persuasion, a talent that Triana felt she possessed, but at nowhere near the level she was observing. Merit Simms could sell, period.

After his brief pause, he shook his head. "I have given this so much thought. I have considered not only our past experiences, but also studied, in depth, what lies before us. We have so far to go within the Kuiper Belt, and it's more dangerous than you know. And then, what lies beyond that? What will we encounter in the void between the Belt and Eos? What do we know about empty space? Or, is it even really empty?

"And more importantly: What happens when we arrive at Eos? Do I even need to point out to you the odds of survival on the new world?"

With this comment, there were several murmurs amongst the crew. Merit paused to allow them to express their own doubts. For an instant Triana wondered if the look on his face wasn't a look of satisfaction. He knew what was happening.

"But," he said, raising his voice above the chatter. "But," he said again, louder, until the room again fell silent. "But apparently questioning the plan is not allowed on this ship. Apparently our Council, which is supposed to represent us, does not allow lowly crew members like me, like you, to approach them with fears and concerns. Apparently we are at their mercy. Did you know that?"

There was no verbal response to this, but the assembled crew members nervously looked at one another, aware that the majority of the Council sat quietly in the back of the room. Two or three of Merit's personal entourage glanced back at Triana and smirked.

"I know," Merit said, "because I tried. I tried to visit with the Council, tried to express my fears, tried to recommend that they consider an alternative. I questioned them about the Cassini, a force more powerful than anything man has ever seen, a force that can either destroy . . . or assist.

"The Cassini have now known for months about Bhaktul. What might have happened since we left Titan? What changes have possibly taken place on Earth in the last ninety days? How do we know that the Cassini haven't used their awesome powers to repair our home? How do we know that we're not risking our lives every single minute of every single day . . . when our families might be healing, and waiting for us to return?"

Now Triana could see Gap clenching his fists. She knew that he was dying to stand up and speak, but he kept his composure. She bit her lip and remained still.

"And do you want to know what happens when you actually try to talk to the Council today?" Merit paused, then pointed to the bandage on his lip. "This is what happens. You get attacked."

Another low murmur spread across the room. Merit lowered his hand and stood still, a victim on display.

Finally he spoke again in a low voice, drawing his audience back in. "All I'm asking is to be heard. All I'm asking is that the will of the crew be honored. We are a ship in trouble. I believe we should turn for home, for the safety and security of our families. But I'm only one voice, a voice that has been beaten down. So tonight I'm asking you to join us, peacefully. With numbers we can finally be heard. If you join with us, we can choose life, together."

He paused again, before closing with a soft, "Thank you."

Immediately his cheering section stood and began applauding. They looked around at the tables near them, encouraging others to rise and join in. Slowly, several other crew members rose to their feet and began to clap. As Merit nodded his thanks, almost a third of the Dining Hall was cheering his speech. He waited for a few moments, made quick eye contact with Triana, the corners of his mouth barely turned up in a smile, then walked toward the door, shaking hands and offering personal thanks. A minute later he was gone.

12

I see that you're about to eavesdrop on Lita in Sick House, so this is a good time to ask you something that I've wondered for a while.

If one of your electronic devices breaks down, I've noticed that you won't hesitate to either take it in to be repaired, or immediately order a new one. On Earth, if an automobile has a problem, you would immediately take it in to the shop. If your washing machine is acting up, you get a repairman out right away.

But if your own body has a problem, you put it off, you ignore it, you pretend that everything is fine. Seems funny to me that your portable music device gets preferential treatment over your flesh and blood. You're a very funny species.

No . . . no, a little higher," the girl said.

Lita pushed two fingers against the slightly bruised skin. "Okay. What about here?"

"Yeah, that's . . . ouch!"

Lita pulled her hand away. "Well, it's at least a bruised rib. Maybe a crack. Seems to be a popular injury this week."

The girl, a fifteen-year-old from Egypt, blew out a sigh of disgust. "How long does that take to heal?"

"Oh, that depends," Lita said, walking over to a locked cabinet. She opened it and removed a small bottle of pills. "No more than six or eight months."

"*What*? Eight months?"

Lita grinned as she poured six of the pills into a small envelope. "Relax, Ana, I'm kidding. You'll be fine in just a few weeks."

"Don't scare me like that. I don't think I could go that long without soccer. My team needs me."

"It was soccer that did this to you in the first place," Lita said, pointing to the bruise. "You guys are playing a little rough, aren't you?"

Ana returned Lita's smile. "You have to be tough to win. I stayed in the game after this, you know. I even scored the winning goal."

"Yes, you told me already. In fact, I think you've mentioned it three times. Listen, take one of these now, another one tomorrow, and only take the other four if you really think you need them. If you're as tough as you think you are, you can bring them back to me."

Ana slid off the examining table and winked at Lita. "You'll get the other four back."

Lita nodded her head. "Uh-huh. Well, we'll see how tough you are tonight when you try lying down for the first time with a cracked rib." She placed the envelope in her latest patient's hand. "One other piece of advice. If I were you I would try to stay away from funny people and pepper for the next few days."

"Why?"

"Because you'll be wishing for another pill if you start laughing or sneezing," Lita said. "Trust me."

Ana smiled and gave a quick wave good-bye. As she was walking out the door she passed Alexa, who was obviously doing her best to look better than she felt. Lita rushed over to greet her assistant.

"How are you feeling today?"

Alexa shrugged. "Ugh, I've felt better. But I'm not missing any more work, I can tell you that."

Lita stood in her path, arms crossed. "You know, there are only so many tough crew members I can tolerate in one day. What's going on with you?"

"I still feel a little queasy. Almost like I'm seasick or something. I don't know if it's better, or if I'm just getting used to it."

"Anything else, or just the stomach?"

Alexa walked around *Galahad's* Health Director and made her way over to her desk. "You are such a worrywart. I'm fine."

"C'mon, Alexa. What else?"

"A little pain, okay? Nothing I can't handle."

"Pain in your stomach? Pain and nausea?"

"Yeah. So, what have I missed around here?"

Lita's face took on a scowl. "Dr. Zimmer not only found the brightest kids on the planet, I think he rounded up the most stubborn ones, too. Why won't you let me help you?"

"Because it will go away. I'm telling you, it's gotta be something I ate. Blame Bon, not me."

"Nobody else is sick. It's not the food."

Alexa looked at her friend. "I'll tell you what. If it's not better in a couple of days you can poke and prod all you want, okay?"

Lita shook her head. "No, if it's not better *tomorrow* I'm going to poke and prod. And don't lie to me, Alexa."

"Yes, Mother," Alexa said, and turned her attention to the work that had piled up on her desk. The conversation was apparently over.

Lita stared at her for another minute as a knot of concern began to grow in her own stomach.

The high-intensity lights in Dome 2 had begun their daily afternoon fade, gradually ushering in the equivalent of an

Earth dusk. One by one the flicker of starlight seeped through the clear panels of the dome, the familiar nighttime companions resuming their mute watch over the ship full of pilgrims streaking toward a new world. Workers on the late-afternoon shift had chosen to bathe the farm domes in a pleasant background veil of sound. The piped-in music was a relaxing blend of deep tones, cascading synth pieces, and a rushing wind; the effect was almost tranquilizing.

Gap held on to Hannah's hand as they slowly made their way along one of the paths. His grip was light, almost caressing. He stole an occasional glance at her face, taking in her soft eyes, the fall of her hair over the shoulder. Her laugh was easy and relaxed, comfortable at last in his company.

The tension he felt around the Merit Simms trouble had melted away—for the time being, anyway. In the back of his mind he knew that it would come racing back to the forefront very soon, but for now he was content.

Or . . . was it more than that? Was he happy?

His thoughts were interrupted by a familiar voice that floated out from within a dense growth of corn stalks. He recognized one of Channy's bright yellow T-shirts pushing through the green plants.

"Hold up, lovebirds," she said.

Gap and Hannah stopped and watched the young Brit emerge, brushing small patches of dirt from her knees. Gap smiled at Channy and said, "Are you lost?"

"Ugh, it wouldn't be hard to do. I can't believe how quickly these things have grown. They're almost over my head."

"So what *are* you doing in there?" Gap said.

Channy looked back and pointed at a small shape that was slinking onto the path about twenty feet away. "Babysitting, as usual. Iris definitely prefers Dome 2 over the other one."

Hannah raised her eyebrows. "So this is better territory for a cat to explore, is that it?"

"Who knows?" Channy said. "They seem about the same to me, but maybe there's just too much noise in Dome 1. It might spook her a bit. It took me fifteen minutes to track her down in the corn." She turned her attention to the clasped hands of Gap and Hannah, a smile spreading across her face. "I'm not interrupting anything, am I?"

"What if I said yes?" Gap said.

"Then I'd be forced to walk away, and then secretly stalk you from a distance. You could save me a lot of trouble if you just said no."

Hannah laughed. "We're just taking a walk. Any spying that you did would be pretty boring for you."

Channy shrugged. "More exciting than anything I have planned tonight." She looked up at Gap. "So . . . have you thought anymore about that garbage Merit was spilling last night?"

Gap frowned. Apparently the break from tension was over. "It's a tough situation," he said. "The guy has every right to express himself, and people have every right to agree or disagree with him. It's not like we can shut him up because we don't like what he's saying."

"Yeah, I know that," Channy said. "But he's so . . . so wrong. He's filling people's heads with a bunch of silly nonsense."

"Again, that's for people to decide."

"Yes, but nobody is telling them that it's nonsense. They're only hearing one side."

She had a good point, Gap thought. So far the fight had been completely one-sided. Not counting Bon's contribution, of course, but that had ended up benefiting Merit's cause.

Channy filled the silence between them. "Why doesn't Tree hold her own meeting and respond?"

"Well, at first I don't think she wanted to give him the satisfaction, you know?" Gap said. "It was almost as if acknowledging his claims gave him some sort of credibility. But now . . ." He trailed off.

"Right," Channy said. "*Now* he seems to have a ton of credibility."

Hannah shifted uncomfortably. Gap wondered if she felt like she was intruding into a mini-Council meeting. He tightened his grip on her hand to let her know that everything was okay.

"I was going to talk to Tree about this anyway," he said to Channy. "Listen, she's a great leader, we all know that. I'm sure she's giving this as much thought—or more—as we are."

Channy seemed unmoved by this. Her gaze turned toward Iris, who had sprawled into a patch of dirt and was rolling onto her back. The light had faded considerably, and the starlight above was taking on a sharper set.

Gap was about to add something to the conversation when the sound of voices caught his ear. Two boys in farming overalls came around the edge of the corn crop, tools slung over their shoulders, intently talking about something until they realized they were not alone. They fell silent as they marched past, one of them acknowledging Gap, Hannah, and Channy with a brisk nod, while the other, a tall, slender boy with a shaved head, stared straight ahead.

Around his upper arm was a distinctive yellow armband with a black "R.T.E." stenciled on it.

No words were exchanged between either group, and within a few seconds the two farm workers had disappeared down the path. Channy balled her fists and seethed.

"That's the kind of stuff I'm talking about," she said, pointing in the direction the boys had walked. "More and more of these people putting on those ridiculous armbands, walking around like they're on a mission or something."

Gap forced a smile. "We're all on a mission."

"You know what I mean," Channy snapped at him.

"Hey, calm down," Gap said. "Don't take it out on me."

"Well, I'm angry."

"I know you're angry. But remember what happened when

Bon let his anger get out of control." Gap paused to let that sink in, and watched as Channy slowly relaxed and crossed her arms.

"All I'm saying is don't overreact," he said. "There's no reason they can't wear whatever they want. I know it's frustrating, but we have to keep our composure, right? That's one good example that Triana is setting for the rest of us. She's just as frustrated as you, believe me. But any confrontation right now is only fuel for the fire."

"So just how long are we going to take this?" Channy said.

Gap ran his free hand through his hair. "Things are going to work out, okay? For the time being maybe we should be grateful that we're getting a crash course on accepting other viewpoints." He touched Channy's arm to get her attention focused on him. "Hey, we have a long way to go. This is the kind of stuff that we need to learn how to deal with if we're going to create a new world someday. We're not all going to agree all the time, you know."

Channy stared at him for a minute, then dropped her gaze to the ground. She mumbled, "Yeah, you're right."

Gap chuckled. "I think part of you is upset because other people have discovered yellow."

A smile inched its way across Channy's face. She looked at Gap and nodded, then turned her attention to Hannah. "You're not saying much. What do you think about all of this?"

Hannah darted a glance at Gap, then back to Channy. "Well . . . uh . . . it's a little uncomfortable, I know that. But . . ." She paused for a second. "But people approach a crisis in different ways. Some people get emotionally involved, and others tackle it from a more . . . well, a more logical angle."

Both Gap and Channy stared at her, waiting for her to continue. She cleared her throat nervously and said, "I happen to disagree with Merit because of pure logic. It just makes no sense to attempt to turn around here in the Kuiper Belt, and to start a slow return trip to Earth. Especially since we have no evidence whatsoever that things are any better there than when we left."

"What would you recommend we do?" Channy said.

Again Hannah took a quick look into Gap's face. "Well, since so many people are wondering about the Cassini, I think it might make sense to talk to the one person who has had intimate contact with them."

Gap and Channy looked at each other. Then Gap nodded slowly. "That's a really good idea."

Channy said, "Yeah, I hate to admit it, but Bon could know more about this situation than anyone." She paused, glancing uncomfortably between Gap and Hannah. "Uh . . . so who's going to be the one to try to drag it out of him?"

There was silence again. Gap looked up through the dome into the star field that was now furiously blazing. He knew that a showdown was inevitable, and the possibility that Bon might hold the key—as he did during their encounter with Titan—was not the most comforting thought of the day.

He gave Hannah's hand another squeeze, and began to lead her down the path. "I'll see you at the Council meeting in the morning," he said to Channy, who had picked Iris up from the dirt.

"Cheers," Channy said, waving one of the cat's paws at them. She held Iris up to her mouth and whispered, "Maybe *you* can talk to Bon."

13

Things were chilly again on Level Six. Triana walked briskly through the curving corridor, rubbing her arms to help the circulation, wondering just how cold it was. She could only imagine the frustration that Gap was probably feeling right now. His pride told him that he could solve any technical problem, and to have a constant gremlin turn up in the heating system of the ship wore through his patience quickly. She had spoken with him moments earlier on the intercom, and asked him if he could break away for at least thirty minutes for the morning Council meeting.

Now, as she approached the Conference Room, she wondered about reversing that decision. It was colder up here than she had expected, and she could always catch Gap up on anything discussed in the meeting. She was torn; on one hand she wanted all of her allies present as they rode through the turbulent times experienced both inside the ship and out, yet she also knew that every little breakdown, every little incident, every tiny error, would all be blown as far out of proportion as Merit Simms could manage. For that reason alone she figured Gap should stay on the job in Engineering.

The point was driven home the minute she rounded the turn leading to the Conference Room and found more than a dozen crew members congregated in the hallway. Many of them leaned against the curved walls, a few were sitting cross-legged on the floor. Merit stood next to the door, his arms crossed, deep in conversation with three or four followers. They appeared to be mesmerized by what he was saying.

For a split second her pace slowed, but then she recovered and worked her way through the tangle of bodies. Merit broke away from his speech and blocked her entry to the Conference Room. "I'm here to formally request to be heard at this morning's Council meeting."

Triana burned on the inside. He had made sure to have as many witnesses as possible, and no doubt secretly hoped that she would turn him down, building his case that the Council did not care to hear the concerns of the crew. With Merit it always seemed to be about power and control.

She kept her face calm and replied, "I think that's a good idea. Let us take care of some other business, and we'll be happy to have you join us."

Merit flinched for a moment. "Uh . . . very good. Thank you." Then, with a manufactured look of victory on his face, he turned to the group. "Everyone relax, it will be a few minutes."

Triana resisted the urge to roll her eyes, and instead gave a curt smile and nod to the assembled crowd and ducked inside the Conference Room. The door closed behind her and she found herself staring into the concerned faces of the Council. Nobody said a word as she walked to the head of the table and sat down.

"I won't keep you in suspense," Triana said. "Merit has requested another hearing, and I've agreed. He'll join us in a few minutes."

When this also was greeted with silence, she continued. "First things first. Gap, what do you need to get this heating problem fixed on Level Six?"

"A new heating system," he said. That seemed to break the ice, and there were chuckles around the table. "I'm quickly running out of options, but I'm not giving up."

Channy, whose neon-bright T-shirt was shielded under a long-sleeved top, said, "Our furnace went out more than a few times when I was growing up. My mum used to bang on it with a hammer, and that seemed to work most of the time."

"I'll keep that in mind," Gap said, "although Roc hasn't suggested that as a solution . . . yet."

The computer spoke up. "I couldn't live with myself if you smashed your thumb."

"I don't think we'll be long this morning," Triana said. "You should be able to get back to it within the hour." She looked around the table. "Unless anyone has something urgent we need to address, I want to talk quickly about the Kuiper Belt, and then we can hear what Mr. Simms has to say."

When this was greeted with mute stares, she tapped a login on the keyboard before her, and a split second later all of the table's vidscreens displayed a three-dimensional rendering of the Belt. A thick red line traced *Galahad's* path through the crowded space.

"I want to let you in on some information that Gap and Roc shared with me the other day. It has to do with the makeup of the Kuiper Belt, and, quite honestly, a bit of bad luck."

She spent a few minutes relaying the report on the Belt's inconsistent thickness, and how *Galahad* had stumbled into a particularly rough stretch. For the time being she withheld the odds of survival that Roc had offered.

"This means," she said, "that things are probably going to get worse before they get better. It also means that we might have to change course several times as we weave through this mess, and for now we don't know what that will mean to our overall schedule."

Lita spoke up. "If it's a choice of getting to Eos a few weeks late, or not getting there at all . . ."

"Right," Triana said. "So be prepared for some tight spots coming up, and remember to help diffuse any concerns you hear from the crew."

With another couple of strokes, she cleared all of the room's vidscreens. "Is there anything to add before we bring in Merit?"

After a moment of silence, Channy leaned forward, her palms flat against the table. "I just have a question, if that's okay."

Triana immediately took note of the unusual tone in Channy's voice. Her typical playful rhythm had been replaced by a sober touch, a characteristic that seemed alien on the energetic Council member. "Sure, what's your question?"

"I'm wondering how you plan on responding to the muck that Merit is stirring up. I mean . . ." She threw a quick glance at Gap. "I know we're supposed to appreciate other opinions and all that, but it doesn't seem to me that the crew is getting the whole story."

Triana looked hard at Channy, then around at the other Council members. Their faces—with the exception of Bon, who was as unreadable as a statue—seemed to express a silent agreement with the petite girl from England.

"That's a fair question," Triana said, "and it's something I've thought about. Until Merit held his meeting in the Dining Hall, there wasn't really a reason to gather the crew together."

"But now he's gaining momentum, and we look like we're hiding," Channy said.

"That's one way of looking at it, I suppose," Triana said. "But in my opinion it would have been worse to immediately try to defend a plan that has been arranged, plotted, and followed since day one. Everyone on this ship has known why we're doing what we're doing, and it made no sense to me to round up 250 crew members and state the obvious. Our mission is on track, and, if anything, slightly ahead of schedule. I saw no reason to defend that."

Gap picked up on the past tense. "Saw? So that means that now you're considering a meeting?"

"Of course I am. Now that Merit has 'stirred the muck,' as Channy put it, it's time to get everyone to refocus on the plan. A refresher course."

Channy sighed. "Okay, thank you. I just haven't liked this feeling lately, like we have our heads buried in the sand or something."

"I understand," Triana said. She looked at the other Council members. "Is there anything else?"

Lita shrugged. "Let's hear the latest speech."

Gap went to the door and summoned Merit into the room. He swept in, his long black hair pulled back into a tail. For a moment he locked eyes with Bon, who glared at him with open disgust.

Standing at an open spot near the middle of the table, Merit held up a sheet of paper and immediately began to speak.

"This is a petition signed by 38 members of the *Galahad* crew. That represents about fifteen percent of the people on this ship, and they demand an open debate on the issues I have raised."

Gap took the sheet of paper and looked over the signatures. "I'm assuming you mean a debate between you and Triana?"

"Or any member of the Council, actually," Merit said. "This crew deserves the right to hear all of their options, presented in a formal, intelligent manner."

"Thank you for sharing that," Triana said, eyeing her adversary with a cool look. "We will certainly take it under consideration and let you know shortly."

Merit chuckled. "We've grown weary of waiting while you 'consider' our requests."

"I'm sorry to hear that," Triana said with a slight smile of her own. "It's the way procedures work on this ship. We don't make hasty decisions."

"Exactly how many names do you need to see on a petition before you'll act? Fifty? One hundred?"

"It's not a matter of quantity," Triana said. "It's a matter of the Council determining whether the request is in the best interests of the crew. If one hundred people wanted us to fly straight into an asteroid I would not open that to debate."

"That's a ridiculous comparison," Merit sneered.

"In your mind, maybe. But my job, and the job of this Council, is to protect this crew from harm to the best of our abilities, and to make decisions that best serve the mission. That mission, by the way, is to pilot this spacecraft to Eos. Turning it around, in the middle of a dangerous stretch of space, is not necessarily that different from driving it straight into a hunk of rock."

"So instead we're supposed to just wait for one of those hunks of rock to slam into us."

Triana paused, then lowered her voice to reply. "As I said very clearly, we will discuss your request, and we'll inform you shortly as to our decision."

Merit looked down at the table, then raised his gaze to meet Triana's. "Then besides my request, let me offer some advice. It would be wise to quickly agree to our request. A lot of tension is building among the crew, and that can many times lead to unfortunate events."

Gap bristled. "Are you threatening us?"

"I'm saying that the best way to deal with pressure is to allow a little steam to escape before something blows."

Triana said, "During your speech in the Dining Hall you invited people to join your movement 'peacefully.' Have you changed your mind about that?"

"I'm not advocating violence, although your side has clearly taken that step already." He looked at Bon, who continued to bore through him with his eyes. "An open, honest debate would allow everyone to hear all of the facts."

"And what facts do you have?" Gap said.

Merit held up another sheet of paper. "A few of my associates and I have worked hard putting together a plan of our own. It would involve a slow turn, safely, through the Kuiper Belt, then back into the solar system toward Earth. Once we inform *Galahad* Command of our decision, they'll clearly plot a flight plan for a return to Earth orbit. The return journey shouldn't take more than two years."

"Two years?" Lita said. "In two years we'll be more than half-way to Eos."

"That's assuming, of course, that we'll survive on our current path," Merit said to her. "We happen to believe that assumption is crazy."

Triana cleared her throat, a clear indication that the discussion was over. "Thank you for your time, and for your observations, Merit. We will let you know soon what we have decided."

He stared at her for a long time, until the silence became uncomfortable.

As he finally opened his mouth to speak, a sudden alarm sounded over the intercom. Triana stood and leaned against the table. "Roc, report."

The computer voice answered immediately. "Collision warning. An extremely large object."

"We'll be in the Control Room in one minute," Triana replied. "Gap, come with me." She hustled out of the Conference Room with Gap on her heels, and they pushed their way through the assembled crowd. There were shouts and questions which were hard to make out over the blare of the alarm.

Merit stepped out into the hallway, making sure to get the attention of his followers before shouting after Triana and Gap: "What more evidence do you need?"

As the two Council members rounded a curve and dropped out of sight, a familiar smile spread across the face of Merit Simms.

14

"How large is it?" Triana said as she bolted into the Control Room.

Roc's voice came through loud and clear. "One hundred and ninety-two feet from end to end, roughly the same shape as an Idaho potato. Which is very ironic, since we'll be the ones who get mashed."

Triana ignored the computer's joke and rushed to one of the vidscreen consoles in the room. Gap had already brought up a 3-D plot, which showed the massive stone tumbling directly into their path.

"I have already changed course to escape collision," Roc said. "We should know in about . . . twenty-five seconds if it was done soon enough."

Triana felt the blood drain from her face. Twenty-five seconds. She steadied herself on the console, and a moment later felt Gap's hand on her shoulder. The seconds ticked by without a sound from any of the six crew members in the room. All eyes turned to the large main vidscreen that Roc had activated.

From the bottom right corner of the vidscreen Triana noticed what looked like a shadow emerge. It lurched upward, carving a path that seemed destined to intersect with *Galahad*. The ship, although flashing through the Kuiper Belt at a staggering rate of speed, still needed some distance for course corrections to take effect. The massive spacecraft could not exactly turn on a dime.

The shadow grew in size, and in a few seconds the potato shape became clear. It was scarred with craters, remnants of a violent history that stretched back to the origin of the solar system more than four billion years earlier. At one time, Triana guessed, it must have been huge, perhaps the size of Earth's moon even, but collision after collision had chopped it down to its current size. Chunks of that original rock now contributed to the scattershot of debris that orbited in this extreme ring, billions of miles away from the sun.

And if their luck was about to run out, then chunks of a certain spaceship would soon become a permanent addition to the ring.

The shadowy hulk slowly rose on the vidscreen, and Triana realized that Roc's course correction had been to dive the ship so that it passed below the rock. A move to the left, the right, or above would almost certainly have been fatal. But, with the boulder rocketing upwards at this angle, *Galahad*'s momentum in a downward streak might spell the difference.

Fifteen seconds later she felt her breathing return. The dark shape was slipping farther above them, and it became apparent that they were spared.

This time.

Soon the boulder disappeared from the screen. Triana let out a deep rush of air through pursed lips, and turned to Gap. "That was fun, huh?"

He shook his head and offered a weak smile in return. "Do you get the feeling that this ship is charmed? We keep missing collisions by just a few feet."

"Don't get dramatic on me," Roc said from the speaker. "We cleared the bottom of that monster by almost two hundred feet. Not even close enough to muss my hair."

"Roc," Triana said, "I have to hand it to you. That was a perfect move you made. Perfect. So now, tell me: Where in the world did this thing come from, and why didn't we see it earlier?"

"It's that ping pong ball effect I mentioned to you earlier. These crazy rocks keep bouncing around off each other, changing direction, speed, rotation. This thing obviously smacked into something just before it zoomed into our path. Our warning system is good, but it can't predict everything."

Triana nodded, then looked across the room. The other crew members stationed in the Control Room were either wide-eyed from fright, or holding their heads in relief. One girl in particular, a fifteen-year-old from Japan named Mika, was watching—and listening intently—to the discussion with Roc.

And she was wearing a yellow armband.

Gap followed Triana's gaze. He felt her start to move toward Mika, and his hand, which was still on her shoulder, stiffened. "Uh-uh," he said to her in a whisper. "Leave it alone."

"What are you talking about?"

"Leave it alone. She hasn't done anything wrong."

"I know that," Triana said. "I'm just going to talk with her."

"If you—"

"Relax," Triana said, pulling his hand free from her shoulder. She walked toward Mika, who broke eye contact and turned back to her work. Triana didn't know the Japanese girl very well, but had lunched with her once, several weeks earlier. She was quiet, but extremely polite and respectful. Triana had always felt comfortable with her on duty in the Control Room.

The display of the yellow armband was disturbing to the Council Leader if for no other reason than it showed that the reach of Merit Simms had penetrated into Triana's outer circle. Mika would have been one of the last people she expected to show support for Merit's cause, and Triana couldn't deny that a pang of betrayal rippled through her as she walked across the room.

"Hi, Mika," she said, stopping beside the girl's chair.

"Hi," Mika said, a sheepish look on her face. Triana realized that it probably took a lot of courage for the girl to show up for duty with the display on her arm.

"Close call, huh?" Triana said.

Mika nodded, and uttered a quiet "Yes. Very close."

"I see that you're wearing one of Merit's armbands. Do you mind if I ask you about that?"

Mika shrugged nervously. "I . . . I have listened to what he has been saying, and . . . and I find that I agree with him."

"Do you?"

Another nod. "Yes." Mika pointed to the vidscreen. "This is a good example of what he's talking about. Another close call."

Triana examined the girl's face. "We knew when we left Earth that things might get difficult at times. And any return to Earth will have dangers as well."

There was no response to this. Triana tried a different approach.

"Are you homesick?"

This brought an immediate reaction from Mika. She turned sharply and looked into Triana's eyes. "No. Well, yes, of course I miss my family. But . . . but that doesn't have anything to do with my choice."

"Are you sure? Have you really thought about everything, or have you just been seduced by a chance to maybe see your brothers and sisters again? A chance that has no guarantee, by the way."

Mika was silent, but kept her gaze on Triana's eyes.

"And once you get there," Triana said softly, "then what? You will have thrown away a chance at a new life, and condemned yourself to a painful death from Bhaktul. By the time we reach Earth, you'll be almost eighteen. And you know what that means."

Mika broke eye contact and looked back up at the vidscreen. A moment later she spoke in her quiet voice. "I will continue to do my job here in the Control Room, and you'll have no trouble from me." She looked back at Triana. "But if the crew is allowed to vote on a change, I will vote for a return to Earth."

The two girls stared at each other. Triana felt like continuing the debate, but realized that this was not the time, nor the place. Instead, she summoned all of her will and offered a smile to Mika. "No matter what you decide, I want you to know that I appreciate all of the hard work you've done."

She turned on her heel and walked back to Gap. He watched her face closely, scanning back and forth from eye to eye. "So, what did you say to her?" he said in a whisper.

Triana sighed. "Just had a little chat. There's no problem."

"No problem? She's wearing a symbol that says she's part of a mutiny. I'd say that's a problem."

"It's not a mutiny."

"Not yet," Gap said. "But you heard Merit. He pretty much said that if we don't agree with him, he and his pals could resort to force."

Triana shook her head. "I'm not ready to believe that yet. Listen, he's very good at manipulation. Don't let him prod you into doing something."

"Like Bon?"

"Exactly. For now, let's not give anyone a reason to distrust the Council. Agreed?"

Gap glanced over at Mika, who was calmly going about her business. "Yeah, okay. But you know what scares me the most?"

Before Triana could answer, the intercom in the Control Room buzzed. Lita's voice called out, "Triana, are you in there?"

With a quick snap of a button, the Council Leader answered. "What is it?"

"I know you've had your hands full, but I need you in Sick House right away."

Triana began to question the urgency, but realized that everyone in the Control Room would be able to hear. Instead she told

Lita that she would be there in two minutes, then asked Gap to keep an eye on things.

"What do you think that's about?" he said in a whisper.

Triana looked into his eyes. "I'm afraid it's probably about Alexa. And if Lita is calling me like that, it can't be good."

At first Triana began to sprint down the corridor toward Sick House, but then realized that in the current climate it might be a bit unsettling to the crew for her to be rushing anywhere. She slowed to a brisk walk, and made a conscious effort to keep any sign of panic off her face. Strong, she told herself, be strong.

The door to Sick House swished open. There was no one in the outer room, no sign of Lita at her desk. With a pang, Triana noted that Alexa's desk also sat unoccupied. "Hello," she called out.

"In here," came Lita's voice from the adjoining room. It functioned as the hospital ward of *Galahad*, with twenty beds lining the walls. With the exception of the harrowing encounter around Saturn and Titan, when twelve of the beds had been in use, the room was usually quiet. Now, however, Lita and two of her part-time assistants were clustered around Alexa Wellington, who was lying unconscious, her head propped up with extra pillows. With soft steps Triana came up beside Lita. The two assistants finished their duties and left the room.

"What happened to her?" Triana said.

Lita kept her attention on Alexa. "Her roommate found her on the floor of their room. She apparently passed out from the pain. Probably . . ." She paused, and swallowed hard. "Probably trying to get ready for work, forcing herself to tough it out."

Triana bit her lip. "Have you found out anything yet?"

"I'm waiting on two tests, but my guess is that it's her appendix."

"Her appendix? Does that mean . . ." Triana's voice trailed off.

Lita nodded, her voice low and trembling. "It means that I'll probably have to operate. And soon."

All Triana could think to do was to put a hand on her friend's forearm. She kept quiet for a moment before saying, "Is . . . is there anything you need me to do?"

"Not that I can think of at the moment," Lita said. She sighed heavily and reached out with a hand to gently stroke Alexa's cheek. "I should never have let her talk me out of those tests. If I had—"

"Stop that," Triana said, squeezing Lita's arm. "You couldn't have known what was going on."

"I should have admitted her to the ward without an argument, that's what I should have done."

"You would still have to operate on her."

There was silence between them for a while. When Lita finally turned to face Triana, she did so with tears in her eyes. "I'm scared, Tree."

Once again Triana could think of no words for the moment. She stepped forward and pulled Lita into a hug, fighting to keep the tears from her own eyes.

It was happening again. Another crisis, another challenge, another . . .

Another test? Was that what this was all about? Was there some cosmic power that was testing their strength, their will? How much more could they take?

Triana stopped herself. This was no time to begin wallowing in pity. Alexa was seriously ill, and Lita had suddenly been thrust into a position that Triana recognized all too well: the responsibility for another's life. The only thing to do now was to rally around her friend and offer every ounce of strength that she could summon. She pushed Lita back to arm's length and looked into her eyes.

"You know you can do this, right?" Triana said. "Dr. Zimmer knew that you were the right person for this job, and I have no doubt of it."

Another tear slipped down Lita's face. She brushed it away and stared back at Triana, then nodded. "Yes, I can do this." After some hesitation, she added, "I guess . . . listen, this made me do some thinking about . . . our situation."

"What do you mean?"

Lita seemed unsure of how to continue. She looked down for a moment. "Don't be angry at me for saying this, but I've been thinking about what Merit said." She looked back up. "With everything that is happening, I mean . . ."

Triana felt her breath grow short. "You're upset, Lita. That's all."

"I'm not saying that I agree with him. But suddenly I'm thinking about it, you know?"

"Okay," Triana said slowly. "There's nothing wrong with that. We'll talk about it, all right? But let's get through this emergency with Alexa first. Agreed?"

Lita nodded, and lowered her gaze again.

Triana forced a smile. "Good. I want to be here when it's time. When will you be ready?"

"I have to be ready right now," Lita said. "We can't wait any longer. We'll get her prepped and into surgery within an hour." She let out a deep breath. "I'll call you before we start."

Triana left Sick House and walked toward the lift, her mind a whirlwind of competing issues. The news about Alexa was disturbing enough. The crew would undoubtedly react with shock, and that would only empower Merit even more. Now Lita had expressed her own doubts about the mission.

Triana had taken for granted that the Council would remain unified in the conflict with Merit. But if one member had concerns, did that mean they all did? How could she know? Or, Triana wondered, was she overreacting to one isolated incident? Lita's uncertainty could probably be written off to stress.

Probably.

15

When Dr. Wallace Zimmer had championed the building of the lifeboat called *Galahad*, he had envisioned a community that sustained itself through smart management of resources, recycling, and sophisticated agricultural techniques to keep the crew healthy and well fed. Various engineers and consultants had devised the most efficient farming systems ever imagined, and placed the ship's crops beneath the glistening domes that were simply named 1 and 2.

The systems, however, required delicate yet consistent management in order to produce the bounty needed to fuel the crew. Dr. Zimmer had been grateful that Bon Hartsfield had emerged from the thousands of mission candidates as the only person truly qualified to run the farms. And he had been tolerant of Bon's gruff personality; to Dr. Zimmer it lent an edge to the Council that was otherwise missing, an element that others might not understand, and yet was—to Zimmer—indispensable.

At the moment Bon was training that gruff personality upon a small electric tractor that had chosen to take the day off. It sat, unmoving, amid a row of bean plants. The farm worker who had been maneuvering it through the crop had spent fifteen minutes attempting to restart the tractor, then had surrendered the effort and summoned *Galahad*'s Director of Agriculture. It was one of the minor duties that Bon understood to be his responsibility, yet irritated him nonetheless. His time, he knew, could be much better spent on other matters, rather than worrying over a stubborn machine.

As they labored over it, Bon noticed that four or five other farm workers had stopped by to lend a hand. Marco, the Portuguese boy who had earlier been commended by Bon, began tinkering with the mechanics of the tractor, to no avail. Finally the utter waste of time took its toll on the impatient Swede, and he turned to the crew member who had originally been working with the machine.

"Liam's not on the schedule today, is that right?" When this was confirmed, he shook his head. "All right, somebody find him and get him up here. He knows more about making these things run than I do, and I don't want to fall any farther behind schedule."

As one farm worker scampered off, two more walked up to offer assistance. Another unproductive ten minutes passed before Bon looked up to see Liam Wright approaching, slowly.

Too slowly.

Bon pulled his head out of the engine compartment of the tractor and watched as Liam sauntered up. Complete silence fell over the assembled group as their eyes fell upon the yellow armband encircling Liam's bicep. Bon could feel the air grow thick with the anticipation of his reaction. He pointed to the tractor's engine.

"We could use your help with this," he said.

Liam's gaze shifted from the open compartment to Bon's face. "Today is my day off."

Bon acted as if he hadn't heard. "It's not in the panel circuitry. We were just about to open the lower module. Perhaps you could help with that."

"Today is my day off."

"There are several of us who can lend a hand," Bon said. "What do you need to get started?"

Liam crossed his arms. "I'm assuming that if I work today I'll get the next two days off. Would that be right?"

Bon openly fumed. "I'm pretty sure that you don't take two days off from eating. If you believe that you're being overworked, that's something you can bring to the Council."

"The Council," Liam said. "Since when does the Council listen to anyone?"

The already thick atmosphere turned even heavier. The crew members who were standing nearby looked back and forth from Bon to Liam. Nobody uttered a sound.

"The Council will be more than happy to listen to any concerns you might have," Bon said through clenched teeth. "For now, I'm sure we would all appreciate your help, especially during your day off."

Liam turned to look at the assembled workers while directing his comments at Bon. "And what exactly happens to me if I choose to do my work only during my assigned time? Will I incur the wrath of the Council? Will I be put on trial?" He looked back at Bon. "Or will I be physically assaulted?"

Before Bon could respond, Marco stepped forward. "That's out of line, Liam," he said. "Whatever issue you might have with the Council is of no interest to us. We're simply asking for your help. Now, will you give that help or not?"

A smile crept across Liam's face. "If we continue to follow our current path through the Kuiper Belt, it really won't matter if this tractor runs or not, Marco."

"So that's your decision? You choose to do nothing?"

Bon said, "Never mind. Go about your business, Liam. We don't need your help. We'll take care of things here." Without waiting for a response, he turned back to the tractor and began to work on the lower module. "Marco, shine that light over here, please."

Liam watched the pair work for a few moments before turning away and walking quickly down the path toward the lift. With the drama apparently over, most of the other workers wandered away to their own duties. For a minute there was silence, broken only by the sounds of Bon's efforts in repairing the engine. Then, he turned to Marco and quietly said, "That wasn't necessary. But thank you."

Marco never looked up from the work. "Let's get this thing running."

Hannah sat at the desk in her room. All of the papers nearby were perfectly aligned with the edge of the desk, as was her stylus pen. A framed sketch of Gap that she had made was also squared to the corner of the desk. The walls around her were adorned with other examples of her completed artwork, mostly drawings in colored pencil, along with a couple of oil paintings she had finished before the launch. Her eye for detail and vivid imagination made her creations very popular with the crew, many of whom had the Alaskan girl's handiwork on their own walls.

Yet at the moment, Hannah's love of art was far from her mind. The vidscreen on her desk displayed a three-dimensional chart of *Galahad*'s course through the Kuiper Belt. A separate file, open in the lower right-hand corner of the screen, scrolled through a series of numbers and equations. Hannah's usually pretty face was furrowed into a frown as she looked at the file.

There had to be a way to maneuver safely through this minefield, she thought. The pressure that was being applied by Merit and his followers might have its roots in the overall inherent danger of the mission, but it was specifically supported right now by the perils they all faced in this shooting gallery. Hannah couldn't deny that the Kuiper Belt had the potential to destroy them, yet in her heart she was convinced that Merit was taking advantage of it to propel his personal agenda of fear. He was either homesick or afraid of what lay ahead, and had latched on to their series of unfortunate encounters to gather support for his movement.

Now that movement was threatening the stability of her world. As far as Hannah was concerned, order was critically important, and Merit represented a disruption in that order.

He also was disrupting Gap's life, which caused her additional anxiety, a situation that would have been totally alien to her only three months ago. Quiet, shy, and content to work in the shadows, she had been completely unprepared for the attention she suddenly received from *Galahad*'s Head of Engineering. She had, like many of the girls on board, been very attracted to Gap from the first time she'd met him. Yet she had never considered the possibility that he would not only notice her, but feel something for her, too. The past three months had been some of the happiest times of her life.

Now that happiness was threatened by turmoil, from the deadly debris that menaced their ship in the outer reaches of the solar system, to the unrest being promoted by Merit.

Turmoil and unrest were concepts that did not fit into her world.

She sighed heavily and shook her head, then refocused on the figures running through the corner of the vidscreen. The real story of the Kuiper Belt was played out here, told not in story form, but in the form of mathematics. Trillions of rock fragments, pre-comets, ice chunks, even sand and dust, all tumbling and colliding, intersecting with each other, changing direction and speed, and completely oblivious to the spacecraft that picked its way . . .

Wait a minute, Hannah thought. She froze, staring at the

screen, her mind racing ahead of the numbers that reflected from her eyes. One idea had snapped into focus, and as usual with her, once in that position it was difficult for anything else to crowd in. She fixed on this one thought for more than a minute, turning it over and around inside her head. Finally she narrowed her eyes and looked up, her gaze settling upon her roommate's unmade bed but not really seeing anything.

"That's ridiculous," she said aloud to herself. And yet she didn't fully believe that, either. *Galahad*'s experience around Titan had shattered the notion that things could be too bizarre to be true. The crew was quickly adapting to the idea that what lay ahead could be more fantastic and weird than anything they had ever imagined.

But what troubled Hannah the most about this particular idea—besides the obvious dangers to the ship—was that, if she shared this thought with others, it could be used as ammunition by Merit.

And that was the last thing she wanted to do.

Besides, she decided, this *was* a pretty wild thought, beyond even the strange phenomenon of Titan. Perhaps, when the moment was right, she would share the idea with Triana. But for the time being she would continue to puzzle it over, and do her best to shoot holes in it before sharing with anyone.

Not for the first time in her life, she secretly hoped that she was wrong.

16

Triana lay still on the bed in her room, her sanctuary from the hectic life as Council Leader. The sound system could have produced any music of her liking, and yet at the moment she had dialed into her most frequent choice, ushering the sound of a murmuring Colorado stream into her room. With the lights low, the water sounds were hypnotic and soothing, allowing Triana the opportunity to close her eyes and meditate. She looked for, and found, the quiet space in her mind that offered relief and escape.

If even for a few moments, it was an escape that was always precious to her.

A few minutes passed, and she opened her eyes. Her gaze instantly went to the photo beside her bed. Her dad, smiling and healthy, carried a younger version of her on his back, doing what he had always done best: enjoying life. The usual mixture of joy and sadness washed over her, a combination that she recognized as both powerful and essential for her well-being. The sadness served as a reminder of the love she carried for her late father, taken in his prime by the killer Bhaktul. The joy drove her to find the best in her dad's life to inspire her own search for happiness. In the past two years that search had been challenging, but these moments of solitude and soul-searching reaffirmed for her that happiness was coming her way.

It was up to her to create it and make it real.

She thought about Lita's admission of doubt. It had surprised her . . . or had it? Could she honestly say that the same thought had never entered her own mind?

Triana looked again at the picture of her dad. He was gone, and Earth could never be the same for her. His death had been the motivating factor in her decision to leave.

But now, after more time had passed, would it be possible to go back and pick up again, to find a new life there? Was she completely sure that happiness on Earth, for her, was impossible?

Stop that, she thought. Bhaktul had made the decision for all of them. There was no going back.

But still . . .

She looked at the clock and realized that it was time to return to Sick House. Lita would soon be ready for surgery. Triana felt a stab of anxiety, but realized that it was probably only a fraction of the nervousness that gripped Lita and Alexa right now.

Swinging her legs off the bed, *Galahad*'s Council Leader sat up and pulled her long brown hair behind her ears. She knew that one aspect of leadership was instilling confidence in others, yet that task would be very challenging in this circumstance. Who among them was ready—especially as teenagers—to literally hold a friend's life in their hand, the way Lita would when she picked up that scalpel? What exactly did one say to a person preparing for that? Triana wanted desperately to empathize with what Lita was facing, but was that possible? Was it really possible to imagine that responsibility?

Triana's thoughts flashed back to their encounter with the stowaway, and her frantic remote control of the Spider which would ultimately save their lives. She had held the fate of *Galahad* in her hands at that moment.

There might be similarities with what Lita now confronted, but only slightly. Triana wondered, were she in Lita's place, if she could even hold the blade steady, while the unconscious figure of her friend lay before her.

Well, she decided, for now it was unimportant. Lita was trained—although briefly—for this task, and Triana was not. Support was the best thing she could offer, and she would devote all of her energies to that.

Her thoughts were interrupted by the buzz of her door. She opened it to find Lita standing there, her eyes hollow and distant.

"It's almost time," Lita said softly. "You said you wanted to be there."

In an instant Triana recognized that Lita could have easily called down to her with this announcement. The fact that she had taken the time to personally escort Triana to Sick House must have meant that she wanted to talk.

"Come in for a moment," Triana said, standing aside. When the two girls were seated in the room, a silence fell over them. Triana waited.

A minute passed. Two. Finally, Lita made eye contact. "I want you to know that I will do my very best."

The comment seemed strange to Triana, almost out of character for her friend. Lita was one of Triana's rocks, a stable, steady force that she relied upon for counsel and guidance during difficult moments. She would, of course, do her best. There was no question about that. Something else had to be brewing inside Lita, and was undoubtedly the reason she was here. Triana chose to remain silent and listen.

"They're finishing the prep on Alexa, so I have a couple of minutes," Lita said. "I . . . I wanted to share a story with you, a story about my mother."

She took a deep breath, then let it out slowly. "You know, of course, that my mother was a doctor. And she was very good. Early in her career she was approached by several universities and hospitals in America, hoping to bring her onto their staffs. She was very tempted, too. At one point she even traveled to Los Angeles for an interview.

"But then something happened. While she was considering the job offer in the States, her best friend fell ill. Cancer."

There was another moment of silence as Lita gathered her thoughts. "I was only an infant at the time, but I've heard many stories. Her name was Carmela, and she had been my mother's closest friend since grade school. In college, while my mother studied medicine, Carmela was interested only in mathematics. From what I've heard, she was brilliant. She and my mother spent hours together in the library, studying for their exams, of course. But more than that. They would share their dreams, too. My mother was sure she would become a top surgeon, while Carmela was convinced she would teach in a major university somewhere.

"They would also talk about their personal dreams. My mother was married with a baby daughter, and Carmela was engaged to be married to her high school sweetheart. They would laugh, I'm told, about how they would have to convince their husbands to move, so that the two friends would always live in the same city. In the same neighborhood, they claimed." A faint smile crossed Lita's face. "They probably would have insisted on buying homes right next door to each other."

Triana smiled, and took Lita's hand for support.

"But the cancer," Lita said, the smile fading. "The cancer."

She fell quiet for a moment. When she spoke again, she tried to keep her voice strong, although it was obvious to Triana that her emotions were beginning to take a toll.

"By now my mother was certified, and working in the hospital in Veracruz. As I mentioned, the offer from Los Angeles was on her mind when Carmela became sick. Two doctors informed Carmela's fiancé, and my mother, that surgery might help.

"Or it might kill her."

Triana held her breath, staring into Lita's eyes, which had again taken on the hollow, vacant look.

"Carmela chose to have the surgery, on one condition. She insisted that my mother perform the operation. She believed that my mother's love for her would make the difference.

"So," Lita said, "that's exactly what happened. My mother summoned all of her courage and faith, and walked into that operating room, with her best friend's life in her hands."

In a flash, Triana knew the outcome. Lita confirmed it.

"Carmela died. She survived the operation, but was gone twelve hours later. The other doctors told my mother that there was nothing she could have done, that she had done the best she could. But my mother was inconsolable. In her mind she had failed her best friend. She had not been able to save her, which is what she had studied and trained for her entire adult life. She watched her best friend die."

At this point Lita's voice broke. Her shoulders shook, and a sob escaped her throat. "And that changed everything. My mother immediately declined the offer to go to Los Angeles. She gave up any thoughts of ever leaving Veracruz. She chose to never again perform surgery, and instead dedicated herself to a small family practice in her hometown."

Lita looked up into Triana's face. "She never got over Carmela's death."

Triana squeezed Lita's hand and felt her own tears coming on. "Lita," she said in a soft voice. "Your mother was a hero. She chose to spend her life helping others. She also chose to do everything in her power to help her friend. Sometimes . . ." Triana hesitated, thinking of her own father. "Sometimes the universe has plans for our friends and family that we can't understand.

"But that doesn't mean that we don't try. The universe could very well have planned for your mother to save Carmela's life. We don't know, just as we *never* know what's in store for any of us."

Triana reached out and placed her hand on Lita's upper arm. "It seems like such a cruel coincidence right now, the fact that you're in the same position as your mother. But . . . but when you think about it, is it really? Your mother was a caregiver, as you are now. Caregivers are going to sometimes find themselves treating their own loved ones, their friends, people they care about. As much as we hate to think about it, this probably won't be the last time you're called upon to do this."

She waited until she saw Lita give a slight nod before continuing. "So, while we have no idea what's in store for any of us, we do know that it's our destiny to do everything we can to help, whenever possible. That's who we are. That's who *you* are.

"I know that your mother would tell you the same thing."

For a while Lita said nothing, looking into Triana's eyes. Triana leaned across and embraced her, and felt Lita's breathing become strong and steady.

17

By now you undoubtedly recognize that I am an amazing observer of human characteristics and behavior. You do recognize that, right?

Here's my latest observation. Human males are somehow genetically related to bull elks and bighorn sheep. Why? Because they all butt heads the same way.

Hey, Gap. Mind if I interrupt for a minute?"

Gap recognized the voice behind him. He stood with his hands clasped behind his head, staring at the same panel that had occupied his attention far too much recently, once again wracking his brain to solve—once and for all—the heating issue on Level 6. It had stabilized for the time being, so on his way to Sick House he had decided to pop in and check on things.

He answered without turning around. "I'm a little busy right now, Merit."

"I won't take long."

"I'm busy here, and in just a couple of minutes I have to be somewhere else," Gap said.

"Sick House, right?"

That was enough to prompt Gap to spin around. Before he could speak, Merit held up both hands as if warding off a blow.

"Whoa, steady boy," Merit said. "Yes, I heard about Alexa. I'm sorry about that. I'm sure she'll be—"

"Before you get any ideas," Gap spit out, "this has nothing to do with our mission or our destination. It just happened. It would have happened to Alexa if we were heading back to Earth, too."

Merit slowly lowered his hands. "I know that. I said I'm sorry, okay?" He paused, allowing Gap to cool a bit. "Just one minute of your time?"

"You have nothing to say that I want to hear right now," Gap said. He looked around. "Where's your cheering section? Traveling without your fan club today?"

A smile spread across Merit's face. "How do you know what I'm going to say? You might be very interested."

"Not likely. I've heard your arguments already. Not very impressive, really."

"Afraid to find out what I might say? You haven't become close-minded, have you, Gap?"

It was Gap's turn to smile. "I'm sure if you blabbered on for weeks and weeks, eventually something interesting might accidentally spill out of your mouth."

Merit took a step back, leaned against the wall and crossed his arms. "I should know better than to verbally spar with someone who practices with Roc on a daily basis. I am overmatched."

Gap stared at him for a moment. He had always noticed the long, jet-black hair, often pulled back into a tail. Now he scanned Merit's face, and noticed for the first time a small scar under his right eye. The bandage from his lip was gone, without any trace of the blow that Bon had inflicted. Apparently Merit didn't feel the prop was necessary anymore.

"Alexa is about to have surgery, and I want to be there," Gap said. "You have thirty seconds."

"Then I'll make it quick," Merit said. "I just wanted you to know that we now number almost fifty. That's twenty percent of the crew. And, although you sometimes seem to get . . . shall we say, emotional? . . . I know that you're one of the brightest people on this ship. Putting aside for the moment your loyalty to Triana—and I honestly do commend you for that—does your brain really tell you that she's right and we're wrong? Have you truly stopped to consider what we're saying? Loyalty is admirable . . . but not at the cost of your life. Wouldn't you agree?"

Gap chuckled. "Let's shoot straight with each other, Merit. First of all, I'm not swayed by your constant use of the word 'we.' This is about you. Secondly, if you're going to appeal to my intellect, it would be a good idea to take a stance that actually makes sense. Your idea of going back to Earth is completely illogical. You accuse me of being emotional; well, your plan is based totally on fear, one of the most destructive emotions there is.

"And finally," he added, "you'll find that people are loyal to Triana for a reason. She's doing the job that was assigned to her—unlike some people—and she's doing it well."

Merit nodded his head. "Nice speech. I'm glad we could talk."

Gap walked around him toward the door.

"One other thing," Merit called out. "If things turn ugly—and they might—you're always welcome to change your mind and come over to our side. Just remember that."

Gap stopped at the open door and looked back. "I would be very careful if I were you, Merit."

"And you as well," Merit said.

Triana and Channy stood next to Alexa's bed. Triana knew that the best thing they could do was cheer up the sick girl, and keep the atmosphere upbeat. She also knew that these weren't exactly her strongest talents, but was confident that Channy would more than make up for it. She wasn't disappointed.

"Don't think for a minute that I don't know what's really going on here," Channy said, fixing Alexa with a mock scowl. "I've seen people go to outrageous extremes to get out of one of my workouts, but this is ridiculous."

Alexa, prepped and ready for surgery, managed to force a smile through the haze of painkilling medication that had left her barely awake. She mumbled, "Can't . . . fool you, can . . . I?"

Channy shook her head. "And if you think this gives you a free pass for months, think again."

Triana took Alexa's hand. "I see you've got a little friend keeping you company." Iris was curled up beside the patient, purring steadily. One of the cat's paws was casually draped across Alexa's forearm.

"Uh-huh," Alexa said. "She's my . . . good luck charm."

"I thought you might enjoy some pet power on your way to surgery," Channy said, scratching the cat's chin. "You know, they say that dogs and cats can sense when somebody's sick. And look, she could have jumped down a long time ago, but she's not going anywhere." In response to the scratching, Iris closed her eyes and began to purr louder.

"You'll have quite an audience, too," Triana said. "Gap's on his way, and your roomie will be here any minute."

Alexa exhaled a grunt. "That's . . . nice. Tell them . . . I said . . . thank . . . you."

"Oh, one other thing," Channy said with a grin. "Hurry up and get well so you can be on my dating game. You've become a celebrity now, which means you'll be a very popular contestant."

It was obvious that Alexa wanted to respond, but instead her eyes closed and her breathing became regular and deep. Channy, a sudden look of fear in her eyes, turned to Triana.

"Is this normal?" she said.

"Yes," came the answer from Lita who was walking into the room. "She's getting a gradual drip that puts her in a light sleep on and off."

Triana bit her lip, then said to Lita. "You need anything from us?"

"No, but thanks," Lita said. "We're going to take her into the operating room now." She gently shook Alexa's arm. "Hey, sleepy head."

Alexa stirred and opened her eyes about halfway. Lita leaned over her and said, "What do you want to eat when we're all finished? Pizza? Ice cream? Liver?"

A trace of a smile crept across Alexa's semiconscious face. Channy picked up Iris and touched Alexa's other arm. "You can borrow Iris during your recovery, but you're responsible for cleaning up any hairballs, okay?"

It was Triana's turn. She felt as if she should say something lighthearted as well, but found that she was becoming emotionally overcome by the situation. A lump formed in her throat. "We'll see you soon, okay?" was all that she could manage to say.

"There's good news," Lita said to Alexa. "You'll sleep through the blood, so you won't have to see anything."

A larger smile spread across Alexa's face. Before she could mutter anything, two Sick House workers entered the room. They stepped up, adjusted Alexa's bed, then rolled it out of the hospital ward toward *Galahad*'s lone operating room. It had never been used up to this point.

Triana looked at Lita. "Blood?"

"She told me the other day that she's afraid of blood. She works in a clinic, and she's afraid of . . ." Lita began to choke up.

Triana put an arm around her friend. "She's in great hands, Lita. You'll be perfect."

"Yeah," added Channy. "Piece of cake."

Lita exhaled and appeared to gather her composure. "All right. I'll . . . I guess I'll see you in a little while." She hugged Triana and Channy, then left to scrub and change into sterile gear.

Channy shifted Iris into a crook of her arm, then shook her

head in disbelief. "She's not even sixteen years old yet, and she's about to operate on someone. I can't even imagine that."

Triana said, "She probably can't, either."

The two of them retreated to the Sick House office. The door to the hallway opened, and Gap walked in with Alexa's roommate, Katarina.

"Did we miss her?" Gap said.

Triana nodded. "Yeah, they just took her in."

"Is she going to be okay?" Katarina said softly.

Everyone was quiet for a moment as the gravity of the situation finally hit home. Through all of the tough scrapes, through all of the near-death experiences, and through all of the drama, nothing like this had happened until now. Once again it occurred to the four *Galahad* crew members standing in Sick House that they were indeed on their own. There was no help to call in, no ambulance that could rush to the scene, no . . .

No adult that they could lean on. They had only themselves.

Triana finally answered Katarina. "Yes. She's going to be okay."

The mechanical waves of sound are unable to travel through the icy vacuum of space, which means that the ultimate silence sits just beyond a planet's atmosphere. The Kuiper objects that jostled and collided with each other gave off eruptions of rock and ice shards, but there was no soundtrack to accompany their impacts, no matter how violent.

Rolling, tumbling, scraping, they pitched along in their mindless trek around the outskirts of the solar system. *Galahad* dared to cut across their path, not unlike a pedestrian tempting fate by running across swiftly moving lanes of traffic.

Any collision between a Kuiper object and the spacecraft would produce an explosion with enough intensity to be visible—if only for an instant—on Earth. The impact would produce a blinding flash.

But no sound whatsoever.

The most sophisticated warning system ever developed kept up a continuous scan of the space ahead of the ship, probing for potential danger spots, alerting the ship's computer to any possible hazards. A typical scan would normally be a lazy sweep back and forth, up and down, repeated at a slow and steady pace.

The Kuiper Belt was a stickier situation than normal, however. *Galahad*'s warning system was tweaked to cover its optimum distance and spread pattern, and swept in all directions at a frantic pace. The cumulative amount of data processed every second during these scans equaled all of the data stored in an average library back on Earth. There was no margin for error.

The lives of 251 teenage pilgrims relied upon a scanning unit no larger than a shoe box, bolted into an equipment rack, and tucked into an isolated corner of the ship's Engineering section.

18

They waited in the Conference Room. The office of Sick House seemed too close to the reality of what was happening, the Rec Room and Dining Halls were too noisy, and their own rooms seemed stifling.

Triana chose not to sit in her usual spot at the head of the table. Gap had the seat beside her, rolling a cup of water back and forth in his hands. Channy opted for the floor of the room, her back against the wall and her legs crossed, with Iris sprawled beside her. Katarina seemed to feel uncomfortable, almost like an outsider who had crashed a Council meeting. She sat quietly across from Triana and Gap.

For more than an hour they made small talk, trying to keep the mood as light as possible. Channy tried to sell them on her dating game, but it became quickly apparent that nobody was interested at the moment. She changed course and discussed some recent workouts, as well as the idea of another soccer tournament. This garnered a somewhat enthusiastic response, but soon that, too, faded.

Gap asked Katarina a few questions about what was going on in the Farms, which was her current assignment on the ship. Her abbreviated answers hinted at the discomfort she obviously felt, so Gap turned his attention to the cat. He quizzed Channy about

Bon's patience with Iris in the Farms, and whether or not she was getting tired of feline babysitting duties. This conversation fizzled after about a minute.

They knew that it was all just one big distraction from the tension that weighed heavily on the room. Now, after a block of silence that only focused each of them on the seriousness of the situation, Triana cleared her throat.

"We're all scared," she said softly.

Gap looked at her with an expression of surprise. "What?"

She nodded. "There's nothing wrong with admitting that. We can sit here and pretend that we're doing okay, but we're all scared. Maybe we should talk about that instead of soccer games and Iris."

Channy got up from the floor and sat down at the table beside Katarina. "You know what scares me the most?" she said. "This could have happened to any of us. I mean, your appendix?"

"Yeah," Gap said. "The month we spent in quarantine before we left Earth might have eliminated a lot of germs or viruses from our future, but not this."

"And that makes me wonder about a lot of other things," Channy said. "What about tumors, or blood clots, or stuff like that? I know we're all young, but with this many people on the ship, things are gonna happen."

Triana could see the concern on Channy's face, and it caused her to lean forward, her elbows on the table. "Can I share something with you about that?" she said. "I . . . I don't talk about my dad very much, even though I'm always thinking about him. But he did teach me a few things about this."

The others sat quietly staring at her. She realized that this was a side of herself that they never saw, and they were not about to interrupt. She gathered her thoughts for a moment, then continued.

"I've never known a happier person in my life. He loved his work, he loved me, and he loved life. Of all the lessons he tried to teach to a somewhat serious little girl, the one that stood out was to enjoy life without worrying about what might happen. It's not like he was a crazy daredevil or anything, but he . . . he didn't always play it safe, either."

Triana paused, her mind drifting backwards, retrieving a moment frozen in her memory.

"When I was thirteen, I remember crying before one of my soccer tournaments. Our team had worked so hard the whole season, and we were picked to go to this big state tournament. I was scared to death that I would play horribly, or that we would embarrass ourselves against these other great teams. I even worried about getting hurt, because a few of the teams were a little older than us, and a lot bigger. I was upset about so many things.

"The night before the first game, my dad sat on the edge of my bed and shook his head. He said, 'Let me tell you something that you obviously have not thought about. You're thirteen, you're about to play in a tournament that thousands of other girls would give anything to participate in, and it could be one of the most fun experiences of your life.

"'But,' he said to me, 'you're all balled up inside. You're worrying about ridiculous things. Do you really want this tournament to end and have your only memories be of worrying about it?'"

Gap, Channy, and Katarina sat still, their attention fixed on Triana. She chuckled, then continued. "He told me something that I've tried to remember as often as possible. He said, 'Close your eyes, and for a few moments visualize the last minute of the last game. You're running down the field, the sun is shining, the grass is perfect, you're laughing, your teammates are laughing, and you have a wide open shot for the game-winner. You pull back your leg, and you fire away.'"

Triana closed her eyes now, taking herself back to that moment, one of many precious memories of her dad. She kept the smile etched across her face. After a few moments, Channy spoke up in a quiet voice, as if not wanting to break the spell, but yet needing to know the answer.

"Umm . . . what happened? What did you visualize?"

"That's the best part," Triana said, opening her eyes and looking at Channy. "I have relived that moment over and over again. I'm lying in bed before the tournament begins, and I'm watching myself take that shot. And you know what? It ends differently every single time."

Channy looked puzzled. "What do you mean?"

"I mean, sometimes I visualize that shot scooting past the goalie, into the corner of the net for the winning score. Sometimes it rockets over the goalie's head, skims off the crossbar, and drops into the net. Other times the goalie blocks the shot, but I get the rebound and fire it past her to win the game.

"It's always different. But I noticed something about it. Every time I see it, it's something good. My dad had me close my eyes and visualize, right? He didn't say to visualize a happy ending. He just put me in that place, and allowed me to sketch my own ending. And I found that my worries disappeared. It was . . ."

She fell silent for a moment, searching for the words. "It was like I was given the brush and could paint any picture I wanted. And it made me realize that I wanted none of those things that had bothered me. I could be the artist of my own future."

Triana looked around at the faces of her friends. "Listen, I know there's a big difference between a soccer game, and what we're going through today. I know the stakes are a lot higher, and the results are much more important.

"That doesn't change the fact that we ultimately control our thoughts. They don't control us, unless we let them. Yes, bad things might happen, and, believe me, I've been through my share of difficult times. But I can't deny that there is still a power that we don't understand, and it comes from right here." She tapped her head. "We might not be able to control everything that happens, and we might be challenged by many things in our lives.

But we only drain ourselves emotionally when we worry about things beyond our control."

Channy smiled at her. "Your dad was pretty cool, wasn't he?"

Triana leaned back in her chair and looked up at the ceiling. "He was the best. We're all individuals, you know, and we have our own settings, I guess you could say. But I'm grateful for everything he shared with me, and everything that he taught me."

Gap reached over and put a hand on her shoulder. "I wish everyone on the ship could have heard what you just said."

Triana felt a tear trying to work its way out, so she took a deep breath and blinked a couple of times. When it seemed like an awkward silence had settled over the room, she turned to Katarina. "Are you okay?"

Katarina nodded, her eyes wide. "I . . . I guess so. I just don't like feeling like there's nothing I can do, you know?"

The other three considered this for a moment. Triana said, "In a way, we're all doing something. We're here for each other, and that's the most important thing right now."

Katarina smiled at her. "You're right. If I wasn't here with you guys right now, I'd probably be going out of my mind."

"Me, too," Channy said. "I know you all get a bit tired of my chattering all the time, but today I kinda need to. It helps."

"Of course it does," Triana said. She offered her own faint smile. "You know I'm not usually much of a talker, but this is exactly what we need to be doing."

"Well," Gap said, setting down his cup of water and running a hand through his hair. "I'm glad to hear you all saying this. If you weren't hanging out with me right now I'd probably be forced to chat with Roc, and I'm not sure I could handle that under the circumstances."

"I heard that," came the computer's voice from the speaker.

A stress-reducing ripple of laughter spread around the room. Triana appreciated the break from the tension, but couldn't help but wonder if a good portion of that stress wasn't triggered by guilt. Yes, they were afraid for Alexa, and yes, they were aware that it could just as easily have happened to them.

But was there another factor at play here, too? Were they troubled by thoughts that they didn't dare give voice to? Did they all wonder, secretly, how this might have played out if they had been home? Were they each considering Merit's arguments, which, in the light of another potential crisis, suddenly seemed more attractive?

Or was it just her?

Triana studied the faces around the table. There was no way of knowing if their minds were wrestling with the same disturbing questions. She felt a knot in her stomach again, and wondered if her own face registered the conflict she felt. If so, nobody said anything.

She suddenly felt a touch of shame, angry at herself for allowing her thoughts to drift this way, when she should be thinking about the life-and-death struggle that Alexa faced. A struggle, she realized, that should have been decided by now. Lita had said that the surgery would take less than an hour. Triana glanced at the clock on her vidscreen.

It had been an hour and a half.

19

Her Zen place; that's how Alexa had said she dealt with blood. She went into her Zen place.

Lita had never been bothered by the sight of blood, until, she realized, it belonged to a close friend. Now she understood exactly what Alexa had meant about the need to somehow detach from the situation. Yet how to detach and still maintain control? What place was this, Zen or otherwise, that offered relief from the pain, the pressure, the weight of responsibility?

Lita felt a catch in her throat and swallowed hard, partly to stifle the stab of grief at her friend's condition, but also to staunch the rising alarm that she had missed something. The surgery had progressed exactly as it had been spelled out in all of the tutorials she had scanned. The programmed video guide had directed her through every step, and she had made sure to not rush anything, to follow each stage precisely as instructed. She had total confidence in her thoroughness.

So why did she have this feeling?

Nerves, she told herself. That's all, just nerves.

The monitors flashed their steady reports: pulse, blood pressure, breathing. Everything looked fine. Lita looked quickly at Alexa's face, so calm and serene. In this unconscious state there was no pain. Would there be dreams?

The thought made Lita pause. She had read that some people did experience dreams during anesthesia, and thankfully most were pleasant. Alexa looked content and peaceful, which made Lita feel somewhat better, but who could say what images were flashing through Alexa's mind during this down time? The idea fascinated Lita.

She shifted her gaze to stare down at the small incision, amazed once again at the incredible machine that was the human body. The appendix was out, the abdominal area had been inspected for bleeding and any pockets of infection, and then had been washed out with a saline solution. It was time to close up.

Lita thought about the progress of medical science. In the old days she would have been sewing up her patient, and later might have evolved to stapling. But today she was fortunate to have a technique similar to gluing, which would leave no scar on Alexa's abdomen. In less than two minutes she was finished.

Lita set down the instrument she had been using and exhaled. One of her assistants looked up and made eye contact. Even through the mask, Lita could tell that her face held a big smile.

For the next minute there was an exchange of congratulations and heavy sighs. Things were cleaned up, carts were wheeled out of the way, and Lita made one more inspection of the wound. "Okay," she said, "let's wake her up."

Another assistant, Manu, adjusted the mixture of gases into Alexa's clear mask, checking and double-checking the figures that spilled across the vidscreen. Lita stepped back and pulled down her surgical mask. The monitors continued to relay a healthy set of vital signs. She walked across the room and stripped off her gloves. In the background she heard the assistant softly calling Alexa back to consciousness. The entire procedure, from start to finish, had taken forty-nine minutes. Next time, Lita thought with a smile, I'll know what I'm doing, and should be able to knock it out in thirty-five.

A few small drops of blood spotted one of her sleeves. It magnified the significance of what had just happened. Pulling off the white smock, she looked back over her shoulder at Manu as he worked beside Alexa.

"Everything okay?" Lita asked him.

He looked up at her. "She's not responding."

Lita quickly walked back to the operating table, looked at Alexa, then up at the monitors. Everything continued to read normal.

"She should at least be stirring a little bit by now," Manu said. His voice carried a touch of panic.

"Let's stay calm," Lita said, but inside her chest she felt the same odd sensation return. Something didn't feel right. She immediately summoned the ship's computer.

"Roc, am I boosting the oxygen level here?"

"No," came the reply. In the next ten minutes they followed every emergency step as outlined in their medical procedures manual. Alexa remained unconscious.

Now the sensation of panic began to overwhelm Lita. Her mind tortured her with a reminder of her mother's experience with Carmela. In frustration she lashed out at Roc.

"There's something we're missing! What are we not doing?"

"Lita," Roc said, "we have done everything called for. She's not responding."

"She *has* to respond!" Lita looked at the monitor again, willing it to show her something, anything, that would explain the situation. It mocked her with normal readings. Turning to Manu she said, "Are you sure you gave her the right mixture during the procedure?"

Roc answered for the stunned boy. "Lita, I monitored everything that was administered during the operation. The dosage was correct, the course of action was followed perfectly. She's not responding."

Lita's chin dropped to her chest and she issued a low groan. "What have I missed? I must have missed something."

"You haven't done anything wrong, Lita," Roc said. "You did everything exactly as you should have. The surgery itself was perfect."

"It's not perfect!" Lita said, raising her voice. "She's not waking up."

"And there is nothing you have done to cause that," the computer replied.

Lita shook her head and felt a tremble work its way through her body. First her mother with Carmela, and now her own failure with Alexa. After a moment she realized that Manu and the other assistant were watching her, waiting for direction. She took a deep breath, then another.

"Let's get her back into the hospital ward and into her bed," she said finally, her voice returning to normal. She laid out instructions for Alexa's care and treatment, then watched as they wheeled her out. She was alone in the operating room.

Leaning back against the wall, she allowed one sob to shake her. Then she tilted her head toward the ceiling and shut her eyes.

He spent about five minutes scrubbing the combination of grease and dirt from his hands and nails before remembering that there was still a lot of work to be done before he could take a break. Now Bon dried his hands and sat down with a sigh at his desk. He and Marco had finally coaxed the tractor into starting, no thanks to Liam. A flash of anger passed through Bon as he recalled the smug look of satisfaction on Liam's face. Between that showdown and the confrontation with Merit, Bon felt mentally fatigued. He wasn't one for taking time off, but suddenly all he wanted was to get away and not have to think about any of it for awhile.

A tap came on his open door. Hannah stood just outside,

her body language making it clear that she felt as if she were intruding.

"Yes, come in," Bon said, puzzled by the visit. Other than a brief connection during the drama around Titan, he hadn't spent any time with her. He knew that she was gifted when it came to mathematics, and that she and Gap were close, but, between his natural reluctance to socialize and her shyness, they had never really spoken.

"I don't want to interrupt anything," she said, taking a few tentative steps into his office.

"No, you're not interrupting," he said. "What's on your mind?"

She sat down across from his desk. "Well, I've been doing some research on the Kuiper Belt." When Bon didn't respond, she nervously looked down at her hands. "It's a pretty scary place. I mean, a lot more dangerous than we thought, obviously. There's a lot more . . . stuff, I guess you could say, than we thought would be out here. Mostly smaller rocks and ice balls. It's going to be very difficult to squeeze through it all."

Bon stared at her. "Sounds like you've been talking with Merit."

"No, no," Hannah said quickly, looking up at him. "I mean, I know what he's saying, and he's right that it's dangerous. But I don't agree with him about turning back."

"Okay," Bon said, sitting back in his chair. "I'm sorry, but I don't really know that much about it. Not my specialty. I'm pretty busy up here. I leave the piloting of the ship to others."

Hannah swallowed, and again looked as if she was cowering from him. "Right, I know that. That's not really why I'm here."

"And just why *are* you here?"

"Well . . ." She paused.

Bon said, "Contrary to what you might think, I don't bite. What do you want to talk to me about?"

She began again. "Well, I've been plugging in a lot of numbers, trying to make sense of what we're seeing out here. There are some extremely large bodies, the size of dwarf planets, like Pluto. There are probably a hundred or so of those. But that's nothing compared to the billions and billions of smaller chunks. They're scattered in a haphazard way. When you first look at it, it seems random."

Bon studied her face. "I suppose you're going to tell me that it's really not random?"

She nodded. "That's right. There are pockets of density here and there, separated by long stretches where it's rather unpopulated. We could zip through those areas without too many worries. At least not compared to the other zones."

"Bad luck," the Swede said to her. "We happened across a thick stretch, I guess."

"No," she said. "We didn't just happen across it. We *have* to go through this crowded stretch if we want to get to Eos."

"I don't understand what you're getting at," Bon said. "Of course we have to go this way." He studied her face for a moment, trying to jump a step ahead in order to figure out where she was going. "Wait a minute," he said, pushing his chair back. "Are you suggesting that these thick pockets of space debris are *deliberately* in this spot?"

Hannah diverted her eyes. "It's probably a discussion for the entire Council, but I wanted to at least talk to you about something . . . sensitive."

"Let me guess," Bon said. "The Cassini."

Hannah nodded, keeping her eyes in her lap.

Bon exhaled loudly. "Listen, I'm getting a little tired of all the questions about them. We left Titan months ago."

"But I'm guessing that . . ." Hannah seemed to find a hidden reserve of courage. "I'm guessing that you're still in contact with them somehow, and I was hoping that you might be able to . . . I don't know, ask a question, or something."

Another long silence fell over the room. This time Hannah kept her gaze fixed on Bon's eyes, as if willing him to answer. He stared back, considering his words. Or, rather, considering the potential impact his words would have.

"I think I am," he said finally.

Hannah swallowed and let out her breath. "You think you're still in contact?"

"Yeah. I think so."

A visible look of relief crossed Hannah's face. "I was hoping you would say that. So, if you don't mind me prying, why do you think so?"

Bon looked out the window into Dome 1. "Just little things here and there. I told Channy that it felt almost like déjà vu, but sometimes it's more than that. A little while ago we had a problem with one of the tractors. A couple of us banged around on it but couldn't get it to go."

He paused, looking back at Hannah. "And then I just kinda . . . I don't know, sat back, closed my eyes, and quit trying so hard. A moment later I knew what I needed to do. And I did it."

"You got it to run?"

"Yeah."

"But couldn't you have already known how to fix it, and you just finally remembered?"

Bon shrugged. "You asked if I thought I was still in contact, and that's what I think. Sometimes things just come to me. Could I have fixed the engine on that tractor anyway? Maybe. But as soon as I let go and emptied my mind, the answer came to me. In my opinion, it came from the Cassini."

Hannah nodded slowly. She unconsciously reached out and straightened a piece of paper on Bon's desk. "Okay. Well, like I said, I'm glad to hear that, because I'd like to make a request."

Bon chuckled. "All right. What is it you want to know? Something about these dense spots in the Kuiper Belt, right?"

"Yeah. I'll explain it in detail with the Council, but when we have that meeting I'd like to know if the Cassini can answer a question for me."

"Well," Bon said, "obviously I can't promise anything, but I'll do my best. What is it?"

Hannah hesitated before answering. "I want to know if these pockets are meant to keep things out, or to keep us in."

20

Triana's heart sank. Light spilled into the Conference Room from the corridor, and Lita stood in the doorway, looking completely drained, almost ready to collapse. In a flash Gap bolted from his seat and helped her over to the table where she sat down heavily. Triana and Channy rushed to her side, both dropping to a knee to look into her face.

"Lita," Triana said. "Are you okay?"

"I don't know," Lita mumbled. "Not really."

Channy was the one who asked what they all were afraid to ask. "Alexa . . . ?"

Lita looked down at Channy, then at Gap, then Triana. Her gaze finally settled upon Katarina, who was frozen in her chair, her eyes wide.

"She . . ." Lita began to say, then shook with a sob. "She made it through the surgery fine, but . . ."

Nobody spoke. Triana placed a hand on Lita's knee to show support.

"I got the appendix out," Lita said softly. "But . . . but we couldn't wake her up afterwards."

Channy shot a quick glance of alarm at Triana. "What does that mean?"

Lita looked at Channy with red-rimmed eyes. "It means that she's in a coma."

Across the table Katarina brought her hand up to her mouth, letting out a sharp cry. Triana felt a shudder ripple through her body, and her mouth went dry. She managed to exchange a look with Gap, who spoke for the first time.

"But . . . that might be normal, right?" he said. "Like a defense mechanism or something?"

Lita shook her head. "No, it's not normal. She should be wide awake right now. But her body had some strange reaction to the anesthesia, and she's not waking up." She turned to look at Triana. "She's not waking up," she repeated.

Now Triana felt her heart ache for her friend. She could only imagine the pain that Lita must be experiencing. Words, which only minutes before had seemed easy to find, now seemed out of reach. And yet something needed to be said.

She gently touched Lita's face, turning it so that they would make eye contact. "Listen to me," Triana said, her voice low but firm. "A couple of hours ago you were terrified because you were about to perform surgery—surgery, Lita!—on your friend. There were doubts running through your head. And you pulled it off. Do you understand that? You're about to turn sixteen, and out here, more than a billion miles from home, you just saved someone's life. Nobody else on this ship could have done that!"

The others in the room were motionless, listening to Triana. Lita seemed slowly to regain her composure. Her body appeared to relax, melting into the chair.

"You are responsible for Alexa being alive right now," Triana said. "She had a reaction to the anesthesia, but that's something you could never have known. Your first priority was to operate on her, quickly. You saved her."

Lita smiled faintly. "I was so scared."

"I know," Triana half-whispered. "I know you were. But you did it. We're all so proud of you." She leaned over and wrapped her arms around Lita, who returned the hug and finally found release in tears.

Channy wept, too. She leaned in and joined the two Council members in their embrace.

Gap sat down in one of the chairs. He respectfully waited a few moments before speaking. "Um, what happens now?"

Lita sat back and dabbed at the remaining tears. "Well, I honestly don't know. Alexa has the hospital ward to herself, so she'll be getting a lot of personalized care. She's breathing on her own just fine. I think all we can do is watch and wait."

Triana pulled up one of the chairs and sat down. "Roc, can you help us out with some answers here?"

"I've just been analyzing the data," the computer said. "Alexa is in a low-level state on the Glasgow Coma Scale, but I don't see any signs of brain damage."

"How long could this last?" Gap said.

"Impossible to answer. It's actually rare for a coma to last more than a few weeks at most, and often it's just a matter of days. Notable exceptions include senators and congressmen, who have been known to remain in a coma for decades. I would prefer to withhold any prediction on Alexa until we see what happens in the next twenty-four hours."

Triana digested this for a minute. "Okay," she said to Lita. "What do you need from us?"

Galahad's Health Director stood up. "I can't think of anything right now." She let out a long breath. "Well, I have to get back to Sick House. Sorry if I freaked out a bit, guys."

Channy shook her head. "Don't be crazy. We think you're amazing."

"Thanks," Lita said with a smile. "I appreciate the support from all of you." She looked at Katarina at the end of the table. "I'm going to take good care of your roomie, okay?"

Katarina walked over to Lita and gave her a hug. "I know you will. Thank you. Is it okay if I at least see her for a moment?"

"Sure," Lita said. "But only for a minute right now. C'mon." She started to follow Katarina into the corridor, then turned back to face Triana. She didn't say anything, but Triana could sense what her friend was thinking. She smiled and nodded at Lita, who spun around with a renewed confidence and walked briskly out the door.

The room remained silent for a few seconds. Then Gap drummed his fingers on the table and said, "Life is never boring aboard *Galahad*, is it?"

Triana said, "Not so far, anyway." In her mind she quickly ran through the inventory of current issues. Heating problems, the Kuiper Belt minefield, Alexa's emergency surgery . . .

And Merit Simms.

The drama from Alexa's appendicitis had distracted Triana for awhile, but she knew that the minute she walked out of the Conference Room she would be walking right back into the controversy that Merit had stirred up.

Gap seemed to read her thoughts. "Just for the record, our troublesome friend came to see me. I have to tell you that I don't care for the tone his little speeches are taking."

Triana shook her head. "I know what you're suggesting, but I find it very hard to believe that he would ever resort to violence."

"It doesn't have to be him, though, does it?" Gap said. "The way he's going about this protest could provoke somebody else to do something stupid. Merit might not even know about it, even though he's to blame."

As much as she hated to admit it, Triana knew that this argument was valid. Tensions were starting to run high and sides were being drawn; an insignificant spark could set off a chain of events that might end in violence. Earth's history was peppered with numerous examples, often with the original instigator out of the picture. And, once it began, it was extremely difficult to stop.

Triana hoped that they had left that particular aspect of human nature behind when they launched. Time would tell.

At the moment, she felt the gravity of her balancing act between respecting Merit's right to protest and maintaining peace, order, and productivity among the crew. She immediately recalled Dr. Zimmer's recorded message: "Finding that fair position might seem tough, if not impossible." He had, as usual, been prophetic with his prediction about crew relations; would she now reward his faith in her as a leader?

The logical response to Gap's concern was obvious to her. "The time has come," she said to him. "We'll have a full crew meeting in two days. It's time that we dealt with this issue head-on."

Channy pumped her fist in the air and let out an excited "Yes!" Gap raised his eyebrows and nodded. "Sounds like a good plan to me," he said.

Hannah walked down the deserted corridor of the ship, keeping exactly two feet from the curved wall. Her eyes remained focused on a spot on the floor ten feet ahead of her. One hand clutched her workpad, the other hung limply at her side. A fellow crew member exited a room directly in front of her, almost colliding, before pulling up and letting her pass. She never saw him.

Her mind was still on the conversation with Bon. The more she thought about it, the more she became convinced that her theory—as crazy as it sounded—might very well be correct. And, if it was, *Galahad* was in more danger than they had originally thought.

So why wasn't she afraid? Why did this excite her when it should have left her terrified?

She realized that the answer lay within her own natural curiosity, a force so powerful it had led ancient mariners to venture out beyond the edge of the horizon, where legend held that the Earth fell away into a void of monsters and devils. The same force had also compelled adventurers to risk their lives to scale the highest mountains, to cross the Antarctic ice pack, to plunge into the murky depths of the ocean, all in the name of exploration and to satisfy mankind's overwhelming desire to see, to learn, to *know* what was out there.

It had also driven thirty scientists and researchers to the moons of Saturn, where they had mysteriously perished in the pursuit of knowledge.

This same force churned inside Hannah Ross. Fear might lurk somewhere within, but it stood no chance against her overwhelming desire to learn. Bon had helped with another piece of the puzzle; now her mind was in overdrive, trying its best to see exactly what picture this puzzle would produce when all was said and done.

It might not be pretty.

The time had come to meet once again with *Galahad*'s Council. She might lack concrete proof of her theory, but her instincts had been right during the crisis at Titan and those same feelings were bubbling around again.

She looked up in time to notice that she had reached her room. Once inside she crossed to her desk, set the workpad down, nudged it slightly to make sure that its edge aligned evenly with the side of the desk, and began to mentally prepare her presentation to the Council before writing it. Snapping on the vidscreen she opened her email account. Before she could compose a note to Triana she saw that the Council Leader had sent out a mass email to the entire crew.

She scanned it quickly. A general crew meeting would take place in two days, 2 P.M., in the auditorium that they called School.

Things were reaching the boiling point. If Triana was going to address all of the crew members, then she would need to know right away. It could change everything.

21

The sounds coming from the hidden speakers in her room mimicked an ocean shore, complete with crashing waves and an occasional gull cry. Although she had spent the majority of her life in landlocked Colorado, Triana loved the soothing atmosphere that was created with these sounds, and was thankful that Lita had suggested them. Lita, practically raised with sand between her toes, had touted the hypnotic background noise as "therapy for the soul." That prescription was exactly what Triana needed at the moment.

She scribbled a few words into her journal, but found that her thoughts were scattered and unsatisfying. After a moment of consideration, she decided that was okay; the emotional release from her journaling served a purpose, scattered thoughts and all. She leaned over the pages.

With another crew meeting coming up, the perfectionist in me is rearing its ugly head again. With all that has happened in the past couple of days, it's time to give myself permission to NOT have all of the answers all of the time.

If we weren't always moments away from being blasted out of existence, if Merit wasn't practically leading a mutiny, and if Alexa was awake and alert, I'd almost say it was time for a vacation. Just think, it wasn't long ago that every summer was a long vacation. Those days are gone.

I could use a mental vacation, that's for sure. The more I allow myself to think about it, the more I realize that I do miss the sun, the wind, the openness of home. I'm angry that these thoughts even enter my mind.

But they do. They're real, and I have to accept them, deal with them, and move on. Take a break.

So, even though I need to work out exactly what I'm going to say to the crew . . . I'm not going to do that right now. I'm putting everything on hold for the next hour, and enjoying the sounds of the sea, maybe doing some yoga, and simply breathing.

A smile crept across her face. She knew that, for her, this was a tall order. There was, however, someone who could help her relax.

"Hey, Roc," she said. "When Roy was programming you, did he ever tell you much about his past?"

The computer didn't hesitate to respond. "Are you bored?"

"What are you talking about?"

"You never start conversations with me that way," Roc said. "What happened to, 'Roc, what's the status on the Kuiper Belt?' or 'Roc, are the tests finished on those Balsom clips on Level Six?' or 'Roc, how does it feel to be the ultimate supreme being in the universe?' You must be bored. Which seems a little odd with everything going on at the present time."

"I'm not bored. I'm . . ." Triana paused. "I'm trying to decide if I want to meditate for awhile and collect my thoughts, or distract myself from those thoughts."

"I'm feeling used again," the computer said.

"Quit being a baby," Triana said. "So, did Roy ever tell you that, when he was young, he wanted to be a comedian?"

"He wisely kept that information from me. But I'm not surprised."

Triana slid out of her chair and sat on the floor, propped up against the edge of her bed. She crossed her legs beneath her and pulled her long hair behind her ears. "Would you like to hear one of his jokes?"

"I'm getting worried about you," Roc said. "*You*? You want to tell me a joke? Are you feeling okay?"

"Just humor me, okay?" she said. "A duck walks into a store. He . . . um, wait a minute."

"Hilarious."

"Just wait a minute," Triana said. "I don't want to mess it up." She murmured under her breath for a moment, reciting the joke to herself. "Okay, a duck walks into a store. He—"

" 'And put it on my bill,' " Roc said. "That joke?"

Triana crossed her arms and frowned. "Thanks a lot. You couldn't just humor me for a moment?"

"Sorry. But I know now why Roy was a computer programmer. Good thing you practiced on me and not in front of a packed Dining Hall or something."

"I said it was Roy's joke, not mine."

"Don't be angry, Tree. Friends don't let friends humiliate themselves with unfunny jokes. Next time, try this one: A guy walks into a store with a duck on his head. Wait, did Roy tell you this one?"

Triana continued to sulk. "No."

"A guy walks into a store with a duck on his head. The guy behind the counter looks up and says, 'What's that all about?' And the duck says, 'I don't know, I woke up this morning and he was down there.' "

"And you think that one was funnier than mine?"

"Not necessarily," Roc said, "but you seem to like duck humor, and that's one of the best."

"I'm sorry I even brought it all up," Triana said.

"Would you rather talk about the Balsom clips?"

After a moment of silence, Triana smiled, and then found her-self chuckling. "Well," she said, "I guess I got the distraction I was looking for."

"What about the one where the duck goes bowling on crutches?"

"No thanks," Triana said. "I'm off the duck jokes for awhile."

"Okay, then I really will talk to you about the Balsom clips."

"Are you still trying to be funny?"

"Nope," the computer said. "It's actually good news, too. The problem with the heating on Level Six can indeed be traced to the Balsom clips."

Triana sat stunned for a moment. "Wait. You said you had done a complete check—"

"Yes, I did do a complete check," the computer said. "I did a complete check of the clips on Level Six. They're fine."

"You've lost me."

"I'm only telling you this," Roc said, "so you can help me find a way to spin it so that Gap doesn't pull an 'I told you so' and hold it against me."

Triana had to laugh. "This is classic. You're telling me that Gap had it right all along with those silly clips?"

"No. Well, yes. But not the way he thought."

"If Gap had it right, and you told him he was crazy, I most cer-tainly will not help you spin it just so you can save face."

"What if I laughed at your duck joke?"

"No," Triana said. "I might enjoy this moment as much as Gap. Okay, so explain your Balsom clip solution. And tell me quickly. We might get pulverized by a Kuiper object any moment, and I *have* to hear this before the end."

"Never mind," Roc said. "I'll wait until the next Council meet-ing. Maybe Channy or Lita will be supportive. Besides . . ." The computer paused, almost as if contemplating the next thought.

"It doesn't make sense. Where the problem originated, I mean. I need time to figure it all out."

The soft chime of the door sounded, and Triana, suppressing a laugh, called out, "Come in." She looked over at Roc's glowing sensor. "This might be the greatest moment of our entire journey."

"Let's not overreact," Roc said as the door opened and Hannah stepped cautiously inside. She looked at Triana, sitting cross-legged on the floor, and stopped in mid-stride.

"Is . . . this a bad time?" she said.

Triana was still grinning. "On the contrary, it's a terrific time. Legendary, you might say."

"Pay no attention to her, Hannah," Roc said. "She's gone space-crazy."

Hannah's smile seemed uncomfortable and confused. Triana pointed to the chair across from her desk. "Have a seat, Hannah. Roc and I were just discussing how important it is for people to admit their mistakes. Apparently *only* people."

"Um . . . okay," Hannah said. She sat down and looked around. "I like your room. And I love that sound of the ocean."

"Yeah, Lita turned me on to that."

At the mention of Lita's name, Hannah grew serious. "How's Alexa?"

"Not so good. She didn't wake up from the surgery, and now she's in a coma. I'll be talking about it with the crew in a couple of days. We hope she'll be awake by then."

Hannah looked stunned by the news. "Well, I wanted to talk with you now, before you have that meeting. I suppose it could wait . . ."

Triana could read the mannerisms of the brilliant girl from Alaska, and knew that this was obviously important. "No, that's okay. What's up?"

"It's a little bit complicated, so you'll have to bear with me. And I don't even know anything for sure. It's just an educated guess."

"Hannah," Triana said. "You have a pretty good track record with your 'educated guesses.' If you think it's important, I'm interested."

With a sigh, Hannah leaned forward, her elbows on her knees. "I've been doing a lot of thinking about the Kuiper Belt, and the way it's distributed."

"You mean the thick patches and the empty stretches?"

Hannah nodded. "It doesn't add up. It should be much more uniform than it is. The fact that it's so heavily populated in some areas was really bothering me. Given billions of years, it shouldn't be so . . . clumpy."

She looked down at the carpeted floor. "Then I had a funny thought. If it's not supposed to be this way, then *why* would it be this way? What would be the purpose?"

"The purpose?" Triana said.

"Yeah. Gravity shouldn't have made it this way. So what else would be responsible?"

Triana stared at her. "And what did you come up with?"

Hannah looked back at the Council Leader. "The Cassini."

There was a long moment of silence. Finally, Triana leaned forward and clasped her arms around her legs. "I think the Council needs to hear this. Right now."

22

"Why do you want to be cranky?"

Gap was leaning against the curved wall of the corridor outside the Conference Room. He glanced down at Channy, who had asked the question, and who was in the middle of one of her stretching routines. They were the first two to arrive for the emergency Council meeting.

"Am I cranky?" he said.

"No, but you will be," Channy said, her face hidden as she touched her nose to her right knee.

"Okay, this is leading somewhere, so I'll play along. Why am I going to be cranky?"

"Because you haven't been to the gym in four days."

"Three," he said.

"Nope, it's four," Channy said, adjusting her torso backwards so that she now lay flat against the floor with one leg stretched out and the other tucked at an impossible angle. "You forget who you're talking with. Four."

Gap rolled his eyes. "I've been a little busy, if you hadn't noticed. Oh, wait, you must have noticed, since you were able to report a snowman up here on Level Six. That *was* you, right?"

A smirk played across Channy's face. "Would I say something like that? Besides, that's not the point. You should be able to find forty minutes out of your day to keep your body from turning to mush. And once it does turn to mush, you'll become cranky and irritable. So, get your tush down to the gym and spare all of us from a crabby Engineer."

Gap performed an exaggerated salute. "Aye aye, Cap'n."

Channy rolled onto her stomach and shifted into a yoga stance called the Cobra. "See, I'm able to find a few minutes to stretch even when I'm waiting around."

"Yes, you're certainly amazing."

"Just like I thought, you're already getting cranky." She pushed up into a different position, then, with a final stretch, jumped to her feet. "So, what do you think this meeting is all about?"

Gap shrugged. "I don't know, but Triana added a little P.S. to my email that said Roc owes me. Whatever that means."

"I'm just happy that she's going to fight back against this Merit Simms nonsense," Channy said.

They looked up as Triana rounded a turn and walked up to the Conference Room door. She said a quick hello, then added, "Seen Bon or Lita yet?"

"Lita called to say that she might not be able to make it," Channy said. "She's still a little overwhelmed in Sick House. I don't know about Bon."

"I do," Gap said. "He grumbled something about 'too many meetings,' then said he'd be here. Just had to make sure first that we all knew he was put out by the whole thing. Now we know."

"Okay, well, Hannah will be here in a minute, too."

"Hannah?" Gap said. "We must have some big news."

Triana nodded. "I wouldn't have called the meeting otherwise. C'mon, let's wait inside."

They had barely taken their seats inside the Conference Room when the door opened and Hannah and Bon walked in together. Although he told himself that the timing was likely a coincidence, Gap couldn't help but bristle. The memory of Bon and Triana embracing flashed through his mind. A moment later he relaxed as Hannah made her way around the table to give him a quick peck on the cheek and took the seat beside him. He shot a quick glance at Bon, who seemed completely uninterested as he filled a cup at the water dispenser.

"We'll get started and catch Lita up later," Triana said. "First, just a quick reminder about the full crew meeting. I haven't heard a peep from Merit since I sent out the email, but I want everyone on the Council to be prepared for any ugly incidents that might occur."

"What do you think might happen?" Channy said.

"Probably nothing. I'm guessing that Merit will use the meeting to take notes on our position, and then go off to work up his response in some sort of dramatic speech. But you never know. He might use the meeting as a platform to recruit more followers."

"Or his cheerleaders might try to disrupt things," Gap suggested.

"Maybe," Triana said. "I don't want us to get worked up over this. Let's treat it like a normal crew meeting, but just keep your eyes open. Remember, we don't want to do anything to fan the flames, right?"

There were nods from around the table, with the exception of Bon, who looked bored.

Triana waited a moment before moving on to the next order of business. "I know that it gets your attention when Hannah shows up at a Council meeting. She started to share some thoughts with me regarding the Kuiper Belt, but I thought it would make more sense for all of us to hear it together."

Aware that all eyes had fallen upon her, Hannah shifted in her seat and kept her eyes on her workpad. When she spoke, her voice was soft.

"As you probably have figured out by now," she began, "I'm someone who really likes order in the universe." There were polite chuckles around the table. "That's why the Kuiper Belt has been so frustrating for me. I'm especially bothered by some sections being as dense as they are, while others are much emptier. Contrary to what we thought, there are no completely empty stretches; there are bits of rock and debris throughout the whole ring. It's just wildly heavier in some spots. I . . . I couldn't accept that."

She finally found the courage to look up and make eye contact around the table. "I started wondering what that was all about. Then it struck me that it's quite a coincidence that we're hitting one of those rough spots on our way out of the solar system and on to Eos. But . . . is it really a coincidence?"

The room was heavy with silence. Punching a few instructions into the keyboard before her, Hannah turned on the room's multiple vidscreens. Then she said, "I plugged in a few figures, and was . . . well, I was a little stunned to see things fall into place."

"Like what?" Triana said.

"Like the fact that any trip out of the system toward Eos would always mean having to go through a 'hot' stretch of the Kuiper Belt."

"What?" Gap said. "That can't be right. The Kuiper Belt orbits the sun, just like the planets. There are bound to be times when a thin stretch pops up."

"That's what I thought," Hannah said. "But in order for us to make the leap to Eos, it requires that we utilize a slingshot maneuver around one of the gas giants. We happened to use Saturn, remember?"

There were nods around the table. Even Bon seemed to be intently listening to the explanation. Saturn had indeed provided the boost that *Galahad* needed to dramatically increase its speed.

"So, when you plug in the numbers—and there are a lot of them—any route from Earth that uses a gravity boost from Jupiter, Saturn, Uranus, or Neptune, and leads to a rendezvous with Eos, would end up going through a dangerous portion of the Kuiper Belt."

When this was greeted with more silence, Hannah continued. "You're probably thinking this is too strange to be true. But I've run the figures so many times that I'm sure there's no mistake. Um . . . and it gets even more bizarre."

Gap snorted. "How could it be any more bizarre than that?"

"Well," Hannah said, "I decided to check on a few other things. For one thing, the debris in the Kuiper Belt orbits at different velocities. Some clumps are moving much faster than others. Some are barely poking along. This, by the way, contributes to the violent impacts that we've been seeing.

"Next, I took the list we have of known Earth-type planets that are circling stars like our sun, all within a nearby radius of our solar system. When you plug in a route to any of them, using a slingshot boost around the gas giants, you'll wind up having to play dodge ball in the heaviest parts of the Kuiper Belt."

Triana scanned the vidscreen before her. Hannah plugged in courses for *Galahad* using different destinations, sometimes using Jupiter, sometimes Saturn, for a gravity boost. Each time the red line of their route crossed through a dense portion of the ring.

"Do you know what this means?" Triana said quietly.

Hannah nodded. "I know what I *think* it means. The Kuiper Belt is not some random collection of space junk." She paused before adding, "It's a giant fence around the solar system. And it's supposed to keep us inside."

Galahad's Council sat still, absorbing the gravity of the statement. They had come to expect the unexpected, and had been shaken by the discovery of a super-intelligent force on Saturn's moon, Titan. With so many wonders, both beautiful and dangerous, all within the confines of their own cosmic neighborhood, what astonishing discoveries could they expect during the remainder of their journey?

Not to mention what might await them at Eos.

It was Channy who asked the most logical question. "Who built the fence?"

There were glances around the table. Triana said, "Should we naturally assume that the Cassini are behind it?"

"Actually," Hannah said, casting a fleeting look in the direction of Bon, "that's correct."

Triana saw the look and turned to the Swede. "Bon, do you have something that you can add to this?"

He took a slow drink from his cup of water before answering. "Hannah came to see me about this earlier. I am still in some loose form of contact with the Cassini. I . . . I can't say anything for sure, but I sense that the Kuiper Belt is their creation, yes."

Gap shook his head in awe. "This is unbelievable."

Triana leaned forward. "You say it's just a feeling that you have. Would it be possible . . ." Her voice trailed off at the same moment she and Bon made eye contact. He answered as if reading her thoughts.

"No," he said. "I won't do that."

Another deep silence enveloped the room. Channy looked from Triana to Bon and back again. "Uh, what are we talking about?" she said.

Gap tapped his fingers on the table and answered, his voice low. "I think we're talking about the translator."

At the mention of the word, Bon stood up and walked over to the water dispenser, his back to the group. Everyone around the table immediately pictured the small, metal device that Bon had used to communicate with the Cassini during the crisis near Saturn. It had turned up among the items recovered from SAT33, the doomed space station orbiting Saturn's moon, Titan.

They called it the translator for lack of a better word, but it worked as a sort of mental connector between Bon and the web-like force that occupied the orange moon. A junction box, it al-lowed Bon to convey specific messages to the Cassini; without it, they probed his mind at will, picking and choosing the information they wanted.

This connection had been possible because of the unique wavelength that Bon's brain emitted. A dozen *Galahad* crew members had exhibited painful symptoms of this bizarre connection, yet it was Bon who was the most in tune. His brain had become the focal point of the Cassini's attempts to communicate with the shipload of teens.

It had come at a severe price, physically. Bon had been wracked with pain that dropped him to his knees, even causing him to lose consciousness. In the months since that episode, he had been reluctant to discuss it. Without a doubt it was an experience that he wished never to repeat.

And now Triana was asking him to do just that.

She bit her lip, aware of the tension that had settled upon them. "If you'd like," she said, "we can discuss this later."

"We can discuss it now," Bon said firmly. "I don't ever want to make that connection again." He turned to face Triana. "Besides, what purpose would it serve? Suppose we find out that the Cassini *are* responsible for the Kuiper Belt? Then what?"

"Then you ask them how we get through to the other side."

Bon snorted in disgust. "If they did put this . . . this fence around the solar system, why would they help us out?"

Triana didn't have an answer. She looked at Hannah, who shrugged her shoulders. Gap and Channy also seemed to have nothing to say.

"Listen," the Council Leader said. "I don't enjoy asking you to do this. Believe me, if I could do it myself, I would. But right now we're in serious trouble. We're trying to tiptoe through a minefield where the mines keep moving, we're potentially seconds away from colliding with something, and we have a growing number of people on board who want us to turn tail and run back home.

"The one thing that could help us the most would be a little more information. If there's any chance to get some help, we need to take it. Suppose there *is* an answer to getting out of here?"

Her tone softened a bit. "Bon, I know it's the last thing you want to do. I just don't know if we have any better option."

For almost a full minute, he stared back at her. Then, without saying a word, he set down the cup of water and walked quickly out of the room.

Channy looked down the table at Triana. "Oh, boy. Now what?"

"I don't know," Triana said with a sigh.

Gap leaned forward, resting his chin on one hand. "You know what I think? I think he'll do it. He growls a lot, but when it comes down to it, he is just as driven as the rest of us to make this mission succeed. He knows that he's going to be in agony, but he'll do it. Just let him walk around for awhile."

Triana thought about this. Then, rubbing her forehead, she said, "Let me go talk to him." She pushed herself up out of her chair and walked out.

Hannah looked nervously at Gap, who said, "Everything's going to be okay." When neither she nor Channy responded, he said it again. Even to his own ears it sounded unconvincing.

Sheesh, can we ever get away from these crazy Titan aliens? Hey, I watched what Bon went through last time, so I don't blame him for stomping out. Hooking up with those guys is a pain, literally.

Besides, we don't need their help, do we?

23

ita had grown up around her mother's medical practice, so she knew the smell of a hospital better than most people. To her, Sick House didn't have that particular odor, and yet it still carried a scent that recalled memories of patients and procedures.

Not all of those hospital memories were unpleasant. One of Lita's most powerful memories was of trailing her mother, Dr. Maria Marques, during a typical morning round. A nurse had frantically rushed up to them, with news that an elderly man had unplugged his IV and monitor, and was demanding to be discharged to go home. The nurses had tried, in vain, to convince the man that he was in no condition to leave the hospital, and that his doctor was on the way. That doctor, however, was tied up in the emergency room. When the nurse had seen Lita's mom, she had begged her to help in some way.

Lita could still remember the way the old man's room had looked and smelled. A handful of small vases held flowers from well-wishers; a tray, carrying unappetizing breakfast items that had been only picked at, sat near the window; a television, its sound muted, flashed overly dramatic scenes from a soap opera, set ironically in a hospital.

The elderly man sat in his own clothes, his faded hospital

gown tossed over the end of the bed. He clutched a small duffel bag in his lap, one toe tapping to a rhythm that played in his head. He fixed his eyes on Lita's mother as soon as she walked in the room. She smiled her electric smile at him.

"Well, good morning, Mr. Romero."

He grunted back, "Who are you?"

"My name is Maria."

"You a doctor?"

"I'm many things. I'm a wife, a mother, a pretty-good cook, a very-good singer, and a wicked canasta player. I do a little doctoring when it fits my schedule."

Mr. Romero grunted again. "I don't want to talk to another doctor. I'm going home."

Lita remembered her mother's patient response. "I don't really like talking to doctors, either. That's why I listed it last." She propped against the bed and clasped her hands together. "Why are you so anxious to get out of here? Aren't they feeding you well?"

The old man stared up at her. "Hospitals are for sick people. I'm not sick."

"You're fighting off a case of pneumonia, Mr. Romero. How would you do that at home? You live by yourself, don't you?"

"I know how to take care of myself."

"I'm sure you do. You're eighty-one years old, so you must know a few things about taking care of yourself. And I see here on your chart that you retired from the plumbing business, is that right?"

Mr. Romero nodded, his head up, a look of pride and defiance on his face.

Maria continued. "My husband thinks he's a plumber sometimes. He's not. He runs a grocery store. But last year he decided to add another sink in our bathroom, and the next thing you know water was shooting everywhere. It looked like a fire sprinkler system had gone off."

"I've seen it a thousand times," Mr. Romero said. "People always think they know better than a professional. They just end up paying us more to fix their messes."

"And that's exactly what happened," Lita's mom said with a laugh. "I never let him forget it, either. If he had just called you in the first place it would have saved us a lot of time and trouble."

She reached out and took the old man's hand. "So I'm sure you understand that these wonderful nurses here, who have been working so hard to fix you up, would hate to see you try to do their job, right?"

Mr. Romero's eyes darted to the two nurses who stood in the doorway. He made another small grunting sound, then looked back at Maria. She smiled and said, "They're doing such a good job, I'd hate to see them have to work even harder to fix something you've tried to do yourself."

He took one more look at the nurses, then nodded. "They're almost finished, right?"

"I think they'll be able to get you out of here in another three or four days. But if you leave now, it might take them a couple of weeks."

Lita remembered standing quietly behind her mother, listening intently to her words. More than that, however, she remembered the impact those words had on the old man. He stood up and reached for his hospital gown.

"Do you really sing?" he said with his familiar grunt.

"Like a bird. Let these fine women get you back into bed and I'll come back and sing any song you like." Dr. Maria Marques had turned, taken her daughter by the hand, and gone about her rounds.

Now, six years later, young Lita Marques stood in a hospital ward, more than a billion miles from Veracruz, Mexico, and took in the scent that carried a mixture of memories, both tragic and hopeful.

Alexa Wellington was the patient in this case, yet she was in no way able to get herself up from bed. Her condition had not changed. The coma was baffling to Lita, and frightening. Had it been caused by a mistake that Lita had made during surgery? Was there something else wrong inside Alexa, something that Lita had not detected? Was there a solution that Lita had not considered, something that would snap Alexa out of the coma and on to a stable recovery?

The questions tormented Lita. She had dedicated herself to solving the problem, choosing even to miss the emergency Council meeting in order to focus on Alexa. She looked at the monitor as it paced through its readings, looking and listening for something that might make everything clear.

She heard the door open in the outer office, and wondered if it might be Triana coming to recap the meeting. Instead the face of Merit Simms peered around the corner.

"Hi, Lita."

"Hello, Merit. Feeling okay?"

"What? Oh, no, I'm fine. I just wanted to stop by and see how Alexa was doing."

Lita walked past Merit, into the Clinic's office. He turned and followed her. "So, what's the word?" he said.

"I didn't know that you and Alexa were so close," Lita said.

Merit smiled. "I don't know her very well. Does that mean I shouldn't care how she's doing?"

Lita returned his smile. "She's resting comfortably, but she's not up for having visitors right now."

Merit put his hands on the top of a chair and leaned against it, his black hair spilling down around his shoulders. "I heard that she's in a coma. Is that right?"

It would be impossible to keep the news from spreading throughout the ship, Lita realized. Plus, there was nothing to be gained by lying. "Yes, that's right. But I don't expect it to last for long."

"Is she going to be okay?"

Lita fought the urge to snap back. Keeping her voice calm, she said, "Alexa will be fine. Her appendix was definitely the problem, it's been successfully removed, and in time she will heal. The coma is a temporary setback, and, although we don't know exactly what caused it, she's getting the best treatment we can give her, and I expect her to recover completely. Is there anything else you need to know at the moment?"

"You don't want to talk with me about this?" Merit said.

"First of all, Alexa has a right to privacy. Plus, I don't like the fact that you show up here, probing for information, not because you sincerely care about Alexa, but to see if it can help you rally support for your agenda. I consider that despicable. I don't know if I should be angry with you, or feel sorry for you."

Merit scanned her face for a moment, then stood up straight. "Or there's a third possibility," he said. "Perhaps you don't completely understand what's going on. My 'agenda' that you refer to is based on the fact that I care about the well-being of every crew member on the ship, not just Alexa. The fact that she's struggling with a health issue right now is a symptom of our problems, not the problem itself. And, if I'm going to speak for a group of people about that problem, I need to have my facts straight."

"So this is research, is that right?"

He shrugged. "If you want to call it that. But I do care about what happens to Alexa, even if she's not my best friend."

Lita tried to read his face. She was irritated by the trouble he had kicked up recently, but there was nothing wrong in what he was saying at the moment. Like any good motivator, he could be very convincing. How much, she wondered, was sincere, and how much was manipulation?

She felt her earlier doubts returning. Home *did* sound good, never more so than right now. Merit got on her nerves, but underneath it all, his promise of better days ahead—on Earth—was tempting. Very tempting.

Rather than let him see the hesitation, she forced herself to refocus. "Well," she said, "now you have the facts. Alexa is in a coma, but she's stable and getting good care. I'm optimistic that she'll pull out of this soon, and everything will be fine. Okay?"

Merit nodded. "Yes. And thank you very much for sharing with me. Even though I probably can't be of any real help right now, please let me know if you can think of anything I can do."

"Thanks," Lita said. "I appreciate that. Now, I hope you understand that I'm pretty busy."

"Of course. I'll see you around."

Lita walked back into the hospital ward. Merit watched her go before turning and strolling out into the corridor. Waiting for him were two of his followers, leaning up against the wall. Merit reached them in three quick strides.

"Okay," he said, "you can get started. Let everyone know that Alexa is not only in a coma, but that she's getting worse. Tell them that Lita is worried that she might not make it. Got it?"

The two boys nodded and turned toward the lift entrance. Merit smiled, pushing a strand of hair out of his face.

24

She knew exactly where to find him. The narrow dirt path was damp, with a few scattered puddles that had collected the run-off from the morning watering schedule. Most of the tropical fruits were grown in this portion of Dome 2, giving the area a distinct smell that reminded Triana of citrus groves, along with an almost muggy feel to the air. Her shirt clung to her skin. Beads of perspiration had popped up on her forehead, either from the humidity in the air or her nerves. Or both.

She had waited almost an hour, giving Bon time to walk and think. It had also given her time to think as well. It didn't escape her attention that she was asking Bon to step up for the second time in four months, to help the crew of *Galahad* out of a tough situation. Why, she wondered, out of such a large crew, was it him, of all people, who was able to connect with the Cassini?

And why, given his dark and brooding nature, did it pain her so much to ask him to make this sacrifice? He wasn't exactly the type of person who evoked sympathy.

The answer to the first question evaded her. The answer to the second question was much more clear.

Triana could no longer deny that her feelings for Bon were real. She had run from those feelings, just as she had run from other things in her past that had weighed heavily upon her. She didn't want to fall for him; in fact, he seemed to make it difficult for anyone to like him that much. But she was troubled right now because she did care deeply for him, and she was about to ask him to suffer unimaginable pain.

She pushed through an overhang of leaves and there he was, sitting on a metal box that housed an irrigation pump. His long, blond hair reflected the artificial sunlight that poured from the crisscrossing grid above. His shoes and socks were in a pile nearby.

"Thought I might find you here," she said.

"And I was sure you'd come looking," he said.

Triana looked around for a place to sit. The soil was wet, and Bon made no effort to share his perch. She crossed her arms and shifted her weight to one side, trying her best to look at ease.

"If you knew I was coming, then you probably know what I'm going to say."

"Yes," he said, "but let me hear you say it anyway."

"All right. I'd like to ask you to attempt another connection with the Cassini."

He glared at her. "Just like that? You think it's that simple?"

"No, Bon, I know it's not simple, and regardless of what you might think, I'm not making this request lightly. But I'm quickly running out of options."

Bon reached over and picked up a clod of dirt, then crushed it, letting the fragments fall between his fingers to the ground. When he didn't answer, Triana softly said, "Talk to me about this."

"It's not something I can explain to you. You wouldn't understand."

"Try me."

He looked off through the plants and took a deep breath. "It's not a simple matter of 'connecting,' as you call it. And even though the physical pain is staggering, it's not just that." He took another deep breath. "When I . . . when I make that connection, it's as if my brain becomes filled with thousands of other people. I lose all control of my senses, my emotions, my thoughts. The communication process is very . . . one-sided."

He looked at Triana. "When I made the connection at Saturn, I didn't think I was going to survive it. I was slowly slipping away, the pain was tearing me apart, and the . . ." He paused. "The presence in my mind was overwhelming. The rush of sound was deafening. The fact that you took hold of me and helped me relay the message is the only thing that saved me. I couldn't have done it on my own."

Triana felt a pang of sympathy. She knelt down, ignoring the muddy stains that covered her knees. "Maybe . . ." She reconsidered her thought, then decided to press on. "Maybe it will be a little different this time. Maybe you and the Cassini have established some sort of . . . I don't know, some sort of relationship now."

Bon shook his head. "You don't understand. They're so far beyond us, so advanced, that they don't form 'relationships.' They do what they do, and they don't make allowances for pitiful little beings such as us. We are like amoebas to them. If they can help us, they will. But they won't change for us."

He closed his eyes and rubbed his forehead. "No, it will be the same."

Triana remained still. She felt that she was making tentative progress, slowly breaking down their own communication barrier, one that had gradually grown between them ever since their one intimate moment months ago. She also realized that she was seeing Bon in a new way.

She had always defined him through his external image, a troubled, brooding young man who built up a tough façade in order to protect himself. She had maneuvered close to him, then backed away, always playing by his rules . . . or the rules that she perceived were his. She realized that all of her actions toward him had been reactions to his temperament, and not based on her own instincts.

But suddenly there seemed to be a part of Bon that was leaking out from behind that façade. When he mentioned the feeling of 'thousands of other people' forcing their way into his mind, it struck her: He's as alone as I am.

Triana couldn't imagine what he was experiencing. She guarded her own thoughts and privacy with intensity, and Bon was clearly the same way. When he made the connection with the Cassini, it wasn't the searing physical pain alone that crippled him; it was the pain of opening every hidden, private cove of his mind to others, of losing all emotional and mental control.

That, she decided, would be enough to bring her to her knees, too. It explained so much about Bon—and the link with the Cassini—that she had never considered.

In a completely impulsive moment, Triana leaned forward, her hand on Bon's knee, and placed a kiss on his lips. When she pulled back, she found his ice-blue eyes boring into hers. After an awkward moment, he put his hand behind her head and gently pulled her forward into another kiss.

"Wait," she said, pulling back again. "I can't let you think I'm doing this to talk you into something you don't want to do. That's not—"

"I know," he said.

"No," she said, pushing away from him. "This isn't the right time for this. It will only complicate things."

He slowly shook his head. "Things are already complicated." He stood up and gathered his shoes and socks. Then, fixing her with a deep stare, he said, "You need to figure out what you really want."

Taking a few steps away, he stopped and looked back. "Get the translator. I'll make the connection." Then he turned and strode quickly down the path.

★ ★ ★

Hannah walked alongside Gap toward the Engineering offices, one of her hands looped through the crook of his arm. His head was down, his mind vaulting from one thought to the next, and he was completely unaware that it was she who was guiding them through the corridor, subtly maneuvering them both in order to remain exactly two feet from the wall.

Gap had so far not questioned Hannah any further about her Kuiper Belt theory and the Cassini. It seemed so bizarre, but if the crew of *Galahad* had learned anything on their journey, it was that the bizarre was commonplace in space.

And, as far as he was concerned, if Hannah was sure that it was true, chances were that it was. Her ability to sift through countless mounds of data and somehow make sense of it all was remarkable; that ability had already proven to be a lifesaver during their encounter with Saturn and Titan. Her contributions to the mission were significant, and she wasn't even a member of the Council.

What of his contributions?

A scowl worked its way across his face as he pondered the thought. What exactly *had* he brought to the table? Upon first examination, it didn't seem like much. He had felt almost helpless during the confrontation with the stowaway; in fact, it was Bon who had saved Triana's life, then Triana who had saved the ship.

During *Galahad*'s perilous journey past Saturn, Hannah had discovered the mysterious force called the Cassini. Then, once again, Bon had stepped up and helped to deliver the ship to safety.

Now there was trouble within and without as they weaved their way through the treacherous Kuiper Belt, and managed an internal crisis with Merit.

Gap assessed his contributions to this point, and the only thing that stood out was the problem with the heating system. And on that count he had failed so far. He was the Head of Engineering, and yet had no engineering successes to his credit.

No wonder Triana had applied her attentions to Bon. For that matter, what exactly did Hannah see in him? Airboarding lessons only carried so much weight. Would she soon reach a point where she, too, wondered the same thing? Since they had been together she had only seen him fail, it seemed. He hadn't been able to stop the ship's dangerous acceleration around Saturn, and this perplexing heating problem had actually induced laughter from her.

The realization of it all suddenly hit home. Self-confidence had never been a problem for him, which made these doubts even more discouraging. Insecurity was unknown terrain for him.

His mind drifted to home, back on Earth. The days spent with friends at school and in his gymnastics club, the nights spent laughing with family. On one hand it seemed so long ago, a fond but fading memory. Was it possible to go back, to savor the time he had left with his family? If he wasn't contributing *here* . . .

"Everything okay?" Hannah said.

The last thing he wanted was to allow these doubts to set. In mere minutes Hannah had apparently picked up on his discomfort. "Sure, everything's fine," he said, turning to give her a quick smile. "Just thinking, that's all."

She gave his arm a squeeze.

They neared the Engineering section, and as it came into sight Gap set an intention. He would spend less time on the Airboard track, less time gossiping with friends, less time playing Masego with Roc. From now on he would pay more attention to the duties that his fellow crew members—like Triana—expected him to perform. He would earn his place on the Council all over again.

One way to do it would be to help Triana defeat the rising tide of discontent aboard the ship; that meant defeating Merit. So far it seemed as if Bon was the only person who had taken Merit on. Gap resolved to play a bigger role than he had.

But, first things first. It was time to make his title mean something on the ship. Without fail he would solve the nagging problem of the heating system.

"Roc," he said as they entered the section and walked up to the control panel. "Let's fix this thing once and for all."

The computer wasted no time with a reply. "If you're referring to your fashion sense, I've already told you that it's impossible. You are destined to always match stripes with plaids."

"The heating system, Roc. Let's go back to the very beginning. I want to take a completely new approach."

"I sense that you have not yet visited with Triana," Roc said.

Gap looked at Hannah, then back at Roc's sensor. "What are you talking about?"

"I'm talking about a miraculous breakthrough in the technology of heating systems for interstellar spacecraft. We've decided to shut the whole system down and hand out candles to every crew member. It's a much more reliable heat source, provided we can keep a supply of matches."

Gap smiled. "I'm a little pressed for time, Roc. Quit playing around and let's get to work."

"No work to be done here, my good man. I'm still tracing the original problem, but the system is repaired."

The smile on Gap's face faltered. "Repaired? A temporary fix?"

Roc said, "Temporary in the sense that it will only last us until we arrive at Eos. After that we'll probably cannibalize the system for use on one of the planets."

Now the smile was gone. Gap scanned the control panel, where each of the readings showed normal and steady. "You fixed it?"

"When, oh when, will you realize my powers?" Roc said. "Next up, the common cold."

"Wow," Hannah said. "That's great!" She tugged on Gap's arm. "Isn't that great news?"

Gap paused, aware of the puzzled expression on her face. By all accounts he should be as delighted as she was, and his reaction must have been bewildering to her. He forced a half-smile and replied, "Of course it's great news. Terrific news. One less problem for us to deal with."

He turned back to the sensor. "Thanks, Roc."

For the first time that Gap could recall, the computer had no snappy comeback. Apparently Roc was as mystified as Hannah, and chose to remain silent.

"Okay, well," Gap said to Hannah, "I've got some other things to take care of this afternoon. Want to catch up later?"

She peered into his face, a look of concern coming over her. "Sure," she said quietly. "Maybe we can grab a bite to eat."

"Sounds good," he said. With a quick peck on her cheek he was out the door, leaving her standing alone at the control panel.

25

The atmosphere was all wrong. Triana stood near a vidscreen in the Control Room, with a half-dozen crew members working nearby, and she could sense it. The air itself was fine, but a strange vibe enveloped the room, a feeling of conflict and tension. No one said anything; they didn't have to.

Her conversation with Bon had been successful, and yet, once again, it had been clumsy and confusing. She could have gone straight to her room and collected the translator, but instead had chosen to check on their progress through the Kuiper Belt. It seemed imperative that Bon make the connection with the Cassini as soon as possible, but a cooling-off period seemed equally important. She decided to give it one more hour, an hour that would hopefully prove to be peaceful.

It wasn't. An alarm sounded, snapping her back to attention.

"Roc?" she said.

"Collision warning," the computer said. "Not as big this time, but tumbling very erratically. This will take a moment."

Triana bit her lip and waited. There was no sense pushing for more information. She glanced over at Gap's empty workstation and wondered where he was.

Roc spoke up. "I'm nudging us a bit."

"You're what?"

"Nudging. You know, pushing, tipping, prodding."

Triana raised her hands. "Fine. Nudge. What's the verdict?"

"Well, that little warning system in the Engineering Section has done it again. With the nudge, we'll miss this particular piece of rock by almost a quarter of a mile."

A quarter of a mile. Triana let her breath out quietly, not wanting to appear flustered in front of the other crew members. But a quarter of a mile was less than fifteen hundred feet. In space, that was nothing. In fact, without the alert from the warning system, and Roc's immediate correction, it meant that mere seconds were all that separated success from destruction.

Seconds.

Triana walked over to Gap's workstation and sat down. She could feel the eyes of the crew following her, estimating her stress, her confidence. It was as if she could read some of their thoughts: "See, Merit was right, we need to get out of here."

How many were with her? How many had joined the ranks of the yellow armbands? Who was a friend? Who might be an adversary? The thoughts weighed heavily upon her.

Was she absolutely sure that she was right and Merit was wrong? Another collision warning had only intensified the conflict that bubbled within her. Who was she to say that her way was . . .

No, she told herself. No! Don't do this. Not now.

She kept her back to the room, punching in mindless computations on the keyboard, meaningless searches for information that had no impact whatsoever on their mission. Anything to keep herself occupied for a few moments while she tried to make sense of everything. If Roc noticed what she was doing, he kept quiet . . . thankfully.

When the intercom sounded, it came as a relief.

"Tree, it's Gap."

"Yeah, where are you?" she said.

"Could you come down to Level Four, please?"

There were only crew quarters on Level Four, including Gap's. She started to ask him a question, then thought better of it. Instead, almost grateful for the distraction, she simply told him that she'd be right down.

A minute later she stepped off the lift and found a cluster of almost two dozen crew members standing around. Gap waved her over to the side.

"What's going on?" she said.

"Another fight," he said, indicating two boys who waited behind him. "Well, mostly just a lot of pushing and shoving. I just happened to be walking from my room to head up to the Control Room when I heard the commotion." He looked over at the assembled throng. "It certainly drew a crowd."

Triana bit her lip. She turned back to face the crew members gathered in the hall. Their faces reflected a mixture of amazement and concern. "Okay, do me a favor, please?" she said to the throng. "Can you give us a few moments to talk here? Either go back to your rooms, or wherever else you might have been going. A little privacy, please?"

It took a moment to clear out. There were several glances exchanged, some that had an almost challenging look to them. Triana heard more than a few grumbles, and briefly wondered if more drama was imminent. But slowly the crowd dispersed, leaving the two Council members and the two combatants, one of whom, Triana finally noticed, was Balin, one of the two boys who constantly followed Merit. Tall and imposing, Balin eyed her coldly as he readjusted his yellow armband which had apparently been pulled out of place during the scuffle.

Triana looked at the other boy. It was Jhani Kumar, a normally quiet boy from India. It seemed odd that he would be involved in something like this. She decided to address him first.

"Jhani, what happened here?"

He looked at Balin before answering her. "Nothing."

"Nothing," Triana said. "Uh-huh." She looked at Balin. "Would you care to answer the question?"

Balin gave a dismissive snort. "I'll see you later." He turned and began walking toward the lift.

"Hey!" Gap shouted. "What are you doing? Get back here."

Balin turned to look back at them. "What are you, the police? I don't have to jump when you speak. You might be on the Council, but you can't order me around."

Gap took a couple of steps toward the boy, who, although taller, flinched backward a step. "It's called keeping order," Gap said. "If you're involved in a fight on this ship, it's our responsibility to solve the issue. You know that's true."

"You heard what this guy said," Balin sneered. "Nothing happened. Can I go now, Officer?"

Triana took Gap's arm before he could advance again. "Sure," she said to Balin. "You're free to go."

He laughed and spun around. In a few moments he was out of sight.

Triana looked back at Jhani. "Why don't you tell me what happened, okay?"

Jhani shifted awkwardly on his feet. "He's a loud-mouth bully, that's all. I'm tired of listening to it, especially when he's spreading false rumors."

"Like what?"

"He was yelling that Alexa Wellington is about to die. He was blaming you and the Council." Jhani lowered his voice. "Alexa is my friend. I went to visit her just an hour ago. She's not about to die."

Triana stared at him. "No, of course she's not. Where did he say he got his information?"

"He didn't. He just said that she was about to die, and that we would all end up dead if we kept following you."

Triana shook her head, then reached out and touched Jhani

on the shoulder. "Okay, that's fine. We'll see you later." As he turned to leave, she added, "And thank you, Jhani."

He nodded and mumbled a response that Triana couldn't hear. Soon she was alone in the hallway with Gap, and was stunned when he turned on her.

"What do you think you're doing?" he said, his face flushed.

"What do you mean?"

Gap pointed towards the lift. "You just let that thug Balin walk away without any accountability at all. It's exactly the same mild-mannered nonsense that's let Merit get away with . . . with . . ."

"With what?" Triana said, her tone matching his. "With speaking his mind? You think I should out-bully him? Is that right?

"No, but I think you should show a little more leadership," Gap said. "I'm sick of this. They are stirring up more and more trouble each day. Now they're even lying about Alexa, trying to scare everyone into rebelling. And you let him spit in our faces and walk away."

Triana kept herself quiet for a moment before responding. She didn't want to say something that she regretted later. When she spoke, her voice was low and determined. "I'm just as unhappy about this as you are, Gap. I don't like what they're doing, either. But I'm in no position, even as the Council Leader, to keep them from voicing their opinions. When Balin walked away I didn't know about the Alexa comments. I will address those rumors when I speak to the crew. Until then . . ." She took a step toward him. "Until then, I will not fight foul behavior with more of the same. I will not stoop to their level. Do you understand that?"

"That's just great," Gap said. "You have no problem talking tough with me, I see, but the creeps on this ship get a lot of sweet-talk."

Triana was speechless for a second. "What is wrong with you?"

196

Dom Testa

Gap didn't answer. Instead he gave her a parting look that seemed full of venom, and marched off down the corridor.

"Gap," she called after him, but he disappeared around a turn.

Her face was pale. Although it should have looked like she was merely sleeping, something about the expression—was it the eyes, the eyebrows, the set of her mouth?—did not look like sleep. Instead Alexa seemed to be deep in thought, eyes simply closed, pondering a great problem.

And it was unnerving.

Channy stood at Alexa's bedside, one hand stroking Iris, who went about one of her daily cleaning rituals, propped against Alexa's motionless side. Monitors kept a vigil over Alexa, keeping rhythm with her heartbeat, her breathing, her life force. There was no other sound in the room.

Channy shivered. The sight of Lita's assistant, usually one of the more outgoing personalities aboard *Galahad*, now lying in a coma, was surreal. Danger had been a constant companion on the journey, yet this scene carried the force of visual evidence; seeing a friend this close to death made their plight real.

Lita walked into the room and offered a greeting and smile as she moved to the opposite side of the bed.

"It's okay that Iris is here, right?" Channy said.

"I honestly haven't checked it out in the databanks," Lita said, "so I couldn't tell you what the true medical answer is. But in my heart I want Alexa to feel comfort, and if that means sharing some energy with a friendly soul like Iris, then I'm all for it."

Channy nodded, then glanced down at Alexa. "Can she hear us talking?"

Lita considered the question. "Let's just assume that she can, at least on some level. There's conflicting theories on that, too, but I come in and talk to her every hour or so, just in case she can." She looked back at Channy. "You okay?"

"Oh . . ." Channy paused. "No."

Lita laughed softly. "Well, at least you're honest. Anything specific, or just the whole weight of it all?"

Channy scratched Iris under the chin. "It's just getting so hard, you know? All of the stuff we've been through already, now the Kuiper Belt is trying to smash us into a million bits, and people who are supposed to be our friends are turning hostile. I thought we were all on the same team."

She lowered her voice to a whisper and gestured toward the girl lying between them. "There's even talk about Alexa dying. Have you heard about that?"

Lita said, "Yes. I've had at least a dozen calls, and a few people have even stopped by in person. Word is spreading pretty fast."

"But it's garbage. Don't they know it's just Merit causing more trouble?"

"Of course it is," Lita said. "Don't let it rattle you. It's exactly the effect he's looking for."

Channy stared at her. "I know, I know. You sound like Triana now."

"And Triana is right. Trust in the truth, Channy, it will get us through this."

Iris stood up, turned to face the opposite direction, then plopped back down and resumed her bath, oblivious to the conversation and the drama around her. Both girls watched this, taking in the bizarre visual combination of the fussy feline against the troubled teenage girl.

Channy's face broke into her usual smile. "I don't know what I would do without this silly cat right now."

Lita reached across and tickled Iris behind one ear. "I'm glad you keep bringing her in here. For that matter, I'm glad *you're* here." She stepped back and looked at Channy. "There are a couple of helpers in the next room who will look in every few minutes. I've got to leave."

"What's up?"

"Triana wants me to meet her up in the Domes," Lita said. "Bon is going to connect with the Cassini again, and she thinks it would be a good idea if I was there."

Channy's mouth fell open. "I never thought he would do that."

"I didn't either. I'll let you know what happens."

"Should I come, too?"

Lita shook her head. "I think it would be better if there wasn't a crowd, you know? If you want to help, stay here for a little while and keep Alexa company for me. Don't be afraid to talk to her, okay? I'm telling you, on some level I think it has a positive impact."

"Umm . . ." Channy said. "What do you think is going to happen? With Bon, I mean."

Lita exhaled deeply. "You saw what happened last time."

26

The evening routine of dimming the lights throughout the ship brought on the imitation of an Earth dusk, and many crew members had come to recognize that the best place to experience it was in the Domes. As the artificial sunlight faded, those who were not on duty or socializing in the Dining Hall or Recreation Room would often sneak away to watch the brilliant starlight emerge from behind the day's glare. It was a popular spot for quiet introspection, a chance to unwind at the end of a work shift.

This evening, however, Dome 2 was closed to the crew. Yellow warning signs blocked the entry with a notice proclaiming that special testing was taking place, and that all traffic should be diverted into Dome 1. One of the Farm workers sat nearby in a folding chair, acting as a makeshift security guard to keep everyone out.

Inside, Triana stood near the center of Dome 2 with hands on hips, a small bag slung over her shoulder. On her face she kept a confident look that she hoped would mask the twisting ball of stress that sat heavily in her stomach. Cleared of other people like this, the dome had a crypt-like silence cast over it, broken only occasionally by the sound of Triana shifting on her feet. To her ears, her breathing was loud and disruptive.

Bon sat peacefully in the dirt a few feet away, his face expressionless, his eyes closed. They were alone.

The setting brought about a twinge of déjà vu in Triana as she gazed up at the spectacle of the Milky Way. It had been only a few months since they had first played out this scene. That fateful connection with the Cassini had taken place in the other dome, with only minutes separating *Galahad* from total destruction. This time . . .

This time, she wondered, did they even have minutes? It was one thing to have a fatal deadline looming over you, and quite another to live in uncertainty, never knowing if or when the blow might come. It was, oddly, a completely different form of pressure, Triana realized. Both might have the same outcome, yet they worked on the psyche in distinctive ways.

Simply thinking about it brought a sudden sense of urgency into her mind, and yet there was no way she could thrust any more pressure upon Bon. She was determined to allow him to set the pace. She chose, however, to remain standing, if for no other reason than to subtly convey a message of determination.

Bon brought a fist to his mouth and quietly coughed. He glanced up at Triana and spent a moment peering into her eyes. "Is it going to be just you and me?" he said.

"No," Triana said. "Well, maybe to start. But I asked Lita to be here."

He nodded, a look of understanding, mixed with a touch of resignation, crossing his face. They both knew that Lita's medical skills were unlikely to come into play; it was a formality more than anything else. After all, what could she really do?

Another moment of silence passed, then Bon held out a hand. "Okay, I'm ready."

Triana nodded and stepped toward him. From within her shoulder bag she extracted a small, lightweight metal ball. It had four short spikes that protruded from the top, bottom, and two sides, as well as small slits that appeared to be vents. It seemed insignificant, yet had saved their lives once already.

Bon eyed the translator. Before setting it in his palm, Triana reached out and took his open hand. "Thank you," she said.

"You realize that this might get us nowhere, right?" he said.

"Maybe. Or it might help a great deal."

He smiled, a gesture that Triana was unprepared for. She felt a hitch in her breathing and a sensation that often preceded tears; she fought against the feeling. Instead, she returned his smile, let go of his hand, and slowly placed the translator in his palm. Almost immediately his smile dissipated, and he gripped the metallic ball at his side.

It happened quickly. A shudder seemed to pass through his body, his eyes clenched tightly, and his head snapped back. Through his gritted teeth Triana could hear a stifled moan escape, the sound of a wounded animal. She immediately dropped to her knees by his side.

A spasm of pain shook him. His head whipped to one side, then the other, and another cry of torture poured out. A dull red glow escaped from the vents of the translator and seeped between Bon's fingers.

Even though she had witnessed it before, Triana still recoiled in shock when Bon's eyes flew open. They glowed with a brilliant orange color, indicating that the turbulent connection with the Cassini was in full force. Then, moments later, the voices returned.

It was a garbled collection of sounds that spilled from Bon's trembling lips, with an almost hollow echo to them, a mishmash of voices, all communicating at once. The overall effect was frightening: the glow from the translator, strengthening for a brief moment, then ebbing, then picking up in intensity once again; the eerie orange tint from Bon's shifting eyes, eyes that seemed to be looking inward rather than outward; and the voices, stacking upon each other, with a sound that felt as if it might pierce Triana's skull. The Cassini had not only tapped into Bon's mind, but had apparently reestablished their link with the other *Galahad* crew members who shared their neural wavelength.

Triana wondered what Bon was hearing, what he was seeing. She could only imagine what he must be feeling. It was exactly as it had been four months ago.

And then, without warning, it wasn't. Bon let out a cry in his own voice, overriding the multitude of sounds, and his eyes seemed to focus again. They kept their orange shine, but for once it seemed as if Bon was fighting for control. Triana resisted the urge to touch him, to help. Something was happening, and she needed to let it play out without interference, no matter how painful it might be for Bon.

She felt a presence behind her and glanced over her shoulder. Lita stood a few feet away, staring at Bon, her own face a collection of emotions that seemed to include awe, pity, and fear. She held a small medical bag, but let it drop to the dirt.

Triana turned back to Bon just as the unexpected happened. Bon let out what sounded almost like a quick snort of laughter. If so, it was full of pain, too, but when it happened again Triana was sure that it was a laugh. Bon pulled his gritted teeth apart and emitted a long, agonizing groan, followed by a third grunt of laughter.

"Bon," Triana said. "Can you hear me?"

It was difficult, given the shudders of pain that wracked his body, to know for certain, but it seemed as if he nodded once in reply. It was confirmed a moment later when he turned his orange eyes to look directly into her face. He nodded again.

"The Kuiper Belt," Triana said. "Talk to them about the Kuiper Belt. Help us."

Bon blurted out another short, pain-filled laugh, his eyes snapped shut again, and his head rolled back. The voices picked up their intensity. It was as if a battle of wills was taking place, a tug-of-war within Bon's head, each side—or many sides—fighting for control. The translator pulsed.

"The Kuiper Belt," Triana said again. "Bon, hold on. Fight for your identity. Tell them to help us."

She saw him shake his head a couple of times, but not in disagreement. Instead it seemed as if he was wrestling back control. His eyes flickered a few times, then settled back on Triana once more. His breathing became regular, and the voices calmed.

This was also new. Triana held her breath, watching, waiting. Then, a new bolt of fear raced through her when Bon's lips parted with a subdued, ominous laugh. It echoed, similar to the hollow sound that accompanied the voices, but it was distinctly Bon.

Laughter. She felt a chill, and noticed that goose bumps covered her arms. One portion of her brain screamed to get up and run, yet she held firm, anchored to the spot beside Bon. After a moment, he fell silent again. His tremors subsided, but the eyes maintained their orange glow. What felt like an eternity passed, the two of them sitting in the soil of Dome 2, separated physically by less than three feet, although to Triana it seemed like a chasm a mile wide. She completely forgot about Lita standing behind her.

The translator's red light dimmed, then winked out. Bon's grip loosened, and the metallic ball fell to the ground. In less than ten seconds, his eyes had returned to their normal icy blue.

It took a moment for Triana to realize that her breathing was almost as labored as his. Her hands were clenched into fists, the muscles in her forearms tight, her entire body clamped and taut as a spring. She willed herself to relax.

Time passed. How much, Triana couldn't say for sure. She kept her attention riveted to Bon's face, trying desperately to read him, to understand what had happened. He gave no indication, and remained silent. Finally, he lay back on the soil with his hands beneath his head, his eyes closed. His hair was matted with sweat, and, for the first time, Triana noticed a light-colored, wispy growth of small hairs on his upper lip. It seemed odd to her that she should notice something like that at such a critical time, but she found her eyes dipping again and again. Between the faint beginnings of facial hair and the experience that had just concluded, Bon seemed a stranger to her. Kneeling in the dirt beside him, she brought a hand out to touch his leg, but then slowly retracted it.

When the unexpected touch of a hand on her shoulder came, she jumped and let out a small cry.

"Sorry," Lita whispered, kneeling beside Triana. "I didn't mean to scare you."

Triana gave a soundless laugh then swallowed hard. "No, it's okay. I guess I was just so . . . wrapped up in everything."

Lita indicated Bon. "Well? What do you think?"

Triana glanced down at him. "I don't know. Something's . . . different, that's for sure." With Lita beside her, she felt confidence return. She reached out and laid a hand on Bon's leg.

A moment later he stirred and opened his eyes. At first he simply stared up at the starlight washing through the dome, his chest slowly rising and falling. Then he turned his head and looked at Triana.

"We're okay," he said.

Triana stared into his eyes, unsure of how to respond. It was such an unusual comment for Bon to make, and not what she would have expected from him. *We're okay.* What exactly did that mean?

Her mind began to decode the simple statement. By "we" did he mean the crew of *Galahad*? Was he referring to the two of them? Or . . .

The thought flashed through her like a lightning bolt. *We.* Was that Bon speaking? Or . . . the Cassini?

His connection with the alien intelligence had shifted. Unlike their initial contact around Saturn, Bon seemed to have negotiated with the Cassini this time. He had managed to direct his attention at Triana, he had responded to her, he had . . .

He had laughed. She was sure of it.

And now he appeared more calm than anyone had a right to be following such an ordeal. He reclined in the soft soil of Dome 2, his head resting on his hands, his pale blue eyes stoically locked onto Triana's. Only the tinge of sweat in his hair gave testimony to the suffering his body had endured only brief minutes ago.

Triana bit her lip, but kept her gaze on him. Finally, she said, "What can you tell me?"

Bon smiled, which only made her discomfort intensify. His voice was soft, but steady. "There's a trick to talking with them, I know that now."

"You had more control, is that right?"

He chuckled. "There's no such thing as control over them. No, it's a matter of not giving yourself away completely."

Triana wrinkled her brow. "I don't know what that means."

Bon turned onto his side and supported his head with one hand. He could not appear more relaxed, Triana noted.

"The first time I interfaced with the Cassini," Bon said, "it was beyond overwhelming. Think of a child opening the door on the world's most wonderful candy store. Except this candy store is brilliantly lit, and it's the size of the universe; it goes on forever and ever, with every aisle carrying upward to the sky, all of it stocked with every delight a child could imagine, and then an infinite supply of delights beyond comprehension.

"It's irresistible. You want to take it all in, you almost *have* to take it in. That's what it's like when I first connect with them. That's probably why it hurts so much." Bon pushed a stray hair out of his face. "When you give yourself over to that amount of sensation, it's impossible to move, to think. The Cassini don't really take over as much as they . . . I don't know, outshine, I guess. Like a candle sitting next to a supernova."

Triana said, "I get that. But what did you do differently this time?"

Bon shrugged. "The only way I can describe it is that I shut my eyes. My inner eyes, I guess. I didn't allow myself to be completely swallowed by the intensity of their essence. It wasn't a matter of fighting back; it was more like . . . sipping instead of gulping." He paused, then smiled again. "Yeah, I guess that's the best way to put it."

"I'm sure that's hard to do," Triana said. "It's probably tempting to dive in, right?"

"Yeah. Except . . ." His smile faded, and he looked down at the dirt below him. "Except that way leads to destruction. We're not equipped to handle that."

Lita inched closer and sat on her heels beside them, but kept quiet. Triana gave Bon a moment of reflection before asking him, "So . . . did you learn anything about the Kuiper Belt? Can they help us?"

Bon remained focused on the ground. He ran a finger through the soil, back and forth, carving a small trench, then filled it in and began over again. After a moment he looked back up at Triana.

"I think we'll be able to get through," he said.

Triana wanted to smile, wanted to celebrate the news, yet something in Bon's tone held her back. He wasn't telling her everything.

"But . . ." she said.

"But," Bon said, "I get the feeling that there might be something waiting for us on the other side."

27

I like to read. Not in the way you do, probably. I'm guessing you like to curl up with a good book, get really involved with the story and the characters, and let it take you on a voyage of imagination. I appreciate that.

When I read, I am digitally soaking up an entire shelf full of volumes in less than a second. Not too exciting, really. Plus, I can't curl, which takes some of the romance out of it.

But I love the knowledge found between the covers of books. Even a work of fiction, which is made up, still has seeds of truth regarding the ways of life. Like, for instance, the fact that just when things seem to be working out okay, you realize that you either left the iron plugged in, or there's something perched outside the Kuiper Belt waiting to eat you.

The corridors on the lowest level of the ship were, as usual, mostly deserted and quiet. A few crew members were likely at the other end of the level, either working out in the gym or taking a few turns in the Airboard room. But this end, which housed the mysterious Storage Sections and the Spider bay, sat in muted light, almost a perpetual twilight. It was the only section of *Galahad* that went unused.

At least for now. Once the ship pulled into orbit around one of the two Earth-like planets in the Eos system, it would come alive with activity.

The Spider bay held the small transport vehicles that the crew would use to shuttle down to the planet's surface. Known affectionately as Spiders because of their oval shape and multiple robot arms, each craft was capable of holding thirty passengers. Plans had called for ten functional Spiders to make the journey in the large hangar bay, but as it turned out only eight of the vehicles were completed in time for the launch. The other two were loaded aboard to supply possible replacement parts.

To complicate matters, one of the working eight had been lost in the near-deadly encounter with the mad stowaway. Merit wasted no time reminding his followers that this left only seven Spiders to safely deploy more than 250 passengers to the planet's surface. The math, he preached, did not work with eight; to rely on seven was dangerously foolish.

The Storage Sections were a mystery indeed. Loaded aboard the ship just prior to launch, they were sealed and impenetrable. Dr. Zimmer had deflected any and all questions from the young crew members concerning the contents, refusing to say anything beyond "you'll find out when you get there." Tucked into the desolate lower corner of the ship, most of *Galahad's* crew had practically forgotten about the massive containers once the ship was outside the orbit of Mars; that was exactly as Dr. Zimmer had planned.

Just around a bend from the entrance to the Spider bay was a lone window that provided a solitary view into space. It was one of Gap's favorite spots, a secluded setting that offered a rare break from noise and company.

He stood there now, leaning against the window with his arms crossed, scanning the spectacular star field. It often struck him as odd that there was no sensation of movement, how the stars seemed almost like a painted backdrop that never changed, even as the ship flashed through space faster than any human-built device ever conceived. He wondered if he would catch a glimpse of one of the Kuiper objects, perhaps a tumbling boulder, as it wound its way around the sun.

His temper had finally cooled. He scolded himself for lashing out at Triana, yet at the same time he recognized that many factors had played a part in his anger. Anxiety, fear, frustration, and self-doubt. They had all mixed together to create a vicious mood, and once again his emotions had bubbled to the surface, overriding his rational side.

Perhaps guilt had played a part, as well. He had vented to Triana about Balin and Merit . . . and yet he, himself, had entertained thoughts of turning back. He had fantasized about reuniting with his family and friends, then had taken out his frustrations on Triana.

The outburst still troubled him, maybe because one other emotion—one that Gap had thought was suppressed—kept clawing its way to the top, demanding attention.

There was no time for such thoughts.

He heard the soft approach of footsteps, and turned his head to find Hannah walking toward him, a tentative smile on her face.

"Your favorite place," she said. "You would be the world's worst hide-and-go-seek player, you know?"

"You're probably right," he said, forcing a return smile. "But it's still the best place to get away and think."

He felt a rush of feelings that surprised him. Part of him was glad to see Hannah, one of the sweetest people on the ship. She was so easy to get along with, so understanding, and so caring. He had to admit that his mood could swing pretty rapidly, and yet she had weathered his shifting emotions without once complaining.

If he began to catalogue her other qualities, they would be impressive. She was brilliant, artistically talented, kind, and even sported a dry sense of humor. On top of all of that, he was attracted to her looks, too. She had so much going for her, and he knew that he was a lucky guy.

So why, when she came around the corner, had he also felt a touch of annoyance? It wasn't simply that he wanted time to be alone; it was *her*. He hadn't felt this way before. In fact, *he* was the one who had insisted on spending so much time together, who had pushed the relationship perhaps faster than it would have normally progressed. And now he was irritated when she showed up? What was that about?

He tried to rationalize the feeling. His inability to solve the ship's heating problem, coupled with all of the contributions that Hannah had delivered, might be causing a temporary surge of jealousy. Or his heated argument with Triana had opened an old wound. Or maybe it was simply the combination of those issues, along with the added stress of a crew in turmoil.

In any event, something was different. Complicating things even further was the twinge of guilt that overlapped his feelings. Hannah had done nothing wrong, so why was he pulling away from her now?

He decided to ignore the conflict for the moment, especially since he suddenly found her head resting on his shoulder. He draped an arm around her.

"It's beautiful," she said, staring out the window. "You would think we'd be used to it by now, but it still leaves me in awe every time I see it."

"That's why it's so easy to find me," Gap said. "I hope I never get tired of it."

They were quiet for a minute, each taking in the scene before them. Then Hannah pulled her head back and looked up at him. "Is there anything you'd like to talk about?"

Now he was caught. He knew that he was lousy at camouflaging his feelings, and to say no would be an obvious lie. He chewed on his thoughts for a moment before responding.

"You'll think it's silly."

"I'll think it's silly if you don't talk about what's bothering you."

He sighed, an uneasy smile playing across his face. "Listen, you're putting me in a tough spot, because no guy likes to show weakness, you know?"

Hannah shook her head. "Do you think I want you to be a machine or something? It's nice to know that there are genuine human emotions floating around inside there." She grinned. "Okay, so I like the strong side of you, too. But a little sensitivity from time to time is . . . attractive. Get it?"

Gap shrugged. "Sure. I get it." He withdrew his arm, walked across the corridor and leaned against the far side, his hands behind him. Hannah leaned against the window and faced him.

The slight distance between them seemed to help him. It was a buffer zone, of sorts, and he found that the words began to flow out of him.

"It was an honor to be selected for this mission. For all of us. I remember how proud my parents were. Even though they were sad, they were also happy, you know? Then, to be named to the Council, I thought my mom was going to burst with pride. When I wrote to her with the news, she wrote back to say, 'Dr. Zimmer has put a lot of faith in you; he sees what I have always seen in you.'"

"She was right," Hannah said.

"Was she? I think I've talked a pretty good game so far, but when you get right down to it, what have I really done?"

Hannah stared across the corridor at him, a look of irritation spreading across her face. "What are you talking about? Stop it right now."

Gap ignored this. "What did I do when we were confronted by the stowaway? What did I do when the Cassini almost did us in? What have I done with this whole Merit Simms trouble?

Nothing. Now my one job was to repair the heating system, and I couldn't even finish that. Roc took care of it without me."

He dropped his chin to his chest. "Tomorrow I'm going to meet with Triana and talk about resigning from the Council."

Hannah covered the distance between them in a flash. She pulled his chin up in her hand. "What is wrong with you?" she snapped. "Where is this coming from? Remember when I said that a little sensitivity was attractive? Well, *this* is not."

He gave her a wry smile. "Great. So I'm failing with you, too."

She let go of his chin and took a step backward. "I can't believe this is the same Gap I fell for. Are you listening to yourself? If you can't be the hero all the time, or the knight in shining armor, or whatever you want to call it, you suddenly sulk and quit? I don't believe that."

Gap had no response.

"Hey," Hannah said, her voice softening. "Whatever you're going through right now, let me help you. Don't be this way."

After another moment of silence, she stepped up and encircled him with her arms. He waited a few seconds, his arms dangling at his sides, before slowly returning the embrace. He looked over her shoulder, toward the window and the backdrop of starlight.

Every eye turned to watch as Triana and Bon stepped out of the lift into the Control Room. Every conversation abruptly ended.

Triana noted with a quick glance that Gap's station was once again vacant. Given more time to reflect on it, she might have been angry that he was consistently unavailable lately. But with more pressing matters at hand she dismissed the concern for the time being, while making a mental note to deal with Gap as soon as possible. Their last meeting had turned nasty, and she wondered if that played a part in his absence.

The room remained quiet as she and Bon walked up to the

interface that allowed direct programming access to Roc and *Galahad*'s ion drive. Triana looked at the Swede.

"Do you need me to do anything?"

Bon shook his head. He had spoken with Triana as they made their way from the Domes down to the Control Room, but had only begun to give her a brief description of what would have to take place in the ship's navigation. He didn't understand all of it himself, but an almost eerie sense of the task at hand was imprinted upon his mind; an hour earlier none of it would have made sense.

"I think I can handle it," he said, inspecting the vidscreen before him. He pulled up a chair and placed his hands on the keyboard. "I'll need Roc for some of this."

"I'm happy to lend a hand," the computer countered, "but would it be asking too much for you to fill me in on what's about to happen?"

Bon looked around the room at the crew members before looking up at Triana. She read his thoughts. "It's okay," she said, "they'll all find out sooner or later. Tell him."

Sitting back in the chair, Bon looked at the glowing red sensor. "I'm going to patch in a code that will help us maneuver through the Kuiper Belt without smashing into something."

"Okay," Roc said, "and when you're finished I'll plug in a code that will make rabbit poop turn into jelly beans."

Bon smiled. "You don't believe me?"

"Of course I believe you. Trillions of chunks of rock and ice, all bouncing off each other, without any pattern to their movements whatsoever, and you have the magic formula to slip past like they weren't even there. Why would I possibly question that? By all means, change the course settings. If you guys need me, I'll be over here putting my will together."

Triana leaned on the console. "Roc, the code comes from the Cassini."

"Oh, you mean the same Cassini that tried to blow us out of

space a few months ago? Why didn't you say so? I feel better already. Listen, most wills use the phrase 'sound mind and body.' Do I lose points by not having a body?"

"You know that the problem at Saturn was a misunderstanding," Triana said. Then, looking at Bon, she added, "Don't mind him. Go ahead, do what you need to do."

"Um, may I ask a question?" Roc said. "How will this affect our course to Eos?"

"To be honest with you, I can't worry about that right now," Triana said. "The big issue is avoiding a collision; getting back on course once we leave the Kuiper Belt will have to be secondary."

She was aware that the conversation was having a troubling effect on the assembled crew members. The tension in the room was obvious, and out of the corner of her eye she noticed Mika, one of Merit's followers, lean over and whisper something to the boy next to her.

Triana tapped Bon on the shoulder once and nodded at the panel. He leaned forward and began to type on the keyboard. Slowly at first, with several pauses, then a little more. For a moment he closed his eyes and furrowed his brow, as if he was trying to remember something. Triana could only speculate as to how he was retrieving the information from the Cassini.

She started to ask him about this, when suddenly an alarm sounded. The loud, pulsing tone made her jump and grab on to Bon's shoulders for support. "What did you do?" she yelled over the alarm.

"Nothing," he said back to her. "I'm only doing preliminary work. I haven't even uploaded anything yet."

"It's not Bon," Roc said. "It's the collision warning system down in Engineering."

"What about it?"

"It just failed. It's out completely."

Triana's eyes grew wide. "How could that happen?"

"Checking," Roc said. "It may take awhile to track down."

Bon turned and looked up at Triana. "That means we're flying blind right now."

She felt her breath catch in her chest. There was no way for them to know what was coming at them, or where it was, or how to avoid it. They were completely vulnerable.

She looked back at Bon, then pointed to the keyboard before him.

"Hurry," she said.

28

The red ribbon that she often used to tie back her hair was still missing, and Lita looked around her room for the third time since that morning. "Why," she wondered to herself, "do we always look in the same spot over and over again?" It was not in the room. She sighed, opened a dresser drawer, and dug around until she came up with a pink ribbon. Close enough for now, she decided.

As she stood before the mirror, adjusting the ribbon, she thought about the episode with Bon in the dome. It had rattled her a little bit, but on some level she realized that maybe she was becoming almost numb to the bizarre events that piled up during this journey. Each strange occurrence made her aware that the universe was not only vast, but was full of more wonders than the human mind could comprehend.

And what of Bon? He seemed fine when he and Triana had left for the Control Room . . . but was he? There was an odd change in him that Lita had noticed, but it was so vague that it wasn't worth commenting on. She kept it to herself, mainly because she wouldn't have been able to describe it anyway. It was simply a feeling. He was the same Bon as before, yet *not* the same Bon. What was happening to him each time he connected with the Cassini?

The only thing to do, she decided, was to wait and watch. Perhaps others would notice it, too. Channy, for one. It was hard to get anything past her.

She turned to examine the room, which could use some tidying up. But she also felt a need to get back to Sick House as soon as possible. The decision was made for her a split-second later when the alarm sounded.

The loud, pulsing tones jolted her for a second. Her first instinct was to call Triana, but she also knew that the Council Leader and Bon were already in the Control Room, and undoubtedly were in the middle of whatever was taking place. Instead, she quickly grabbed the medical kit that she had carried up to the dome, and dashed out the door.

Three minutes later, with the alarm now muted, she stood at her desk in Sick House. Two of the clinic's workers had questioned her immediately, but no, she told them, she had no more information than they. It was hard to concentrate on the mundane tasks that faced her while her imagination worked through all of the possible emergency scenarios. Finally, she tossed her stylus pen onto the desk and walked into the hospital ward to check on Alexa.

Each time she had entered the room in the past few days her heart ached. Although she had done everything with textbook efficiency, her friend and coworker lay unconscious, and the feeling of responsibility was heavy. Lita stood beside the bed and smoothed the covers. Once again she briefly wondered if Alexa sensed what was going on around her, and again felt certain that she must.

"You should have seen it," Lita said in a soft voice. "Bon did his mind-merge trick again with the Cassini." She smiled as she gently pulled Alexa up, adjusted the pillow beneath her, then laid her back again. "I guess they gave him the key to the back door out of the solar system. But an alarm went off a few minutes ago, so I hope he knows what he's doing."

She took a step back and looked at the monitor which reflected Alexa's vital signs. "Of course, I suppose we should be lucky that we have a Cassini ambassador aboard the ship, right? Somebody who speaks their lingo, anyway. Although I have to tell you, this time when he connected he—"

Lita stopped short when she heard it. A small hiss, barely audible. She stepped closer to the monitor to see if it was coming from there, then looked behind her to see if someone had entered the room. But they were alone.

When it happened again she was startled to hear a high-pitched moan underneath the sound. She quickly darted back to the bed and looked down into her patient's face.

Alexa's eyes were open halfway.

Lita felt her heart race. "Alexa!" she said, grasping the blonde girl's hand. "Alexa, can you hear me?"

Again she heard the hissing sound, with more of the moan, and this time there was no doubt it was coming from Alexa. "Hey, Alexa. C'mon, you can do it. C'mon."

She grabbed a cool wash cloth that was on the night stand and patted Alexa's forehead. It was something her mother had always done for her whenever she was sick, and it just seemed . . . right.

"Alexa?" she said. "Do you know where we are?"

Alexa's eyes drooped shut for a moment, then opened again, this time a little more than halfway. She seemed to be staring into nowhere, until seconds later when her eyes shifted and made contact with Lita's. Lita felt a surge of excitement.

"Hey, welcome back. Did you have a nice nap?" Her emotions began to take hold of her again, and she could feel tears roll down her cheeks. She didn't care. Keeping one hand holding on to Alexa's, she leaned over and pressed the call button to summon some of her help from the other room. Two of her assistants quickly scampered into the hospital ward, their eyes growing wide when they saw Alexa.

"Run a scan on her right away," Lita said without taking her eyes off her friend. "Blood, respiration, cardiovascular." She paused, then added, "And neural. I want a brain scan, too."

While the workers began their preparations, Lita leaned close to Alexa's face. "You've been asleep for awhile. Are you able to talk?"

The wheezing sound came, but no words at first. Then, as if she was thinking hard about something, Alexa scrunched her eyebrows and closed her eyes. Her lips moved, but she seemed to have difficulty forming words. One of the assistants handed Lita a cup of small ice chips, and she gently put one into Alexa's mouth.

"Not too fast," Lita said. "Your mouth is probably like a desert."

Alexa's face relaxed as she moved the ice around her mouth, then asked for another by opening wide. Lita smiled and put two more chips in.

Soon Alexa was able to make more sounds. She moaned, not in a painful way, but as if she was working out her vocal cords. She took two more ice chips, then looked back up at Lita and croaked her first word.

"What?" Lita said, leaning forward. "Say that again."

Another croak. Lita looked up at one of her assistants, Mathias. "Did you catch that?"

The boy shrugged. "Sounded like 'Santa.'"

They both looked down at Alexa, who frowned and slowly shook her head. She licked her lips and, mustering her strength, clearly said, "Sedna."

"Sedna?" Lita asked. "S-e-d-n-a?"

When Alexa nodded, Lita and Mathias exchanged glances again. "Doesn't mean a thing to me," he said, then went about his work.

Lita chuckled at her friend, then fed her another ice chip. "Are you loopy?"

Alexa cleared her throat, and this time her voice was much

easier to hear. "You . . . asked where we were. We're . . . at . . . Sedna."

"Well," Lita said, "I don't know anything about Sedna, wherever that is. But if that's where you're hanging out right now while you get well, then I'm okay with that." She smiled at her friend. "What if I got you a cup of tea? Remember, nothing comes between you and your tea."

Alexa didn't answer. Instead, she closed her eyes and appeared to rest comfortably. Lita helped gather the data on *Galahad*'s first-ever coma recovery patient, and was pleased with the information. Alexa seemed to be fine physically, and her neural scan displayed no brain damage, either. There was a slight arch in one wavelength that hadn't been there before, but nothing significant.

She was just finishing up when the intercom buzzed. It was a call from Triana. Lita walked over to her desk to answer it.

"Hey, I was just about to call you," she said. "We've had some excitement down here, and I forgot all about the alarm a while ago. What was that about?"

Triana said, "The collision warning system in Engineering went out."

"It went out? You seem pretty calm about it."

"That's because it popped back on again," Triana said. "Without us even doing anything. So we flew without any warning system for almost ten minutes."

"And Bon? What about his code, or whatever that was?"

Triana let out a long breath. "Well, he uploaded something. I'll be honest, it's a total leap of faith, because it has taken us off course, and I'm a little nervous about that. But supposedly it will get us through the Kuiper Belt."

Lita thought about this for a moment. "So we won't need the warning system, is that right?"

"I don't know. I'm trying to have faith in our little friends back at Titan, but I'd just as soon have the warning system as a backup, you know? Anyway, I'm going to address all of this at our crew meeting in a couple of hours. Wanted to see if you were going to be there. What's this excitement you mentioned?"

Lita smiled. "Our sleepy-head patient has come back online."

Triana digested this for a moment. "You're telling me that Alexa is awake again?"

"That's right."

"That's great!" Triana said. "And she's okay?"

"As far as I can tell. A little disoriented, maybe. She mumbled something strange, but I think it's probably just like waking up after an intense dream. She probably couldn't tell the real world from the dream world, I'm sure. But yeah, she seems fine."

"Congrats to you and your staff," Triana said. "What a relief. I can't wait to announce *that* at the meeting."

Lita grew serious. "Yeah, I was thinking about this meeting . . ."

"And?"

"And I'm just curious how you're going to handle it. After everything that's happened lately, I'm a little worried that it might turn ugly."

Triana paused before answering. "The only way to handle it is to be honest."

"That doesn't seem to buy much with some people anymore," Lita said.

"Yeah, I know," Triana said with a sigh. "But I've had this discussion with Gap already. There's no other way to go with it. It's not like I won't be firm, but regardless of what happens I can't abandon my ethics. I know that emotion often overpowers rational thought, but where would we be if we all ditched reasonable and logical thinking just to battle someone else's emotional outburst?"

Lita had been standing during the conversation, leaning against her chair. Now she pulled the chair out and sat down. "Listen, you're the Council Leader on this ship, but you're also my friend. You know I support you one hundred percent. I just . . ." She hesitated before finishing. "I just worry that always taking the high road in all of this will only lead to us plummeting off a cliff at some point, you know?"

Triana said, "I'll ask you the same thing I asked Gap: What do you suggest?"

Lita sat quietly. She picked up a little glass cube on her desk, one of her personal mementos from her hometown. It was filled with sand and pebbles from the beach at Veracruz, a visual reminder of the seashore that had supplied so many of her happiest memories. She had spent countless days running through the surf with her family, and had also spent several evenings alone with her mother, sitting in the sand, watching the moon rise over the water. She cherished those memories, as well as the wisdom that her mother had worked so hard to transfer to her oldest daughter. So much of that wisdom involved dignity and moral decisions.

Triana's steadfast determination to fight disorder with dignity reminded Lita of her mother's lessons. How could Lita possibly find fault with that?

"You're right," she said to Triana. "I'm just . . . never mind."

Triana chuckled, then said, "I never knew how passionate this Council was. Channy wants to get tough, Gap wants to fight, you're a little feisty, and Bon punched someone in the mouth. Maybe *I'm* way off base."

"No," Lita said. "We're lucky to have you in charge. If it was up to us, there'd be chaos by now. You've been steady. Then there's me . . ." Her voice trailed off.

"You've had a lot to deal with," Triana said gently. "Don't beat yourself up for thinking about turning back. We've all thought about it."

Lita sat back, surprised. She had never considered that Triana, of all people, would have those feelings. Yet why not? There was a sense of comfort there, compared to the harsh reality they faced each day in space. Of course Triana would feel that, too.

It was selfish, Lita realized, to assume that no one else could experience what she was going through. Yet before she could respond, Triana changed the subject.

"So, will you be at the meeting? It starts in two hours."

"Are you kidding?" Lita said with her own laugh. "If you can't control all of us thugs, I'll need to be there with my little medical kit."

"Things will be fine," Triana said, then, after congratulating Lita again for the good news on Alexa, signed off.

Lita swirled the sand around in the cube, then put it back on the desk and walked into the next room to check on her lone patient.

29

In the seven months since leaving Earth, there had been only three previous all-crew meetings aboard *Galahad*. Triana believed strongly that not only were they unnecessary in most instances, but that too many meetings would dilute their significance. She instead encouraged department leaders to make their own decisions as they saw fit, and to report any problems or concerns to the Council, which usually met about once per week.

As she walked into the large auditorium, Triana felt an oppressive heaviness in the air. The usual chatter and laughter of the assembled group was restrained, much quieter than one would expect from a gathering of more than two hundred teens. Triana felt the gaze of each eye as she made her way to the front of the room, much as she had when she watched Merit's speech in the Dining Hall. Her path down the aisle took her past many friendly faces, and several crew members greeted her with a smile and a wave.

But it seemed that just as many either frowned or looked away.

She approached the front row of the room and was relieved to find Lita, Channy, and Bon seated, talking amongst themselves. Or, to be more precise, Channy was talking, while Lita and Bon sat passively.

There was no sign of Gap. This time the irritation within her quickly swelled into anger. Whatever issues he might be experiencing, Triana could not accept that they warranted his continual absence. She looked around to see if he might be seated nearby, but although she spotted Hannah about five rows back, Gap was nowhere to be found. She decided that her first order of business after the meeting would be to locate the Council member and have a serious discussion about his future in a leadership role.

For now, however, it was important that she focus on the crucial meeting at hand, and not let Gap's apparent lack of maturity disrupt her thoughts. All of her concentration would be required to overcome the hostility of Merit and his disciples.

Her eyes were drawn to a knot of activity toward the back of the auditorium, and she knew at once that it had to be Merit. He was all smiles, shaking hands with everyone around him, waving to others nearby, and playing the role of popular underdog to the max. Triana felt her heartbeat accelerate, and forced herself to remain calm. This would undoubtedly be her toughest test of the journey, and she could not afford to let him throw her off track.

She walked up to her fellow Council members. Channy jumped out of her seat and gave Triana a hug.

"I am so glad this is finally happening," the Brit said. "You'll be great, I know." Triana smiled, but couldn't think of anything to say in return.

Lita spoke up from her seat. "Alexa sends her regards, and says that she wishes she could be here to cheer you on."

"She still doing okay?" Triana said.

"She seems to be fine, except for that disorientation I mentioned. Guess that's a pretty good tradeoff for waking up, though."

Triana agreed, then looked at Bon. "Have you seen Gap?"

He shook his head. "No. Is there a problem?"

"I honestly don't know. Just wondering why he's not here."

All three of the Council members gave her a blank look. Finally, Lita said, "I'll try to hunt him down after the meeting. Maybe I can find out what's bothering him."

Triana nodded, although she knew that the responsibility was hers. She turned and walked up the steps to the auditorium stage, positioned herself behind the podium, and stared out at the suddenly silent room. The only crew members not present—other than Gap and Alexa—were those whose duties kept them from attending, and they were watching on vidscreens around the ship. When she spoke, Triana was pleased to hear her voice come out loud and strong.

"I won't pretend that everything is happy and peaceful on this ship today."

She noticed that the words had the immediate effect she had hoped for. Her objective of speaking honestly and forcefully was intended to, at the very least, maintain the respect of the crew, regardless of their position. She certainly had their attention right away.

"A growing number of you have questioned the mission that we trained very hard to accomplish. Many of you have expressed dissatisfaction with the Council and its decisions. And some of you have also requested that we discuss the option of turning around and plotting a course back to Earth. I have called this meeting to answer these concerns and requests."

She took a deep breath. "I will also fill you in on our latest connection with the Cassini, and how they're helping us through the Kuiper Belt."

Triana paused to let this sink in, and to allow the inevitable buzz to ripple across the room. Those wearing yellow armbands had used the concept of Cassini support to back their campaign of a return to Earth; if the mysterious alien force was now suddenly helping to pilot *Galahad* to safety, it was a blow to Merit's movement. Triana took a quick glance at him, and their eyes met briefly. He wore a faint smile, as if he recognized the strategic move Triana had successfully executed, elevating their battle to a new level. When the murmurs died down, she continued.

"I must admit that I have found it personally disappointing that a few of us have so quickly abandoned the spirit which powered our mission from day one. Each of us made incredible sacrifices to be here; we left family and friends behind because we believed in what we were doing. We believed that it was our destiny to take the human race to the stars.

"Of course it hasn't been easy, and I won't stand up here and lie to you and promise that the worst is behind us. We don't know what lies ahead. And, even more sobering, we have no idea what awaits us at Eos."

She paused again and took in the entire room. "Every one of us knew this when we made the decision to leave. We were strong, then. We also knew that we were leaving behind a future that promised only disease and death, and chose instead to create a future filled with hope. I'm saddened to think that, even though we have conquered every challenge presented to us, a number of us would prefer to give up."

Triana could sense the unease that her words created in the room. She knew that Merit's message had never been portrayed in this manner before; no one had equated his movement with the concept of quitting. Her goal of presenting the R.T.E. idea in a new light was having an effect. She pushed on.

"There has been growing criticism of the Council, spearheaded by individuals who seek to trumpet their ideas while disregarding the concept of order and discipline when it doesn't serve their purpose. The Council was never created to rule as a monarchy; you have the rights and abilities to change the Council as you see fit. But, bear in mind that when you begin to eliminate any sense of organization, and rush to alter the governing body every time it disagrees with your personal agenda, you're encouraging chaos. Order and discipline must always be pre-served, or we'll be no better than animals when we reach our destination, be it Earth or Eos."

Another low murmur spread across the room as the impact of Triana's words hit their mark. In the front row, Lita subtly nodded her approval to her friend. Bon stared up at Triana with a look that she could only interpret as respect. It strengthened her resolve.

"I have taken note of the recent suggestion that we turn the ship around," she said, and again the room fell silent. "There are three points I would like to address. One, the dangers involved in attempting to turn around within the Kuiper Belt are statisti-cally greater than maintaining our straight path. Two, there has been no contact from Earth that suggests any change has taken place in regard to Bhaktul's Disease. Where is the sense in flee-ing from death, only to allow insecurity and fear of the unknown to lead us right back into its grip?

"And third, some have implied that the Cassini would fix all of our problems on Earth, painting a picture that resembles the Garden of Eden awaiting us. This is the lowest form of propa-ganda, because it plays on your emotions rather than your ratio-nal senses. Its goal is to get you to feel, rather than think. It's dangerous, and cannot be backed up with facts of any kind."

Triana took a deep breath. As she began to speak again she looked up to see Gap enter the back of the room. He stood by the door for a moment, then slowly made his way down the aisle to the front row. Triana watched him, trying to make out the ex-pression on his face. He appeared to be calm, and, as he sat down beside Channy, looked up at Triana and nodded once.

She looked across the sea of faces. "As we make our way on this voyage, we find that we are truly children. Not just in a phys-ical sense as individuals, but as a race of beings. Our experience with the Cassini taught us that we have so very far to go, so much to learn, and probably quite a bit that needs to be un-learned. If we allow it, it can frighten us and prevent us from expanding our knowledge and our intellect. If we allow it, it can destroy us, rather than teach us how to live in the galactic community. Those decisions are up to us.

"Three hours ago Bon reestablished contact with the Cassini. He specifically requested their help in navigating through this dangerous ring called the Kuiper Belt. Twenty minutes later he used their response to program a new course for *Galahad*, one that will put us on a safer track, and will speed us onward to Eos. There are too many details to try to share in this meeting, but we will post all of the information on the ship's intranet. You are encouraged to examine the specifics, and to submit your questions and feedback."

Triana looked back at Bon for a moment. "But there is so much more that we have learned from this particular exchange, much more than we discovered during the incident at Saturn. I've asked Bon to speak to you about it. I think you'll find it . . . fascinating."

She stood aside. Bon hesitated, then rose from his seat in the front row and slowly climbed the steps to the stage. As he walked to the podium, the room remained deathly silent. This was something completely unexpected; Bon, renowned for his quiet demeanor and often-surly attitude, had never addressed any gathering of crew members beyond his duties in the Farms, and was something of a mystery aboard the ship. His bond with the Cassini also lent an aura of wonder about him.

He reached the podium and, for the first few moments, kept his gaze down. Then, he slowly looked up and addressed the crowd.

"It's difficult to explain my communication with the Cassini. I have tried to describe it to Triana as a complete surrender to an energy that we can't possibly begin to understand. I get the sense that they are far older than our solar system, possibly as old as the universe itself. We could probably talk for hours about their history and their purpose. But, for the sake of time, let me tell you the essence of the Cassini."

He looked back down for a moment, and appeared to gather his thoughts. Triana noticed that no one in the auditorium moved; they were as captivated as she in the mystery of it all.

Lifting his gaze to the assembled crew, Bon continued. "For lack of a better word, I believe the Cassini are . . . policemen."

Yet another rumble spread across the room, as crew members looked at their neighbors and attempted to decipher the meaning behind the statement. Bon remained passive on the stage, apparently content to let them discuss the possibility. When they again fell silent and directed their attention at Bon, he resumed.

"We are a flawed species. It's impossible for us to imagine a life form—if that's even what we can call the Cassini—that has evolved to the point of near-perfection. As the universe has expanded outward, they have progressed with it. I get the impression that they now exist . . . well, everywhere. They might actually be one immense life form, with segments scattered across the universe.

"One could ask, after so much time and evolution, what is left for them to accomplish? My best guess is that they now reside in star systems like ours, as a kind of guardian for the life forms there. They create various barriers around the systems, and monitor movement. That means monitoring movement both into and out of the system."

Bon paused and licked his lips. This was the most he had spoken at one time since boarding *Galahad*, and to Triana he seemed to be reaching his maximum tolerance level. She decided to assist him.

"What that means," she said, stepping up beside the Swede, "is that when we imagined the Kuiper Belt to be a harmless, natural phenomenon of our solar system, we couldn't grasp the idea that it was an intentional ring of debris and chaos, created to pick off anything attempting to enter or leave. It might seem,

on the surface, to be a rather primitive defense system, but consider this: We have an incredibly sophisticated warning system
and navigational tools at our disposal, and we have barely slipped
through the first third of the Belt."

Bon picked up on this thought. "The Cassini, as I see it, have
witnessed a mind-boggling number of civilizations in the universe come and go throughout their billions of years. They
obviously are superb judges of what is best for each of those
civilizations. Because of our violent history, it's no wonder that
we've never received visitors from another world. The Cassini
have chosen to keep us isolated.

"And now, we have the opportunity to leave the nest, to experience life in another part of the galaxy. The Cassini must eval-
uate us and make an important decision."

He looked out at the crew of *Galahad*. "They are deciding if
we're worthy of survival."

30

Triana allowed the crew to chatter for a few moments. Bon's theory of the Cassini as galactic policemen had stunned them at first; his suggestion that they might also operate like a judge and jury, determining which species survived and which were either isolated or terminated, created mild panic. Triana had predicted this response. She noticed that, amidst the commotion, Merit sat still and spoke to no one. She could imagine that his mind was working on this new information, preparing a pitch that would use it to his advantage.

After two minutes, Triana asked for quiet. Although scattered pockets of conversation continued around the room, she spoke over them.

"I'm sure you have questions. We will try to answer them as best we can."

A boy in the middle of the room stood up. "You say the Cassini are trying to decide if we're worthy of survival," he said. "Yet they gave Bon some sort of key to navigate out of the Kuiper Belt. Doesn't that mean they have given us a green light?"

Triana looked at Bon. He seemed increasingly uncomfortable on the stage, but he answered the question.

"It's not a one-time course correction. The fact that I connected with them again bought us some time, but we'll need multiple adjustments in our course over the next few weeks. During that time I get the distinct feeling that we'll be . . . observed. Don't ask me how. If we fail to live up to their standards—whatever those might be—my guess is that we'll be left on our own. Which means almost certain destruction."

Another question came from the third row. "Are the Cassini fixing things back on Earth?"

This time Bon needed no prompting. He said, "They are obviously very powerful, but they are not gods. They don't wave a wand and clean up a planet's atmosphere. The term I used was policemen. They are able to keep track of what comes into and what leaves the solar system, but I do not see them stepping in to save our planet. There is a cycle of life in the universe; some civilizations survive, some do not. Their job is merely to insure that one does not negatively impact another."

Triana jumped into the discussion. "Remember, they have reached a level of evolution that we can't begin to comprehend. Simply by trying to study our little human machines, they essentially squashed the research station at Titan, and almost 'helped' our ship to destruction. Fixing little problems is not their focus."

A third question was raised. "How do you know all of this for sure?"

"They don't!" came a shout from the back of the room.

Heads turned, and crew members strained to see who had called out. But Triana knew immediately who it was.

Merit was on his feet. "Of course they don't know any of this for sure," he said, this time in his natural speaking voice. He took a few steps out of the row and stood in the aisle. Triana knew that it was to afford a better view of himself to the assembled group, and to allow him to move while he spoke, which was his style.

"Am I allowed to speak?" Merit said, looking up at Triana. "Or, is this meeting similar to one of your Council meetings, where we must beg an audience with you?"

Triana felt a surge of anger. She opened her mouth to speak, then happened to catch sight of Gap. He mouthed something to her, then repeated the gesture to make sure she understood what he was saying. "Let him talk."

Puzzled, she looked at Merit, then back at Gap. He nodded once to her, then turned his attention to the back of the room like everyone else.

This was a surprising turn. Of all the people on the ship, Gap would be the one who would want to stifle Merit. Why would he want the crew to hear Merit's message? Her instinct told her to play along, as dangerous as it might be.

"You are free to speak," she said, "as long as this becomes a dialogue and not a speech."

Merit smiled and began a leisurely walk to the front of the room. His pace was measured, and looked to Triana to be almost rehearsed for effect. After a few steps he stopped and spread his arms wide and spoke in a commanding voice.

"I want to thank all of you, my friends, for your presence today, because it forces the all-powerful Council of *Galahad* to listen to ordinary crew members, like me. Believe me, if you were not here as witnesses, none of our voices might be heard. We're making progress."

His smile widened and he took a few more steps down the aisle before again stopping and addressing the crowd.

"How very convenient that only one person on this ship is able to communicate with the Cassini, and that person happens to be on the Council. I'm reminded of the ancient civilizations that followed their high priest, the only person deemed capable of talking with the gods. Of course, no one dared question the high priest, for fear that the gods would smite them if they disobeyed."

Triana felt her temper flare again. Gap glanced up at her, this time gesturing with his hands to calm down. He turned back toward Merit.

"In the past week or so," Merit continued, "more and more of you have considered our dilemma, as well as our possible choices. You have made it clear that you would prefer to abort this dangerous journey and return to Earth. And I can see from the many armbands on display today that those numbers increase daily."

He took a few more steps toward the stage, putting his hands behind his back and lowering his gaze to the floor. The pose, Triana was sure, was calculated to give an appearance of deep concern and heavy responsibility.

"But now," he said, "we are told that, according to a Council member, the Cassini cannot help anyone on Earth." He paused and looked up, arching his eyebrows. "Does anyone in here remember the amazing power that we witnessed back at Saturn? Is there one among you who believes that the Cassini are powerless security guards?"

There was a small hum of discussion throughout the room. Triana saw several clots of crew members nodding their heads in agreement.

Merit took another step, then spun and faced the stage. His voice grew stronger. "Should we ask our fearless leader, Triana, why we should believe her? Should we ask her why we should once again place our lives in danger, zigzagging through a deadly minefield billions of miles from home?"

Triana forced a smile onto her face. "Thank you, Merit, for taking a breath, and allowing me to respond to your campaign speech." There was a smatter of chuckles, but many in the room looked up at her with distrust.

"There were multiple witnesses to Bon's first connection with the Cassini," she said. "The results of his first contact speak for themselves, and we owe our lives to that bond."

"We are discussing his latest chat," Merit said. "Would you mind telling the crew who witnessed *that* little talk?"

Triana realized that she had walked into a trap. She knew that her hesitation in answering had already damaged her. Her only recourse was the truth.

"This latest connection was in the Farms, witnessed by me and by Lita."

"Of course," Merit said. "You and yet another Council member."

"I was not aware," Triana responded, with more acid in her voice than she had intended, "that during a time of crisis we needed to gather representatives from groups that have a grudge with the Council." She took a breath to calm herself. "Until a majority of the crew elects to change the Council membership, we will continue to act in the best interests of everyone aboard this ship."

"Of course, of course," Merit said, again pacing toward the stage. "We're all aware that we have no choice—today, at least—but to have total and complete faith in the high priestess of our colony."

Triana made eye contact with Gap again. He seemed to read her mind, knowing that she wanted to verbally spar with Merit. He shook his head slowly. Triana was perplexed by his actions, and grew increasingly nervous that he was encouraging her to accept this assault. She bit her lip and remained quiet.

Merit had reached the steps, and now methodically climbed up to the stage. He stood ten feet to Triana's right, then pivoted to face the crowd.

"Why don't we try some easier questions?" he said. "Besides the obvious threat outside the ship, have we forgotten about the problems within? One of our friends lies in a hospital bed, and has just today awakened from a coma. A coma!"

Triana was startled that Merit already had the news of Alexa's recovery. It was another brilliant tactic on his part: take some of the only good news that Triana might deliver, and deliver it himself—keeping the attention on him—while spinning the news to paint a dire picture. One card that she had hoped to play, and he had already trumped it.

"We need heat to survive," Merit said, "and until recently we had no idea why the temperatures were falling on the crucial sixth level."

On the front row, Gap cracked a faint smile. Triana stared at him, but he kept his eyes on Merit, seeming to enjoy every minute.

"But forget about freezing to death," Merit said, again spreading his arms in a dramatic gesture. "That would be a slow, excruciating death. We would at least know what was happening, unlike the biggest danger we face: being instantly disintegrated by a giant boulder smashing into us with no warning."

Gap's smile grew more distinct.

Merit said, "I wonder how many of you have any idea what happened earlier today. I'm sure you heard the warning sirens, but you might not have had time to learn what that was all about."

Heads turned in the auditorium, and there were more whispered exchanges. Merit took two steps toward Triana and gave her a look that she swore resembled a predator's face closing in on the kill.

"Let me tell you what that alarm signified," he shouted over the buzz in the room. "We have one tiny weapon in our battle against the Kuiper Belt's treachery. A sophisticated warning alert system that tells our ship if we're about to get obliterated by a massive rock. Well, that warning system went down today for a few minutes. All of us were completely vulnerable. It's practically a miracle that it came back online before we were hit."

The room exploded in sound. Several crew members were on their feet, pointing at Triana and yelling. Even the crew members who had remained loyal to her and the Council appeared shaken. In the front row, Lita and Channy seemed stunned at the hostility directed toward the ship's Council Leader.

Beside them, Gap was laughing.

A lightning bolt of fear raced through Triana. Suddenly it dawned on her: Gap's behavior, his angry confrontation with her in the hall, his absence from duty . . .

He had rebelled, and obviously joined the opposition. True, he had seemed to be no fan of Merit Simms . . . but how else to account for what had just happened. He had stifled her attempts to debate with Merit, placing her in an almost defenseless position now. She had no idea how the Council would survive this catastrophe.

She stared down from the stage, oblivious for the moment to the shouting and screams coming from the crew. She felt the rage of betrayal as she watched him laugh. And within that rage she felt a burning sense of pain. Although they had never connected in the manner she knew he had desired, Triana never doubted that Gap cared for her. To think that he would destroy her like this was agonizing.

Her lip trembled and she clenched her fists. Merit assumed a passive stance on the stage, obviously aware that his mission had finally been accomplished and that no further words were necessary at this point.

The uproar in the auditorium began to settle. Unsure of what to do or say, Triana glanced at Bon who seemed to be as startled as she. Lita and Channy were doing their part, apparently engaged in heated discussions with several crew members in the row behind them. Something needed to be done.

Just as Triana opened her mouth to speak, she spied Gap standing and raising his hands. He was yelling.

"Excuse me! May I say something, please? Hello? Can I please say something?"

What was this, Triana wondered. The final dagger in the heart?

"Excuse me," Gap yelled again. The room began to grow quiet. Gap moved to the steps and joined Triana, Bon, and Merit on the stage. Triana couldn't help but notice the look of curiosity on Merit's face. He apparently was as clueless as she about Gap's motives.

"If I could have just one moment of your time," Gap said, and the room's noise level dropped enough for him to be heard. "Thank you. I want to say a few things about what Merit has told you today. He could not be more right about the warning system. It is, indeed, our last layer of defense out here."

Gap looked at Triana, the slight remains of the smile lingering on the corners of his mouth. She couldn't decide what his look meant, but it almost appeared . . . vindictive.

"And Merit is right that it failed today. It was down for about ten minutes. That means ten minutes where we could have been blown right out of space."

He walked over and stood next to Merit, who shifted his gaze out over the crew, much like a king surveying his subjects. He nodded to indicate that Gap was speaking the truth.

"But that's not all," Gap said. "You don't know the whole story yet."

Triana's chin dropped to her chest and she closed her eyes. Inside, she felt her heart break.

31

There was no sensation of time. Triana stood quietly, her head down, but her mind was whirling. Besides the crushing weight of despair, she couldn't help but question everything. How could this have happened? How could she have better handled the crisis with Merit? Was there some way she could have steered the ship through the Kuiper Belt without the near-collisions, the drama, the fear?

Could she have managed the Council better? Could she have taken more of a leadership role in the eyes of the crew as they wound their way through the minefield? Was there some way she could have prevented the near-catastrophe with Alexa?

All of these thoughts tumbled across her mind, sending her down a tunnel of doubt and insecurity. Yet, when she came out the other side, she found, to her surprise, that her confidence and dignity took over. She raised her head again and looked out toward the crew.

"No," she thought to herself. "I have not mishandled this in any way. My father taught me well, Dr. Zimmer taught me well, and if I had to do it all over again, I would not change one thing. I have the courage to stand here now, to face my peers, and to know that I have done the best that I could."

She steeled herself for whatever Gap was going to say. She crossed her arms and held her chin high.

"I should have realized this from the start," Gap said to the audience. "When the problems with the heating system on Level Six came and went, it was odd to me, but I thought it was a defective part that had been built into the ship.

"I just spent some time in Engineering looking at the culprit." He reached into a pocket and pulled out a small metal block, slightly grayish in color. It fit into the palm of his hand. "This is called a Balsom clip. I don't expect you to know anything about it, so I won't bore you with too many details. But it's a sensor that regulates the temperature on the ship. Each level has a series of them. They work in connection with each other. It's so complicated, I didn't even really know how they played off one another until recently. But when one breaks down, it might not create a problem until farther down the series."

Triana was confused. Where was he going with this? Roc had told her that the problem definitely came from a faulty clip, but what did that have to do with this meeting?

Gap continued. "This little bugger right here was the problem. Funny, isn't it, that something this small could cause so much trouble?" He held it up to the crowd and slowly swiveled it, letting them get a better look.

"But guess what?" he said. "Each of these parts, including the replacements, is numbered and coded. And this," he raised the Balsom clip again, "is not one of the clips that was in place when we launched."

The room was quiet. This information seemed important, yet produced only looks of puzzlement from the crew. Triana took her eyes off Gap for a moment when she noticed that Merit's shoulders had slumped ever so slightly. He certainly no longer held a kingly pose. She bit her lip. The significance of Gap's revelation began to dawn on her.

"This," Gap said, indicating the clip, "was a spare part seven months ago. But a few hours ago I pulled it out of the heating controls for Level Five. It's been tinkered with. Not enough for a full breakdown, but enough to cause it to flicker on and off."

Triana suddenly understood. It was sabotage.

"We'll probably never know who did this," Gap continued. "But I think I know why it was done. Nobody on this ship would want to have the heating fail completely, but a consistent breakdown would cause an awful lot of distress among the crew. Isn't that right?"

Triana continued to watch Merit, who looked speechless. She couldn't recall ever seeing that before.

Gap placed the clip back into his pocket and said, "This made me wonder: what other part of the ship was so crucial to our comfort and safety? Well, in this shooting gallery called the Kuiper Belt, isn't it obvious? The collision warning system. And don't you find it interesting that it went down for ten minutes, and then popped back on?"

Looks were exchanged between the assembled crew members. Gap stood quietly while they seemed to mull this over. Before he could continue, however, Merit raised his hands and addressed the room.

"I see what's going on here, don't you?" he said. "First we're supposed to believe that somebody sabotaged the heating system, and now—conveniently—someone has tampered with the warning system." He crossed his arms and looked at Gap while shaking his head. "So this is the best you can do, is that right? Rather than admit that we're in serious trouble, you manufacture a villain." He looked back at the crowd. "But we're not falling for it this time."

Triana watched him closely, analyzing the way in which he worked the room, rallying his troops. But the assembled crew members seemed confused, torn.

Merit raised his voice for emphasis. "I suppose we have another stowaway, is that what you're saying, Gap?"

Gap shook his head. "No, it's not a stowaway. It's you."

There was an instant stir in the auditorium. Merit's arms fell to his sides, and a look of disbelief covered his face. "Me?" He began to laugh. "*Me*? Oh, Gap, you might have been able to confuse people at first, but this?" His gaze shifted to the crowd. "Do you see what you're dealing with now? When they can't solve a problem, this is how they react."

A loud buzz enveloped the room. Triana stood still, watching, waiting. She concentrated on Gap's face. He seemed calm, and very sure of himself. She was sure that he wasn't finished yet.

When the room began to grow quiet again, Merit took a couple of paces toward Triana. "Are you behind this nonsense?" he asked her. "Was this your idea? To have your pawn attack while you sit back?"

It was Gap who answered. "No, Triana doesn't know about this. Only you and I know the truth here."

Merit whirled. "That's right. We both know the truth, that you're lying, doing anything you can to deflect responsibility. Tell me, Gap, what is your evidence? Usually when one makes an accusation like you have, they have some evidence." He faced the crew. "I think we'd all love to see your evidence."

Slowly another smile worked across Gap's face. "Evidence? I think I can do that." He cast a quick glance at Triana, then back toward the rows of crew members.

"We don't use video surveillance on this ship," he said. "We haven't thought it was necessary. I mean, who would want to cause harm, right? But . . ." He paused. "But protecting this crew is part of my job. It's why I'm on the Council. After realizing that someone had messed with the heating system, I programmed a remote camera to watch over the warning system."

He turned to Merit Simms. "Merit, you weren't even on duty this morning in Engineering. Can you explain to the crew what business you had opening the warning system's front panel?"

Merit fell motionless on the stage. Every eye in the room bored into him, and the silence was deafening. He fidgeted, unable to speak for almost half a minute. Gap waited patiently, then said, "If you'd like, we can lower the screen and play the video for everyone."

Triana's heart beat faster. Everything—*everything*—had changed in a flash. She stood frozen in place, taking it all in, hardly believing what she was hearing.

Seconds ticked by. Merit clenched and unclenched his hands. He stared at Gap, who stood with his arms crossed, his weight on one foot, displaying a look of complete control.

Finally, Merit looked up to face the crew. "I need you to understand that I never once meant to harm anyone. You have to believe me." A strand of black hair fell across his face. He left it there. "I knew the heating problem would be repaired. And the warning system should only have blinked out for a few seconds. That's all . . . a few seconds. I . . . I don't know what happened."

"I'll tell you what happened," Gap said. "You almost killed every one of us."

Merit didn't respond at first, then slowly nodded. "I know. And . . . I am truly sorry. All I ever wanted to do was . . . was scare you into doing the right thing." He pushed the stray hair back and addressed the crew. "You have to understand. I still believe in my heart that this journey is too dangerous. I'm . . . I'm afraid. Every day could be our last day, don't you see?"

A low chorus of boos began to roll across the room. In a moment a yellow armband flew through the air, landing at Merit's feet. Within a few seconds a handful more fell to the floor.

"What I did was wrong, but you have to understand my motives," Merit said, his usually strong voice collapsing into a whining plea. "Please, you have to listen to me. We could die out here, don't you understand? I just . . . I just want to go home. Don't you? We need to . . ."

The boos grew louder, cutting him off. He started to speak again, then closed his mouth. Without looking at Gap or Triana, he walked down the steps, then briskly up the aisle toward the exit. More yellow armbands fluttered towards him, many striking his chest and face before dropping to the floor. He pushed open the auditorium door and was gone.

Triana realized she had been holding her breath. She let it out with a whoosh, then walked over to stand beside Gap. "I . . . I don't know what to say," she said.

Gap's gaze remained on the door at the top of the room. "Not necessary," he said softly. "Besides, this could have gone very badly."

"What do you mean?"

He turned to look into Triana's eyes. In a low voice that only she could hear he said, "There is no remote camera near the warning system."

She stared at him, dumbfounded. A moment later Gap turned, hurried down the steps, and exited the room to a round of applause and many slaps on the back.

Thirty minutes later, Triana walked into the Control Room. The crew members who had remained on duty during the meeting, and had watched on video monitors, quietly went about their business. Nobody said a word to her, but the atmosphere had dramatically changed. Everyone seemed especially alert as they went about their duties; there was a crispness in their movements that hadn't existed two hours earlier.

Bon was sitting at the interface panel, rapidly punching strings of code on the keyboard. Triana sidled up beside him and watched for a moment, reluctant to interrupt his work. Then, with a final flourish, he hit ENTER and sat back.

"That should take care of the next leg through the Belt," he said. Turning to look at Triana he added, "After this, I'll have to connect again to receive another update."

"How do you feel about that?" she said.

He shrugged. "It's not the most pleasant experience in the world, but I can handle it now."

Triana studied his face for a moment, trying to see through those ice-blue eyes and read his thoughts. Had he really accepted the idea of the Cassini connection so easily? Just a few hours earlier he had been unwilling to attempt it; now he was quick to acknowledge that it would be happening again, possibly several times.

It was more than that, however. Bon's attitude wasn't one of tolerance. It was . . . anticipation?

A new—and frightening—thought came into Triana's mind. Did Bon now *enjoy* that connection? She had wondered, even during the first encounter around Saturn, if the link to the Cassini caused damage to Bon's brain. But what if it was a sensory stimulation that created a dependence? Could Bon slip into an addiction to the power of the Cassini?

She mustered a smile that felt forced, and held out her hand. "You still have the translator on you, right?"

Bon looked puzzled. "Yes. It's in my pocket. Why?"

Triana said, "I just think I should hold onto it for you."

She could tell from his expression that Bon wanted more of an explanation. He made no move to extract the metal device from his pocket.

"Listen," she said, quickly rationalizing her request. "We have no idea what might happen each time you connect with them. I think it would be a good idea if I held onto the translator, to make sure I'm there when it's time." She smiled at him again. "Just a safety measure, that's all."

Bon silently stared at her. She knew that he didn't buy the explanation, but she also knew that he wouldn't have his own reason for keeping the translator, either. A moment later he placed it into her open palm.

"Thanks," she said. "How much longer until you need to hook up with them?"

He mumbled something that sounded like, "I don't know yet," then stood, preparing to leave. Triana felt an awkward moment pass between them, and felt that something needed to be said.

"Thanks again for everything. I mean that." When Bon only nodded a response, she added, "I'll see you at the Council meeting in the morning." He walked past her toward the lift.

Triana turned to watch him, and was startled to see Mika standing beside her. The Japanese girl had left her post and was quietly waiting for a chance to speak to Triana.

She also no longer sported a yellow armband.

"Hi, Mika."

"Triana, I wanted to . . . to apologize for any anxiety I might have caused in the Control Room." She appeared to fumble for words. "I . . . I was too quick to . . . to lose faith in our mission, and I . . . feel like I let you down. It won't happen again."

Triana offered a gentle smile. She reached out and put a hand on Mika's shoulder. "I appreciate that. Don't worry about what happened. You were never disrespectful or rude. We simply . . . disagreed. But you did your job, and never let our differences interfere with your work. I'm glad you're here."

A visible look of relief crossed Mika's face. She nodded acknowledgement of Triana's comments, then walked back to her post.

Triana spent another five minutes checking in by intercom with all of the various departments on *Galahad*. Again she noticed the crisp response from each crew member who answered her call.

She was once again in command.

32

Once upon a time, back when I was a little baby computer, I had a long talk with Roy, my creator. I asked him what the hardest thing was about building the world's most incredible thinking machine. That's me, by the way.

He said, "It's not the building. It's the rebuilding."

Meaning that it was one thing to put me together. When he had to take me apart to fix things, however, it was always a little more difficult getting things back to normal.

And isn't that the truth with just about everything?

What are we going to do about Merit Simms?"

The Council sat around the table in the Conference Room, and Lita's question hung in the air.

"I mean," she continued, "we don't have a jail on this ship. We could confine him to his room for a while, but, really, what good does that do?"

"We could throw him off the ship," Channy said with a grin.

Triana had already considered the issue for hours. Tossing and turning during the night, she had reflected on several choices, including Lita's idea of detention. It seemed almost silly, however, to send Merit to his room. Was that really the way bad behavior

The Cassini Code   249

would be dealt with during the journey? Even dangerous behavior?

Dr. Zimmer had done his best in planning the system of government on *Galahad*, yet had assumed that only minor squabbles and differences would require disciplinary action. He—nor anyone else, for that matter—had imagined a crew member recklessly threatening the lives of everyone on the ship.

Although Merit's actions had been designed to only induce fear, and to manipulate the crew's loyalties, they could have spelled disaster. He had not been seen in the eighteen hours following the meeting in the auditorium. Triana assumed that he would lay low for at least a few days.

In the meantime, it was up to the Council to determine the punishment, if any.

"May I make a recommendation?" Bon said from the end of the table.

Triana was startled. Bon never offered suggestions; in fact, he usually needed prodding to even open his mouth during a Council meeting. "Uh, sure," she said.

Bon leaned forward, his elbows resting on the table. "I don't believe that we should reward this person by giving him a vacation, even if it's in his room. I vote to put him right back to work, with perhaps an extra shift each week. And, when his next rotation of rest comes around, he should forfeit that and immediately report to his next station."

Triana smiled. Bon's work ethic was unquestionably the strongest on the ship; of course he would advocate hard work for any misconduct. She looked around the table for reaction, and was greeted by looks of thoughtful approval.

"It makes sense, really," Lita said.

Gap nodded. "I agree."

"If you won't boot him off the ship," Channy said, "then okay, put him to work."

The unanimous decision helped, but at the same time Triana

realized that the lack of a policy dealing with dangerous behavior could come back to haunt them. A world of no consequences would only mean chaos. Her to-do list had suddenly picked up a priority item.

She moved on to the next item on the agenda. "Tell me about Alexa."

"I think she's going to be fine," Lita said. "It might take her a couple of weeks to get her strength back, but physically she's okay. The only thing . . ." She let the sentence fall away, seemed to think about it, then continued. "Well, she doesn't seem to be the same Alexa as before the surgery."

"What do you mean?" Channy said.

"Um . . . I can't really put my finger on it. She seems pretty . . . serious."

Channy laughed. "You think? She just had emergency surgery, then lay in a coma for a couple of days. You want jokes or something?"

Lita smiled. "It's not that. Her personality seems a little different." She looked at Triana. "I'm not saying anything's wrong with her. Her brain scan is normal, no apparent damage. But this has changed her somehow."

Triana thought about those words for a moment. Finally, she looked at Lita and said, "I think we've all changed, you know?"

The discussion moved to a lighter topic for a minute, as Channy announced that her plans for a dating game would now continue. She enthusiastically predicted at least a dozen crew members would participate. There was a mixture of groans and chuckles when she raised her eyebrows and looked around the table for volunteers.

Gap had been relatively quiet throughout the meeting. Triana had noticed, and wondered if she should later meet privately with him. For the time being she asked him for an Engineering update.

"The heating unit is working perfectly," he said. "If there's any silver lining to what Merit did to make it malfunction, it's that we now know exactly how the Balsom clips behave when they're damaged or failing."

"How did he do that, anyway?" Channy said.

"He's on his second tour of duty in the Engineering section these days, and he had a lot of time to study up on what he needed to do. Plus, it's not like we sat there guarding the heating system, right? He could have done everything in the middle of the night, or whenever. Nobody would have thought twice about him being there."

Lita said, "So we shouldn't be worried about those clips going bad?"

Gap shook his head. "No. I would be surprised if we ever have to pull out a spare clip again on the rest of the trip. It's a pretty solid unit, which is why the malfunction was so frustrating in the first place."

"But you figured it out," Triana said, doing her best to soothe whatever issues were apparently still festering inside Gap.

"Well . . ." he said, looking uncomfortable. "I didn't think to check the clips for another level, and that might have saved us a lot of time."

"Quit being modest," Triana said with a laugh. "You did a good job. You even outsmarted Roc."

"Can we talk about something else?" the computer chimed in.

"Yes, we can," Triana said. "What's the status on the warning system?"

"Same story as the heating unit," Gap said. "Merit loosened a key circuit within it, knowing full well that a backup circuit would kick in. It's just that the warning system didn't identify it as a complete malfunction, and instead tried to either repair the first circuit, or go around it. It caused the unit to completely shut down rather than use the backup."

"It's been reprogrammed," Roc said. "From now on, at the first indication of any problem, it will use any and all backup systems. It's not anyone's fault, really. The system was a brand new invention, and obviously nobody on Earth had ever needed one before. Plus, who knew that we would be driving through such heavy traffic?"

"Speaking of which," Triana said, "the Cassini's secret path through the Kuiper Belt seems to be perfect so far." She looked at Bon. "Any thoughts yet on when you might need to check in again?"

Bon sat still for a few moments before answering. "It's a feeling, that's all I can really say. As strange as it sounds, I think they'll let me know when it's time to talk. In the meantime, we'll just have to trust that they're . . . okay with us."

Lita looked worried. "Meaning . . . they still haven't decided if we get a pass, is that right?"

Bon nodded. "Yeah."

"But they must be happy about how things have turned out now," Channy said. "I mean, there's no more fighting on the ship, and . . . and . . ."

Triana cut in. "We don't even know what they're looking for. We can't assume that they only grade us on how we get along. In fact, I would think it *has* to be more than that."

"You're right," Bon said. "For a species to grow and prosper, in their eyes, not only must they be civilized, but they must prove that they have something to offer to the rest of the universe before they can reach out and affect others."

Channy looked glum. "Well, what would we possibly have to offer?"

There was silence for a few seconds, and then Triana began to laugh. "Oh, Channy, don't be that way. What if we're judged on positive energy? You usually bring more of that to the table than any two crew members combined."

A smile spread across Channy's face. "Hey, you might be right. Okay, positive energy it is." She turned to Lita. "You know, love is the most positive form of energy there is. Just think how much we would glow if you joined the dating game."

There was laughter around the table. Triana began to feel better than she had in a long time. She looked back at Gap, ready to wrap up the meeting.

"One last thing," she said. "Our course has changed through the Kuiper Belt, so we'll need to begin plotting a correction eventually. But I guess we'll need to figure out where we are before we figure out where we're going."

"Yeah, I've already started that process," Gap said. "We're running in something like a zigzag pattern through the Kuiper Belt right now, only a little more complex than that. There is one thing that's pretty cool, though, and it can't be a coincidence, I don't think."

He punched a couple of buttons on the keyboard before him, and all of the room's monitors pulled up a tracking view of the Kuiper Belt. "If things don't change too much in the next week, we'll get a pretty good view of another dwarf planet, similar to Pluto."

"Hey, that's awesome," Lita said. "What is it?"

Gap highlighted a small, reddish dot on the screens. "It's one of the last major bodies in the Kuiper Belt. Not as big as Pluto, but still interesting. I think we'll zip by close enough to get some great pictures, at least."

Triana raised her eyebrows. "Maybe the Cassini use it as an anchor for the secret passageway, eh? What's it called?"

Gap looked up at her. "It's called Sedna."

Lita had been raising a cup of water to her lips. She froze, her eyes looking over the rim of the cup at Gap. "What?" she said loudly.

"Sedna. S-e-d-n-a."

Triana saw the look of surprise on the Lita's face. "What's the matter?"

Lita slowly put the cup on the table and said, "Oh my God."

"What is it?"

Lita didn't answer at first. She said to Gap, "And we would never have come anywhere near this . . . this Sedna . . . before we changed course?"

Gap shook his head. "Not even close."

Triana grew concerned. "Lita, what is it?"

The young girl from Mexico slowly turned to face the Council Leader. "I knew it. I knew there was something different about her."

"What are you talking about?"

Lita took a deep breath. "Remember when I said that there was something different about Alexa? There was a funny blip on her neural scan when she came out of the coma. I couldn't explain it, but didn't think it was important. But now . . ."

She took a couple of minutes and told the story of Alexa's foggy comments upon awakening from the coma.

"You said she was mumbling," Triana said. "Are you sure it was Sedna?"

"I spelled it, just like Gap did."

Gap and Triana exchanged glances. Channy whispered, "This is too weird. She . . . she's become psychic. The coma turned her into a psychic!"

Bon looked away, deep in thought.

33

Dusk arrived on *Galahad*. They had gone to dinner together, and now, as the lights slowly dimmed, Gap and Hannah strolled down one of the paths in Dome 2. During the meal, he had caught her up on some of the details of his day in Engineering, but had repeatedly steered the conversation away from any mention of his success at thwarting Merit.

He also did not mention the bizarre circumstances unfolding around Alexa.

Hannah walked slowly, staying two feet from the edge of the path. Occasionally she would brush her hand against Gap's, but he made no move to grasp it.

This was their first time alone since the tense moment in Engineering. He had not volunteered any information regarding his decision to leave the Council, and she wondered if he had discussed it with Triana. Finally, during a lull in the conversation, she brought it up.

"I haven't decided for sure," he said. "I want to think about some things."

"You realize," she said, "that the crew thinks of you as a hero right now. It wouldn't make any sense for you to quit."

"I'm not a hero," he said. "But let's not talk about this right now, okay?"

She nodded. They walked in silence for a few more minutes, passing other crew members who had also chosen a walk in the dome for the ship's version of a sunset. In the distance they heard the sound of irrigation pumps beginning their nightly chores, a low, rhythmic thump that reminded Hannah of a heartbeat.

The awkward feeling between them was not getting any better. Hannah felt torn, wanting to discuss how she was feeling, how *he* was feeling about the two of them, yet not wanting to inflame the already sensitive aura that had somehow descended upon them. She was confused about what had happened. One day everything had been fine, and now . . .

"I want to apologize if I've been difficult lately," Gap said, nudging her out of her thoughtful state. "I know it hasn't been much fun for you."

"That's okay, I understand," Hannah said.

"You've been terrific, as always," he said. "It's just that . . . things have been tough, you know?"

She nodded, keeping her head down.

"I don't know what's going to happen with me and the Council. I don't even know if I should be in charge of Engineering right now. Maybe somebody else could bring a fresh view to the Council, shake things up a little bit."

They walked in silence another minute before he spoke again. "I guess what I'm trying to say is that I'm a little overwhelmed right now, a little confused about what I need to be doing, you know? And . . . ." He paused. "And I think, to be fair to you, that you and I should take a break right now, too."

Hannah stopped in her tracks. It took Gap a few seconds to realize that she had dropped back. He turned and walked back to her.

"What are you saying?" she said. "You're breaking up with me?"

"I'm just saying that I'm really confused right now-"

"You're confused?" she said. "That's it? You're dumping me because you're confused?"

"I'm not dumping you," Gap said. "I'm not very good company right now, and you deserve a lot better."

Hannah stared at him, her lower lip quivering.

"Please," Gap said. "I just want you to understand."

"Understand? You're dumping me. At least have the guts to be honest."

Gap shook his head. "I really don't want this to get ugly. I'm not saying I don't want to be with you, but it's just not a good time for me right now. It's not a good time for *us* right now."

Hannah stared at him, tapping a finger against her leg. After a few moments she slowly shook her head.

"I thought the whole 'it's not you, it's me' speech only happened in books and movies," she said. She started to walk away, then turned back. "You know, when things are going tough, the last thing you should sacrifice is the one person who knows you best and cares about you. You should lean on them, Gap, not push them away." Her voice cracked as she added, "Sometimes the answer—and the right person—is right in front of you."

This time when she walked away she didn't look back.

Lita didn't look up from her work when she heard the door to Sick House slide open. It wasn't until she felt the presence of someone hovering at her desk that she raised her head to find Bon patiently standing there.

He looked uncomfortable. Lita was sure that he associated the clinic with his own hospital stay several months earlier, and she wondered what could have brought him down here from the Farms. When she asked, he nodded toward the hospital ward.

"Any chance I could visit with Alexa for a minute?" he said.

"Uh . . . sure," Lita said. "She's awake. I think she just finished dinner." She stood up and walked around her desk. "C'mon, I'll take you in."

"Any chance I could visit with her alone?"

Lita stopped and looked into Bon's face. "Well . . ." She quickly sorted through all of the possible arguments, but really couldn't find one that didn't come back to the fact that she was simply curious about his request. "Yeah, I guess that would be okay." She waved him ahead. "Just five minutes, okay?"

Bon thanked her, then walked past her into the ward. Lita stared after him, her mind racing. She had already wondered about the changes in Bon; now he had come to visit Alexa, who also was no longer the same person she had been days ago.

She felt the hairs on the back of her neck stand up.

Sweat was dripping from Channy's face, and she loved it. The workout had been full, the largest attendance for an evening session in months. Now she sipped from a cup of water and exchanged greetings and jokes with several of the crew members as they filed toward the locker rooms.

"Is that all you got tonight?"

"What are you talking about? I saw you stop and rest a few times when you thought I wasn't looking."

"Hey, Channy, not so fast after dinner. I thought I was going to hurl."

"Maybe you should skip the second helpings for a while, you think?"

Kylie, her roommate, walked up to her, a smile covering her face. "I can't remember the last time I saw you so happy."

Channy shrugged. "Why not? The workouts today have been terrific. The crew seems pretty happy, too."

"I think they're embarrassed," Kylie said, helping herself to some water.

"What, you mean because they put their faith in a scoundrel when they should have been supporting Triana all along?"

Kylie laughed. "Yeah, something like that."

They were interrupted by Addie and Vonya, who approached slowly, their eyes darting back and forth between each other, as if pooling their courage.

"Uh, hi," Addie said, glancing at Channy and then looking at Kylie.

"Hi," Channy said. She could tell that they likely wanted to speak with her in private, but she also remembered their last encounter after a workout. They had had no problem speaking in front of Kylie when their attitude had been confrontational, so it would have to be okay this time, as well. "Is there something on your mind?"

"Well, yes," Addie said, throwing another look at her friend, pleading with her eyes for support. Vonya chimed in.

"We just wanted to let you know that we apologize for being so . . . so snippy with you. Things were a little crazy, and we . . . we didn't handle it very well."

Channy took another sip of water without taking her eyes off Vonya's. She could have bailed them out by quickly accepting the apology, but she decided to let them dig their way out a little longer.

"Yeah," Addie said. "You've always been great, and we treated you pretty badly. Can we move past all of that?"

Channy stared at the two girls for a moment without reacting. Then, a smile slowly crept across her face. "That means a lot to me. Thank you, both. And yes, we're still friends, so no worries, okay?"

A visible look of relief spread through Addie and Vonya. They each mumbled a thank you, then hurried off to the showers.

Channy turned to Kylie and raised her eyebrows. Kylie wiped some perspiration from her forehead with a towel and said, "You look like you're about six inches off the ground."

"It's better than you think."

"What do you mean?"

"When it comes time to do my dating game," Channy said with a grin, "people will sign up out of guilt. I'm sure to have a full house."

Bon stepped into the hospital ward and could see that Alexa was the only patient in the room. He immediately flashed back to his own stay, back when the connection with the Cassini was fresh . . . and painful.

Alexa turned to look at him, and kept her gaze on him as he walked from the door to her bed. Something in her look registered with Bon, a sensation that hit him right away and remained constant. There was a power radiating from her, something that he wouldn't have been able to explain to anyone else. It was something he wouldn't have understood himself until recently.

He stood beside her, quietly, for a minute. They simply looked at one another. He heard a trilling sound, and noticed that Iris was curled up beside Alexa, sleeping soundly.

"How are you feeling," he finally said, and when she smiled he realized how rehearsed—and unlike him—it sounded.

"I'm fine," she said. "Ready to get back to work, to tell you the truth."

"I understand," he said. "Uh . . . do you mind if I talk to you about something?"

"No, that's fine. What is it?"

Bon indicated the edge of her bed. "Okay if I sit down?"

Alexa looked amused by the request. "Sure."

He perched beside her. Iris woke up, yawned, then tucked her head back under her leg and closed her eyes. "I'm just a little curious about how you're feeling after waking up from the coma," Bon said. "Or, to be more accurate, *what* you're feeling."

She looked into his left eye, then his right, then back again. "Explain."

Bon took a long breath, then began to tell her about the ship's zigzag course through the Kuiper Belt, and how they had just discovered that their path would take them near the large body known as Sedna. He watched to see her reaction when the name was mentioned. There was none.

"You referred to Sedna when you came out of the coma," he said. "Can you tell me how you knew about it?"

A brief smile flickered across Alexa's face, then she looked away. "I don't know how to answer that. How do you know your birth date? How does anyone know their parents' names? I just . . ." She trailed off.

Bon considered that for a moment. He glanced at the sleeping cat, then back into Alexa's face. "May I ask a favor?"

"Sure."

"Would it be all right," he said, "if I touched you?"

This time her smile remained. "Are you going to heal me?"

"Just humor me."

Alexa shrugged again, and held out her hand. Bon hesitated, then grasped it.

His eyes went wide. His body went stiff, shaking slightly. A minute later he gently placed her hand onto the bed, then he stood up.

"You felt that." It wasn't a question.

"Yes," she said. She licked her lips nervously, then reached down and began to scratch Iris behind the ears. The cat lifted its head, yawned again, then stretched.

"I can't explain what I'm feeling," Alexa said. "But when I go to sleep, I wake up with a very . . . strange sensation. Like I've been somewhere while I was asleep."

Bon didn't reply, so she continued. "When I woke up from a nap about an hour ago, just before dinner, I knew that you were coming to see me."

"Are you afraid?"

She appeared to think about the question. "No. Not really. Just . . . intrigued, I guess. I don't know what's happening."

Bon leaned against the bed and crossed his arms. "I . . . I understand. Probably better than anyone else could, actually. I haven't felt . . . normal since we left the space around Saturn."

He paused, shifted his weight to his other foot, and continued. "I don't think you and I are experiencing the same thing, necessarily. But . . ." Another pause. "But it's nice to know that someone else has changed."

Alexa took a few seconds before answering. "Maybe we should use a different word. I think I'm the same person I was yesterday; I've just been . . . modified."

"Fair enough," Bon said. They stared at each other for a moment before he added, "Any other visions, besides the one about my visit?"

Alexa moved her hand from Iris's ears to her chin. "Yes. But it was more of a feeling, rather than a vision."

"Would you like to share?"

She looked up and met his gaze. "We're going to make it through the Kuiper Belt just fine."

Then she paused before finishing the thought. "But there's something waiting on the other side."

34

It was close to midnight, the end of a very long—and interesting—day. Triana put on a long T-shirt and eyed her bed, but knew that sleep would never come until she emptied the receptacle of thoughts that was filled to the brim. She sat at her desk and spent a few minutes leaning over her journal.

Once again I can't help but think of everything that has happened and wonder what lessons I might have learned. Dad always said that there were lessons in life every day, and that it was up to us to find them.

I know that I stayed strong with my convictions, and I did not sacrifice my beliefs in a time of crisis. But if that almost cost us the mission, what lesson do I extract from that? It's so hard sometimes, so hard.

I do know one thing for sure: we have so many obstacles in our path, and yet over the next four years the biggest challenge will likely be in learning how to deal with each other.

She set down her pen, stood up, and stretched. There was more to say, but she wasn't sure how to put it into words.

"Oh, just say it," she muttered to herself, and sat back down.

Bon and Gap are two perfect examples. They have both changed in the last few days. For Bon, I'm starting to worry about the effect that his connection with the Cassini is having on him. It's not his fault, that's for sure. I asked

She marked these last two words out and started the sentence over.

I begged him to re-establish contact with these super beings, or whatever they are, so now I can't come back and fault him for what it might be doing to him. I know that we probably would not have survived this ring of fire called the Kuiper Belt if they hadn't shared their code with us. I just wonder what long-term effect this is going to have on Bon.

And, once again, I have to wonder where we stand personally. We have kissed now, and I can't deny that I liked it. A lot. But what does that do to our situation? Anything? Nothing? I am more confused than ever about all of that.

And then there's Gap. His inner turmoil is surprising, but at least I understand it. I've experienced more than my share of that, too. All I will say right now is that I miss the fun Gap we were lucky to have on the Council, and I hope he comes to grips with his insecurities. Is there something I should be doing to help this? Or is this such a personal issue that I need to mind my own business?

And Alexa . . .

I honestly don't know what to make of her. I'm going to give her at least a couple of weeks before I begin to worry about her condition.

As for myself, I have to be honest and admit that Merit Simms accomplished more than he thinks he did. I have put on the brave face since day one, and yet I'm scared, too. He at least stood in front of two hundred of his peers and came clean. I attributed all of his motives to a lust for power, when perhaps most of it was much simpler than that: He's just afraid. His mask might take a different form than mine . . . but we both apparently wear them.

And finally, I hope that, as a team, we're able to live up to the expectations that the Cassini have in order to be considered true "citizens of the galaxy." I suppose it's another example of their code, only this time it's a code of conduct. Of course I'm concerned about that, but they can't demand total perfection, can they?

Triana set her pen down again and thought about that last line. Total perfection. If that was the standard needed to venture out to the stars, then the human species was never destined to make it. Surely, she thought, the Cassini were not unreasonable keepers of the galactic passes.

She closed the journal and made her way to her bed. She lay back with her hands beneath her head and stared up at the ceiling, waiting for the peaceful rescue of sleep. As she often did, she began to mentally critique her own job performance over the last few days, wondering if her dad would be proud of the way she had handled things. Or Dr. Zimmer, her mentor and stand-in father figure after her dad had passed away. He had warned her about handling crew controversy. What would he think of her decisions? Would he at least be proud that she had rejected Roc's offer of secret recordings? Would he—

She suddenly sat up. The thought had flashed into her mind so quickly, something that she had buried in all of the recent turbulence, and now it screamed for her attention. How could she have forgotten about this?

Dr. Zimmer and his video message replayed in her mind.

For a moment she debated whether to get up and add a postscript to her journal entry. Instead, she lay back down and bit her lip. This, she knew, would keep sleep at bay for at least another hour.

Somewhere on *Galahad*, she remembered, a fellow crew member had the blood of Dr. Zimmer coursing through their veins.

remember one of my earliest conversations with Gap, so many months ago, long before we left Earth. He asked me an interesting question, and for Gap that's quite an accomplishment.

He wanted to know if I was ever jealous that I wasn't human. Sounds like a question that Gap would ask, doesn't it?

Let me think about this for a moment. You humans sometimes get so caught up in your emotional crises that you almost destroy each other. I, on the other hand, remain calm and rational. You make mistakes, some of which can cost you your lives, while I am practically flawless. You go from happy to sad to anxious to overjoyed to depressed, all within the space of an hour. I am reliably stable at all times.

So what do you think? Am I jealous?

YES! Please don't tell Gap, but it's true. Something about you crazy humans, and your unpredictable swings, is strangely appealing to me, and I can't begin to tell you why. The only thing I can assume is that it's what lets you know that you are truly alive, and THAT is something I will never experience. So, yes, I'm a little envious. Just a little. If given the chance, like Pinocchio, to become a real boy, would I?

No. And not just because of that whole freaky nose thing. SOME-BODY has to think clearly around this place, and it might as well be me.

Having said that, I do wonder about your ability to get along. I've been thinking about that, and I've reached this conclusion. Yes, you can, *but it takes compassion, trust, and patience. Oh, and one other thing: empathy. Lots and lots of empathy.*

Which, I think, our little space voyagers will need in large supply as they continue their journey. Seems that we're seeing a few changes in the moods and attitudes of our fun bunch, and I'm pretty sure it's only the beginning.

What a time to be tested, if that's really what the Cassini are doing. And yet, when you get right down to it, aren't all of you being tested on a daily basis? Think about it.

Actually, think about it later, because right now you should be thinking about what's on the other side of the Kuiper Belt. Alexa might have "the vision," as some people call it, but could she go back to sleep and try to dig up a few more details, please? If I understand the whole idea of the Cassini's ring of debris, it's meant to not only keep us from leaving the solar system until we're ready . . . but it's also supposed to keep things out that don't need to be here.

Just how angry are these visitors who have been waiting at the front door, ringing the bell for who knows how long? You don't suppose they would try to take it out on our innocent little Earthlings, do you?

I guess we won't know until The Dark Zone.

Let's meet back here, okay?

Tor Teen Reader's Guide

About This Guide

The information, activities, and discussion questions that follow are intended to enhance your reading of *The Cassini Code*. Please feel free to adapt these materials to suit your needs and interests.

Writing and Research Activities

I. Return to Earth
  A. The Galahad adventures take place because human life on Earth is facing extinction from Bhaktul's Disease. Imagine you are a crew member aboard *Galahad*, and you are beginning to have second thoughts about leaving your family and friends to face their fate on Earth. Write three to five journal entries describing the life you left behind, your role aboard *Galahad*, and your feelings about the risks you are now encountering as the ship weathers the threats of the Kuiper Belt.
  B. Merit Simms calls his movement "R.T.E." or "Return to Earth," and his followers wear armbands to show their solidarity. With classmates or friends, brainstorm a list of present-day and historical political movements and

social causes with slogans and, possibly, recognizable symbols. How many can you name? How many of these causes have you supported by wearing their symbols or helping to campaign or raise money? In small groups, choose one cause to examine in closer detail, and present your results to the class. Who leads the cause, and what is its message or goal? How is the effort organized, and how is it supported? Has examining real-life movements and causes impacted your consideration of Merit Simms? Why or why not?

C. Make a top-ten list of reasons people should join Merit in the demand to return to Earth. Or, make a top-ten list of reasons to support the Council. Then, in the character of a *Galahad* crew member, write a speech explaining your position. Read your speech aloud to friends or classmates.

II. Calling the Cassini

A. Imagine Triana has asked you to explain the Kuiper Belt to the *Galahad* crew. Using library or online research, prepare a multimedia report with graphs or charts, PowerPoint or other presentation software, models, drawings, or photographs and other dynamic elements. Present your report to friends or classmates acting as the crew, and invite them to ask questions for you to answer.

B. Divide classmates or friends into "for" and "against" groups to debate the plan to allow Bon to try to reconnect with the Cassini. Use information from the novel and additional research about space travel and extraterrestrial life to support each position.

C. Imagine you are part of the Cassini extraterrestrial life form. Write a letter to the *Galahad* crew describing yourself, your species, and your role in policing the universe, or explain why Bon's theory is wrong. Use clues from the text and from the Galahad book *The Web of Titan*, if you have read it, to frame your ideas.

D. Do you believe in extraterrestrial life? Should scientists try to contact aliens? Would you volunteer to try to communicate with aliens, as Bon does with the Cassini? Develop a survey to learn what friends or classmates know about extraterrestrial life, including the questions above, among others. Use bar graphs and short essays to organize and report the results of your survey.

E. Hold an "Extraterrestrial Day" in your classroom or community. Make a recommended reading list of classic alien novels, such as the Ender books by Orson Scott Card and *The Left Hand of Darkness* by Ursula K. Le Guin. Show alien-themed movies, such as Steven Spielberg's *E.T.* and Gene Roddenberry's *Star Trek*. Serve astronaut ice cream or other space-friendly foods.

III. To Be Human

A. Triana's role as Council Leader makes friendships difficult for her. Have you ever had a responsibility that made relationships with your peers more challenging? Create a poem, song, drawing, sculpture, or other artistic work based on the phrase "when friendship gets tough."

B. Merit Simms sabotaged the ship partly because he was afraid. Does fear always make people abandon their sense of right and wrong? Think of a time you were in a frightening situation. How did you feel, physically and emotionally? Did you behave differently than you ordinarily would? How does an encyclopedia define "fear"? Based on your observations and research, write a defense or condemnation of Merit's actions.

C. Although he is defeated by Gap and Triana, Merit Simms's rebellion does call into question the effectiveness of the Council system for governing *Galahad*. Write a detailed outline analyzing the positive and negative elements of this system, including your recommendations for changes or improvements.

D. At the end of the novel, Bon realizes that Alexa has also been somehow changed. In the character of Bon or Alexa, write a journal entry exploring the question "Am I still human?"

E. In the epilogue, Roc admits that he is jealous of humans. In the character of Triana, Gap, Lita, Bon, Channy, Hannah, or Alexa, write an email to Roc explaining why he should be glad and/or sorry that he is not a human being.

Questions for Discussion

1. What technical problem is causing trouble aboard *Galahad* at the start of the novel? How does Gap react to the crew's jokes about the problem? How does the chill on Level Six reflect a change in the attitudes of some crew members?

2. What elements of the Kuiper Belt's structure make it a particularly challenging passage for a spaceship? What strategies are Triana and Roc developing to navigate through this area?

3. Why is Channy trying to organize a "dating game" for the crew? Do you think this is a good plan? What romantic uncertainties exist between crew members early in the novel, and how do they affect the workings of the ship?

4. Why does Triana decline Roc's offer to spy on Merit Simms in chapter 4? Does she apply the same code of ethics to her deci-

sion not to give the *Galahad* crew a complete picture of the risks of making it through the Kuiper Belt?

5. When he first appears before the Council, where does Merit Simms propose Triana take *Galahad*? What are his arguments? Do you think he is persuasive? Why or why not? Do you think Triana's statement that "the Council will take your suggestion under consideration" is sufficient?

6. How do her accounts of her mother's medical student days parallel Lita's own experiences? Is this a benefit to Lita, or does it inhibit her actions? Do you ever think about "following in the footsteps" of a family member? What has led you to this possibility? Does the prospect excite or frighten you?

7. How do Channy, Bon, and the other Council members begin to detect Merit's influence aboard *Galahad*? Do these moments affect their convictions to stay on course to Eos? If you were a *Galahad* crew member, do you think you might have been drawn to Merit's side? Why or why not?

8. What manipulative strategies does Merit use when he speaks in the Dining Hall in chapter 11? Is Merit a bully? Why doesn't Triana respond to his criticisms? Had you been in Triana's position, would you have kept silent?

9. As *Galahad* continues through the Kuiper Belt, Triana, Lita, and other Council members also confront the temptation to return to Earth. What thoughts and feelings prompt the Council members to consider reversing course? What conclusions do they reach?

10. At the end of chapter 15, what new theory about the Kuiper Belt does Hannah develop? How might her insight relate

to—or contrast with—her thoughts about her relationship with Gap? What does she decide to do with her theory?

11. How does supporting Lita through her first surgery strengthen Triana's bond with her? How does Alexa come through the operation? What does the experience teach both girls? How does this result affect the crew?

12. In chapter 18, Triana tells Channy about her father's advice to "visualize" her way through stressful situations. What insight about this technique does Triana realize? In what situations might you try such a technique? Could this strategy be helpful to the *Galahad* crew?

13. Is Channy right that Bon may be best equipped to respond to Merit's implications that the Cassini may know of, and may have cured, Bhaktul's Disease? How does Channy's instinct relate to Hannah's theory about the Cassini and the Kuiper Belt?

14. How does Triana help Bon in chapter 24? What does Bon learn, or conclude, from his second connection with the Cassini? How does he use this information to help navigate *Galahad* through the Kuiper Belt?

15. How does Gap solve the problem of the Level Six heating malfunction and help Triana defeat Merit Simms? Do you think Merit needed to use sabotage techniques to win people to his cause or might he have been equally persuasive without doing so? Could the Cassini—or Roc—have employed the kinds of trickery used by Gap and Merit to achieve their goals? Why or why not?

16. Do you think Merit's punishment is sufficient? Even after Merit's defeat, does homesickness remain a threat to the *Galahad* mission?

17. Does his success in fixing the heating problem and thwarting Merit Simms influence Gap's decision to break up with Hannah? What has Gap come to understand about himself that led him to this action? Does this have a parallel in the new connection between Bon and Alexa? Do you think this new bond will change Bon's relationship with Triana?

18. What clues from Bon and Alexa's visions indicate what might be waiting for *Galahad* beyond the Kuiper Belt? Do you think the crew will pass the Cassini's "test"? What sort of test do you think the crew is undergoing?

19. In the afterword to *The Cassini Code*, Roc admits to being jealous of human beings. How might you describe this jealousy in terms of human qualities? Do you think Roc is right to be jealous?

20. Do you think that empathy is the human quality that will best help the crew pass the Cassini test and proceed into deep space? Or is empathy human beings' greatest weakness? Defend your answer.

The
Dark
Zone

What exactly is the difference between the brain and the mind? This question has baffled people for centuries. It's been the topic of thousands of articles and essays, along with numerous research studies. It has been analyzed, debated, hashed, and rehashed. Some have argued that it's possible for a human to have a brain but no mind, and yet they say it's not possible to have a mind without a brain. I tended to agree with this last statement, until I read about something that used to be called "daytime television."

Classic definitions will tell you that the brain is, for the most part, a computer made of living cells, billions upon billions of neurons and synapses, firing away in an attempt to move its human host from point A to point B without stumbling over something, without getting eaten by something big and hungry, and without wearing socks with sandals. The mind, it has been suggested, is the conscious, thinking component, the "higher self" that supposedly separates humans and primates from lower life forms such as reptiles, bacteria, and politicians.

There are a couple of reasons why I bring this up. For one, as an observer of the brilliant kids who stroll the corridors of the great starship called Galahad, I am constantly intrigued by the ongoing internal conflict between the brain and the mind. Sure, these teens were handpicked from around the world to carry out a mission to save humanity; to leave their families behind and travel across interstellar space to the *planetary system known as Eos; to escape the deadly clutches of a disease borne by a rogue comet's tail and preserve the history and legacy of their species; to . . .*

Well, we've already established that they're brilliant, which is why they're able to make this journey without any adults aboard the ship. They are essentially the perfect laboratory specimens for me to study the brain/mind relationship.

Here's what I've determined: regardless of how sharp a person may be, the battle between the brain's automatic (some might say instinctual) response and the mind's emotional response can often lead to conflict, chaos, and . . . and . . . sorry, I can't think of another word that fits here and starts with "C."

You get the idea. I'm often amazed at how the so-called superior mind of the human species will obsess over details that it should, by all reasonable accounts, ignore. Ah, you say, but that's what makes you human, right? Okay. Then I'm left to wonder how you ever did rise above the bacteria. Your incredible minds, it seems, truly beat the odds.

The other reason I bring this up—remember, there were two—is because I'm an interesting subject myself. My name is Roc, and I'm undeniably the most astonishing artificial brain ever conceived. My role on Galahad is to oversee the ship's primary functions, of course, but I also provide the insight, the intuitive good sense, and a healthy dose of dazzling wit and charm. But . . . do I have a mind?

Why don't we let you decide for yourself? There's plenty of evidence to sift through, and I would strongly recommend that you start at the beginning of the Galahad saga with a volume known as The Comet's Curse, *followed by* The Web of Titan, *and then* The Cassini Code. *Each of these tales will catch you up on the drama and excitement that has followed our merry band of star travelers from Earth, past Saturn, and through the very border of the solar system. And, along the way, you'll naturally develop a strong appreciation and—dare I say it?—a warm affection for your humble narrator. Then you can make the call on whether or not a mind exists within my circuits.*

Brain versus mind. Rational thought versus emotional influence.

Smooth peanut butter versus crunchy. None of it gets any easier when you're billions of miles from home, rocketing out of the Kuiper Belt and into the great unknown. My friends aboard Galahad are the smartest, most courageous young people you'll ever meet . . .

But they're only human.

1

There was no sound in the room other than muted sobs. No laughter, no whispers, no private conversations. More than two hundred teenagers, crammed into a sterile space, yet completely quiet. It was an unnatural silence, which added to the somber mood. Occasionally a cry escaped from one of the teens, which provoked a similar response from another, then another. Then once again the deathly veil dropped, and silence reigned.

The shroud-covered body lay alone on the table, identity disguised. It held the attention of every person in the room, for it represented what none had believed possible.

Galahad's first death.

A crew member separated from the crowd and trudged up the steps to stand behind a hastily arranged podium. Choking back tears, they spoke quietly, reciting memories of their late friend, offering words of encouragement in a vain attempt to make it seem that everything would be okay.

Nobody responded. They stood silently, most with hands clasped behind their backs, filling most of the available space in the Spider bay of the ship called *Galahad*. As the speaker walked slowly back down the stairs, music began to drift across the room. It brought about a fresh wave of tears.

Silence dominated again. Then, slowly, the crew members began to disperse. One by one they approached the body; some reached out and placed a hand upon it, others simply stared. After pausing for a moment, they shuffled past, across the vast hangar, and out the door. It took almost thirty minutes for everyone to pay his or her respects individually. In the end, five people were left, huddled together, not wanting to believe it could have happened, not wanting to say good-bye. They embraced, then together approached their fallen comrade and placed upon the shroud a bouquet gathered from the ship's farms; not true flowers, but the closest symbol they could manage.

A minute later they convened in the Spider bay's control room, sealing it off, and stared sadly through the glass. With a spoken command, a door opened in the hangar, exposing the room to the icy vacuum of deep space. Starlight cascaded through the opening. It was a simple reminder: we are far from home.

There was hesitation, a collected feeling of loss, and a reluctance to let go. The next move would send the body into space, to drift for eternity. No one wanted to move, to take the next step, to banish his friend to the depths of empty, lonely space. But at last the word was given, and the ship's computer began the final sequence.

The robotic arm, until now concealed below the table that held the body, extended toward the bay's open door. With a gentle shove it was done; the shroud covering the body fell away, revealing a cocooned human form, layered in specially treated wraps. It cleared the opening and began its endless journey. Within a minute it had receded from view, first a small white object slipping away, becoming a faint pinprick of light, and then gone.

Once again the five companions in the Spider bay's control room embraced, allowing their grief to mingle, physically holding each other up. They remained that way as the bay's outer door closed, blocking out the starlight, sealing them once again into the warmth of their metal nest.

And then the scene froze . . . and faded away.

It was a familiar smell, but Alexa Wellington couldn't place it at first. Still disoriented from the deep sleep, she lay on her bed and kept her eyes closed. The misty line between wakefulness and dreams had dissolved, but once again the vision had been so strong, so intense, so . . . real . . .

She was, as usual, reluctant to let it go. In the last six weeks her dreams had become more and more vivid. They didn't come often, perhaps only two or three that she could remember each week; but they were unlike any dreams she had ever experienced before. For one thing, there was no dreamlike quality to them. In one of her quiet conversations with Bon Hartsfield, Alexa had likened them to minimovies, only with the screen inside her head in full 3-D and high definition. Until she awoke and opened her eyes, her mind would not interpret them as anything except real.

On top of that, they were complete dramas; they had a beginning, middle, and end, unlike the typical dream that generally jumped from place to place as well as backward and forward in time. These were stories that played out as if scripted. Often they were quite pleasant, while others were very unsettling. This particular dream was the most disturbing yet.

Taking a deep breath, Alexa opened her eyes. Other than the soft glow from the computer monitor across the room and the faint emergency light above the door, the room was dark. She could just make out the still form of her roommate, Katarina, sleeping. All was quiet. The scent that had greeted her upon waking was artificial; Katarina had apparently dialed up her favorite sleep aid, a soft fragrance of lavender that seeped through the ventilation ducts.

Alexa resisted the urge to glance at the clock, for she had found that her mind would then only focus on the time, mentally calculating how long it would take to fall back asleep. It might be midnight; it might be 5 a.m. She didn't want to know.

Of course, concentrating on the time might distract her from the troubling dream that had unfolded minutes ago. The nightmare's tragic setting was only one concern; the fact that her dreams had lately started to come true was terrifying.

She took another deep breath, held it, and then slowly exhaled. Try as she might, she couldn't shake the vivid image of the deepspace funeral. Who had been lying beneath the shroud? Who were the friends clustered in the control room, grieving together? Their faces were obscured, their gender a mystery. She had felt that they were somehow close to one another, but that didn't help; there were 251 teenagers aboard the ship.

Another thought occurred to her: Should she tell someone? If indeed her dreams were somehow portals to the future, allowing her to glimpse ahead, was it irresponsible to keep this vision to herself? On the other hand, what purpose could it serve? The dream had given no indication of the cause of death, which meant that realistically no preventive steps could be taken. If word leaked out that Alexa was now predicting death for one of the crew members . . .

And just whom exactly would she tell? Triana Martell? That would be the obvious choice; the ship's Council Leader would be understanding, and would treat Alexa with respect. But Triana had so many responsibilities, and dealt with more pressure than most teenagers could imagine. Why add to her concerns when there was nothing that could be done about it?

Lita Marques would also be very understanding, and, as Alexa's immediate supervisor in *Galahad*'s clinic—lovingly referred to by the crew as Sick House—knew her better than anyone. Lita was a good friend, a good listener, and easily the most compassionate person Alexa had ever met.

And yet was it a good idea to burden her with this information? A mere eight weeks ago Lita had operated on Alexa and removed her appendix. In fact, the surgical procedure had inadvertently brought on the dream visions that now plagued her.

Alexa had not awakened immediately after the operation, and instead had briefly lain in a coma. Something had happened to her during this unconscious stretch, something nobody could quite explain.

Although she had done nothing wrong, Lita blamed herself for the frightening turn of events. Alexa couldn't see troubling her with this new development.

Then there was Bon.

The quiet, somber Swede had few real friends aboard the ship. He kept himself busy with his work, running the agricultural program within the two massive domes that topped the spacecraft. Few people had ever been able to get emotionally close to him. And yet, over the last few weeks, he and Alexa had connected.

It began with a visit he made before she was discharged from Sick House. During their brief conversation she realized that he had sought her out because of something they had in common: both were experiencing bizarre mental flashes that had altered their worlds.

For Bon it was his tenuous connection with the alien entity that the *Galahad* crew had encountered while zipping past Titan, the mysterious orange moon of Saturn. That connection had eventually saved the ship from certain destruction within the debris-strewn minefield known as the Kuiper Belt. For Alexa it was her sudden prescient abilities.

It was a bond forged of their uniqueness. As Alexa had said to him recently, "We are the ship's freaks. Nobody else could possibly understand." Bon had scowled at hearing this, but had offered no argument.

She had shared many of her dream visions with him over the weeks, but not all. How would he take the news that a death aboard the ship might be imminent?

She decided to wait.

With a sigh she gave in and twisted her head to look at the clock, just as the time clicked over to 1:55 a.m. "Go to sleep," she whispered to herself.

Deep inside she knew it would not come easy.

The Dining Hall on *Galahad* was packed. Triana walked in at 7:15, late for her breakfast meeting with Channy Oakland and Lita. The three girls made it a point to start the day together at least once a week, occasionally to discuss Council business, but mostly for social reasons. She scanned the busy room and spotted Channy waving from the far corner. Channy was easy to pick out of most crowds; all one needed to do was look for the brightest T-shirt in the room. Today's choice was hot pink.

"Sorry I'm late," Triana said after loading a tray with some fruit, an energy block, and simulated juice, her usual breakfast combination. "It took me longer to answer emails than I expected."

"Everything okay?" Lita said.

Triana nodded as she sipped her juice. "Lots of questions about what's going on back home. Not that I could really offer much information."

"It had to happen eventually, right?" Channy said, a grim tone overriding her usual upbeat British inflection. "I mean, I'm surprised we kept contact for as long as we did."

"It's still tough to swallow, no matter how prepared you think you are," Triana said.

Lita looked thoughtful. "So I guess we can officially declare ourselves out of the nest. No replies to our messages must mean that Galahad Command has closed for good."

The three girls reflected on this for a moment before Triana said, "It's not that we really needed their help for anything in particular. With Roc we pretty much have the technical know-how. It's the . . . uh . . ."

Lita finished for her. "It's the emotional tie."

"Yeah." Triana looked around the room. "Although the crew seems to be in pretty good spirits. I can't remember when I last saw this place so busy in the morning."

Channy laughed. "It's because of this." She held up a small bowl with a sticky residue around the insides.

"What's that?"

"Oatmeal."

Triana raised her eyebrows. "You're kidding. We have oatmeal?"

Lita smiled. "Bon impresses again. He told a few people that it would finally be ready, and the word spread like wildfire."

Turning to look over her shoulder at the serving line, Triana said, "Why didn't I see any?"

"Because it's all gone, that's why," Lita said. "I don't think anyone was prepared for the rush."

"I got here at 6:45 and scooped up one of the last bowls," Channy said. "Sorry, I guess I should have saved you some."

It was Triana's turn to chuckle. "Don't worry about it. I'm sure I'll have plenty of chances over the next few years." She looked around. "Who knew that oatmeal could bring so much joy?"

"If you ask me," Lita said, "it's not simply the fact that we have any particular new food. I think it's simply change, and that's something this crew could use."

"What do you mean?" Channy said.

"It's not healthy to fall into a rut," Lita said. "This is just my opinion, of course, but we could all use a shake-up in our routines. Tomorrow is the ten-month anniversary of our launch, and besides a few dramatic moments, and the switching of job assignments, we have pretty much all fallen into the same patterns, day in and day out." She looked at Channy. "It's no different than what you preach to us every week in the gym, about alternating our workouts. After a while your body adapts, right? It's not as effective."

Channy nodded. "Right. But you're talking mentally?"

"I'm talking about all of it: physically, mentally, emotionally."
She indicated the food dispenser line. "A new food choice is a little
thing, but look at the reaction. It's a welcome change; not all
change is embraced, but it's almost always good for people."

Triana smiled. "Any suggestions, Doctor?"

Channy piped in before Lita could answer. "Oh! I know! What
if we had something like, I don't know, um . . . okay, how about
Shake It Up Day, or something like that? You know, everyone has
to do everything differently for one day."

Lita's laugh was gentle and pleasant. "I know that you love to
plan special events, Channy, but I wasn't thinking about just one
day. I'm talking about a lifestyle adjustment."

"I know, but at least it would bring it to everyone's attention."

Triana shrugged. "I'm probably the biggest creature of habit
on this ship. I'm pretty sure it would do me some good to mix
things up a bit. I don't know if we need a special day dedicated
to it, but it's something that we should discuss in a Council
meeting."

Channy grinned. "Just don't forget about tonight."

Her two companions went through the motions of adjusting
the items on their trays, neither making eye contact. Finally, Lita
said, "Tonight?"

"Oh, stop pretending you don't know," Channy said with a
huff. "The Dating Game? This evening? Auditorium? Big fun?
Remember?"

Lita and Triana looked at her, then at each other. Triana kept
quiet, leaving it up to Lita to respond again. "I'm pretty busy with
reports this week."

Channy crossed her arms. "It's one hour out of your life, Lita."
She shook her head at both girls. "I swear, you two are the biggest wet noodles I've ever met. Would it hurt that much to put
yourselves out there?"

Triana at last broke her silence. "I know you really want us to participate, Channy, but maybe next time." She offered a wry smile; Channy returned a pout.

"Fine. You could at least stop by and be part of the audience. I promise I won't bring you up on stage. But I could use some more bodies in the crowd."

"I'll pop in for a few minutes," Lita said.

"I'll do my best," was all that Triana offered.

For the next ten minutes the conversation drifted through a variety of topics, mostly with Channy's enthusiastic comments, Lita's thoughtful responses, and an occasional observation from Triana, who often chose to listen and quietly consider. During this time the room began to thin out, as more and more crew members cleaned up their tables and set out on their daily duties.

Galahad's crew worked in six-week shifts within the various departments on the ship, before rotating into a different assignment. It was understood that this would allow each person to become proficient in many areas. Along with the advanced schooling that accompanied their work, the idea was for *Galahad* to have a seasoned, well-educated crew when it arrived at the Eos star system, their eventual destination.

At any given time a group of about sixty people were on a break from work, but even then their education continued. Many found that the break only led to boredom, and when their next assignment arrived they gladly returned to the rotation.

Lita stood, stretched, and picked up her tray. "Back to work for me. Anything exciting for you guys today?"

"I'm going to ask Bon if we can clear a path around the outer perimeter of Dome 2," Channy said. "A few people in the afternoon workout group suggested that it might be more fun to run up there. It would be more like running outside. I think they're very tired of the treadmills."

Lita laughed. "Good luck. If I hear the walls shaking today I'll know that you asked Bon."

"I know he's very protective about his crops," Triana added, "but that's actually a pretty good suggestion. Let me know if you want me to go with you."

"What about you?" Lita said. "What's your day like?"

Triana stood and pushed back her chair. "This will be an interesting day in the Control Room. We are officially shooting out of the Kuiper Belt now, and I've heard some rumblings about what might be on the other side."

Channy sat still, looking up at the Council Leader. "And what do *you* think is out there?"

"A whole lot of nothing."

"Just empty space?"

"Just empty space," Triana said. She waved good-bye to Channy and walked toward the door with Lita.

As they exited into the curved hallway and prepared to go their separate ways, Lita looked into Triana's eyes. "Do you really believe there's nothing outside the Belt?"

Triana sensed the anxiety in her friend. "Honestly, Lita, I have no idea anymore. It's getting to the point where nothing would surprise me."

"Bon and Alexa seem a little worried about it."

Triana sighed. "I know. But what can we do?"

Lita didn't answer at first. Then, with a smile, she said, "We're tough. We can handle anything, right?" She turned and walked toward the lift.

Triana bit her lip. For two months she had wondered what they would be facing when they shot out of the minefield of debris that circled the solar system. Soon they would find out.

His name was Taresh, and he held the attention of about twenty-five *Galahad* crew members who hunched over their workpads. This particular session of School focused on history; in particular, the rise and eventual end of British colonization. With their stylus pens hastily scribbling notes, the students' eyes darted back and forth between their workpads and the young man from India who spoke onstage in the Learning Center.

From the beginning, the man who had organized the *Galahad* mission insisted that the crew members participate in their own education. Dr. Wallace Zimmer had provided the necessary information in the ship's computers to instruct the young pupils in all areas, a measure that ensured that Eos would be settled by a highly educated population. Yet, rather than have them sit through lecture after lecture by Roc, Dr. Zimmer put a heavy emphasis on students carrying much of the load.

Regardless of the subject matter, *Galahad's* crew members were expected to take their turn onstage, sharing specific information that they had researched for that particular lesson. It not only encouraged each student to expand his or her individual acquirement skills, it developed a sense of teamwork. Whether they were outgoing or shy, it didn't matter; at various points, everyone would take his turn in front of the group.

Taresh had volunteered to share the story of India's past. A native of Patna, a city on the banks of the Ganges River, he was a good choice to teach his fellow travelers about the region. Easygoing and well liked, he exuded pride about his home country that was evident to everyone in the room. With the help of graphics that Roc flashed on the large screen behind the stage, Taresh quickly recounted the story of India's vast wealth of cotton, silk, spices, and tea, and how Britain established outposts that soon came to dominate the country. The British East India Company evolved into territorial rule, complete with a government infrastructure, armies, and more. Taresh concluded his comments by addressing the rise of self-government, and official independence in 1947.

Seated in one of the chairs, and entirely absorbed in the information, was Gap Lee. The Head of Engineering on *Galahad* and a Council member, he enjoyed School, especially these times of student-led discussion. In particular, Gap admired the way Taresh held himself, and the graceful manner in which he related the story of his country's heritage.

Gap felt a similar pride for his home country of China. He knew that for ages, the people of his country had clashed with the people of India, often over disputed territory between the two great nations. Now, with Earth billions of miles behind him— and growing more distant every second—it was difficult for Gap to fathom those differences, and how they could go unresolved for so long. Taresh was a friend, and Gap was saddened that countless generations of their people had chosen a warlike path over peace and cooperation.

Too often it had been the same story for the people of Earth; here, however, in the cocoon known as *Galahad,* such cultural and territorial disputes seemed old and irrelevant.

Taresh finished his report, and a smattering of applause followed him to his seat next to Gap. A five-minute break would follow before the class shifted its attention to mathematics.

"Well done," Gap said, clapping Taresh on the shoulder. "I've heard the name Gandhi so many times, but I never really knew what he was all about."

"I felt the same way when we studied Greek history last week," Taresh said, saving the data on his workpad. "Familiar names, but I couldn't have told you anything about them."

A boy in front of them turned around. "I still don't understand why we have to learn any of this anyway."

Gap looked into the eyes of Micah, who hailed from New York. "What do you mean?"

"Well, we've left all of this behind us. Why bother to drag it to Eos? What good will it do when we start over on a new world? I don't get it."

Gap glanced at Taresh, who jumped in to answer.

"It's important to learn as many lessons from the past as possible."

"I don't see how," Micah said. "Shouldn't we spend more time on math and science, and forget about all of the nonsense that our ancestors caused? If you ask me, it's better to ignore their mistakes."

Gap shook his head. "I can't agree with that. The reason we study the mistakes from the past is so that we'll recognize what works and what doesn't. Besides, it's not all about mistakes. There were some great people who did some amazing things; just reading about their wisdom inspires me sometimes."

"And remember this," Taresh added. "The path that we've all taken is a part of who we are. How can you appreciate what you have if you have nothing to compare it to?"

Micah looked thoughtful. "Yeah, that's true. I never looked at it that way before."

Taresh chuckled. "I know that sometimes it just seems like a bunch of useless facts that we'll never really need. But that's because we forget to look underneath. The story of our past is a great tool for creating a better future. It's not just facts and figures; it's our foundation. It's the same with traditions."

With a nod, and a new look of respect on his face, Micah turned back around. Gap looked at Taresh. "So what's new in your world?"

"I'm about to start a turn in Sick House in two weeks. I'm glad, too, because medicine is one of my interests."

"That's cool. Lita's a good teacher, too," Gap said. "What have you been doing for fun?"

"Would you believe board games?" Taresh said with a smile. "Seven or eight of us have gotten hooked. We meet in the Rec Room twice a week after dinner, and it's a blast. You should join us sometime."

"Might be a good change from playing Masego with Roc," Gap said. "I've still never beaten him, and I think lately he's been letting me get closer, just to keep my hopes up."

While he was talking, Gap glanced around the room. People were sitting in groups, chatting, and others were walking in and out of the door to the hallway, preparing for the second half of the class. He started to say something else about Roc, when suddenly he caught sight of a familiar face in the back row.

It was Hannah Ross. She kept her head down, and appeared to be sketching something. The fact that she was in the back of the room probably indicated that she preferred not to be seen by Gap. He understood.

Two months earlier he had ended a relationship with Hannah, and they had not spoken since. He saw her occasionally, but it was rare. And in those awkward moments, she made sure to avoid contact or conversation.

The breakup had come during a stressful, disturbing point in Gap's experience on *Galahad*. In the weeks that followed, he had questioned his own decision, often tempted to stop by and visit the quiet girl from Alaska. The closest he had come was an email, a long, detailed letter explaining his motives. In it he admitted that he missed her, and wondered if she would have any interest in meeting for dinner.

Hannah had not responded.

Now, at the back of the Learning Center, she continued to keep her gaze on her workpad. She had to know that Gap was in the room.

"Well?"

Gap realized with a start that Taresh had been speaking to him. "I'm sorry, I was drifting," he said.

Taresh turned to look in the direction that Gap had been staring, then looked back at his friend. A knowing expression was on his face. "I said we're going to be meeting up in the Rec Room again tonight, if you'd like to come by."

"Uh, sure, I'll try to make it if I can," Gap said, shifting back in his chair to face forward. "Anybody I know in your group?"

"Channy started playing a couple of weeks ago," Taresh said.

"Really? Channy?" Gap was surprised that the chattiest member of the crew had not said anything about it during a Council meeting.

"Yeah. She, um . . ." Taresh appeared to search for words. "She . . . has been very friendly lately."

Gap laughed. "What are you talking about? Channy is always friendly. You know that."

Taresh raised his eyebrows. "No, I mean she's been very friendly."

It finally sank in. Gap's mouth dropped open. "Ohhhh. Interesting."

"Don't say anything to anyone," Taresh said, dropping his gaze to the floor. "I'm not trying to embarrass her. I just don't know . . . how to handle it."

"Do you like her? I mean . . . she's very cute." Gap suddenly felt uncomfortable about the conversation. In a strange way, he almost felt as if he was talking about his sister.

Taresh shrugged. "Yeah, she's cool. I don't know."

A soft tone sounded in the room, announcing the end of the break. Both boys seemed relieved.

The door of the lift slid open, and Triana was immediately aware of a heaviness that blanketed the Control Room. She wondered for a moment if something had gone wrong, until she glanced to the far corner and recognized the figure who sat before a keyboard, his back to the room. He likely had not said a word, nor done anything to intentionally produce the feeling that swam about the room, yet Bon's mere presence often cast a dense shadow. The word "brooding" had been used by more than one crew member when describing the tall Swede; the result was that he usually worked without interruption or small talk.

Triana crossed to the workstation and looked over Bon's shoulder at the vidscreen before him. A jumble of code played out, countless strings that meant nothing to her, and, strangely enough, probably meant as little to Bon. He was a vessel, a container of information, a messenger of sorts. Yet the information he carried had saved the lives of everyone aboard *Galahad*.

Without knowing exactly how it worked, Bon was able to sync telepathically with the alien force they called the Cassini. Ageless and intellectually advanced beyond human comprehension, this powerful force occupied Titan, the methane-wrapped moon of Saturn. During the brief encounter as *Galahad* whipped past, Bon discovered that his mind was being used as a conduit to the alien entity. He was able to sink into a painful, frightening connection with the Cassini using a device known as the translator, whereupon data was transferred in a sort of mental uplink. The crew of *Galahad* had used that data to navigate its way out of the deadly Kuiper Belt, avoiding collision with the trillions of pieces of space debris that circled the edge of the solar system.

Each stage of the navigation, however, had required an individual uplink. Triana had grown concerned that Bon was somehow becoming addicted to the powerful connection. She knew that his link to the Cassini had altered him in some way, something that neither she nor he could describe. Even though his connections were agonizing, it seemed he was too eager to repeat the experience. Wary, and more than a little distrustful of the effects he was suffering, Triana chose to hold onto the translator herself, and only allow Bon to use it in her presence.

He had made another connection the previous evening, kneeling among the dirt and plants in Dome 2, where he felt the most at ease. Triana had watched the spasms take over, watched Bon's head snap back, his eyes turn a terrifying shade of orange, and a mash of voices pour forth from his mouth. It meant that the Cassini had taken hold of him.

Although it lasted barely a minute, Triana always found herself shaking by the time it ended, often clutching herself with both arms, anxious for it to end, unable to relax until Bon's normal shade of ice-blue seeped back into his eyes.

This would likely be the final set of instructions for navigating out of the belt. Already the number of rock chunks and ice balls had plummeted; what lay before them, other than a second ring called the Oort Cloud, was cold, empty space.

Truly empty, they hoped.

Triana placed her hand on the back of Bon's chair. He responded by looking up at her, his usual blank expression revealing nothing.

"Well?" she said. "Finished?"

"Yeah," Bon said, punching one final key with a flourish. "Not much of a change, really. I think we're basically out."

The words sent a shiver through her. The Kuiper Belt had been a two-month game of dodge ball, with destruction always a possibility. And yet, at the same time, it had also acted as a security blanket, preventing anything from outside the solar system from reaching them. *Galahad* had now rocketed into the great unknown.

"I'll let the crew know," she said, quickly regaining her composure. "Any other information from our friends?"

Bon shook his head. "No, just this final course correction. I got the feeling that they were washing their hands of us . . . for now. Of course," he added, "it would probably be a good idea for me to check back in to make sure."

Triana looked down at the Swede. On more than one occasion he had subtly suggested that she allow him to keep the translator. She tried to read his face, but came up empty. "Right," she said quietly. "Well, we'll talk about that."

She turned and made her way to an empty workstation and sat down. "Roc," she called out, "analysis of the space up ahead."

The computer's voice responded. "Dark and empty. Reminds me a lot of Gap's head."

"Be nice," Triana said with a smile. "What about our course to Eos? How far off have we veered?"

"Not too bad, but it will take some more adjustments once we're safely out of any danger of getting creamed by a stray boulder. Not that the super brains on Titan seem to care about our travel plans."

Triana said, "I know, you don't care for them. But they did get us through this mess safely. Can't you show a little gratitude?"

"Hmph, if you say so."

"All right, go ahead and pout because you weren't the hero this time. Anything else to report?"

Roc was silent for a moment before answering. "Nothing. All systems on the ship are fine, the path ahead is pretty much clear, and I think I set a new record for solving Rubik's Cube."

"Congratulations."

"Don't think I don't hear the sarcasm in your voice," Roc said. "Let's see *you* try it with no hands."

Triana pushed back her chair and stood. "I'll be in Engineering if you need to brag about anything else."

Bon had finished his work, and joined her as she walked toward the lift. She sensed that he wanted to say something to her, but kept quiet. They had just stepped into the lift when she heard Roc call out from the Control Room.

"Uh-oh."

Triana put her hand up to stop the door from closing, then stepped back out of the lift. "What is it?"

Roc's playful tone had evaporated. "There's something up ahead. And it's not a chunk of rock or ice."

Triana's gaze shot quickly up to the large vidscreen. It showed only inky blackness, with a panorama of softly twinkling stars. She squinted, trying to make out any unusual object.

"Correction," Roc said. "Lots of somethings."

3

With all of the drama you juggle each and every day, it's a won-der to me that humans are able to sleep at all. Roy—my creator—once bragged that he only needed three hours of sleep each day; any more than that, he said, was a waste of his valuable time. Experts would tell him that he's (a) not allowing his body to recover from the stresses of the previous day, and (b) not allowing his brain to process and filter all of the information that it soaked in during that day.

I know that you're already enormously jealous of me, but here's another tidbit that you'll hate: I don't sleep at all. Not even a catnap.

That means I don't have to deal with nightmares, which occur dur-ing REM sleep, or night terrors, which happen earlier in the sleep cycle, and are seldom remembered.

I don't know what you'd call Alexa's dreams . . . just be glad you don't have them.

It was the worst part of her job, but Lita understood that it had to be done. She had followed her mother's path into medicine in order to help people, and to bring a gentle, human touch into circumstances where people were rarely at their best. All of that inspired her. Writing these reports, however, did not.

In earlier days, she realized, it was much worse. Back then it was pure paperwork, and entailed endless hours hunched over a desk with mounds of paper piled up on all sides. Today it was all keyboards and touch screens, and could be accomplished in a fraction of the time.

It didn't make it any more enjoyable, however. "I'm a book-keeper as much as a doctor," she thought, keying in another entry from the previous day's physicals.

Keeping all 251 crew members fit was a top priority of the five-year mission. They had been quarantined during the final thirty days before the launch from Earth. Holed up inside the Incubator, isolated from all outside human contact, it was hoped they would begin their journey without carrying along the worst kind of baggage: Earth's collection of infectious diseases. Then, once on their way, it was Bon's job to produce a healthy balance of foods in the two domes that sat atop the ship, and Channy's responsibility to drive each of them during their daily workouts.

Lita's role was to monitor their medical data on a regular basis, which meant brief assessments every ninety days. Space travel was a challenge to the human body; fortunately the ship's artificial gravity eliminated the problem of bone and muscle atrophy, and the combination of proper diet and exercise kept their cardiovascular systems running smoothly.

Still, Dr. Zimmer had stressed the importance of staying on top of everything, not allowing any condition to fester and lead to complications. The physicals, while necessary, meant several hours of record keeping. Lita's top assistant, Alexa, handled the bulk of the filing, but it was easily a job for two.

Lita pushed her chair back from the desk and rubbed her eyes. The constant staring at the vidscreen always sapped her energy. She looked across the room and found Alexa staring back at her.

"Having fun?" Lita said before noticing the expression on her friend's face, a look that caused her to sit up straight. "Hey, everything okay?"

Alexa continued to stare through her for a moment, then blinked and offered a slight smile. "Uh, sure. Just thinking."

Lita hesitated before offering the question that was on her mind. "Been dreaming again, haven't you?"

Alexa blinked again, then looked down at her work. She said nothing.

"Wanna talk about it?" Lita said gently. "I know it troubles you; maybe it wouldn't be as . . . as heavy . . . if you talked about it."

When Alexa still didn't respond, Lita wondered if she had made the situation worse by adding a new level of pressure. The truth was, she wanted Alexa to open up and discuss the prophetic dreams that tormented her, but she wanted her to do it without feeling as if she was being analyzed or tested. For weeks Lita had allowed her friend the privacy that she seemed to long for; at the same time, might it be better if she shared the fears that obviously weighed on her?

They had developed a close bond from the moment they met, and the two years they had trained and worked together had only cemented their relationship. When it had fallen on Lita to operate on Alexa in order to save her life, she might just as well have been rescuing her own sister. And, when things had initially turned scary, Lita's pain was unbearable.

Since then, a veil had somehow dropped between them; their relationship was still good, but a shift had occurred. Lita knew that most of it was the result of the gift of future-sight that had befallen the medical assistant following her surgery—if *gift* was the right word. Lita suspected that it was more likely a curse.

The week before, Alexa had marked her sixteenth birthday, a day that normally would have found the two of them celebrating. Instead, Alexa had requested the day off, complaining of a headache, and spent the entire day in her room. Lita had dropped by with birthday greetings, but their visit had seemed rigid, uncomfortable.

Lita mourned the loss of their special connection, but held out hope that it was temporary.

For now, she decided that a good friend should never shy away from trying to help. "I know this is awkward for you," she said to Alexa, "but we've been friends a long time. I really think it would make you feel better if you talked about it."

After another moment of hesitation, Alexa looked up at Lita. "I have talked about it, actually. I don't know if it makes me feel any better, but . . . but Bon and I talk about things every few days."

Bon and Alexa.

Although Lita knew that their bizarre mental transformations had created a unique link between them, it was startling to imagine Bon showing that much interest in someone, or opening up to her. His personality was nothing like Alexa's.

Or, at least, it hadn't been. Things on *Galahad* had changed so much in less than a year.

"Do you feel like it helps you?" Lita said.

Alexa shrugged. "Yes and no. I guess it feels good to talk about it with someone who understands . . ." She paused, a sudden look of alarm on her face. "Not that you don't understand. I mean, he just . . . I mean—"

"It's okay, I get it," Lita said with a smile. "You're both experiencing things that the rest of us might never really understand. It's natural for you guys to grow close." She chuckled. "Well, I take that back, it might be natural for *you,* but not our Nordic Grump."

Alexa smiled back. "Oh, he's not as bad as most people think."

With raised eyebrows, Lita said, "Oh, really?"

A blush spread across Alexa's face. "Stop it. We just talk. You're starting to sound like Channy."

Lita raised her hands, palms up. "I'm not saying anything." Then her face grew serious again. "But you said yes and no. What's the no?"

"Well, it gets stuff off my chest, but . . . but verbalizing it almost makes it seem more . . . I don't know, concrete, I guess. When it's just a dream, I can treat it that way. When I talk about it, though, it's like I'm . . ." She trailed off.

Lita said, "Yes?"

Alexa exhaled loudly. "When I talk about it, it's like I'm planning it, or something. Like it's all my doing."

"You know that's not true, though," Lita said.

"Of course I do, but you know how our brains work. Rational and logical don't always win out."

Lita nodded. "Well, I can tell from your face that you've had another experience. I just want you to know that you can talk to me about it, too. I might not have Bon's exact frame of reference, but I might be able to help you sort things out."

"And I appreciate that, I really do," Alexa said. She smiled. "I might be a weirdo these days, but I'm still glad you're my friend." She seemed to think hard for a moment. "And you're right, I did have another episode last night. I . . . I just don't think I can talk about it right now. I haven't even told Bon yet."

"Okay, I won't pressure you," Lita said. "As long as you know I'm here."

Alexa smiled again, then bent back over her work.

Lita decided to give her some privacy for a moment. She stood up and walked out to the corridor. A good five-minute walk would do her good anyway, blow out some of the carbon, clear her mind a bit, and prepare her for another hour-long session of staring at a vidscreen.

As she walked she wondered what it must be like to carry the burden that Alexa did. Some people wished for the ability to see the future; apparently those who could do so would trade it away in an instant.

"Would I want to know?" Lita thought, walking with her head down and her hands behind her back. "Would I?"

* * *

The cursor on the vidscreen before her blinked patiently, but Channy's fingers rested without movement on the keyboard. Three drafts of the letter had come to life, and almost immediately had been discarded. The fourth didn't seem to be coming at all.

Talking with Taresh had come easily at first, when there were no feelings involved. Now that he occupied her thoughts on a regular basis, she found that her words sounded clumsy and forced. Things had been fine until the night before, when she had awkwardly pursued questions about his family, his hobbies, and—she sighed just remembering it—his cultural background. When he had finally lapsed into a quiet stage, Channy realized she had been very obvious.

But, she asked herself, so what? What's wrong with letting someone know that you're interested? Why should games always be a part of the early relationship dance?

She hadn't convinced herself.

After leaving Triana and Lita at breakfast, she decided to make a quick stop at her room and compose a brief note to Taresh. Its primary function was to save face from her enthusiastic gushing of the night before, but also to reinforce the fact that she was interested in more than just a simple friendship. Subtle, yet direct, she decided.

Except subtle was a suppressed gene in Channy's molecular makeup.

"C'mon," she said to herself, wiggling her fingers above the keys. Nothing came.

She stood up with a huff, pushed back her chair, and marched a small circle around her desk. "What's so hard about this?" she said. "Just tell him. 'Hey, I like you, I think we could have a lot of fun together, I'll let you skip an occasional workout in the gym.'"

She stopped, turned, and paced in the opposite direction. "'Look, no pressure, I understand you want to take it slow, so do I, we can maybe have lunch tomorrow, may I kiss you, please? No, forget I said that! I was just kidding. No, really, I think you're an amazing guy, and—'"

She had come full circle again around the desk, and plopped back into her chair. "Aarrgh! This is not difficult, Channy! Quit being so odd!"

What made it all the more frustrating was her own reputation. Often hailed as the ship's unofficial matchmaker, she prided herself on her ability to detect hidden romantic feelings between crew members. More than once she had murmured sly comments to those involved, which brought either a hail of denials—guilty, lame denials though they were—or flushed looks of embarrassment.

So how could she, *Galahad's* resident Cupid, suddenly find herself at a loss when it came to her *own* emotions? This was unacceptable.

On more than one occasion she had been called on it. Lita had often responded to Channy's romantic meddling by asking, "And what about you?"

She had been crafty in deflecting all such questions, using her wit and charm to divert attention away from her own love life. No one had pressed the issue, which had been a blessing for Channy because of the secret that she kept hidden from everyone.

Deep down, she was terrified of falling for someone.

Whenever the possibility had presented itself, she had moved in another direction, afraid of taking the chance, of opening up her heart. It was much easier, she decided, to occupy herself with everyone else's pursuits. No chance of getting hurt when you kept yourself out of the game.

The trick had been to keep a clamp on her emotions and not allow herself to spiral in too closely to someone. Taresh, however, had caught her off guard. His soft-spoken demeanor made for an interesting combination with his strong presence. It had an intoxicating effect on the young Brit, and she was stunned when it dawned on her: she had fallen hard for him.

Her inexperience, however, soon became apparent, culminating with the embarrassing exchange the night before. It was the reason she believed some damage control was called for.

This left her now, sitting again, staring at the flickering cursor on the vidscreen.

She sighed. Her hands flew across the keys, two quick paragraphs, hastily written. Punching the final period, her finger hovered above the Send key. After another moment of hesitation, it fell hard on the key, and the message was away.

Five seconds later she groaned aloud. "Oh, no, what have I done?"

She sat back and laced her fingers together over her head. She stared at the vidscreen's mocking text: Message Sent.

In an instant her mind raced through every possible fix. She would immediately write back to Taresh and tell him it was a joke. No, she would simply act like she'd never sent it, never acknowledge anything, and ignore him for a month. No, she would ask Kylie, her roommate, to snoop around and find out if Taresh was saying anything about the email to his friends.

No.

No, she would own up to it. She would accept the fact that she had fired off an email in an emotionally unbalanced state, that she had opened herself to embarrassment and ridicule. She would live with the consequences, no matter what they might be.

And then she would go to the Spider bay, open the hatch, and jump off the ship.

An alarm sounded in Triana's head. Roc, for all of his glib humor and often reckless attitude, knew when to stow the comedy and get down to work. There was a definite tone he was able to summon in that manufactured voice that said, "This is no joking matter."

That tone was in effect now.

Triana walked briskly back to the empty workstation in *Galahad*'s Control Room. "Explain, Roc. What's out there?"

"Can't get a visual fix on them. I count . . ." He paused. ". . . between eight and ten. Small. Fast. Very quick in their maneuvering. Makes it hard to get a good read on them."

"Wait," Triana said, "slow down. Did you say maneuvering?"

"I did. It's what brought them to my attention in the first place. Things out here . . . well, they tend to go about their business in one direction, right? Until they bump into something, or get tugged by gravity. But even then they just bend a little bit." The computer hesitated before adding, "These little devils are darting in several directions."

"Location?" Triana said.

Roc seemed to calculate for a moment. "Straight ahead, swirling along both sides of our path. They were scattered when I first picked them up, spread out over a pretty large distance. But now they've collected themselves. They're like . . ." He didn't finish.

Triana turned to Bon, who had followed her to the workstation. "Please find Gap and get him up here." She then looked back at the vidscreen, peering through the star field, searching . . . for what? Her mind tried to fill in several blanks at once.

The dread that had clawed for attention the past few weeks pushed its way back in. Triana recalled the suggestions made by both Bon and Alexa that something might be waiting on the other side of the Kuiper Belt. Neither of them could say what that something might be, nor could they offer any explanation for their feelings. Which, Triana decided, had made it even worse. Every horror movie fan knew that the terror didn't come when the monster jumped out at you; no, the real panic lurked in the shadows, torturing you with what *might* be there.

She bit her lip and looked around the Control Room. The smattering of crew members on duty—it never totaled more than five or six—seemed as nervous as she, most of them taking quick, furtive glances at the vidscreen. Roc's vague description of the unexpected company ahead had altered the mood; if Bon's heavy disposition had cast a gloom over the setting, it now had an overlapping tinge of fear.

The crew of *Galahad* had already experienced more than their share of the mysterious unknown, but that didn't make each new incident any less ominous. They were constantly reminded of their vulnerability.

And, she thought grimly, they would always be the outsiders, the new guys on every new block. Always trespassing.

Another three minutes passed before Triana heard the lift door open. She glanced around to see Gap striding up to her. He apparently read her face instantly.

"What's going on?" he said.

Triana shrugged. "Roc says there are . . . things up ahead. Unidentified, and hard to pin down."

Like everyone else in the room, Gap peered up at the large vidscreen. "Things? Not rock or ice chunks, I take it."

"They're maneuvering."

Gap's head snapped around, and he stared hard at Triana. "Maneuvering? So they're not natural." He paused. "What do you think—"

"I have no idea what to think," Triana said. She turned her attention back to the panel before her. "Roc, how long until they reach us?"

The computer's voice replied, "Oh, they're not approaching. They're circling in our path, waiting for us to reach *them*. At least we have some prep time. I estimate we'll make contact in roughly . . . fifty minutes."

Gap nudged Triana. "Let me in here a minute." He punched a few keys, looked at the results on the small screen before him, then keyed in a few more entries. A minute later he looked up at Triana.

"Yeah, they're on both sides of our path." He stood up and looked toward the large vidscreen again. "Ever seen a marathon? You know how people line the sides of the streets to either applaud the runners or hand them a cup of water? That's what this is like; we have a little group of spectators waiting to welcome us."

A shiver went down Triana's neck. "Have you been able to tell anything else about them? What size are we talking about?"

Roc said, "Best guess would be about the size of a large bird. This, by the way, lends itself to the comparison I was going to make earlier, and one that is much better than Gap's silly marathon analogy."

"Which is?" Triana said.

"I'd say they're behaving more like vultures, circling over the spot where a varmint is about to collapse in the heat of the desert."

Triana's shoulders sagged. "Great."

"And," Roc added, "they have the mobility of birds, too. What we've got here, ladies and gentleman, are space vultures."

The words hung in the air of the Control Room, and Triana felt the atmosphere of dread tick upward another notch. Her mind sifted through their options, but only one idea came to her.

"Should we change course?"

"These things are incredibly quick," Roc said. "They have already responded to our approach and placed themselves in position to intercept us. We can't run away from them.

"I'm afraid," the computer continued, "that we're left with no choice but to plunge right through them." After a pause, he added, "Gee, I hope they're friendly."

4

Channy sat with her feet dangling from the stage of the auditorium, staring out at a sea of mostly empty seats. She worked hard to keep a look of irritation off her face, and kept reminding herself that it was still early.

Behind her, on the stage, a crew of hastily assembled volunteers arranged a series of chairs, while others finished placing decorations that mostly resembled Valentine's Day at an elementary school. Oversized pink and red hearts, along with improvised images that were meant to represent Cupid in a variety of poses, either hung from drop lines or trumpeted from the backs of chairs and podiums. After starting and stopping a few times, the soft sounds of what passed for romantic music drifted from the room's speaker system.

Channy bumped her heels against the front of the stage and drummed her fingers across the floor. She watched one of the auditorium's doors open and admit a smiling Lita, who strolled down the aisle.

"Hey, it looks really good, Channy. Very bright, very festive."

"Very empty," Channy said, gesturing toward the seats.

Lita sized up the situation and offered a look of pity. "It doesn't start for another fifteen minutes. Nobody will ever want to be the first one here, you know that."

"I smell a disaster."

"Oh, stop that," Lita said, swatting Channy on the leg. "It's the first Dating Game, and you knew it was going to be a challenge." She pulled herself up onto the stage and sat with her arm around *Galahad*'s Activities/Nutrition Director.

"I know you don't want to hear this," Lita said, "but now you know why I suggested you do this in the Dining Hall. At least the first one." She waved her arm to indicate the room. "This is a very big space."

"Because it's a big event," Channy said defensively. "Or at least it should be. You have to think big, you know."

Lita seemed to measure her words before answering. "You have no problem thinking big, Channy. It's too bad not everyone shares your enthusiasm all the time. But you know how human nature works."

Channy grunted. "You mean to act like big chickens?"

"No. Sometimes people have to warm up to things, that's all."

A door opened at the top of an aisle and a girl peeked inside for a quick moment, before disappearing again and closing the door. Channy shook her head.

"That's happened about ten times. If there were even a few more people in the seats they would come in and sit down. They'd sit as far back as they could, but at least they'd come in." She turned to look at Lita. "Where's the rest of the Council, anyway? You'd think I'd at least get some support there."

"Something's happening in the Control Room," Lita said.

"Right. A likely story."

Lita shook her head. "No, seriously. Triana didn't tell me much, but said that they're checking something out." She paused and patted Channy's shoulder. "C'mon, you know Triana supports everything you do on this ship."

"Except this. She's afraid I'll stick her up here on stage as a contestant. And what about Bon? What about Gap?"

"Gap's in the Control Room with Triana. And who are you kidding about Bon?"

Channy quietly stared into the room.

"You still have fifteen minutes," Lita said.

"Five."

"Okay, five minutes. Just start a few minutes late and I'll bet you'll see a bunch of people wander in. You know that curiosity will start to work on them."

As she said this, the door opened and three crew members walked in, snickering among themselves as they took seats in the back.

"See?" Lita said, beaming. "It's already started."

"Wonderful," Channy said sarcastically. "At this rate we'll have more contestants on stage than in the seats."

"Well, I'll be in the seats," Lita said, hopping off the stage and turning to look back. "Do not—repeat, do not—call me up there. In fact . . ." She turned back toward the door. "I'll go find Alexa to sit with me. That's another warm body for you."

"Grab everybody you see on the way," Channy called out to her. "Threaten them with tetanus shots if they don't come."

should do something," Triana thought. "There should be something that I can do."

And yet the harder she concentrated on the situation, the more she realized that they were helpless to do anything at the moment. *Galahad* sped toward a rendezvous with as many as ten unidentified objects that loomed ahead, circling like vultures, as Roc had put it. There was no way to stop, no way to maneuver, which would be useless anyway, given the agility of the mysterious strangers. There remained but one question.

What would happen at the point of contact?

Triana kept her voice low as she spoke to both Gap and Roc. "Can we survive a collision?"

Gap responded with a similar hushed tone, never taking his eyes off his control panel. "We don't even know what they are, so there's no way to predict what would happen. I can't believe they would just let us slam into them, though. A suicide job makes no sense. Besides . . . wait a minute." He punched in a quick adjustment on the keyboard.

"What?" Triana said.

It was Roc who answered. "Well, isn't this interesting."

"What is it?" Triana said again. "Tell me."

"Apparently they don't want to stop us," Roc said. "I think they intend to hitch a ride."

Gap's face displayed shock as he looked at Triana. "We are officially the fastest object in the history of our solar system. We should zip past these . . . whatever they are . . . in a microsecond. But . . . this is incredible."

Before Triana could sputter another demand for information, Roc chimed in. "They have gone from circling in one spot to an acceleration that doesn't seem possible. They have adapted to our course, and are suddenly rocketing along almost as fast as we are. That changes our time of contact, of course. With their new speed and trajectory, we have a whopping ninety-five minutes until we are rubbing shoulders . . . or wings . . . or whatever these things have."

Gap shook his head. "I don't know how they did it, but suddenly they're pacing us." He looked up at the room's vidscreen. "Nothing should be able to accelerate that fast."

Triana was again aware of the atmosphere in the Control Room, and tried to modulate her response to cloak any sign of panic. "Well, I guess that rules out any intention of collision." She bit her lip for a moment before continuing. "Is there something we can do to keep them away from the ship? Maybe some sort of electrical charge on the outside?"

The silence from Gap and Roc answered the question.

"Well," she said, "what about rocking the ship, or going into some sort of controlled spin?"

"No," Gap said. "I think we need to accept the fact that these things are going to catch us and grab hold. I'm not sure that would cause any problems, actually."

"Unless they cut their way into the ship," Roc added. "Or oozed some sort of acid that ate its way through the skin of the ship. Or physically started eating the ship. My, imagine that; actually eating the steel of our ship."

"Stop," Triana said.

"How can that not fascinate you?" the computer asked. "Or what if they—"

Gap interrupted. "Tree, do you, uh, want to make some sort of announcement to the crew?"

The idea had flashed through her mind. Would it make sense to warn the crew of their impending contact, or better to just wait and see what happened. After a moment's hesitation, she shook her head.

"Later. Let's see if the situation changes in the next half hour or so." She took a few steps away from the console and stood with one hand on her hip, the other cupped around her chin. She studied the large vidscreen that refused to divulge any sign of the vultures.

One thing after another, after another, after another . . .

Triana could pick up the uncomfortable vibe of the room, the tinge of fear that seeped from each crew member. She marveled at how quickly the aura of the group had shifted from when she had first walked in. Bon was absent, and the unease he triggered was now replaced by alarm of the unknown.

It was a feeling that apparently the crew of *Galahad* should get used to, she realized.

She turned to Gap. "We're certain about the time until contact?"

He glanced at his monitor, and then back to her. "Yes. Just over ninety minutes."

"Okay," she said, walking toward the door of the lift. "I'll be back in forty-five. If anything changes, call me immediately. I'll be in my room."

A puzzled look spread across Gap's face, but he mumbled a quick "sure" before bending back to his monitor.

Three minutes later Triana sat down at the desk in her room. As the Council Leader, she had the luxury of solitude, the only crew member without a roommate. At times like this, she was grateful.

"Roc," she called out.

The computer responded at once. "Don't you just love this? Another big adventure. Some people go their whole lives without a whiff of excitement, and yet we could practically bottle the stuff."

"I think I speak for the rest of the crew when I say that we could use a nice, long, boring stretch. Like about four years' worth."

"Are you sure?" Roc said. "It's all in your perspective; just think how battle-tested you'll be once you reach Eos. At this rate, there won't be a thing that could surprise you at your new home. Wouldn't want to sail all the way there without a little conflict now and then; you'd show up lazy and complacent."

Triana responded with a grunt of skepticism, then changed the subject. "Listen, I didn't want to talk about this in the Control Room, in front of the crew."

"I knew that's what you were doing," Roc said. "Either that or a quick bathroom break."

She ignored this. "After our misunderstanding of the Cassini, I'm a little hesitant to assume the intentions of anything we might encounter out here in the middle of nowhere. But it would be irresponsible of me to not assume that these . . . vultures, or whatever you want to call them, are dangerous."

"I agree," the computer said.

"And it would also be irresponsible of me, as the Council Leader, to not take every precaution possible to protect this ship."

"Again, I concur."

Triana paused for a moment before continuing. She tapped a finger on her desk and said, "I hate to be the aggressor in a situation like this, but . . ." Her voice trailed off.

Roc filled the empty silence that followed. "You know, even though I'm not human, I know your species, and I know your history. I have read practically everything ever written—well, except some of those romance novels; I get easily embarrassed—and your history texts are full of instances where people fall back on one particular rule."

Triana obliged the computer by asking the obvious question. "And what rule is that?"

"Shoot first, ask questions later."

There was another long silence. "Well," Triana finally offered, "that's kinda what I was getting around to. My question for you is: Do we have anything to shoot with?"

"What do you mean? You know this ship isn't equipped—"

"I know what we've been told," Triana interjected. "I know that Dr. Zimmer didn't have the time or resources to build a traditional weapons system into the ship."

"So," Roc said, "what are you suggesting?"

Triana tapped her finger a few more times. "I'm suggesting that there might be something in the Storage Sections for us to use."

"Ah-ha," Roc said. "Silly me. I never saw your mind going in that direction."

Triana chose to remain silent for the moment and wait for the computer to answer her charge. But her mind, in fact, had gone in that particular direction the moment she had learned that the vultures were pacing the ship. *Galahad* was essentially a modern *Mayflower*, delivering the human race to a new world, full of new opportunities, new challenges. But it also was a ship of peace; there were no weapons of any kind aboard.

Or were there?

The crew had been trained in every aspect of the immense ship, and they were intimately aware of every square inch of their home-away-from-home . . . with one exception.

Dr. Zimmer had insisted that the teenage crew remain in the dark about the last components to be loaded aboard before launch. Dubbed only as the Storage Sections, they occupied the majority of *Galahad*'s lowest level. Dark passageways surrounded these impenetrable vaults. The contents were a mystery, one that would not be revealed until the young explorers entered the space around Eos, now a little more than four years away.

"It's for your own good," was all that Dr. Zimmer would say when pressed. "You won't need any of it until you arrive. The best thing for you to do is simply forget that the Storage Sections even exist. Go about your days without even thinking of them."

But it was impossible to assemble a crew of the best and brightest and not expect insatiable curiosity. If Zimmer had known it would have this effect, he hadn't let it influence his decision. The crew would not know the contents until the end of the ride.

But Roc *did* know.

When it was obvious that he would not volunteer any more information, Triana stopped tapping her finger and sat back. "I'm not asking for an inventory, you understand, right? I'm only suggesting that if there's something in there that could help us defend ourselves, this might be a good time to open up."

She paused before adding, "In fact, it might be our *last* time to open up."

"We don't know what these vultures really are," Roc said. "They might be harmless."

"They might not be."

"Perhaps they intend to just look at us."

"Perhaps they intend to do more."

"You like arguing, don't you?" Roc said.

"And you don't?"

"I can't tell you what's inside the Storage Sections."

Triana let out a slow breath. "Even if it could save us."

The computer mimicked her dramatic exhale. "I'm not able to confirm or deny that anything exists within those units that might, or might not, be able to help. Humans are prone to break sworn promises; I'm not capable of that. I don't blame you for asking; in fact, I think it's rather ingenious of you to ask. But stop asking."

For the third time, silence blanketed the room. Triana waited for the stalemate to end, then accepted defeat.

"Okay. Can you think of anything we might do to protect ourselves?"

The computer seemed to consider the question for a minute. "Well, I'm sure you don't want to hear this, but the best thing to do is wait until we know more about these things. Then there might be an obvious answer. You might not need your average, everyday shoot-'em-up gun."

Triana bit her lip. She didn't like the idea of playing defensively, but couldn't see another option at the moment.

In eighty-five minutes, she realized, they might run out of options entirely.

5

The girl on the stage was quite obviously nervous, sitting on her hands, swinging her feet back and forth under the chair. Her attention swept between her friends sitting in the auditorium and the two boys sitting across from her. Both boys were going to immense pains to seem casual and comfortable, sitting back in their chairs, even leaning back on two legs from time to time; but nervous tics and laughter betrayed this facade.

Channy stood in the center of the stage and addressed the modest crowd. "This has flown by pretty fast, but now you all know how it works, so I'm sure we'll have more contestants next time. As you can see, nobody got embarrassed up here, and nobody had a massive heart attack and fell out of their chair."

She waited for the polite laughter to subside before saying, "So, thanks to a few brave souls who came forward as volunteers, we all know how easy this is. Which brings us to our final contestant this evening." She turned to the nervous girl seated next to her. "Antoinette is sixteen, was born and raised in England . . ."

Channy paused and addressed the crowd, exaggerating her British accent: "Of course, all of the coolest people on *Galahad* hail from the U.K., right?" This brought even more laughter, and a few hoots from the crowd. In the third row, Lita turned to whisper to Alexa.

"She's a natural at this, you know?"

"I'm glad she's having fun," Alexa whispered back. "She's put a lot into the whole thing."

Lita glanced around before responding. "For all of her worrying, it's not a bad turnout. Probably fifty people, wouldn't you say?"

Alexa nodded, and both girls turned their attention back to the stage.

"Antoinette is currently assigned to the Farms," Channy said. "Although she notes, 'I'm anxious to rotate out in a few weeks, because I dislike dirty hands and fingernails.'" This brought a few more chuckles from the crowd, spurred on by Channy's dramatic gestures and facial expressions. "I don't know, Antoinette, I'm sure Bon would give you a day off if you broke a nail."

Lita and Alexa joined in the laughter. Onstage, Antoinette turned a shade of red and kicked her feet a little more quickly.

"All right, let's say hello to the two very cool gentlemen to my left," Channy said. "Andrei is seventeen, comes to us from Moscow, and apparently does not believe in haircuts. He is presently on his six-week break, lucky guy, and enjoys working out and solving extreme math problems." She smiled at him. "Brains and brawn; a Mr. Galahad if I ever saw one."

She then focused on the other boy. "Next to Andrei we have Karl, a native of Düsseldorf. He is currently assigned to the kitchen crew, and enjoys Airboarding and chess. Oh, and today, believe it or not, is Karl's sixteenth birthday." There was a smattering of applause and whistles at the mention of this. "Sorry, my friend," Channy said, "but you will not automatically get the hand of Antoinette as a gift; you must earn it.

"Antoinette has chosen the simple question option. This means that she is eliminating a lot of the usual back-and-forth silliness, and is instead trusting her instincts." Channy held aloft a small index card. "She has already answered this random question, and her answer is stored on the workpad. We will have each of the gentlemen answer the same question, and then post all three on the giant vidscreen behind us. The game is simple: the young man with the answer most similar to Antoinette's will be the winner, and away they will go to a private romantic dinner, where they will get to know each other better and see if those instincts were correct."

Channy took a step toward the front of the stage and lowered her voice. "Of course, if neither of the gentlemen is even close to Antoinette's answer, then she gets to select one of them using a completely different form of instinct, if you know what I mean."

This was greeted with more hoots from the crowd, and Antoinette again went red. Andrei and Karl grinned and continued their relaxed act.

"Okay, gentlemen," Channy said with a flourish, "workpads ready. In twenty-five words or less, please answer this question: What will we find on Eos that will make it the most romantic place in the galaxy? You have two minutes. Begin."

At this cue, a crew member enabled the recorded music that Channy had selected for the Dating Game, and the soft, melodic tones filled the auditorium. The crowd began to talk within their small groups, supplying their own answers to the question, while Andrei and Karl took a moment to think before hunching over the workpads on their laps. Lita and Alexa looked at each other and giggled.

"How much you wanna bet they both say multiple moons, or something like that?" Alexa said.

"Hey, that was the first thing that popped into my head," Lita said with mock indignation. "You have a better answer?"

"No," Alexa admitted. "I only said that because it was the first thing I came up with, too." She looked up at the stage. "I think the object is to try to get into Antoinette's head and guess what *she* would say."

"But that's not right," Lita said. "If it's a game of matching instincts, then the guys should go with their own gut. Otherwise the date is already based on a lie."

"I know that, and you know that," Alexa said. "But look at those two guys. Watch the way they keep glancing at each other. I don't think they really care about Antoinette's answer; they just want to win."

Lita smiled. "I have to give Channy a lot of credit. This game is not only fun for the contestants, it's fun for us, too. Suddenly we're all analysts and relationship experts."

The music came to an end, and Channy moved back to center stage.

"All right," she said, "it's time to compare answers and see which lucky guy has earned a date with the lovely Antoinette." She turned and faced the giant vidscreen at the back of the stage. "The question was: What will we find on Eos that will make it the most romantic place in the galaxy? Let's have Andrei's answer first, please."

There was an electronic version of a drumroll before the screen flickered and the connection was made with Andrei's workpad. The crowd laughed as Channy read his response.

"Northern lights like Earth's aurora borealis, except these lights would dance in sync with the songs of the birds."

Channy put a hand on one hip and gave Andrei a critical look. "My friend, birds don't sing at night."

"They might on Eos," Andrei said with a grin. The crowd clapped its approval of his defense, and he egged them on by giving the "come on" sign with his hands.

"Riiiggghhhttt," Channy said. "Okay, you get points for creativity, but remember, the idea is to come close to the lady's answer. Before we put her answer on the screen, let's see what Karl had to say."

She turned again to the screen and narrated. "Perpetual rainbows."

Oohs and aahs rumbled from the crowd. "Wow," Alexa said to Lita. "They really like his answer."

"Are you kidding?" Lita whispered back. "I *love* his answer!"

Alexa raised her eyebrows. "Well, if Antoinette doesn't get him, *you* should ask him out."

"I might," Lita said with a laugh.

Channy turned back to the audience. "Two excellent answers, wouldn't you say? Let's see if either of them comes close to Antoinette's choice. Are you ready?"

The crowd applauded and whistled. "Okay," Channy said, and faced the nervous girl on the stage. "Antoinette, I tried to read your face when each answer popped up on the screen. As you know, I'm pretty well tuned in to people's emotions." The crowd snickered, and she shot them a warning look that brought laughter. "Oh, it's true, we all know it." She looked back at Antoinette. "I distinctly saw a reaction, and if I'm right, it means that a certain young man from Germany will be dining with you this week."

She pointed to the vidscreen. "What will we find on Eos that will make it the most romantic place in the galaxy? May we please see the lady's answer?"

The vidscreen flickered again, went black, and then lit up with Antoinette's answer. The crowd cheered as Channy read it. "Rainbows every evening! Wow! An exact match! Karl, you're incredible!"

The crowd jumped to their feet, and the applause grew louder. On the stage, Karl stood up, walked over to Antoinette, and took her by the hand. Her face turned a deeper red, and she laughed nervously. Across the stage, even Andrei clapped and grinned.

"Oh well, the one that got away," Lita said with a sigh.

"There's always the aurora borealis guy," Alexa said. "That's romantic, too, you know."

Channy put her hand on Antoinette's shoulder and addressed the crowd. "Can I read people, or what?" She thanked everyone for coming, and announced that a second Dating Game would be forthcoming. There was more applause, and as the music swelled again, the audience turned for the doors.

Two minutes later, Channy was standing in the aisle with Lita and Alexa, beaming.

"See?" Lita said. "A major hit. You were worried for nothing."

"Could've been a few more people in the seats," Channy said.

"That won't be a problem next time," Alexa said. "Did you see the way people were talking when they left? You put on such a great show, it will be packed next month."

"Thank you," Channy said. She batted her eyes. "Anything I can do to promote love. Hopefully this inspired people to stop being so shy all the time."

"Hmm," Lita said. "Did it inspire you?"

"Maybe," Channy said, lifting her chin. "Maybe it did."

On one hand, Triana felt that it was important to hurry back to the Control Room. Another part of her brain, however, suggested that walking—and thinking—could be more beneficial. Away from people, away from the situation, she hoped to at least find clarity, if not answers.

The clock was ticking. In a little over an hour, *Galahad* would plunge into a swarm of darting objects that littered the path ahead. It would be their second alien encounter since leaving Earth.

The first had almost destroyed them.

The lift doors opened onto the lower level of the ship. A left turn would take Triana toward the gym and the Airboarding track. Instead she quickly moved to the right, into the dim corridors that snaked through the Storage Sections. She was confident that she would have this portion of the ship to herself.

She paused momentarily by the large window that looked out upon the dazzling panoramic star field of the Milky Way before putting her head down and moving on.

Her thoughts skipped through a checklist of possibilities regarding their impending rendezvous with the vultures. There might be contact, a collision of sorts, and the consequences of this baffled Triana. The vultures might attack, but what form would that take? There was always the possibility that the vultures might scatter and allow *Galahad* to pass unmolested, but the Council Leader didn't think this likely.

She rounded a turn and slowed her pace, focusing to match her breathing to her steps, a technique that her dad had recommended to help her get centered during times of stress. In a flash her thoughts turned to the man who had meant so much to her.

Her memories stirred, then settled on a sun-filled afternoon, soon after her thirteenth birthday. Sitting in the passenger seat of their car, she had twisted the hair tie around her fingers, stretching it almost to the point of breaking. Her dad maneuvered the car gently along the road that wound into the foothills of the Rocky Mountains just outside of Denver. He glanced at his daughter's hands, watching her stress manifest itself in the bending and stretching of the cloth tie, a faint smile on his lips.

"Still worried?" he said, shifting the car into a lower gear as they began to climb a steep hill.

"No," she said. Then, after a pause: "Yes."

"Wanna talk about it some more?"

Triana watched the replay of her younger self, anguishing over a painful moment that time had somehow sanded away. She did remember, however, what her grumpy reply had been: "Will it change anything?"

Her dad waited before answering, using the time to glance out at the trees racing past, the afternoon sunlight dappling them as it cut through a V in the mountains. Triana always treasured their drives together, most of which were filled with warmth and laughter; many times, however, the front seat became a sanctuary, their private refuge from a confusing world, a place where they could dissect the events of the day, or whatever might be troubling the dark-haired teen.

"Your question says it all," her dad said. "Your energy is concentrated on trying to change something that is out of your control." He threw a quick glance at his daughter before looking back at the road. "There are a lot of things in our lives that we can control, and a lot that we can't. When you get wrapped up in trying to change something that is beyond your power to change, it causes frustration and despair."

Triana continued to work the hair tie, but had now begun to bite her lip. She let her father's words sink in before replying. "So what do I do?"

He took his right hand off the wheel and gently placed it over both of hers. "You stop worrying about things you can't change, and divert your energy to the things you can. One of the most powerful days of your life will be when you learn to tell the difference."

His touch had its usual calming effect. After momentarily tensing, she felt her hands relax. Her breathing slowed, and she leaned her head back against the deep cushion of the seat. She turned to look out the passenger window, taking in the rush of colors, the sharp outline of the craggy hills rising up to pierce the sky, and for a moment a feeling of gratitude replaced the stress that had eaten away at her.

Without her realizing it, the hair tie slipped from her fingers.

Now, almost four years later, Triana paused in the dim corridor of *Galahad*'s lowest level and leaned her back against a wall. The time had come to take inventory of what exactly was in her control, and what wasn't.

The ship would soon reach the contact point with the alien forms they referred to as the vultures; that was inevitable, and no amount of worrying would change that. Her reaction would have to wait until the moment their paths intersected.

Bon's attitude had shifted somewhat since forming a tenuous connection with the Cassini, yet he was often still difficult to communicate with. Again, her reaction was the only thing within her control.

The crew would be apprehensive when they found out about the vultures. That, however, was somewhat within her control because it was one of the responsibilities of leadership: managing the crew.

Her thoughts were interrupted by joyous shouts echoing through the halls, and she knew it likely was a passel of Airboarders celebrating another successful tour of the track and now on their way to the upper levels of the ship. She tapped her heel against the wall and let her mind sift through the remaining obligations of her day, all of which could wait until after the encounter with the vultures.

As she turned to make her way back toward the lift, she could feel her father's warm hand covering hers, and his calm voice: "Learn to tell the difference."

6

Time alone on *Galahad* was a precious commodity, and getting away from 250 crew members could be a challenge. With the crew quarters and most of the primary work and meeting facilities concentrated within the middle decks, it was no surprise that individuals would gravitate to the extreme upper and lower levels to seek escape. Many would sneak away to the lonely corridors near the Storage Sections and Spider bay in the bowels of the ship. With the dim lighting and narrow passageways—not to mention its reputation as the hideout of a maniacal stowaway early in their mission—the area was often described as spooky, and attracted only the hardiest souls.

This left the Domes as the primary getaway location. Prior to launch, noted psychologist Dr. Angela Armistead had briefed the mission's planners that *Galahad*'s young explorers would be naturally drawn to all of the domes' sensory delights, including starlight, gentle breezes—even manufactured ones—and the many smells that would remind them of open fields on Earth. Dr. Zimmer had consequently informed Bon Hartsfield to expect dozens of crew members to tromp through the farms of *Galahad* on a daily basis.

Bon understood as well as anyone, given his own upbringing, and grunted agreement.

Now, as dusk descended upon the ship, he knifed along a path that cut between one section of wheat and another of corn. As the keeper of this domain, he was intimately aware of the least-traveled pathways, and rarely had difficulty finding solitude. He could usually count on this particular route to be quiet, and had shared his secret with only one person.

He pushed aside the arm of a cornstalk that reached across the path, and there she was, sitting cross-legged on the soil in a small clearing. Beside her lay a small, portable lantern that emitted a soft glow, along with two personal water bottles, one of which she held up to him as he came to a stop.

"Thirsty?" Alexa said. Bon accepted the water and stood beside her.

She looked up through the mesh of clear panels that separated *Galahad*'s food supplies from the harsh vacuum of space. "This is my favorite time of day. I love it when the lights go down and the stars turn on."

"Turn on?" Bon said.

She laughed. "Yeah, why not?" Pointing almost directly overhead, she said, "Tonight it was Arcturus that turned on first. That red one, right there."

Bon glanced up momentarily, then back at the blonde girl on the ground. "It's a red giant. Probably similar to what our own sun will look like in a few billion years."

Alexa raised her eyebrows. "Yes, but that's not the good stuff."

Bon shifted his weight to his right foot. "The ancient Polynesians used it to navigate back and forth from Hawaii. Is that the good stuff?"

"No, that's the science. I'm talking about the romance. In Greek mythology, the story of Arcturus was rather sad." When Bon didn't answer, she leaned back on her elbows and stared up into space. "A story of love and jealousy. Would you like to hear it?"

"Mythology doesn't really interest me," Bon said. "There were two kinds of people in those days: those who sat around and made up stories, and those who used the stars to actually get work done."

Alexa laughed. "And there's no question which line you descended from."

A smile flickered across Bon's face. "You're right about that. I'm a farmer, from a long line of farmers. You can thank the stars for teaching my ancestors when the time was right to plant and harvest."

With a bow of her head, Alexa said, "On behalf of my silly romantic ancestors, thank you, thank you very much." She patted the ground beside her. "Have a seat; you make me nervous standing there."

Bon knelt and gently gathered an earthworm that was edging along the soil. He placed it a few feet away, then sat down. "You said in your email that you wanted to talk about something in particular tonight."

His directness never failed to catch Alexa off guard. She took a moment to collect her thoughts before looking into his face.

"I've . . . I've had another vision."

Bon studied her eyes. "You've had several, but you've never looked like this."

She nodded, and her voice fell to a whisper. "This was different."

They sat quietly for a moment. They heard distant laughter from a handful of crew members, but it was obvious they were heading in another direction and would not disturb this small clearing. Alexa fidgeted, looking upward again, toward the starlight that fought its way through the slowly dimming natural light of the dome.

"I wasn't sure I should talk to you about this. Well, talk to anyone about it, actually. But . . . but I knew you would understand better than anyone."

Bon ran a finger through the soil beside him, carving a

miniature channel, before filling it in and starting again a few inches to the side. "Maybe understand isn't the right word. You have visions; I get . . . feelings. They're not the same thing."

"But you understand how difficult it is to be on the receiving end," Alexa said, and offered a smile with a shrug. "You're at least a good listener."

He kept his gaze down at the ground. "Tell me what happened."

Alexa took several deep breaths before responding. "I saw death."

Bon's head snapped up, but he let his face ask the obvious questions.

"I don't know who," Alexa said, "and I don't know how. All I know is that I saw someone's funeral." She spent a minute recounting all that she had seen in her dream, the words picking up intensity as they spilled from her. Bon listened, his finger once again scoring grooves into the dirt. When she lapsed into silence, he spoke.

"You said that people spoke at this . . . this funeral. Couldn't you make out any details, any information about the person?"

Alexa shook her head. "I heard the sounds of people talking, and I understood that it was a eulogy. I don't remember hearing anything specific." She seemed to struggle to find the best description. "You know how you overhear a conversation, and you somehow know what they're talking about without grasping any exact details? Besides, it was a dream, or a vision, or . . . something. It made sense at the time, while I was floating in the middle of it."

Bon nodded. After a moment of hesitation he said, "Do you have any guesses at all? Anything that feels like . . . I don't know, an instinct?"

A small chuckle escaped from Alexa. "Remember, that's *your* specialty. I have the visions, you have the feelings." Then, when he didn't answer, her face grew serious again, and she reached out to place a hand on his knee. "Bon . . . I'm really scared."

He looked at her hand for a moment before covering it with his own. "Yeah, I know. But not all of your visions have necessarily played out, right?"

"I don't know. Some of them have been so unrelated to anything in my experience, I don't know if they're happening or not. I mean, they *seem* to be real."

Bon raised his other hand, palm up. "Right, but isn't it possible that what you're seeing are just possibilities? We barely understand even a fraction of the way the universe works, but we know that there are an infinite number of possible outcomes. It's like . . . like an infinitely long hallway, with an infinite number of doors, all with a different future. Isn't it possible that your mind is simply opening doors at random, and seeing something that might—or might not—happen?"

They both seemed to consider this, although Alexa's face betrayed skepticism. The sounds of scattered activity around the dome filtered across the fields to their isolated setting, along with the gurgle of an irrigation pump two or three rows away.

"Are we going to get wet?" Alexa said, peering through the leaves.

A wry smile worked across Bon's face. "I adjusted the system to skip this spot for another hour."

Alexa grinned back, and gave his knee a small squeeze. "Wow, it's nice to know the manager of the place."

They remained that way for a minute, taking in the sounds, the smells, the atmosphere of their oasis of solitude. Finally, Alexa removed her hand and pulled her hair behind her ears.

"I suppose you might be right. I'm not even sure what I could do, anyway. I don't think I should tell Triana." She hesitated, as if waiting for agreement. When it didn't come, she asked. "Do you?"

Bon shrugged. "What if you wait to see if it happens again? You're right; I don't know what anyone could do without more information. Maybe you'll . . . I don't know, see something else that might help."

"I'd have to go back through that same door," she said.

The gurgle of the irrigation pump was replaced by the thump of water pressure kicking up a notch. From twenty feet away they could hear water flicking across leaves. Alexa began to think that Bon's attention had been diverted back to his work until he fixed her with a look.

"Perhaps," he said, "you have some control over which door you open."

She studied his face, as an image of endless possibilities opened before her.

Gap hunched over his workstation in the Control Room, shifting back and forth between two monitors, oblivious, it seemed, to the activity going on around him. Triana twice attempted to communicate with him, but gave up; with only minutes remaining until *Galahad* streaked through the cluster of vultures, his mind was locked onto the task of determining the outcome.

The fact that there were too many unknowns in the equation didn't seem to make a difference to him.

With a sigh, he finally pushed back from his station and looked around the room to find Triana. She threw another fruitless glance at the large vidscreen before walking over to stand next to him. He seemed to understand what question her raised eyebrows implied.

"The best I can figure out," he said, "is that there are close to ten of these things out there. They're not that big, which makes them tough to nail down, and they're in constant movement. They flit around almost like moths near a light."

Triana nodded, even though this wasn't exactly new information. She knew that Gap was doing the best he could, with an enthusiasm she hadn't seen from him in a while. He recently had battled discouragement over his contributions—or his perceived lack of contributions—to the mission; in a way, for Gap the intrigue brought on by the vultures was good medicine.

Roc chimed in with his own observations. "Their wingspan is approximately one meter across, their composition is unknown, and their sense of drama is impeccable."

"Can anyone make an educated guess what will happen when we cross paths?" Triana said. "I'm hearing a lot of 'I don't know,' so how about a few cases of 'I think.'"

"I think their mission is to either check us out as we shoot by, or try to board us," Gap said.

"I agree," Roc said. "They are obviously quite advanced technologically, if they were able to spot us, plot our course, and arrange to intercept us; crashing into us would not make much sense. Ever seen a bug hit a windshield? Yuck."

Triana looked at Gap. "All right. How much time?"

"Two minutes."

With a determined step, Triana walked to her command post and punched the intercom, which fed the entire ship.

"If I could have your attention," she said, keeping her voice as calm as possible. "We have picked up some sort of escort out of the Kuiper Belt. Eight to ten objects, roughly the size of large birds. They are pacing us, and appear to want to make contact." She paused, and could only imagine the impact these words were having upon a stunned crew. Swallowing hard, she began again. "I have no idea what we can expect; maybe a jolt, maybe something more violent. But whatever it might be, it's going to happen in about one minute. Please prepare yourself."

She snapped off the intercom and wondered exactly what that preparation would consist of. Holding on to something? Sitting down?

Roc began a countdown. "Thirty seconds to contact . . . twenty . . . ten . . ."

Triana found herself unconsciously reaching out and grasping the arm of Gap, who responded by putting one hand on her back. They both stared at the large vidscreen.

Suddenly Gap cried out. "Did you see that?"

Triana strained her eyes. "I didn't see—"

But then she did. At the extreme edges of the screen, on both sides, wispy black shapes, almost appearing to be doing cartwheels, spinning, vibrating, flew into her field of vision. They flashed briefly, a muted shade of blue-green, and then were gone.

Half a minute elapsed, with no sound from anyone, and no apparent reaction from *Galahad*. Triana gradually let go of Gap's arm. He kept his hand on the small of her back. They looked at each other without saying a word.

Finally, one of the other crew members on duty in the Control Room spoke up. "What happened? Did they miss us?"

Gap bent back over the panel before him, but it was Roc who answered.

"At the point of intercept we were able to positively identify eight of them. They are no longer registering. Wait, check that. I have one vulture, trailing us . . . now peeling off."

Triana considered this. "And the other seven?"

"I have to assume," Roc said, "that they have indeed grabbed hold of us, and are comfortably attached to the outside of our ship."

7

like games. As part of my programming and training, I was taught hundreds of them. I'll tell you right now, I have no use for Duck Duck Goose; I got no legs, which means I get killed every time. I'll stick with the cerebral games, thanks.

Not only do I enjoy poker, but I love the way poker's colorful language works its way into human relationships. Playing something "close to the chest," or "vest," comes from the way poker players hold their cards close so that no one else can see them. Well, it's the same with budding relationships: neither side seems to want to reveal too much to the other.

Plus you seem to always try to "keep a poker face"; you keep important information in reserve, which means you have "an ace up your sleeve"; and you never want to "tip your hand." I'm telling you, poker players and budding romances have an uncanny amount in common.

Triana and Bon have been playing a kind of poker game for months . . . and I still don't think they are ready to "lay their cards on the table."

t was late, the ship's lights had dimmed for the night, and the Dining Hall was almost empty. Triana sat in her customary spot near the back, facing the door, and picked her way through a plate of mixed vegetables. She had not eaten since breakfast, and yet found that she was forcing herself to take in the nourishment. In the four hours since their encounter with the vultures, she had been unwilling to break away from the Control Room, although no new information was forthcoming.

They had indeed picked up some uninvited guests; seven entities that they described as space vultures had apparently latched onto *Galahad*. A report from crew members indicated that one of the vultures was firmly attached to the outside of Dome 1 like a leech. Its dark color would normally have camouflaged it against the black background of space, but following Triana's warning message many of the farmworkers had been peering upward through the domes. Several gasped when a dark shape blotted out a small section of stars.

The other six could not be seen, but Roc assured Triana that they were there. He was busy programming many of the ship's external cameras to begin a sweeping scan to locate the remaining vultures.

Triana poked at a piece of carrot before opting for a hunk of green pepper. One of the last groups of crew members in the room began to clear their table and make for the door, which opened and admitted Bon. He quickly picked up a tray and filled it with fruit and vegetables, an energy block, and a cup of water, before turning and making eye contact with Triana.

She watched him hesitate, and knew what thoughts were tumbling through his mind. He would ordinarily have chosen to sit by himself, but the absence of other people in the Dining Hall would have made it rude—even by Bon's standards—to ignore her completely. With what appeared to be a resigned sigh, he carried his tray to her table.

"I can't remember the last time I ran into you here," Triana said.

"Then you must not usually come this late," he said, pulling out the chair across from her and sitting down. "I always wait until things have cleared out."

"Surprise, surprise," she said with a smirk. "You? Avoiding people?"

He fixed her with his blue eyes. "I work late. This is more convenient."

"Uh-huh." She picked up a wedge of cucumber and took a bite, then held up the remnant. "In case I haven't told you in a while, this is all delicious. You do know your stuff, I'll give you that."

He didn't respond, his usual style in dealing with compliments. Instead he concentrated on quickly eating. Triana waited a moment before changing the subject.

"Did you happen to see the blob hanging outside Dome 1?"

Bon nodded. "Not much to see. A black triangle." He took a bite from his energy bar. "What are your plans now?"

She shrugged. "It's one of the things we'll talk about in the Council meeting tomorrow. As of right now they don't seem to be doing anything. Of course, we don't know that for certain."

They sat in silence for a moment before Bon spoke up. "I suppose we could ask our friends about it."

Triana had been lifting a glass of juice to her lips. She stopped and stared at him. "You mean the Cassini."

He nodded.

She set the glass back on the table, took the napkin from her lap, and wiped her mouth. All of this allowed her to process the thoughts that were tumbling through her head.

"I guess this is as good a time as any to talk about this," she said. "I have some thoughts about your connection with the Cassini, and I'd like for you to hear me out."

She took his lack of response as permission to continue.

"I'll just come right out and say it: I'm concerned about your recent . . . fondness, I guess, for making that connection."

His eyes never left his tray. "What do you mean?"

"I mean that you seem much too eager to link up with them, especially considering the pain that it causes. The obvious comparison would be the drug addict who needs his fix." She moved her tray to one side, clasped her hands together, and leaned forward. "I know you, and I know you'll brush that off, but think about it. The link is agonizing for you, and yet you are beginning to crave it. Talk to me; what is happening during this connection that has you so . . . addicted?"

He looked up at her. "You didn't have these concerns when I was getting the information we needed to escape the Kuiper Belt."

"Yes, I did. I shouldn't have waited this long to talk about it with you."

He set down his half-eaten bar. "The pain isn't nearly as bad as it was in the beginning."

"You mean you're building up a tolerance."

"If that's what you want to call it."

"So it won't be long until you feel nothing at all? Just a quick high, with a side of orange eyes?"

He grunted. "Listen, this conversation is ridiculous. I'm not a Cassini addict."

Triana looked back and forth between his eyes. "You're avoiding my question. What happens to you during the connection? There's obviously something that attracts you."

Bon sat back and pulled a strand of his long dark hair out of his face. "I didn't ask for this responsibility, remember? In fact, I seem to recall a time when you begged me to make contact with them. Why are you pestering me?"

"Because I—" She broke off at the sound of her own voice, surprised at how loud it had burst from her. The handful of crew members on the other side of the room looked around, then returned to their own discussion. Triana felt a flush creep into her face, embarrassed at her sudden lack of control. Bon appeared to study her.

"You mentioned responsibility," she said in a calmer voice. "Well, don't forget that I have a few myself, including the well-being of the crew. That includes you. If I have concerns over your mental connection with an alien force, it's my duty to discuss those with you, and if I feel it's necessary, make any command decision that I believe is required."

A sneer spread across Bon's face. "I see you're able to recite the manual."

Triana choked off the impulse to lash back at him. She felt anger rising in her, reminiscent of the emotions he had brought out of her for so long, emotions that had lain dormant recently. For months she had battled confused thoughts about Bon, drifting back and forth between anger, frustration, and . . .

And what? Could she even put a name to all of the emotions he triggered? If he irritated her so much, why did she sometimes find herself thinking about that one moment, sealed in her memory, when they had kissed? Why during Council meetings did she keep her gaze on him longer than normal? Why did his new association with Alexa cause an unfamiliar ache?

She let his words settle a moment, then pushed back her chair and stood. Gathering her tray and her composure, she said, "We're essentially out of the Kuiper Belt. If we mutually agree that another connection is necessary for the safety of the ship, it will happen. If not, it won't. Any questions?"

He looked up at her, his eyes cold, and slowly shook his head.

"Good," she said. "See you at the meeting."

The images on the Rec Room wall had been dialed in by a crew member from South America. The montage included scenes from the Amazon, complete with the subtle soundtrack of jungle life, followed by the sweeping majesty of the Andes. That image would dissolve into a video clip of a crowded beach in Rio, then shift to the wonder of Machu Picchu. The backdrop was different each evening, depending upon whose turn came up in rotation.

Channy barely noticed. Of the thirteen people who had attended Game Night, all but three had said good night and trundled off to bed. Besides Channy, that left Ariel Morgan and Taresh. Under normal circumstances, Channy would have enjoyed having Ariel to chat with; the spark plug from Australia was always good for a laugh because of her sarcastic wit. But tonight Channy wanted more than anything to spend a few minutes alone with Taresh. The fact that he had also stayed gave her hope that he felt the same way.

Or, more likely, he wanted to respond to her email. Channy was desperate to hear his reaction. Or was she? He had not sent a reply; did that mean he was angry about it? Was he embarrassed by it?

Was it possible that he loved it, and couldn't wait to tell her?

The answer would have to wait, because Ariel seemed to be in no mood to leave the Rec Room. She perched on the end of a table and dangled her feet over the side, a wide grin covering her face.

"I have a great idea," she said. "Airboarding."

Channy lowered her chin and raised her eyes. "What? Now?"

"Of course! We're obviously the diehards in this party group. If the others want to go to bed, fine. But we should go make a few turns while the adrenaline is still pumping."

"Uh, my adrenaline has just about sputtered," Channy said, looking at Taresh for some backup.

He was sitting against the wall, tipped back on his chair's rear legs. A look of alarm streaked across his face.

"Uh . . ." He looked between Channy and Ariel, not sure which of the two required his answer. "I don't know, I'm a little tired . . . I guess."

"Oh, come on," Ariel said, swatting at one of his legs. "What's thirty minutes? It'll be fun."

"I've only done it twice," Channy said. "And I've been up since five this morning, you know, in the gym. I think I'd like to be completely rested when I—"

"Of all people," Ariel said with a comic scowl. "I would have thought you'd be with me on this." She glanced back at Taresh. "And your excuse? You weren't in the gym at five, were you?"

Taresh offered a faint smile. "If I said that I was, would I still have to go Airboarding?"

Channy could barely suppress the grin that forced itself onto her face. She studied Taresh, suddenly aware of a glint in his rich brown eyes that she hadn't noticed before. The look he leveled at Ariel was at once both challenging and good-spirited, and when he broke that link to fix his gaze upon Channy, she felt a catch in her breath. His smile broadened and seemed to imply that the two of them were somehow conspirators, partners in a private game.

Now, more than ever, she longed to be alone with him; if that meant being obvious to others, it was worth the attention and ribbing.

"Ariel," she said, "you should go ahead without us. I think I just want to relax here for a few minutes. Besides, there's something I'd like to talk to Taresh about, anyway."

The girl from Australia sat silently for a moment, then nodded. "Okay, I see." She stood up and pushed back her chair. "If you wanted to be alone, you should have just said so." As she strolled toward the door she added, "You kids be good."

The door closed behind her, and Taresh eyed Channy. "I hope she doesn't think we're rude. I'm just really not in the mood for boarding this late."

"I don't think she thinks that," Channy said. She lowered her eyes and her voice grew soft. "Of course, she only has to mention this once or twice and people might start talking about us."

Taresh remained motionless, his chair still propped against the wall. His face was impassive. "I don't know what they would have to say. We haven't done anything. You simply said that you wanted to talk with me about something, right?"

"Right. But you know how people are."

A touch of playfulness coated his voice. "Well, I know how *you* are."

She grinned, and her gaze darted up to briefly meet his before dropping again. She felt her pulse increase and a flush dance across her face. She considered and then rejected several possible replies to his comment; she didn't necessarily like the fact that he might think of her as a gossip, but at the same time she enjoyed the attention he was paying to her. How would it look if she corrected him, especially when they both knew that what he'd said was true?

Then, in a heartbeat, her giddiness turned to alarm when he said, "So, you wanted to talk with me alone. Is it about your email?"

His manner had not changed, the tone of his voice was steady, and he still appeared relaxed as he leaned back in his chair. Channy wished that she was able to project the same image of ease, and yet at the moment every signal she gave off was dripping with tension. She knew that every instant she waited to respond to his question only added to the awkwardness of the situation.

She scrambled for something that would strike a balance between a lighthearted reply and one that would not completely dismiss what she had sent as frivolous. Why, she wondered, hadn't she hit Delete instead of Send?

As if to soften her distress, Taresh finally brought his chair back down to all four legs, then leaned forward with his hands resting on his knees. He gave her a sympathetic look.

"For what it's worth," he said, "I feel like you're someone special, too."

Channy felt a rush of air escape from her chest, and only then realized that she had been holding her breath. "Really?" was all that she could manage to say.

Taresh nodded. "I do. All of your responsibilities, and yet you keep everything so . . . I don't know, so loose. You're always laughing, always having fun. It makes it fun to be around you. So, yeah, I think you're someone special."

"Oh," Channy said. She quickly tried to digest what he was saying. It certainly was not what she had in mind when it came to being "special." Was he being coy? Was he guarding his feelings? Did he really only think of her as special in that way, or did he harbor other feelings as well? She couldn't read him well enough to know.

It dawned on her that since he had broached the subject, she had managed to say all of two words: Really and Oh.

"Well," she said, attempting to sound as relaxed as possible, "that's very sweet of you to say. I try to have fun, you know? Everyone's under a lot of stress, and I think it's important to have a release, more than just a workout in the gym, right? I know we all have different ways of blowing off steam, and for some people it's running on the treadmill, and for others it's doing something completely different, like reading, or just sitting up in the domes watching the stars, kind of like meditating, I guess. I like to laugh, and so . . ."

With a start she realized that she had gone from saying nothing at all to babbling uncontrollably. Taresh was staring at her, his eyes wide, trying to take in everything that she was saying. He nodded politely.

Channy couldn't recall ever feeling so clumsy. Her years of training in gymnastics, her grace and balance in dance class, her natural charm in front of large groups . . . all of it had deserted her. She twisted her hands together.

And yet, from somewhere deep inside, she at last tapped into a reservoir of courage. Swallowing hard, she reached across and laid a hand on his knee. "Okay, so I'm not very good at this, all right?"

Taresh remained silent, either unsure of her direction, or unable to think of a way to make it easier for her.

"I know I talk a big game when it comes to romance on this ship," she said, chuckling. "I know that I have developed a reputation as a bit of a Cupid character, or something like that. And I know that I tend to stick my nose into other people's business on a regular basis.

"But I think you're finding out firsthand that I'm really not all that good at this kind of stuff. I'm sorry if my email made you . . . uncomfortable." Taresh began to shake his head, but she kept going. "I'm not trying to put you on the spot, or anything like that. I just thought it was important that I share those thoughts with you, that's all."

She paused, then slowly pulled her hand off his knee. "I don't expect you to respond, and I certainly don't expect you to automatically feel the way I do. I . . . I just wanted you to know that, even though we don't know each other all that well, that I think you're pretty special. That's all. And that maybe . . . well, maybe we could spend some time getting to know each other."

By the end her voice had dropped, and was barely above a whisper. She had broken eye contact, and now stared at the floor between them.

Silent seconds passed before Taresh reached out and slowly rubbed the back of her hand, a gesture that Channy couldn't decipher. When he spoke, his voice was soft and gentle.

"I didn't mean to dismiss anything you said in your email, Channy. I appreciate everything you wrote to me, and everything you've said tonight, too. I guess I just don't know exactly what to say. I mean . . ." He paused. "I do think you're a special person, and I really do enjoy the time we spend together. Any other feelings I might have . . ."

She kept her gaze on the floor, until he eventually finished his sentence.

"I just have to think about everything, that's all. There are things in my life that are . . . complicated. It doesn't mean that I'm not attracted to you, or that I don't like being with you. It's just complicated, that's all."

"I understand," she said.

He smiled, and used his index finger to raise her face to meet his. "No," he said, "you couldn't understand, actually. But hopefully I'll be able to explain it to you soon. In the meantime, can we do what you requested, and just get to know each other a little better?"

She felt tears begin to collect in her eyes, and willed them away. "Yes, of course," she said. "I think that would be perfect."

8

have finished my study of great poetry and music, and have reached the conclusion that falling in love shaves off about twenty percent of your IQ and makes you miserable."

Triana set down her pen and looked at Roc's glowing sensor. "What are you talking about?"

"It's true," the computer said. "Pick up any book of poetry or listen to any popular music, and chances are the author has either lost his marbles or wants to curl up in a ball and suck his thumb. Losing one's marbles, by the way, is an old expression that means going slightly insane."

"I know the expression."

"Not only that," Roc added, "but the romanticizing of love leads to ridiculous scientific conclusions."

"Such as . . . ?"

"Such as the lyric 'love makes the world go round.' Gravitational forces, while relatively weak in the scheme of things, are unaffected by human emotions."

"Right," Triana said.

"And when Romeo says to Juliet, 'with love's light wings did I o'er-perch these walls,' we have a breakdown in the laws of physics, all because of this one emotion."

"This is quite a study you've completed. Any particular reason you took this on?"

"My never-ending attempt to understand the human creature," Roc said. "So much of your lives is built around your obsession with love, and yet it makes you loony. You have other emotions, some of them very powerful, but they don't come close to making you do so many dumb things."

A scowl worked its way onto Triana's face. "Have you been eavesdropping on people again?"

"What an insulting thing to suggest."

"Well, have you?"

"It's not eavesdropping, it's research. How can I assist you if I don't completely understand you? Next I'm going to study kissing, which strikes me as a very poor form of communication. Not to mention unhygienic. Yuck."

Triana sighed. "It's late, and I'd like to finish this journal entry before bed. Is there something important you wanted to discuss?"

"I know you wanted an update on our little vulture pals," Roc said. "Can't seem to get a clear picture of them, but I still believe we have seven of them stuck to the skin of the ship."

"We're going to talk about that during our Council meeting in the morning," Triana said. "I think we need to go out and take a look, don't you?"

"Aye, Cap'n, I agree. An EVA."

Triana nodded. "In the meeting I'll need your help with explaining it. Anything else tonight?"

"Besides being a research specialist and budding expert on the human condition, I'm also a mailman. You have a new video message. Good night, Tree."

The announcement caught her off guard for a moment before she realized that it had to be another message from Dr. Zimmer. The nonchalant manner in which Roc had mentioned it almost struck Triana as funny. She picked up her pen and tapped it against the journal that lay open on the desk before her.

Dr. Zimmer had been more to Triana than just the project director; he had been an advisor, a confidant, a surrogate father of sorts. He had quickly recognized the depth of the teenage girl from Colorado, and had taken on the responsibility of nurturing her throughout *Galahad*'s training period. No one, with the lone exception of her real father, had ever understood Triana as well, nor had ever known quite how to communicate with her when it came to personal feelings. Dr. Zimmer had forged a unique bond with her, an affection that was rarely acknowledged verbally, yet was genuine nonetheless.

He had died shortly after *Galahad*'s launch. However, in his final days he had recorded a variety of private messages for her, and she never knew when one would show up in her in-box. She looked forward to them, not only because of her affection for the man but because each one gave her some insight into human relations that stimulated her intellectually and emotionally. Dr. Zimmer provided a parental connection and influence that she dearly missed.

She chose to finish her thoughts on the night's journal entry before opening the message.

I try my best to keep my personal feelings from interfering with my responsibilities as the Council Leader. But my dealings with Bon really make that a challenge. When I argue with him over the translator, how much of that is really for the good of the ship—and Bon—and how much of it is my own frustration with him? Am I trying to punish him somehow for not showing more interest in me? Am I acting like a jealous lover because he now seems to have found a connection with Alexa? Or am I right to make the decisions I have, and my emotions are simply causing me to second-guess everything?

Triana rested her head on her fist and contemplated adding more about Bon, but decided that this was enough. The idea that her actions were being motivated in large part by her emotions had not occurred to her until she sat down to journal, and it produced a sick feeling in her stomach. Writing it down, however, had helped; now that it was spoken, more or less, it could be dealt with.

One final issue, however, demanded her attention.

Maybe it's because it happened so fast, or maybe it's because they haven't really done anything, but I am starting to wonder why I haven't felt more of a sense of urgency over the vultures. Have we been through so much, so quickly, that now something that once would have astonished us is treated so casually? There are seven alien entities attached to our ship, and yet no one seems to be panicking . . . or even worrying that much, it seems. Now, tonight, I am beginning to feel like that's a dangerous mind-set to have. Yes, they're relatively small, but these things are potentially more dangerous than anything else we've encountered so far. I have decided to announce at tomorrow's Council meeting that we will immediately get out there and investigate, and, if necessary, remove them. Almost no need to ask for volunteers, because I know without a doubt that Gap will insist on going. And, honestly, I wouldn't want anyone else doing it.

As with most of her entries, she kept it shorter than she normally would have preferred. Paper was a precious commodity on *Galahad,* and her bound journals constituted a large portion of the personal items she had been allowed to bring on the journey. Still, it felt good to put her thoughts onto the pages.

She stood and stretched, then filled a cup with water. It was close to midnight, and the next day would be extremely taxing. Yet there was no way she could go to bed without watching Dr. Zimmer's message.

At the sight of his face she felt a sting in her heart. She realized that it was easy to get caught up in the day-to-day activities of running the ship, and to sometimes forget about the life that she had left behind. But one look into the eyes of her mentor brought everything home again in a flash. It stirred memories not only of Dr. Zimmer but of her dad as well.

The scientist was putting on his best face, given his condition during the recording. Bhaktul's Disease had begun to systematically ravage the man, and would eventually take him completely. For now he summoned a smile, the lines around his eyes crinkling. Triana recalled his previous message to her, and his observation that she would age and mature throughout the course of their journey, and yet he would not change; he was frozen in time in both her memory and these video clips.

"Hello to you, my little interstellar traveler," he said. "Oh, what I wouldn't give to be there with you, to see the miracle of creation in its purest form, so unlike the artificial world we have built around us here on Earth.

"I trust that you are healthy and happy. After my last recording I realized that I was so focused on speaking to you that I neglected to have you pass along my best wishes to the Council, and to the rest of the crew. Please let them know that they are in my thoughts."

He shifted slightly in his chair, and Triana could sense the discomfort that he tried so hard to disguise; she knew him too well.

"Since Roc has seen fit to deliver this next message, I conclude that you have safely emerged from the Kuiper Belt and are now entering a fairly empty stretch of space. Empty, at least, compared to what you've just experienced."

Triana softly chuckled. He could never have imagined—nor, for that matter, could any of the other scientists and astronomers on Earth—just how treacherous the Kuiper Belt really was.

"I would also imagine," he continued, "that everyone on board has pretty much settled into a routine by now. Oh, I'm sure there are some grumblings and disagreements, but hopefully nothing that you can't handle."

Again, Triana smiled, thinking of the crisis situation with the crew that had been narrowly averted just weeks earlier.

"I think it's important, Tree, that you're prepared for the additional stresses that are coming as a result of the natural connections that are taking place right now." Dr. Zimmer paused, looked down for a moment, and then laughed. "Listen to me, I sound like such a clinical scientist. By 'natural connections' I'm obviously referring to the personal relationships that are starting and, unfortunately, ending. Sorry, the vocabulary of a lifelong bachelor can sometimes be a little . . . cold and emotionless.

"But I'm sure you know exactly what I'm talking about. You yourself have perhaps felt some of this stress, and if so, you probably find that it often gets in the way of rational thought. I simply want you to understand that it's okay, you're not the first one to experience it, and you certainly won't be the last."

Triana felt a lump in her throat. Her father never really had the chance to have much of a talk with her about boys, and now Dr. Zimmer was doing his best to touch on something that not only made him feel uncomfortable, but was something in which he knew he lacked much personal experience. It was touching to the teenage girl, and made her love the man even more. His rambling, stumbling approach to discussing teen angst was adorable to her.

"What makes it even more difficult, however, is the fact that all 251 of you are confined to such a small space, relatively speaking. As these relationships follow their normal course, there will be friction and ultimately hurt feelings. Again, I'm no expert, but I would highly encourage you, as the Council Leader, to keep your eyes open for any signs that it's affecting the safety and performance of the crew. It's sad but true that not all relationships will work out. Talking about it will help, I know that. I would even go so far as to recommend group meetings to allow people to share their feelings, if necessary, to let them know they're not alone with the quickly changing emotions they're experiencing."

Triana had never considered this, but found herself nodding. She wondered if she would be able to discuss her topsy-turvy feelings.

"But regardless of how these things work out, the ultimate responsibility of every crew member is to the safety of the ship and the success of the mission. It's difficult enough to find life balance here on Earth and to function normally during times of stress; in your situation, it can be critical.

"I suppose what I'm trying to say, Tree, is that all of us working on the *Galahad* mission knew that you kids were going to be facing conditions that are much more difficult than the average teenager would ever deal with, both physically and emotionally. I spent many hours talking with Dr. Armistead about this, and she was quite blunt. As she told me, the fact that you were specially selected through a vigorous process really wouldn't have any effect on the emotional aspect; kids, even amazing kids like you, are still kids, and your emotional evolution was determined a long, long time ago."

He paused, and what seemed to be a spasm of pain rippled through his face. He turned to one side and coughed into a handkerchief, and when he faced the camera again Triana was sure that she saw tears in his eyes. She was sure that this time they were tears of pain. He knew that he didn't have much time left, and yet he was determined to spend that time offering every bit of wisdom and support that he could to the kids who had captured his heart—and his imagination—for the last years of his life.

"Tree, before I let you go," he said, "I wanted to say something about the news I dropped on you last time. I'm talking, of course, about the child that I never told you about."

He paused again, and Triana involuntarily sat forward. During his last recorded message to her, Dr. Zimmer had stunned the Council Leader by announcing that he had fathered a child, and—most shocking of all—that child was a crew member on *Galahad*. His or her identity was a mystery.

"A part of me questions why I felt the need to tell you anything," the scientist said. He rubbed a hand over weary eyes. "You never would have known. For that matter—" He broke off and stared from the screen. "My child doesn't even know, and believes their natural father to have died before their birth. The mother and I thought this would be best, a decision that I have also questioned many, many times since then. There were times that I often thought about showing up at the door, and introducing myself to my only child. I planned the conversation in my head a thousand times, played it out over and over again, imagining their face as I broke the news. But . . . I never had the nerve.

"And, eventually, a stepfather came into the picture. I couldn't disrupt the household after that, and felt that I had missed out on my chance to get to know them."

Dr. Zimmer again rubbed his forehead. "Then, of course, I began the *Galahad* project, which consumed my life. I reached out to the mother and suggested that there could be a spot on board. She was hesitant at first, but realized that it was a chance to save her child's life. She agreed."

At this point a concerned look spread across his face. "I don't need to point this out, but I want you to know that this crew member has every right to be aboard. Yes, there was favoritism shown, I will not deny that; but at the same time, I believe in my heart that they could have easily been accepted anyway. They are just as qualified and gifted as any other person on the ship. I don't want you to think a spot was taken by someone who shouldn't be there."

He looked down, obviously ashamed at not only his actions

from the past but his passionate plea for Triana to somehow accept this mystery crew member. When he spoke again, his voice was barely above a whisper.

"I don't know why I feel it's so important for you to know that, but . . . but I have thought a great deal about it since I first told you. I know you, Triana, and I know that deep down you always wanted me to be proud of you, and to feel worthy." He looked up again. "I suppose I want the same thing."

There was silence for a long time. Triana sensed what was coming, and raised her hand to place it on the vidscreen, a split second before Dr. Zimmer did the same.

9

A grin stretched across Channy's face. She sat cross-legged, her back against the curved wall in the hallway outside the Conference Room. The object of her delight was Iris, the cat that had become the unofficial mascot of the ship, rescued from a small metallic pod orbiting Titan, Saturn's largest moon. Channy could often be found escorting Iris to the domes, where the cat would spend many happy hours exploring the fields and rolling in the dirt.

At the moment, she lay sprawled across the hallway, her legs stretched out, her eyes mostly closed but her tail giving away her attentive state by twitching at the very end. Crew members rounding the turn laughed as they stepped over the animal, and many of them stopped to either rub her belly or delight her with a quick scratch behind the ears. Iris was soaking up the attention, and Channy was sure that was why the cat had positioned herself as she had; there was no getting around her without some form of acknowledgment.

"She's a bigger ham than you," Channy heard someone say with a chuckle, and looked up to see Gap leaning against the wall with his arms crossed. "And," he added, "I never would have thought that possible."

Channy looked back at the cat. "She is an affection hog, isn't she? It's almost like people have to pay a bit of a toll to cross over her. One rub or scratch per person."

As if she recognized that she was again the center of attention, Iris sat up and began one of her many daily bathing routines. She licked at one paw and rubbed the side of her head with it, her eyes closed, and a soft purring sound rolled from her throat.

"I take it we're the first to arrive for the meeting," Gap said. When Channy nodded, he added, "Lots to talk about, too. I'm anxious to hear what Triana wants to do about the vultures."

Channy gave a noticeable shudder at the word. "I'm creeped out to think about them stuck to the ship. Can't we get rid of them?"

Gap shrugged. "Probably. Oh, and I'll bet we talk about your Dating Game. I heard it was a smash hit. Congrats to you."

"Thank you. You never had a doubt, did you?"

"No, but I heard that you did," Gap said. "What's next on the agenda for you?"

"Ugh, nothing right now. I want to savor the success of the Dating Game before I worry about anything else. You?"

Gap slid down the wall to sit next to her and rubbed a hand through his hair. "The most exciting thing in my life today is getting this cut. I'm a shaggy dog. I need to go see Jenner and have him chop it off."

Channy laughed. "I swear you get more haircuts than anyone else on board. Besides, it doesn't look bad to me. Trying to impress someone?"

"Right."

"Speaking of which, what's going on with you and Hannah?"

A cloud passed over Gap's face, and Channy quickly continued. "I mean, if you don't want to talk about it, I understand. But you two were so cute together, and . . ." She trailed off.

"I think the world of Hannah," Gap said, nodding at two crew members who strolled past and briefly stopped to pet Iris before continuing down the hall. "But she seems to need her space right now."

"Have you tried talking with her?"

"Yeah, I tried." Gap realized he was saying more than he intended; Channy had a way of pulling that out of people without much effort. He turned to her and smiled. "Enough about me. What's going on with you? I hear you're part of a games group in the evenings. How come you haven't said anything about that?"

He noticed a momentary look of panic that streaked across her face before she recovered with her usual grin. "Oh," she said, "it's just a few people that get together once in a while. I thought you knew."

In a flash Gap thought of all the times Channy had needled him about his love life, and decided this was the perfect time for some payback. He kept an innocent look on his face as he said, "No, this is the first you've mentioned it. Anyone I know in the group? Maybe I should drop by and play sometime, eh?"

The anxious look on her face lingered a bit longer this time, and he could tell that she was weighing her response.

"Um . . . well, you probably know some of them," she finally said. "I'm not sure there's really enough room right now. You know," she added quickly, "you have to have an even number for so many of the games. Partners and stuff, right?"

He nodded in understanding. "Of course. Well, if someone can't make it, I would love to sit in, okay?"

She smiled again, obviously relieved to have dodged him. "Sure."

Gap had to get in one more shot. "My friend Taresh told me about it, so maybe I'll come with him sometime and just watch."

He had to stifle a laugh when she almost choked. The timing was perfect, however; before she could reply they looked up to see Triana and Lita approaching from their left, while Bon briskly walked up from the right.

"Another hallway meeting?" Lita said. "I'm starting to think

we might get more done out here than in the Conference Room."
She kneeled down and gave Iris a scratch on the chin; the cat responded by closing her eyes and once again stretching out across
the carpeted floor.

"As much as I enjoy the relaxed atmosphere of the hall, let's
go ahead and move inside and get started," Triana said. "I assume
that Iris is joining us."

Channy, who appeared to have recovered from Gap's comments, rubbed the cat's belly a few times, then scooped her up.
"If she gets antsy I'll have Kylie stop by and take her up to the
domes."

The five Council members took their seats around the conference table. Triana opened her workpad, scanned her notes,
then laced her fingers together and addressed the room.

"Before we get down to the serious business at hand, I wanted
to acknowledge a few things. Channy, I apologize for missing
the Dating Game. As you know by now, we had a bit of drama to
deal with in the Control Room."

Channy waved her hand. "Yes, I know how much you were
dying to join us." There were chuckles from around the table, including Triana's own guilty laugh. "I almost believed you invented
these new creatures just to get out of attending, actually."

"Well," Triana said, "I just wanted to congratulate you on another successful social event. I've heard rave reviews from Lita
and a couple of other people. Thank you for your hard work in
keeping the crew entertained. Honestly, I don't take that lightly,
and I'm grateful to have you on our team."

Channy looked touched. "Thank you, Tree."

Triana turned her attention to the opposite end of the table.
"And I want to also acknowledge you, Bon, for the sacrifices
you've made—physically and emotionally—in helping to lead
us out of the Kuiper Belt. I know that your connections with the
Cassini are not very pleasant, but your links provided us with a
safe path to follow. So, thank you."

There were assorted words of agreement from the other Council members. Bon looked uncomfortable.

"You . . . um, you're welcome," he said, and cast his gaze down at the table. Triana knew that attention was always the last thing he wanted; she punched a key on her workpad and redirected the conversation.

"But although we are out of the danger zone with the Kuiper Belt, it would seem we have a whole new issue to deal with. By now you all know that we have picked up some unexpected passengers. I'll let Roc fill you in with the latest information."

"They're icky," the computer said. "That's my latest information."

Gap leaned forward. "Have you been able to get a close-up look with one of the exterior cameras?"

"No, they're in awkward places, and our cameras are set to scan outward, not so much inward. But one of them is clamped onto Dome 1, so we had a crew member scramble up onto a maintenance catwalk and get close enough to snap some shots. Icky."

"Why do you say that?" Channy said.

"Ever seen the suction side of a snail, or octopus tentacle?" the computer said. "Those things give me the creeps. Blegh."

Triana steered the conversation back to business. "A few more pertinent details, please."

"Seven alien entities," Roc said. "They have extraordinary maneuvering capabilities, they can accelerate to remarkable speed in the wink of an eye, they can turn on a dime—you guys wouldn't know that expression, since you're part of the postcurrency generation—but trust me, it means we could never outrun or dodge them.

"As of right now we can only guess as to their makeup, including their source of energy, their guidance systems, and the sticky stuff that keeps them glued to the skin of our ship."

"Okay—" Triana said before Roc interrupted her.

"Wait, one more thing. I know I called them vultures earlier, and if you really like that name, you're welcome to keep using it. But I'll tell you right now that what they really act like are parasites."

Channy grimaced. "Parasites?"

"The official definition means 'an organism that lives in, on, or around another organism for the sake of feeding, without benefiting or killing the host.' From the ancient Greek *parasitos,* which meant 'one who eats at another's table.' How's that for detail?"

"Feeding?" Channy said.

"Well," Roc said, "so they haven't started feeding on us or any-thing . . . yet. But they have suctioned themselves onto the ship like a copepod on a shark. So, yes, I am more inclined to call them parasites than vultures. They must want something."

This induced silence from *Galahad's* Council. Triana looked around and saw each of them considering this last comment.

"I've discussed this with Roc," she finally said, "and I think the obvious answer is an EVA."

Channy blinked. "An EVA? Extra vehicle something?"

"Extravehicular activity," Roc piped in. "What used to be known as a spacewalk."

Gap said, "I'm assuming that this would be in a Spider, right? So we go out and either shoo these things away, or . . ."

Lita fixed him with a look. "Or what? Kill them?"

"I'm not sure that sweeping them off the ship with a broom would do much good," Gap said. "What would prevent them from glomming right back on again?"

Lita's voice crept higher. "You think we should kill them?"

"We don't even know if they're alive," Gap said. "We have no idea what these things are."

"I agree," Lita said. "That's why I'm not in favor of just auto-matically destroying them. We don't know that they mean us harm, do we?"

"We don't know that they don't, either," Gap said. "But there's another possibility, too."

"Which is?"

"I go out in one of the Spiders, grab one, and bring it back for us to study."

Channy let out a groan. "You want to bring one of those things into the ship? Are you kidding me?"

Gap looked at Lita and then Triana. "I think we have some sort of . . . I don't know, a container, or something, that we could put it in. Don't we?"

Lita's expression brightened. "That's right, we do. It's perfect, because it can actually simulate the conditions of space." She turned to Triana. "Okay, if we're talking about capturing one, I think that's a great idea. Think of the knowledge we could gain from this."

Channy cut in. "Think of the danger."

"Of course there's a risk," Lita said. "But there's also a risk if we just leave them out there and don't learn anything about them."

"I'm with Roc," Channy said. "They're gross, and we shouldn't bring them inside."

"I used the word 'icky,'" the computer said, "but I vote for bagging one. As long as I don't have to touch it."

Lita said, "Tree, this is an amazing learning opportunity for us. We might actually get to study an alien life form."

"What if it's not life?" Channy said. "What if it's just a killing machine?"

"That's a little dramatic, isn't it?"

"How do we know?"

"If I had a head, I'd have a headache by now," Roc said. "Can someone turn a hose on these two?"

"Wait a minute," Triana said. "Everyone take a breath." She waited until she had the Council's attention, then leaned back in her chair. "Here's what we know: these parasites, or vultures, or whatever, can outmaneuver us, and can outrace us. They are either programmed to attach to us, or have some form of intelligence—if they're alive—that has them curious about us, and they have chosen to hitch a ride. They have been clamped aboard the ship for . . ." She looked at the clock on one of the room's vidscreens. "For about sixteen hours. And in that time they haven't moved, they haven't eaten their way into the ship; they haven't done anything that we can tell.

"Here's what we *don't* know: whether they're sentient beings, whether they're simple life forms, or whether they're programmed machines." Here she paused and looked at the faces staring back at her. "And, we don't know what they want. So, I think picking one up would at least allow us to find out what they are, and might help us figure out that last part: what they want."

There was silence for a full minute. Triana bit her lip and, for no reason she could think of, looked down the table at Bon. He was staring back at her. For a moment he seemed completely unreadable, as if unwilling to offer any feedback whatsoever. Then, barely perceptible, he gave a slight nod.

"Our mission is not necessarily one of exploration," she said. "Our assignment is to safely carry our knowledge and our history to a new world, to start over. To save our species, really.

"And yet, we're human; we are creatures of discovery. Through the years our path has been a difficult one because we chose to make it that way. We have never taken the easy route, and when we've been confronted by the unknown, it quickly becomes our task to make it known."

She paused a moment, then, tapping her finger on the table, said, "Now we're confronted with a new mystery. These things, whatever they are, made the first move. I believe the next move is ours."

A grin spread across Gap's face. "That's great. When do I go?"

"I would think as soon as possible," Triana said. "We don't

know what they're doing out there, and I really don't like playing defensively."

"Someone should probably go with him," Lita said. "I'll go."

Triana shook her head. "No, I won't have two Council members out there at the same time. But I think someone from the Medical Department might be a good idea."

Lita looked thoughtful. "Either Alexa or Mira. Mira's a bit of a go-getter."

"And I think Alexa has had enough excitement for a while," Triana said. "Please talk with Mira and get her up to speed." She turned back to Gap. "Work with Roc on setting up your plan, and let's shoot for tomorrow morning."

10

You never visit me in my office," Alexa said, staring out of the large picture window near Bon's desk. Her attention was captured by a small tractor that pulled a flat cart through Dome 1. The cart was laden with what appeared to be bushels of bright red fruit, perhaps strawberries. As she watched, the driver maneuvered a tight turn, then backed the cart up to a loading dock staffed by half a dozen other farmworkers. In seconds the team went to work, lifting the bushels from the cart in a synchronized system that almost resembled military drill precision.

She turned around and leaned on the glass. "No comment?"

Bon stood behind his desk, jabbing at his keyboard. "I try to avoid hospitals at all times. It has nothing to do with you."

"If you say so."

He glanced up from his work. "Besides, I thought you liked it up here."

"Oh, I do. I just thought it would be nice for you to stop by every once in a while, just to say hi."

"Just to say hi?"

Alexa grinned. "Yeah, well, I guess that's not really your nature, is it? Okay, never mind." She nodded toward the door. "C'mon, let's walk."

They left the office and made their way down the path that would take them into Dome 2. Neither spoke until they emerged under the canopy of artificial sunlight that simulated early afternoon. A rich medley of smells greeted them, a combination of citrus from the nearest crop and freshly tilled soil from the adjoining lot. Alexa found herself inhaling deeply, enjoying the infusion of natural odors after another morning spent working in recycled air. She rubbed her bare arms, feeling a light coating of moisture from the mist of nearby irrigation.

Bon steered them toward a bench that sat in the shade of some sprawling orange trees.

"Where is everyone?" Alexa said, noting just a few farmworkers scattered in the vicinity. "Usually there're more people wandering around up here on their breaks."

"They're all piled into Dome 1," Bon said. "That's where the show is."

"The show?"

"That thing stuck on the outside of the dome."

"Oh," Alexa said, and felt a shiver flash through her. The mere mention of the alien object attached to the ship ushered in a dark sensation, a feeling of dread.

Bon sat down next to her on the bench. "Something wrong?"

She looked past him, her eyes focusing on nothing, and it took a moment for her to answer. "I don't know. I get a strange feeling about those things." She shook her head and tried to smile at him. "It's creepy just thinking about them stuck to the ship like that."

"Well, you might get to see one up close and personal pretty soon. Gap is going to try to catch one and bring it into Sick House for you guys to study."

The heavy sense of dread again shook Alexa; she immediately identified it this time as foreboding. She pressed Bon for more details, and he shared what he knew.

"Lita is very excited about the chance to examine it," he

concluded, leaning forward, his elbows on his knees. "No doubt you'll be in the middle of it."

Alexa nodded slowly. "As I should be. I don't know why I feel like this." She attempted another smile. "It's probably nothing. Like I said, just creepy, that's all."

They sat in silence for a minute, taking in the sounds and smells of the farm, before she spoke again. "Is this one of those occasions where you might check in with the Cassini?"

Bon grimaced. "Apparently that's a subject for debate." He recounted most of his conversation with Triana.

"So she thinks you're addicted, is that it?" Alexa said.

"That about sums it up."

"And . . ." Alexa hesitated, then pressed on. "Are you?"

Bon turned to look at her. "I expect that from her, not from you."

She sank back from his glare. "Don't get angry. It's a fair question. Remember who you're talking to here."

He stood up and paced a few steps, one hand running through his hair. With his back to her he said, "I'll tell you the same thing I told Triana: I didn't ask for this. I was chosen."

Alexa recoiled at this. "Chosen? So now you've been chosen? You've never said that before."

"Well, isn't it true? There are 251 of us on board, and I'm the one who gets tapped to receive this information?"

"Because of a random configuration of your brain. It could have been anyone."

Bon turned to face her. "A Council member? You think that's a coincidence?"

She looked up at him. "Bon, are you listening to yourself? The Cassini communicate on a particular wavelength, and it just happens to sync with you. There were a few other crew members who had a touch of it, too, as I recall. Maybe not to the same extent—"

"Fine," he said. "But the point is, I do have the ability to communicate with them, and so far it's been pretty helpful."

Alexa sighed. "Nobody is questioning that. But we also have no idea what it's doing to you. Don't tell me the pain spasms are nothing." After a pause, she added, "And don't tell me that you can't see it from my—and Triana's—perspective. Even your reaction and attitude sounds like the angry denial of an addict."

"I was waiting for one of you to say that," he said, his voice low. "That's a no-win situation for me. If I don't disagree, then I'm essentially agreeing. And if I disagree, then I'm in denial. Either way supports your argument and leaves me guilty."

Alexa considered this for a while. "Okay, so I guess we're at a stalemate here. By your argument there's nothing I can say, either, without you thinking of it as a trap. So let me ask you a personal question instead, and be honest. Have you lost your fear of the connection?"

"My fear?"

"Yeah. Don't put on a macho act for me; that connection had to be frightening. Is it still?"

He stared at her, but didn't answer.

"I'm guessing that the answer is no," she said. "And if that's true, think about it. The most powerful alien force we could imagine, potentially doing damage to you, causing intense pain, and leaving you with thoughts and feelings you don't understand . . . and you've lost your fear of that? That doesn't tell you anything?"

Bon looked down at his feet, then back to her. "You just don't understand. It's not about fear; it's about information."

"No," Alexa said, "it's about control. They have assumed control over you, and you can't see it." He looked away again, and she softened her tone. "Bon, at least acknowledge that the people confronting you on this have valid concerns; Triana is responsible

for your safety and the safety of the ship. And I—" She stopped
and looked away.

"Yes?" Bon said.

With her eyes still averted she said, "And I care about you,
that's all."

The tall Swede again ran a hand through his hair, a look of
resignation on his face. He walked back to the bench and eased
down beside her.

"You're not fighting fair," he said softly.

She didn't answer, and rested her head on his shoulder.

Gap stared at the game board on the vidscreen before him, perplexed. Only seconds earlier he had been convinced that this
time he would finally defeat Roc at a game of Masego. Now, as
he scanned the tactical moves instituted by the computer, he realized that he had blundered once again.

"Incredible," Gap said. "How could I let that happen?"

"Not crossing to the H-line three moves back," Roc said.

"It was a rhetorical question, thank you."

"I can never tell with you," the computer said. "Besides, you
once said that you learn something from each loss; I wanted you
to learn the value of moving to the H-line when you get the
opportunity."

Gap sat back in his chair and examined the board again.
Masego challenged him mentally, and he had enjoyed the
competitive element from the first day that fellow crew member
Nasha had introduced him to the African game. But it was also a
source of great frustration; no matter how much he practiced—or
concentrated—he could never get the better of Roc. He shook his
head and blew out a breath. "Okay, one more, and then I have to
take care of some errands."

In a flash the vidscreen reset to Masego's starting pattern. Roc
wasted no time making his first move, and said, "I hope you're

better at strategy when you pilot a Spider. There are no do-overs in space."

Gap considered his first play of the game. "Thanks for your confidence. I'm sure I'll do fine." He touched the screen to indicate his move. "Plus, I'll have you chirping in my ear the whole time, I imagine."

"I'd better. An EVA requires precise maneuvering. You're going to be hugging pretty close to the ship; I'd hate to see you knock off a piece that we might need later."

"I'm not going to knock off anything, except one of those suction monsters."

They played in silence for a few minutes, each probing, advancing, blocking. The game of strategy required each competitor to think several moves in advance. The din of the Rec Room would often spike, yet Gap maintained his concentration.

"If you don't mind me asking," Roc said, "I've noticed that you haven't been to the Airboard track in quite a while. Lost interest? Or maybe a little nervous about injuring your shoulder again?"

"You are a nosy thing, aren't you?"

"So you *do* mind me asking."

"No," Gap said. "If you really want to know, I decided that I was spending too much time there, and not enough time focusing on my job."

"That's a shame."

"What? Being more responsible is a bad thing?"

"No," Roc said. "That's good. But your once-deft skills in Airboarding could come in handy if there's a crisis in the Spider."

Gap chuckled and touched the screen with a new move. "You are so nervous about this EVA. And never fear, my little mechanical friend, those skills do not go away after a few weeks off. I could hop back onto a board right now and you'd never know I'd been away."

Roc responded by lighting up the vidscreen with his own move; Gap saw instantly that he was doomed.

"All right," he said. "I concede. Good game." He sat back and crossed a leg over a knee. "Okay, since you're so worried about it, let's talk about this EVA for a minute. What's really bothering you about it?"

"Two obvious issues spring to mind," Roc said. "For one thing, these vultures can flat-out move. They can fly circles around you, and at lightning speed. It's not like you'll see one coming; more like it will be in one spot at one moment, then in your face the next."

"And the other issue?"

"We have lived in a virtual stare-down with them since they intercepted us; neither side has done anything. But the minute we go out there like some space-age exterminator getting rid of bugs, the game changes. If they read it as an attack—which, in essence, it is—then we don't know what they will do to the Spider or the ship itself."

Gap scowled. "Wait, they attacked us in the first place."

"Did they? Would they read it like that? There's been no damage to the ship; they seem fairly benevolent right now, almost like old-time hobos hitching a ride in a boxcar. But as soon as you start ripping one from the skin of the ship they'll probably not take too kindly."

"You didn't say a word about this in the Council meeting," Gap said.

"Oh, please. I'm not saying anything that anyone else couldn't have thought of. Besides, I'm still in favor of you going out there; why would I try to talk Triana out of that? You should go. I'm just answering your question, that's all."

Gap chewed on this for a minute, then said: "Okay, since it's just the two of us talking here, tell me what you think these things really are. What am I about to bring inside the ship?"

"I've given that a lot of thought," Roc said. "As fast as they are, as organized as they appear, and as efficient as they seem, I can't help but feel like they're the muscle, not the brains."

"What do you mean?" Gap said.

"Consider what they're doing. Some alien species wants to patrol the outer ring of our solar system, either looking for a way in, or hoping that something will pop out, like we did. There's an awful lot of space to manage. You tell me, who's gonna get that assignment? Not the big dogs, that's for sure. It's one of the reasons I'm questioning if these really are alive, or more like semi-intelligent drones."

"And their job is, what?" Gap said. "To just make contact and call for reinforcements?"

"I don't think they'll call anybody here," Roc said. "Again, this is all guesswork, obviously, but it wouldn't make sense for a mother ship to be close. I would think these things are probably scattered everywhere, just doing a little reconnaissance. And, if they find something good—like us—then I would think they call it in."

Gap rocked back in his chair, his hands laced behind his head, and looked up at the ceiling while he thought. Slowly he said, "But a call would take a long time to reach . . . wherever it was going."

"I've been thinking about that, too," the computer said. "I have a theory that explains not only how they would speed up that call, but how they move so fast in the first place."

"Care to share?"

"Not yet. Let me think about it a little more. But if I'm right, they wouldn't bother to send anyone here when they could just have them meet us along the way."

This brought Gap's attention back to the glowing red sensor. "That sounds ominous."

"But like all of my ideas, it makes complete sense," Roc said. "Now that I've probably given you nightmares for tonight, care for another game?"

Gap shook his head. "No, I have to get back to work."

He waved to a couple of crew members as he walked out the

door and toward the lift. His mind was suddenly on active alert, and Roc's dire suggestion lingered. The computer was right about one thing: it was entirely possible that nightmares would be in order tonight.

11

The final session of School had finished for the day, leaving the large auditorium vacant. Channy sat on the edge of the stage, reliving the euphoric feeling of the Dating Game, looking out over the sea of empty seats. Behind her, Iris padded lithely across the stage, stopping occasionally to sniff at something on the floor, her tail twitching only at the tip.

Channy waited and watched the doors in the back of the room. She had told herself that she would not be the first to show up, that she would make him wait for her. In the end, her excitement hadn't allowed it, and instead she had arrived a full fifteen minutes early. She rationalized it by telling herself that Iris needed the exercise after being cooped up in her room for several hours.

With one hand she rubbed at the corners of her mouth; she wasn't used to wearing anything on her lips, and the thin layer of gloss felt unnatural. Kylie surely wouldn't mind that she had borrowed it just this once.

She glanced down at the shirt she had picked out, a flashy red cotton polo shirt. There was a slight crease near the right shoulder, which she tried pressing away with her fingers.

Cupping her hand before her mouth, she exhaled and checked her breath, silently cursing herself that she had brushed her teeth twenty minutes before leaving her room, rather than waiting until the last minute.

She quickly dropped her hand to her side as one of the rear doors flew open, and Taresh strolled in. He spied her and gave a quick wave, then walked down the aisle toward the stage. She tried not to stare at him, and forced herself to look back at Iris. The cat had wandered to the edge of the stage and plopped onto her side, one paw hanging off into space, her eyes following the progress of Taresh as he approached.

"I'm not late, am I?" he said.

"No," Channy said. "I was a little early. Wanted to give our furry friend here a chance to stretch her legs." She glanced at the cat sprawled a few feet away and laughed. "Although it doesn't look like she's stretching anything right now, does it?"

Taresh dropped into a seat on the front row. "Yes, the life of a cat. Doesn't she sleep something like fourteen hours a day?"

"More than that, I think. Or maybe she just wants us to *think* she's sleeping, and she's actually listening to what we're saying. Either way, you're right, seems like a pretty good life."

Taresh looked around the empty room. "Funny that you picked this spot to meet. I like to come here by myself sometimes, to get away, to read a little bit. Not too many people think about coming here; they're usually either in the Dining Hall or Rec Room." He turned his attention to Channy and grinned. "Can't imagine that you ever look for anyplace without people."

She wagged a finger at him. "Are you picking on me already? I'll have you know that I enjoy some quiet time every once in a while." When he responded with an incredulous look, she added, "At least once a month."

They both laughed, but Channy got the sense that he was nervous about their meeting. He had likely been nervous from the moment he entered the room, which explained why he had chosen to sit in the seat rather than join her up on the stage. She decided to quit stalling.

"Well, you said that you wanted to talk again," she said, "and I know that the domes have been pretty busy lately. So . . ." Her voice trailed off.

Taresh sat forward in his seat. "Yeah." He looked down at the floor, and seemed unsure of what to say. Channy couldn't think of anything to help him get started; *he* was the one who had requested that they talk. She gripped the edge of the stage with both hands and watched him.

Finally he cleared his throat and spoke. "I was impressed by your honesty in expressing your feelings. I know that it took a lot for you to send the email, and then to say something about it after Game Night. I guess it's time I said a few things, right?"

All Channy could do was nod; her stomach was tangled, but she summoned all of her strength to appear calm and comfortable.

"You should know that I am interested in getting to know you better, like we discussed that night," he said. "But—" He broke off and looked back down at the floor for a moment, as if searching for the right words. "But I told you that things are complicated, and you deserve to know what that means."

Now he stood up and began to pace in front of the row of seats. Channy felt a wave of anxiety pass through her.

"For generations my family has lived in the region of India called Bihar. I grew up in Patna, just like my parents and grandparents. My family has always worked hard, always wanting more for their children than themselves. That was true with my parents, their parents, and their parents before them.

"Family is so very important in my heritage. We look after one another, we respect each other, and we love very deeply. I guess you could say that we value our heritage more than anything, because it is what has kept the bonds of our family so strong throughout our history."

Taresh stopped pacing and made eye contact with Channy. "Over the last several years there have been many in our culture who have parted with the old ways. They have introduced not only Western technology and lifestyle, but Western behavior and beliefs. They have ultimately disregarded their family traditions and background, and have surrendered to new ways.

"My family has been very careful to balance these influences. While my grandparents and parents have gradually blended some Western ways into our lives, they have always been dedicated to preserving our Indian culture, and to preserving our strong family line."

He paused. Channy watched him intently, but although she heard what he was saying, her mind scrambled to understand the context. What exactly was he trying to get across? She chose to remain silent, and Taresh continued.

"When I was nominated for the *Galahad* mission, you have no idea of the stress it placed on my family. On one hand it provided a chance for my family line to continue, to survive and spread to the stars. And yet, my mother and father were also very concerned. As my father said, 'What good is it to preserve a heritage if that heritage is blurred?'"

He began to pace again. "In the end my family gave their blessing to me to reach for the stars, but on one condition. They asked me to give my word that I would remain true to my past, true to my sense of cultural identity." He grew quiet for a moment, and, when his pacing brought him even with Channy, he stopped and looked at her again.

"I agreed. I gave my word that I would not lose that identity."

Channy sat still, absorbed in what Taresh was saying, but still confused. She thought she understood . . . and yet it made no sense to her.

"I'm trying to understand," she finally said softly. "Are you saying that . . . that you can't see me because . . . because I'm not from India?"

He exhaled loudly and rubbed his forehead. "I'm saying that that's what my family requested, yes. Our sense of cultural identity in my family is very strong. But . . ."

"But?"

"I'm my own person, too. I have thoughts and feelings that I often don't understand. I know that when the opportunity came for me to apply for this mission, I was so excited that I was willing to agree to anything."

Channy looked deep into his dark eyes. She was afraid to interrupt him now.

"I am torn, Channy. I obviously am interested in you, and that has troubled me a great deal. I want to be my own person, I want to go with whatever my heart says. But . . . it's difficult."

He slowly walked up to where she sat on the edge of the stage. He drew close, but kept his hands at his sides, unwilling—or unable—to reach out and touch her.

"You have no idea how troubled I have been. I do care about you. When you wrote that email, I wanted to respond right away. When you spoke to me in the Rec Room, I wanted to respond. But at those times, the faces of my mother and father loom before me, and their words cut through me. I think of them, and my grandparents, back on Earth, and think of the blessing that they gave me by allowing me to make this journey. I think of everything that I owe them, all of the work that they have done, all of the sacrifices that they made for me, and I think of the trust they put in me when they hugged me good-bye. I think of their dedication to our history and culture, and it's difficult, Channy. It's very difficult. I know this is hard for you to understand."

She nodded. "You're right," she said, her voice barely audible. "It's very hard to understand." She tried to control her breathing, which had accelerated. "You say you care about me, but . . . but you can't explore those feelings because . . . I'm not of your culture? No, Taresh, I don't understand."

He opened his mouth to answer, but stopped. Channy reached out and placed a hand on his shoulder.

"I care about you, too," she said. "I care enough to practically make a fool of myself, but it's because there's something in you

that I'm attracted to. Now, to find out that you have the same feelings, but can't respond because of . . . this . . . ." She felt that she
was on the verge of tears, and willed them away. In their place, a
touch of anger seeped in.

"If this is what you decide," she said, "how many people of
your culture are even on the ship? Fifteen? Twenty? Are you saying that they're the only people worthy of your attention?"

Taresh reached up and covered her hand with his. "I'm saying that I am struggling with this. I haven't decided, okay? But
it's also not something that I take lightly. I need you to be patient
for now and let me think through everything."

She nodded, and, as with the tears, consciously worked to
drive away the irritation that had taken over. "I'll try."

He leaned forward and lightly embraced her. Then, with a shy
smile, he turned and walked back up the aisle toward the door.

On the stage, Channy watched him leave. A moment later she
felt something rub up against her, and looked down to find Iris
stretched out with her back against Channy's leg. She absently
scratched the cat's chin, and again felt her eyes fill with water.
This time she let two single drops course down her face.

Months had passed, and yet Gap still felt uncomfortable in the
Spider bay control room. He had unintentionally witnessed
something pass between Triana and Bon in this very room, when
his feelings for Triana had left him vulnerable. Now, even following his own brief relationship with Hannah, he still felt awkward
stepping into this room; memories rushed upon him, clouding
his thoughts.

Triana stood beside him, her attention focused on the small
vidscreen that displayed a diagram of the route that Gap would
take to locate the vultures. The only other person in the room
was Mira Pereira, a tall sixteen-year-old from the Algarve coast
of Portugal, who would be accompanying Gap in the Spider.

Roc had been speaking, and Gap had heard only scattered words.

"I'm sorry," he said, "my mind was jumping ahead. What was that again?"

"You're certainly instilling a lot of confidence," Roc said. "Perhaps I should speak . . . very . . . slowly . . . ?"

Triana looked up from the vidscreen. "Everything okay?"

"Everything's fine," Gap said. "So, we're sure that we want the one on the dome?"

The Council Leader laughed. "Wow, you did check out for a moment, didn't you? Yes, that's what we've been talking about. I don't know if the others are causing damage or not, but I'd feel a lot better if we could pull that one off the dome. That makes me a lot more nervous than the others."

She pointed to the screen. "Everything is plotted and laid in. This program has been downloaded into the Spider that you'll be taking. Let's do a visual check on all of the vultures first, and get their exact location logged. Then you can finish with the target on Dome 1. I'll be in communication with you the whole time, but Roc will control most of the Spider's movement at first. Once you get close, you'll take over with manual control. It's going to be pretty delicate maneuvering when you get close to these things. Any questions from either of you?"

Mira nodded. "I understand that this is a reconnaissance mission primarily, and a collection mission at the end. But I'm still not clear on how we defend ourselves if something goes wrong."

"The short answer is that we don't," Gap said grimly. "Obviously we have the arms of the Spider at our disposal, but the speed of the vultures pretty much makes those useless."

"It's one of the reasons we want to bring one inside in the first place," Triana added. "Hopefully we'll be able to learn more about them, and find out if we even need to worry about defense." She studied Mira's face. "It's not too late to back out, if you'd rather not take this on."

"Absolutely not," Mira said with a grin. Her dark eyes sparkled. "I wouldn't pass this up for anything."

"Good," Triana said. "Okay, let's get you guys loaded and ready to go."

The three of them walked into the vaulted hangar, where the eight remaining Spiders awaited. The small, egg-shaped transfer vehicles had been given their names because of the multiple arms that splayed out from the sides and front. One of the Spiders was not functional, and had only been loaded for potential spare parts. Two others had been lost to space right after launch; in the space it once occupied now sat the small metal pod that had been rescued from the orbit of Titan. Its lone occupant had been Iris.

Gap approached one of the Spiders and began the procedure to open its door. Triana stood to one side and inspected the polyglass container that they hoped would soon house one of the vultures. The large rectangular box was already secured to one of the Spider's arms; it would be up to Gap and Mira to somehow capture the alien entity and get it safely stored inside.

The Spider door slid open with a hiss. Gap helped Mira climb inside, then pulled himself up and in. He turned and looked back at Triana.

"Need me to pick up anything at the store while I'm out?"

She laughed. "Anything chocolate. Preferably dark chocolate."

"Will do. If I'm not back before dark, leave a light on, okay?"

Triana gave him the thumbs-up. "Good luck. I'll probably monitor from the Control Room instead of down here. Roc will oversee the launch."

He waved to her, and she suddenly felt a twinge of fear pass through her. The lighthearted banter, she realized, was simply their way of camouflaging the stress that both must be feeling. This was more than just an ordinary housekeeping stint on *Galahad*'s exterior; they were once again confronting an unknown force. Although Gap was enthusiastic about the assignment, Triana knew that his insides were likely twisting and turning; *hers* were, and she wasn't the one taking the risk.

She returned his wave, then walked toward the exit. At the door she looked back to see if he was still watching her, but the Spider's hatch was sealed. In minutes it would be on the hunt.

12

Maybe you've wondered what would happen to you if you got caught in outer space without a protective suit or helmet. Of course, some of you have also wondered what would happen if you could squeeze inside a microwave oven, but let's try to stay focused here, okay?

Scientists have debated how long you'd be able to survive in space, but the point is that it's not very long (maybe one to two minutes if you're extremely lucky), and the results are not pretty at all. Pretty grisly, actually.

So hopefully Gap closed the door properly.

Gap adjusted the tilt of his seat and cinched up the safety harness, pulling it snug against his upper body. He stole a quick glance to his right to make sure Mira was strapped in as well. Behind them, twenty-eight seats sat empty. The Spiders were primarily designed to transport the crew from *Galahad* onto the surface of Eos, but were equipped with multiple arms for various duties on the exterior of the ship. Larger arms could tackle heavier payloads, while a series of smaller limbs were designed for precision work. The interiors were simple, almost bare, with space at a premium.

The two pilot seats at the front sat surrounded by an instrument panel, which now bathed Gap and Mira in a golden glow. The majority of the Spider's maneuvering functions could be carried out by Roc, but most of *Galahad*'s crew members had trained for weeks on their operation. Gap had been one of those with intensive study and practice behind the craft's function; he was comfortable at the controls, and had even taken a couple of the Spiders out for routine maintenance checks over the past several months. But, given the gravity of this particular situation, he still felt butterflies in his stomach.

He flipped on the radio. "Hello, Roc," he said. "Beginning preflight check."

The computer's voice filtered through the speaker system. "Roger that."

"What?" Gap said.

"Old-time jargon from the days of fighter pilots," Roc replied. "I've never had the chance to use it, and couldn't pass up the opportunity. I kinda like it. Roger that. It means 'okay, understood.' Sorta like ten-four, but much cooler sounding."

Gap shook his head. "Okay, whatever." He looked at the checklist on the small vidscreen in the console, and proceeded to work his way through the steps necessary to launch the Spider. A few minutes later he looked back at Mira, who had finished her own list. "Ready?"

She smiled and gave him a thumbs-up. "See," she said, "I know a few fighter pilot moves myself."

"Spider bay is clear, preparing to open outer door," Roc said. "Oh, wait. Has everyone gone potty? I don't want to have to stop this car again until we're finished."

"Roc, just open the door," Gap said. He kept a straight face, but inside he appreciated the lighthearted air that the ship's computer brought to the mission. Things were tense enough; Roc often brought just the right touch of wit to take the edge off.

Inside the pressurized Spider no sound could penetrate from

the bay, but Gap and Mira watched wide-eyed through the window before them as the bay door slowly and silently rolled open. A spectacle of starlight danced through the widening breach. For a moment Gap had a frightening vision of a cluster of vultures swooping through, into the ship. But the feeling passed with the first jolt of movement that told him they were being shifted into launch position.

The Spider edged toward the opening, and soon the star field monopolized the view. They stopped at the very edge of the bay door.

"Final check complete," Roc said. "Listen, one more thing before we sling you out into space. Good luck and all that, but if you don't make it back, Gap, can I have your stamp collection?"

"I don't have a stamp collection."

"Well, then never mind. Hold on, kids, here we go."

The Spider's maneuvering jets flared to life, and the mechanical arm below the craft jerked it forward, through the opening, and into the void. Even though he had experienced this before, Gap found himself inhaling sharply, and heard Mira do the same. It was an involuntary reaction. Space blanketed them, and the immensity of it—and the majesty—was staggering. Billions of stars winked greetings, and yet the blackness between them was heavy and deep. Not for the first time, Gap felt humbled by it all, a reality check that placed humans and their meager creations into a truly cosmic perspective.

Jets fired from the port side and below, and the Spider nudged gently to the right and began to ascend *Galahad*. Gap keyed the radio. "Triana, you with us?"

Her voice spilled from the speaker immediately. "Right here."

"We're on our way. Just starting to make the climb. All systems are green and go."

"Good," Triana said. "How's it look out there?"

"Magnificent. You should get out here more often."

"Don't have much time for joyrides these days," she said with a laugh. "We're monitoring from your front cameras; that's gonna have to be good enough for now."

The Spider edged up the side of the ship. "Keep your eyes peeled," Gap muttered to Mira, who nodded mutely. Together they scanned the gray surface of *Galahad*, and the Spider's camera system fed images to Roc, who for now controlled their ascent.

A minute later they crested the ship. To one side lay the massive domes, their interior light blazing through the panels and radiating into space. The Spider hung in place momentarily before spinning to approach the rear. The plan, laid out before their mission, called for a circuit of *Galahad*'s starboard side, beginning at the rear, and working around side and bottom. Then they would repeat the circuit on the port side. The final task would be the capture of the vulture attached to the dome.

With Roc guiding them initially, Gap had focused all of his attention on the search. Now he assumed control of the craft as they glided twenty feet above *Galahad*'s hull, calmly applying pressure to maintain a consistent velocity. Mira leaned forward and touched the control panel, activating twin searchlights and concentrating their beams onto the metallic gray surface of the ship below them.

Several minutes passed in silence. They had worked across the top and barely begun to drop over the back side of the ship when Mira uttered a cry. "Wait, wait. Hold up."

Gap throttled back and peered through the window. "What do you see?"

Mira pointed to a spot just a few feet over the edge. There, attached to the back side of the spacecraft, was a dark, triangular shape, roughly two feet wide. Gap nudged the controls of the Spider, and brought them a little closer.

"Triana, are you getting this?" he said.

"Yes, we see it," she said. "Are those wings tucked up to the side?"

Gap studied the vulture. "I think so. That would explain why it appears smaller now. And . . ."

There was silence for a moment before Triana prompted him. "Yes?"

"Well," he said, "I wouldn't call it breathing, but there's some kind of movement going on. Roc, what would you call that?"

"It looks like it's venting," the computer said. "Those rectangular slits around the circumference; they're opening and closing in a sort of rhythm. Doesn't appear to have a particular pattern that I can discern right now, but . . . hmm."

"Hmm?" Triana said. "What is it?"

"I'm just disappointed that I so quickly jumped to a conclusion. I automatically assumed that the vulture might be venting something out into space. But it could just as easily be absorbing something *from* space. Or doing both, I suppose."

"I'm going to move a little closer," Gap said. He deftly adjusted the controls of the Spider and dropped to within ten feet, which allowed him to take stock of the vulture. It was jet-black, with a strange ribbed effect that reminded Gap of a kite. It was roughly triangular in shape, its surface pebbled. Folded along the sides were two extensions that resembled wings.

Mira pointed again. "It's emitting some kind of light."

Gap studied the alien entity. "She's right," he said to Triana. "Are the cameras picking that up? Up there by the . . . I guess you'd call that the head. Do you see that?"

As they watched, a soft, blue-green glow seeped from one corner of the vulture, lightly at first, then briefly picking up intensity before fading again. To Gap, it almost seemed like an eye opening and closing. He felt a shudder ripple through him.

Roc's voice piped through. "A little more data is coming in now. Other than those brief flashes of visible light, it's not putting out any heat or radiation, which is very odd, and makes me question whether it's alive. But even a machine gives off something. Well, the machines we're used to, anyway. There are sixteen vents across the surface, and I was correct, of course, about the lack of any pattern to their opening and closing. A few of them seem to be fairly active, a few others less so, and two have only opened once so far."

"Any idea about how it's holding on to the ship?" Triana said. "Could it be magnetic?"

"No way of knowing until we get one inside," Roc said. "But I'm not picking up on anything magnetic, unless you count my personality."

"Of course," Triana said.

"Should I poke at it with one of the Spider's arms?" Gap said.

"I'm sorry," Roc said, "but did you just ask if you could *poke* at it?"

He could hear Triana chuckle through the speaker. "You are such a boy. This is not some frog that you've found in a creek. Let's wait until you get to the one on the dome. Let's go look for the others."

Gap took one last look at the vulture, then gently lifted the Spider away and began to guide it down the back of *Galahad*. Within a few minutes they had reached the ship's lower side. Mira adjusted the spotlights to give them a clear view in their search.

"Ugh, I don't know why, but I hope we don't find any down here," Gap said. "I don't like the idea of these things clamped onto the ship's underbelly."

The words had barely escaped his mouth when Mira spoke up. "Sorry. Two of them dead ahead."

They were within a few feet of each other. As Gap drew the Spider close, he could see the methodic opening and closing of their vents, and an occasional blue-green glow. Although sound waves did not carry through the vacuum of space, he could almost imagine a sort of electrical hum that might accompany the light. Something about the motion and light—without the soundtrack that humans were used to—added to the creepy feeling as he watched.

He noticed something else as well. The combination of movement and light, executed in such a relaxed manner, was almost hypnotic. Gap found himself drawn in, his hands resting limply on the Spider's controls, his face slack. The vultures, meanwhile, behaved as if nothing was out of the ordinary, as if they had been clamped onto this particular starship for years, oblivious to the artificial craft hovering mere feet away.

But were *they* artificial? Gap punched up the link to the twin cameras on his vidscreen and zoomed in. He swept across the backs of the vultures, looking for anything that might indicate if they were alive, or merely drones. And yet, he realized, how could he—or anyone else with only Earth-bound experience—know what forms life might take in the universe? The Cassini had taught them that.

Triana's voice came from the speaker. "I can't tell any difference between these two and the first one. Roc, are you picking up anything new?"

"Very slight variation in size, but negligible. Comparisons of the vent activities are processing right now, but don't appear to have any connection. Same with the light emissions; no pattern that I can make out."

"Could they be talking to each other?" Mira asked.

"We can't rule that out," Roc said.

After a few minutes observing the two specimens from different angles, Gap pulled the Spider away and continued the search. Forty minutes later they had discovered three more vultures on the port side: one on the top, one on the back, and one on the bottom. They each exhibited identical characteristics as the first three, with one exception.

"Now why do you suppose the light from this one is constant?" Gap mused aloud. The Spider hovered above the lone vulture attached to the top of *Galahad*'s port side. "The others were slowly winking, and this one has a steady glow to it."

"Maybe it's a short in the wiring," Roc said. "We should shake it."

Triana said, "You know what I'm thinking? This one might be the leader of the pack."

"A squadron leader," Roc said. "Here we go with the fighter pilots again."

"And," Triana continued, "if that's the case, then the light probably *does* signify some form of communication, just like Mira suggested. Maybe the other six stay in contact with this one."

"And, if that's true, I wonder if this guy is in touch with a mother ship somewhere," Gap said. There was silence as this sank in.

Mira looked thoughtful. "Well, if this one *is* the captain, should we maybe try to snag it and leave the one on the dome?"

"No," Triana said after pausing to think. "We don't know anything for sure, so let's stick with the original plan. Besides, I'm still nervous about that thing attached to the dome. We're much more vulnerable there than on the hull."

"Plus, who knows how the others might react if we kidnap the boss," Gap added. "I think we're finished here. It's time to go catch a vulture."

He pulled back on the Spider's controls and spun the small craft in a 180-degree turn. The bright lights of *Galahad*'s twin domes loomed up ahead, beckoning. As they crept closer, a pale shade of green bled through, and shadows played against the clear panels. When the distance had closed to about one hundred feet, Mira looked at Gap and raised her eyebrows.

"You see it?"

She turned her attention back to the crest of the dome and Gap followed her gaze. There, a sinister dark outline emerged, like a bird-shaped hole in the plate. Gap felt a shiver steal through his body and at the same time heard a small sigh escape from Mira. They both understood that their role as silent observers had come to an end; they were about to become the first human beings to ever make physical contact with an extraterrestrial organism.

There was no way of knowing how that organism would react.

Triana's voice came through. "Let's do this in stages. Start with the same distance you hovered above the others. Then move in closer, and let's see how it reacts to something invading its space. If there's no movement, we'll proceed with the capture."

"We're still assuming that *we're* capturing *it*, right?" Gap murmured as the Spider's lights coated the vulture.

"I hope so," Roc piped in. "We can't afford to lose another Spider."

"Thanks," Gap said. He adjusted their speed and piloted the small craft to a spot fifteen feet above the panels. "Roc," he said, "let's bring down the lighting in both domes thirty percent. The glare is a little tough to handle out here."

"I'll make an announcement," Triana said. "I don't want to freak out the people working up there right now."

Two minutes later the radiance dimmed. "Um . . . just a touch more," Gap said. "There, that's good." He looked at the image of the vulture displayed on the vidscreen. "Is it me, or is this one a little smaller?"

"Good eye," Roc said. "Just under two feet in width. That's with wings folded, of course."

"A baby," Mira said with a smile.

"Same venting, same oscillating glow," Roc added.

"I'm taking us closer," Gap said. With a nudge he soon had the Spider within six feet. Everyone remained silent for a full minute, waiting and watching for any response from the vulture.

"Sheesh, does it even know we're here?" Gap said.

"These things began tracking us when we were hundreds of thousands of miles out," Triana said grimly. "I'm pretty sure it knows exactly where you are."

"The light pattern has changed," Roc said. "Barely noticeable, but definitely a different cadence and tempo."

"It's bound to be as curious about us as we are about it," Mira said. She turned to look at Gap. "It's probably asking for instructions."

"I say we don't wait around for it to get an answer," Gap said, and wiped a sweaty palm on his pants leg. "Tree, you ready for us to pick it up?"

She let out a long breath. "Okay, go ahead."

Gap brought the Spider into a better position, level with the vulture, so that he and Mira could see it through their forward window. At a distance of about five feet he nodded to Mira. She tapped instructions into the panel before her, and then leaned forward and inserted her hands into the glovelike controls. With a combination of fluid movements, two of the forward arms of the Spider unfolded and stretched out toward the vulture. Mira deftly maneuvered them within inches before bringing them to a stop.

As he watched, Gap felt a trickle of sweat work down his forehead. "Okay," he said, "let's get the box."

He spun in his chair and engaged the controls of another of the Spider's arms. It held the polyglass container that they hoped would carry their target aboard the ship. It would also provide a spacelike environment, including a vacuum. He grunted as the arm jerked toward the vulture.

"I'm glad you've got the spatula," he said to Mira. "You're much smoother with these things than I am."

A moment later he had the box in position. He let go of the arm control and began to input new instructions on his keyboard. With a glance through the window he watched the door of the container silently slide open.

"Okay," he said. "She's all yours."

He was strangely relieved when, out of the corner of his eye, he watched Mira rub the back of one hand across her forehead before settling back against the controls. They both heard Triana issue a subdued, "Good luck."

The claw hand on one arm of the Spider spread apart, then inched slowly toward the dark figure that clung to the dome. Gap leaned forward and watched as it made contact, and stopped. Mira released some pressure on the controls, then picked it up again. The claw pressed against the vulture, but seemed unable to budge it.

"Umm . . ." Mira said. "How hard do I want to push on this thing?"

Gap thought about it. "Well, we don't want to damage it. But we have to pry it off somehow. Go ahead and push a little more, see if you can't slide that hand under it."

Mira nodded, and squeezed the controls again. The Spider's arm again made contact, but seemed to get nowhere.

Triana spoke up. "Try using both arms, Mira. Maybe you can pry an edge up just enough to slide the other claw under there."

"Okay," Mira said. With her other hand she guided the second arm into position, then rotated its claw and brought it down gently against one edge of the vulture. She gritted her teeth. "I think it's going to be tricky trying to get a grip."

It happened in a flash. There was a quick flare of blue-green light as the vulture sprang from *Galahad*'s dome and shot up against the windshield of the Spider. Mira let out a scream and jumped back from the controls, while Gap simultaneously shouted and threw himself backward. They both disconnected their safety harnesses and scrambled out of their seats, retreating several feet into the interior of the Spider, panting heavily. The vulture's wings had unfurled as it bolted from the dome, creating a terrifying image as it smashed up against the small craft. Now, as Gap and Mira turned back to watch, the wings slowly retracted as the alien entity settled into position and immediately fell still.

Triana's voice boomed through the speaker. "Gap, Mira, are you guys okay?"

"Oh . . . my . . ." Mira sobbed, clutching her chest. "I think I just about had a heart attack."

Gap swallowed hard, and then reflexively laughed. He called out to the intercom. "Yeah, we're okay. We both just aged about five years in one second. I take it you saw what just happened."

"Incredible," Triana said. "I can't believe how fast it moved."

Now Mira laughed, too, as the adrenaline rush subsided. "You're telling us. You should see what it's like coming at your face."

Moving cautiously, Gap approached the windshield to inspect the vulture that now gripped the Spider. He reached out to lean against the back of his pilot's seat, then leaned forward to get a better look.

"I don't know if you can see it very well," he said to Triana. "I'll tell you this, though; the view from this angle is very different than the view from above."

"We're getting a shot now," Triana replied. "But describe it."

"The color is basically the same, that same jet-black, only here it's also got some streaks of yellow that run through it. Thousands of little hairs, or fibers, or something; I'm guessing that's what it uses to grip on to the ship. They're arranged in rows, or grids. More like tens of thousands, actually.

"If you've got a camera shot that's working, zero in on the middle of this thing. I'm no biologist, but that looks very similar to a . . . a mouth, wouldn't you say?"

Mira had crept up beside him. She knelt down and scooted closer to the window. "It's some kind of hollow opening," she said quietly.

Gap laughed. "Um, I don't think it can hear you out in space. You don't have to whisper."

She turned and looked at him with a smirk. "I'm not taking any chances."

Gap addressed Triana again. "Yeah, it's hollow, about five or six inches in diameter. Looks like some sort of valve at the core, but it's not moving. No sign of the vents that we saw on the top side. But . . ." His voice dropped off.

Now he knelt beside Mira and moved within a few inches of the window. "The light that we saw coming from them; here's the source." He craned his neck to look up through the glass. "It's not some sort of eye, or gland. It's the . . . the skin, or whatever it is. Here, near the edges, small sections just . . . light up." He pointed it out to Mira. "Do you see that?"

She nodded. "Thin stretches, about an inch wide or so. There's no break in the skin or any other marking. Just small strips around the edges that emit color, on and off, like a beacon." She looked back at Gap. "It's like a living pulse."

He studied her face. "But is it alive?"

Triana spoke up. "We can't leave you guys out there much longer. Any way to try to peel it off the Spider?"

Gap stood up and stepped back from the window. He thought for a moment, then let out a long breath. "We might be able to turn the arms back onto the ship. But I'm willing to bet that it won't let go of the Spider any easier than it did the ship. Why not just drive it into the Spider bay?"

Mira's mouth fell open. "You mean without putting it in the container? Just bring it into the ship, attached to the window?"

Gap shrugged. "Might as well. Once we get it trapped in the bay we should be able to figure out a way to capture it. The longer we wait out here the more we're giving it the chance to get bored with us and fly away."

"I hate to agree with Gap," Roc said, "which is the understatement of the year; but I do believe he's right. Besides, what other choice do we really have?"

Silence greeted this statement, and Gap could picture Triana biting her lip as she considered the possibility. Finally, her voice came through: "All right. Come on in. But we'll have to get this thing into the box as soon as possible; there's no telling what the ship's environment will do to it."

Mira and Gap exchanged a look, then climbed slowly back into their seats, the forbidding silhouette of the vulture hanging over them, mere feet away. Gap gently swung the Spider around, keeping an eye on the vulture as he worked the controls. Mira retracted and stowed the arms, preparing all systems for docking. In a few minutes they approached the bay doors.

"Ready or not, here we come," Gap said.

He relinquished control back to Roc, then sat back as the Spider glided through the opening and came to rest in the bay. The vulture never budged.

And it was now inside *Galahad*.

Behind them, the outer bay door closed. "Pressurizing," Roc said.

Gap watched the vidscreen as it displayed the atmospheric conditions within the bay. He glanced at Mira. "Now all we have to do is figure out how to get this thing off the Spider. I don't know if we brought a cattle prod along on this—"

A flash of light cut him off. The vulture's wings spread out as if it was preparing for flight. Then, without warning, it slipped a few inches down the windshield, and fell straight down, out of view.

Gap and Mira sat stunned. "Uh . . ." he said to the intercom. "Anybody want to tell us what just happened?"

After a moment of hesitation, Triana answered: "Our guest just fell off the Spider. It didn't fly; it fell. It's lying in a heap on the floor of the bay."

13

Channy sat before the mirror in her room, looking closely at her face, trying desperately to not pick out every imperfection. Her gaze drifted from her eyes, to her nose, to her teeth, back to her eyes, the slight blemishes in the chocolate hue of her skin, then to her hair. She turned her head one way, then the other, catching her reflection in the corner of her eyes. After a few moments of inspection she put her elbows on the counter and leaned her chin on her hands.

"Not exactly a natural beauty, am I?" she said.

Kylie, sitting on her bed across the room, set down the clothes that she was folding and scowled across at her roommate. "Excuse me?"

"I mean, I'm not even properly proportioned. Look at the space between my nose and my mouth."

"I don't believe what I'm hearing," Kylie said. "The space between your nose and your mouth; you're joking, right?"

"I had a chance to get my teeth fixed properly about a year before we left," Channy said. "Now I wish I'd done it. That was stupid, wasn't it?"

Kylie went back to folding her shirts. "I'm not having this conversation with you, Ms. Oakland. You sound ridiculous."

"That's because you don't have to look at it in the mirror

every day." Channy sat back and sighed. "I'm sure that Taresh sees all of it."

She grunted as a wadded-up shirt hit her in the back of the head. Turning, she saw that Kylie had reloaded, and was preparing to throw another one at her.

"What are you doing?" she said.

"If I was closer I would have thumped you with my hand," Kylie said. "Taresh most certainly does *not* see anything wrong with you, and you know that."

"Well, then he doesn't see anything right with me, either."

Kylie crossed her arms. "You're sounding pathetic, Channy. You told me what he said; he's having an issue with cultural differences, not your looks."

Channy snorted. "Cultural differences. Whoever heard of such a thing?" She turned back to the mirror and inspected her face again.

"Okay, I've known you for a long time now," Kylie said. "You have never been this way before. What happened to the happy, fun-loving roomie that I was lucky enough to get?"

"She fell in love," Channy said in a low voice. In the mirror she made eye contact with Kylie. "There, is that what you wanted to know?"

Kylie set down the shirt she had bunched in her hand. "In love? Channy, slow down a moment, okay? You might be infatuated right now, but it's probably a little soon to say that you're in love. I mean, you hardly know him."

"I know enough."

"No, you don't. You've spent a few hours with him after Game Nights, and talked a little bit. But you don't really know him."

"And how much exactly do I need to know before I can have feelings?" Channy blurted out. "Why is everyone else on this ship allowed to be happy with someone, but not me? Answer that!"

Kylie settled back on her bed and let the silence between them grow for a while. When she responded, her voice was gentle.

"Channy, let me ask you something. I'm not trying to pry into your past, or your personal life. But . . . how many boyfriends have you had?"

Channy didn't answer. Instead, she got up and walked over to her bed and stretched out, her hands behind her head, staring at the ceiling.

"You haven't had a boyfriend before, have you?" Kylie said softly. She waited a moment, then walked over to her friend and sat on the edge of the bed. "Hey, it's okay. I'm not trying to be mean, I'm just trying to make a point. This is new territory for you, just like it is for everyone at some point. And it's scary sometimes."

Channy nodded, stole a quick glance at Kylie, then looked away. Her eyes began to water.

"All I'm saying," Kylie said, "is that you might want to take it easy. Not because what you're feeling is wrong, and not because you and Taresh might not be right for each other. But you should slow down because this is all new for you, and you're a little out of control."

"I'm not out of control," Channy whispered.

Kylie smiled. "Uh, you just criticized the space between your nose and your mouth."

Channy looked back at her again, but this time let the gaze linger, long enough to convey to her friend that she was in no mood to joke. Then she rolled onto her side, her back to Kylie. "I don't feel like talking about this anymore."

"I'm not trying to embarrass you, or hurt you," Kylie said. "I'm trying to help."

"I know you are."

There was an awkward moment of silence, then Kylie perked up. "I'm going to get something to eat in just a minute. Wanna go with me? We could—"

"No, I'm not hungry," Channy interrupted. "But you should go. I'll talk to you later."

"Okay," Kylie said. She stood up and took a step back toward her bed before turning around. "Listen, at least think about what I said. Things might work out fine for you two, or they might not. But you need to trust that what he's telling you is the truth. If he thought you were hideous, he wouldn't hang out with you so much. I'm sure he really likes you, Channy. But let him work this out."

When there was no response, Kylie walked out of the room, leaving the rest of her laundry on the bed, and her roommate curled up, staring at the wall.

The Spider's hatch had opened, but Gap was in no hurry to rush out. At the opposite end of the craft, crumpled on the floor of the bay, was a two-foot-wide alien being. Its status as life form or robotic vehicle seemed unimportant at the moment; what mattered was the fact that it had the ability to move at lightning speed, and once it grasped something, it was almost impossible to pry loose.

Mira stood behind Gap, one hand resting on his shoulder in a gesture that made it clear she would have no problem using him as a shield. They both craned their necks through the opening, looking down and around to see if anything had scuttled over to this end of the Spider, but the floor was clear.

Gap called out to Roc. "Any sign of movement since it jumped off?"

"There was no jumping involved," the computer said. "It fell, no control whatsoever. Dropped like a rock and landed hard. And no, it hasn't moved a muscle . . . or pulley, or whatever it uses inside. It's just lying there. In fact, it almost looks like a puppy, kinda cute, all nestled up in a ball, like it's tuckered out and needs a good nap. Of course, I still wouldn't pet it, even if I had arms."

Triana's voice rang out from the bay's speaker system. "Gap, Mira, just hold tight for a minute. Don't climb down. I've got help coming your way."

"What kind of help?" Gap said.

"Two crew members are gearing up right now in EVA suits. I recommend you do the same before you step out. I know the atmosphere is fine, but every bit of protection helps."

Gap pulled back from the hatch and keyed open one of the storage bins. A handful of specially equipped space suits hung there.

"Don't know if these will do any good," he muttered to Mira, "but she's right; probably better than nothing."

Five minutes later they were giving each other a quick visual scan to make certain that everything was secure: suits, gloves, boots, and helmets were checked and rechecked before they nodded through their visors at each other. Gap heard Mira's voice in his ear through the intercom system.

"Should we still wait?"

"Probably," he said. "Not that I want to gang up on the thing, but I'd feel safer with numbers on our side. Easier to surround it."

"I'm okay with that," she said. "This is turning out to be quite an assignment."

They caught sight of movement through the glass of the control room, and looked over to see a handful of crew members milling around inside. Two of them wore EVA suits; they waved at Gap and Mira, then made their way into the bay and cautiously approached the Spider. Gap saw that they were each clutching portable grappling arms, similar to those on the Spider. He addressed them by name—Mitch and Zhenta—and made sure that proper introductions were made with Mira.

Zhenta, whose parents were originally from Egypt, indicated the front of the Spider. "What's the plan?"

Gap peered through her faceplate. "First, we remove the container box, and get it just as close as we can. Then, we close in from all four sides, and you and Mitch grab the . . . thing. Should be a lot easier than when Mira tried it."

"Okay. Let's go bag a creature," Mitch said.

Gap took a deep breath—he could almost sense the others doing the same—and together they rounded the corner of the Spider and began to stride toward the front side. They paused at the far corner, then Gap took the lead and peered around the edge of the metal craft.

There, about ten feet away, lay the vulture. Even in this vulnerable position, crumpled and at awkward angles, it still struck Gap as an imposing force. The deep black seemed like ink, an unnatural darkness, while a small glimpse of its yellow streaks provided a brilliant contrast and a fierce, aggressive aura. It gave every indication of being either dead, unconscious, or offline; the throbbing bright blue-green color from its edges was missing, and the vents that had at least mimicked breathing were motionless.

And yet, the vulture still radiated danger in a manner that Gap couldn't justify. He simply understood, on some level, that although it might be dead, he wasn't about to go up and kick it.

He also knew that he was the leader of this small group, and it was up to him to make the first move. With a silent wave of his hand, he took a few steps toward the creature and sensed the others following him. Within his helmet the sound of his breathing was loud, almost distracting. He never took his eyes from the vulture; the image of it bursting from *Galahad*'s dome onto the Spider replayed in his mind. His rational side told him that with its speed, two feet away, ten feet away, or thirty feet away would make no difference; but his instinctual fears still caused him to almost tiptoe as he approached. Now, as he stood above it, he felt his heart racing, and his breathing intensified.

He directed Mitch and Mira toward the polyglass container that was still attached to the Spider's arm. In three minutes they

had removed it and, with its door still open, placed it—gently—
on the floor beside the vulture.

Then the four of them gathered around and stared down at
the motionless mass. It certainly seemed dead, and Gap immediately began trying to process what might have happened. The
temperature? The atmospheric pressure? The artificial gravity?

He shook his head and exhaled. There was no time for this
right now; it would be Lita's job to answer those questions, and
it was *his* job to get the specimen to her.

"Okay," he said softly. "Let's do it."

Zhenta extended her portable grappling arm toward the vulture, and was able to slide it under one side. She pushed a little
harder, then harder still, until at last the creature appeared to
budge. "Ugh, it's heavy," she said. "We might need to have two
people on each arm."

Gap reached over and helped her with supporting the arm. At
the same time, from the opposite side, Mitch duplicated Zhenta's
actions. A few seconds later he had a firm grip on the vulture,
with Mira lending a hand.

"Are we good so far?" Gap said, looking at the group. "On
three. Very gently, right? One . . . two . . . three."

Straining, and putting their leg muscles into it, the four crew
members slowly lifted the vulture from the Spider bay floor. The
strong and sturdy grappling arms swayed under the mass, but
they managed to raise it a foot off the ground. "Okay, let's get it
inside," Gap said, and they began to rotate toward the box.

One of the vulture's wings shifted, causing the group to suddenly stop and gasp, but they quickly realized that it was simply
a result of the movement.

Mira laughed softly. "We're jumpy."

"For good reason," Gap said with a grin.

They lowered it into the polyglass container. One wing was
hung up on an edge of the box; Zhenta removed her grappling
arm and gently maneuvered the wing down inside.

Gap exhaled loudly. "Whew, good job. Okay, Roc, seal that sucker up."

The container's opening slid shut. Immediately a yellow light began to blink on a side panel, indicating that a seal had been achieved. It would take a few minutes before a vacuum was achieved inside, and the atmosphere and temperature adjusted.

"Did someone order a vulture in a box?" Gap said over the intercom in his helmet.

"Nice work, you guys," Triana said. "Let's roll a cart in there and you can move it up to Sick House. Lita's expecting you. Then, Gap, if you and Mira would stop by the Control Room, please."

"On our way," he said.

Twenty minutes later, he and Mira entered the Control Room to a small round of applause from the crew members working there. Triana beamed at them and clapped Mira on the shoulder.

"Just another day at the office?"

"Oh, sure," Mira said with a laugh. "Pretty boring day."

"Knowing Lita, I'll bet she's excited to get started," Triana said to Gap.

He nodded. "Yeah, she was like a little kid anxious to open birthday presents. She practically fogged up the outside of the box with her face right up against it."

Triana said, "I want to go over things with you, and get any thoughts you might have about what you saw."

"I have a question," Mira said. "After the dome vulture came at us, did any of the other ones react? Are they still in the same position, or did they move?"

"No changes," Triana said. "We have cameras positioned on all of them now, and there was no movement. There was, however, a reaction."

"Let me guess," Gap said. "The lights."

"Yep. As soon as the drama started with you guys, they all lit

Dom Testa

up a little more. But especially our squadron leader. There was practically a symphony of light coming from him."

"So they are definitely communicating with each other," Gap said. He looked thoughtful. "I just wish we knew if that meant communication with something else."

"Your mother ship idea?" Triana said.

He raised his eyebrows. "That's what I'm afraid of."

"Why, oh why, won't anyone ask for my input?" Roc said suddenly.

Triana rolled her eyes. "You don't need an invitation. What do you have?"

"Well, our little winged friends not only stepped up their light show, their flapping show morphed, too."

"The vents?"

"That's right. A sudden and rapid shift in the venting activity. I'm convinced that it's tied in with their communication. And, not only that, I think it's somehow tied into how they get their power."

There was silence as the group thought about this. Then Triana said, "Power from where?"

"I'm working on that," Roc said. "I have a theory . . . but it's a little crazy, and I'd like to get some information from Lita's work before I go much further."

As if on cue, Lita's voice broke through the intercom. "Tree?"

"Yes, Lita."

"Thought you might like to hear the news. We are no longer a morgue, and once again a hospital."

Gap and Triana looked at each other. "It's moving?" Gap said.

"Oh, it's moving. The return to a vacuum and spacelike conditions resuscitated it, apparently. The lights, the vents, everything.

"And not only that," she added, "it doesn't seem very happy at all."

14

She was due back in Sick House to help Lita begin the process of examining the vulture, but at the moment Alexa was sitting quietly on the edge of her bed, alone in her room. Since waking from a fitful night of sleep, she had chosen to be alone. No breakfast in the Dining Hall, not that she was hungry anyway. Katarina had obviously suspected that something was wrong, but other than a polite inquiry she had left her roommate to her own thoughts. And, though it was tempting to call Bon, Alexa reasoned that it was too soon to bring it all up again.

But this dream had been as disturbing as the last.

She had reconstructed it several times in the four hours since snapping awake, but could reach no conclusions. This time details seemed vague, which was unusual for one of her visions. Yet, again, it seemed so real. Perhaps, she decided, if she went through it one more time before going to work it would make sense.

There was darkness, a deep, heavy darkness that swallowed her. It came about swiftly; there had been bright light, then surprise, then the darkness. But surprise because of what? The sensation was unmistakable; its cause was a mystery.

The darkness had a quality about it that brought on her

anxiety: it was suffocating. Not just figuratively, but literally. It was the feeling that stuck with her the most after awakening. She remembered wanting to claw the darkness away because it was somehow affecting the space around her. Had it somehow polluted the air, making it unfit for breathing? Had it somehow absorbed the air, leaving none behind for her to breathe? It was a painful feeling, sharp and daggerlike.

On top of it all, she had been powerless to do anything about it. Her arms were unable to move, as if she was paralyzed. Her need to push the darkness away was maddening, and yet it was quite obviously in total control.

What did it mean? She kept coming back to the same thought: she was in space, without protection, without a suit or helmet. The darkness of space had engulfed her, and there was no air to breathe.

But where were the stars? Why was it so utterly dark? And why could she not move? How could she have stumbled into this predicament? How could she have possibly managed to find herself alone, outside the ship, in the vacuum of space?

Unless she wasn't alone. Was it possible, she wondered, that this was the future of everyone on the ship? Had she seen a vision where *Galahad* itself no longer existed, and the entire crew was adrift in space? And did their encounter with the vultures play a role in their destiny?

She sat forward on her bed and rubbed at her temples, trying to massage the frightening image from her mind. She realized that her futile attempt to make sense of these dreams was causing even more pain. Perhaps, she concluded, it wasn't possible to decipher the meaning; and, she reminded herself, it wasn't clear if all of her visions were destined to come true. There were so many theories of multiple universes, with infinite possibilities and outcomes; what if she was merely tapping into a menu of *potential* futures?

It helped ease her mind . . . but not much.

She had eventually spoken to Bon about the funeral dream, but this vision she would keep to herself.

With a weary sigh she pushed herself to her feet and went about her usual morning routine to prepare for a day of work. It would be a long, difficult stretch once she got to Sick House.

By the time Triana arrived, a throng had surrounded the poly-glass container—although they kept a respectful distance. There was a low murmur of voices, as if they didn't want to take a chance of upsetting the specimen. At first glance, it appeared to Triana that the vulture was distressed enough already; it darted around the interior of the container, pausing for only brief moments before continuing its frantic activity.

She stepped up beside the other crew members and watched. The vulture shot from corner to corner, edge to edge. Although it was a challenge to keep up with its movements, Triana tried to examine the various parts of the creature that she had previously seen only on the vidscreen. The vents fluttered in what seemed a random pattern, with all but a few of them active. The soft, blue-green light seeped from underneath, except when the vulture arched upward to the top of the box, whereupon the light took on a more vivid, cutting appearance, almost laserlike. And when it paused long enough on the sides, Triana was able to catch glimpses of the hollow, mouthlike opening on its belly.

She admired the stark black color, punctuated by a handful of bright yellow streaks on its underside. Funny, she thought, that it could appear both terrifying and beautiful at the same time.

From the opposite side of the container Lita caught her attention without saying a word. The two Council members eyed the vulture, then the amazed faces of their crew mates gathered around. Triana nodded as if to say, "once again we face the great unknown." There was work to be done, but she understood that it was important for the crew to participate in the discovery.

Looking back into the box, it dawned on her that the vulture was not acting manic; it was simply a trapped animal, doing what instincts drove all creatures to do at that moment: search for a way out. It just happened that these particular creatures moved with lightning speed at all times, which gave the impression that it was frenzied. In fact, it was quite likely, she thought, that the captive was more composed than the captors.

Gradually the crew members began to peel away, most shaking their heads, their conversation animated.

Triana looked over her shoulder and saw Alexa enter the room, then immediately stop when she saw the vulture. But unlike the looks of amazement and wonder that she had seen on the faces of the others, Triana caught a glimpse of what seemed to be terror in Alexa's eyes. The medical assistant stood frozen, her hands at her sides, for a long time. She seemed reluctant to draw any closer to the creature that tore around its transparent cage.

Lita had seen her, too. "Pretty incredible, isn't it?" she said.

Alexa didn't answer at first, then looked up at Lita and smiled. To Triana the smile seemed forced and uncomfortable.

"Beyond incredible," Alexa said. The remaining crew members who had come to gape at the captured being pushed past her and left the room.

"I'm glad you're here," Lita said. "I'm going to turn on the probe so we can start gathering a little more hard data." She laughed and added, "You'll have to get a little closer if you want to help."

Alexa took a few cautious steps forward, but gave the container a wide berth as she moved around to stand beside Lita. Her gaze was again locked on the vulture; she seemed to not have even noticed Triana standing there.

Lita crept up to the box. She knelt down and examined one of the end panels, then looked back at her assistant. "Well?"

"Oh, sorry," Alexa said, and inched closer. Triana was convinced they were the hardest steps Alexa had ever taken.

"You okay?" Triana said.

"Um . . . yes. Just kinda in awe, I think."

"Like all of us," Lita said. "Okay, once I get this running, check all of the readings. We don't want anything to affect the vacuum. Shout out and I can shut it down right away."

"Do you need me to do anything?" Triana said.

"Sure. Keep your eye on our little friend and let me know if it starts to react strangely."

"And how in the world will I be able to tell?" Triana said with a laugh.

Lita grinned at her. "That's a good point. And to be honest, I really don't know."

She turned back to the panel before her. When Dr. Zimmer had run through all of the potential tools that the crew might need during their journey, he was aware that there might come a time when they would need to examine objects they encountered along the way. He had ordered the construction of various containers that could simulate the environment of space. Some of the more complex scientific devices aboard, the boxes were capable of maintaining the vacuum and weightlessness of space, and could be temperature controlled. They had taken almost a year to design and build, with the idea that their most likely use would come once they entered the planetary system around Eos.

Yet now, less than a year into the mission, one was being put to use in ways they had never imagined.

"Here goes," Lita said. Pressing her lips together, she took a quick look into the box, then snapped on the power. Immediately a tiny vidscreen came to life, displaying more detailed information about the settings, and—more important—diagnostic readings on the creature within. The information was also sent directly to Roc.

Lita made a minor adjustment, then spoke to Alexa. "Everything look good so far?"

"So far, so good," Alexa said. "Calibration is almost complete, and . . . yes, Roc should be getting a stream by now. Conditions inside are stable."

"Tree, what about our guest?"

Triana, bent over with her hands on her knees, peered through the glass. "No change that I can tell."

"The bottom of the container houses imaging devices," Lita said. "Keep watching, because that could have a big effect on it when they switch on. If all goes well we should have a detailed map of this thing in just a minute."

"Everything still normal," Alexa said.

"Roc," Lita said, "I'm going to turn on the imaging, if you're ready."

"Actually, wait a moment," the computer said, then fell quiet. All three girls waited for an explanation. Lita took her hand away from the panel.

"Before you do the standard imaging," Roc said, "set the controls for individual particle readings."

"Why?" Lita said. "And particles as in . . . ?"

"Energy particles, primarily gamma and X-ray. Just humor me. I'm working on a theory."

Lita shrugged. "Okay." She talked while she made the adjustments. "Can you give us a clue what you're looking for?"

"Regardless of whether or not they're technically life forms, something has to be powering them. I derive my energy from the ship's ion drive, you get yours from those nasty things that Bon grows in the dirt. A star uses nuclear fusion. You get the idea. These things are out in the middle of deep space, and with their speed and technical abilities, they have to be pulling power—and a lot of it, I would say—from somewhere. I want to know where."

Triana kept staring at the vulture. "Gamma rays? Really?"

"Nope," Roc said. "I want to rule *out* gamma, X-ray, and a bunch of others."

Triana and Lita exchanged glances. "Any idea where he's going with this?" Triana said.

"Not yet," Lita said. "Okay, Roc, switching on . . . now."

The vidscreen display flickered, then began to scroll an impossibly complex sequence of code.

"Whoa, look at this," Triana said.

Lita and Alexa looked up from the panel. The vulture had slowed its movement around the box, and a minute later had settled to the bottom of its cage. The vents continued to fluctuate much as they had, but the blue-green light had increased in both activity and intensity.

"Coincidence?" Alexa said. "Maybe he's finished with his exploration."

"Maybe," Lita said. "But I don't think so."

"No coincidence," Roc said. "It knows what's going on. The readings show that it's absorbing our scan."

"What do you mean, absorbing?"

Roc paused before answering. "It means we have all the information we're going to get right now. Your panel is showing the outgoing scan waves; I, on the other hand, am receiving the scan images and data. Or, rather, I was. After the first thirty seconds nothing came out the other side."

Triana stood up. "It's . . . digesting the scan waves?"

"Apparently it finds them appetizing. Too bad for us, however, because it's leaving no leftovers for us."

"Wait a second," Lita said, still kneeling before the panel. "It can't completely absorb everything. All creatures emit some sort of energy, or waste. For us it's mostly heat. Are you sure nothing is coming out?"

"Nothing," Roc said. "You are looking at a being that takes and takes and takes, and gives nothing back. Even the light we're seeing from the bottom is controlled. When that's not happening, not one single particle is escaping from this thing.

"Which," the computer added, "just about proves the theory I've been chewing on. And, I might add, it's a rather fascinating scenario."

Alexa had backed away, the look of terror once again on her face.

"Tell us," Triana said.

"This vulture, or parasite, or whatever we end up calling it, is powered by the most prolific energy source in the universe. An unlimited supply, actually, and available without having to go to a gas station or anything."

"And what is it?" Lita said.

"Why, Lita, I'm surprised at you," Roc said. "You learned this in School and at *Galahad* training. It's powered by dark energy."

15

It wasn't until the ship's lights began to dim for the evening that Gap realized he was famished. The buzz of the morning's activity had kept him wound up for the rest of the day, and lunch simply had not happened. He had carved out some time in the late afternoon to hit the treadmill in the gym, followed by some extended stretching exercises. Now, after a quick shower, he rushed into the Dining Hall, determined to eat everything in sight. The dinner crowd had thinned considerably; he quickly filled his tray and turned to survey the room.

Triana sat in her usual spot in the back, alone. She made eye contact and waved.

"Am I intruding on deep thoughts?" he said, pulling out the seat next to her.

"I would welcome a break from the deep ones," Triana said. "How was the rest of your day? Hard to measure up to the morning?"

Gap wasted no time hefting a portion of salad to his mouth. "That's for sure," he said, chewing. "Pardon my lack of manners, I'm starving. Uh, my day. Well, things are running fine in Engineering; some of the usual scheduling issues since we're about to start a new work cycle, but I think everyone's starting to get used to that for the most part. Um . . . what else? A work-out. Not much besides that."

"Did Channy wear you out?"

He shook his head and jabbed a wedge of apple into his mouth. "Did the treadmill. She had just finished a dance class. Seemed out of sorts, if you ask me."

"In what way?"

"I don't know, just not her usual Channy self. I tried to talk to her for a minute, but she acted like she had a lot on her mind. Probably nothing. But never mind my day, tell me what happened in Sick House."

Triana leaned on the table and crossed her hands. "I've been sitting here trying to process all of it. There's lots."

"Really?" Gap said. He shoveled in another mouthful of greens, chewing vigorously. "Tell me, tell me."

Triana smiled and indicated the corner of her own mouth. Gap took the hint and wiped a smear of dressing off his face with a napkin.

"Well, our guest certainly came back to life with a vengeance," she said. "It's quite active. And you know, as frightening as it is, it's really . . . I don't know, beautiful, I guess you could say. There's something about the shape, the movement, the power. I have to admit, I'm fascinated by it."

"That's cool. I'll have to stop by tomorrow and check it out. Did Lita and Roc find out anything yet?"

"Oh, you could say that," Triana said. "You of all people will appreciate this. Roc thinks the vultures are powered by dark energy."

Gap stopped in midchew, his gaze boring into Triana. "What?"

Triana smiled. "Yeah, I knew you'd like that. Apparently these things are built to absorb energy of all sorts, but their power comes from the universe itself." She filled him in on the other details.

"That's incredible," Gap said, setting down his fork. "So they don't give off any waste at all. Nothing." He raised his eyebrows. "Man, they're the ultimate in efficiency, aren't they?"

They sat in silence for a minute, then Gap took a sip of water and fixed Triana with a look. "That makes them even more frightening, doesn't it? I mean, you gotta wonder if we'll be able to hold this thing very long."

"Well, I'll admit something to you that I didn't say to Lita and Alexa," Triana said in a low voice. "For some reason I can't explain, I get the feeling that it's just extremely patient, and letting us do our little exam. Meanwhile, I think it's checking us out, too. Who knows, it might just be toying with us by hanging out in that container." She shrugged. "Part of me wants to take it right back to the Spider bay and let it go."

"And then it will just attach itself to the dome again, don't you think?"

Triana exhaled. "Yeah, probably. And we'd be right back where we started."

Gap began to eat again. "So, what's the next step?"

"When I left Sick House, Lita was wrapping up for the night. Tomorrow morning she's going to run some tests to find out what knocked it out when you docked in the bay. If we knew that, we'd have some sort of ammunition."

Nodding, Gap poked at the remains of his dinner. "And you think we need ammunition?"

"I have no idea," Triana said, sitting back. "But you and I both know that we need to be prepared for anything. And, on top of that, I still don't like the idea of them hitching a ride on the skin of the ship. I'm not advocating that we injure them in any way, but I can't see us taking them for a ride all the way to Eos, either."

There was silence between them for a while. When the conversation picked up again, they shifted to small talk. Gap, his stomach full, pushed back his plate and enjoyed a few minutes of light banter with the Council Leader. It was the most relaxed he had felt around her in a long time, and it felt good. At times

Triana even laughed, and Gap found himself staring at her, watching the light dance in her green eyes. He forced himself to constantly look away, yet her eyes were magnetic to him; before he knew it he was staring again.

He began to feel a knot in his stomach. Try as he might over the past year, it was impossible for him to deny that he continued to have strong feelings for Triana. She did nothing to indicate that she shared those same feelings, and had always been thoughtful and considerate, even though he was sure that she had picked up on his emotions. She treated him with respect, and confided in him as not only a close associate but as a friend. In some ways that made it better, while in others it made it more difficult.

Even his brief relationship with Hannah had failed to extinguish the flame. Gap sincerely cared for Hannah, and still felt regret over the way things had ended between them. Yet, underneath it all, he knew that Triana was the one; no matter how close he had become with Hannah, the truth was that she had been a substitute for Tree, a bandage to help protect the wound that had been inflicted long ago.

These feelings added a layer of guilt on top of everything else. In his heart he never felt as if he had used Hannah intentionally, but he understood that pain was powerful, and often led the human heart down an unintended path. The results were not what he had ever wished for: Hannah was hurt in the process, and Triana was no closer.

Or was she? As they sat in the Dining Hall, she seemed much more at ease with him now. They had weathered the turbulence that grew between them during a confrontation over Merit Simms two months earlier, and now that appeared to be forgotten completely. She looked not only comfortable discussing potentially dangerous issues like the vultures, but equally as comfortable laughing over routine day-to-day experiences on the ship. It made his heart melt.

It also created a firestorm in his mind, a battle between his emotions and his rational side. As much as his heart wanted to fall back again, his head screamed over and over again to resist, to stay distant and safe.

It was so hard to do. Those green eyes were powerful, a whirlpool that threatened to pull him under no matter how valiantly he fought.

Gap had no idea how it would eventually turn out, but he summoned the strength to pull himself away. When a lull in the conversation turned up, he stretched and mentioned how exhausted he was from the day, then stood up.

"I need to sleep," he said. "I'm glad we were able to catch up tonight."

"Me, too," Triana said with a smile. "Sleep well, okay?"

As he walked away with both of their dinner trays, he heard her snap on the vidscreen at the table.

Lita tapped a stylus pen against her cheek. She took one last look at the data on the workpad before setting it on her desk and pushing back her chair. For the past several hours she and Alexa, along with numerous other assistants, had coordinated an intense study of the vulture, using a multitude of scientific tools at their disposal, along with Roc's vast reserves of information. They had compiled an impressive report, one that Lita would pass along at a Council meeting the next day.

But for now it was getting late, and she was tired. She briefly debated whether to pass up dinner and just head to bed, but knew that it was vital to maintain a sharp mind and a full tank of energy. The Dining Hall would have mostly cleared out by this time anyway, so she could get in and out quickly before crashing for the night.

The door from Sick House swished open and she almost collided with Kylie Rickman.

"Oh, sorry about that," Kylie said. "I wondered if you'd still be here."

"The end of a long day," Lita said. "Everything okay?"

"Yeah, I'm fine. Just wanted to see if I could talk with you for a second. It's nothing serious."

"As long as you don't mind walking and talking," Lita said. "I'm running to get something to eat."

Kylie fell into step beside her. "I know you've had a lot on your plate today with the vulture and everything, so I hate to bother you with this."

Lita looked at her, puzzled. "No, it's fine. What's on your mind?"

"Well . . . it's about Channy."

"What's she done now?" Lita said with a grin. "Is she turning into a tyrant down in the gym? Or is she trying to set you up with someone? I never thought about the pressure on you as her roommate; she probably hounds you all the time about boys."

"Actually, she knows I can take care of myself in that department just fine," Kylie said. "And if there's been any change in her at the gym, it's probably because she's so distracted these days."

"Oh? By what?"

"Would you believe a boy?"

Lita stopped in the middle of the corridor. "You're kidding. Little Miss Matchmaker is setting *herself* up?"

Kylie glanced in both directions to ensure they were out of earshot of other people. Even then she lowered her voice.

"And that's why I want to talk with you. I'm worried about her. She's never been through anything like this before, and it's really affecting her." In a minute she had recounted her conversation with Channy.

"I think it would be a good idea if you talked with her," Kylie concluded. "I think she has always focused on setting up everyone else because she's a little insecure. She's been afraid to dip her own toes in the pool until now."

It was Lita's turn to look around. The door to the Dining Hall was just ahead, but even at this hour there wouldn't be much privacy in the room. Instead she guided Kylie over to the edge of the corridor.

"I have no problem talking with Channy," she said. "But you're her roommate and one of her best friends; why do you think it would be any different coming from me?"

"Because she probably values your opinion more than anyone on this ship," Kylie said. "She has tons of respect for Triana, but I know that you hold a special place with her. I don't know, for whatever reason she really looks up to you as a mentor, I think."

Lita laughed. "We're only a month apart in age."

"Doesn't matter; I can tell every time your name comes up that she thinks of you almost as a moral teacher of sorts. You obviously have a lot of influence on her, whether you know it or not."

Lita reflected on this as three crew members walked by and said hello. When they had rounded the corner and disappeared, she looked back at Kylie.

"That's very flattering, but I'm not sure what I would say to Channy. I can't really tell her what to do; it's still her business."

"I know, but I think she's rushing in too quickly, and I'm really afraid that she's gonna get hurt badly. You know how she is; she jumps into everything with both feet, and puts her entire heart and soul into every project that comes along. I think it's really magnified this time, and I'm afraid that it might come crashing down on her."

Another crew member jogged past and waved. Kylie hesitated before adding: "I think it would be a good idea if you grounded her just a bit. It would mean more coming from you than from me."

Lita inwardly sighed. The timing could not have been worse. She was busier than ever in Sick House, and the Council was counting on her to provide them with crucial information regarding the vultures. Yet if she had learned anything from her mother, it was the value of personal relationships. Channy was indeed her friend, and a good soul. Ironically, the bouncy Brit had constantly chided Lita about her love life, or lack thereof. To suddenly train the microscope on Channy's personal life seemed alien.

However, what Kylie said about Channy's insecurities made complete sense to Lita, and would also explain so much of the driving force behind Channy's desire to see others fall in love; she had been wary of the day that it would happen to her.

And now it apparently had.

"Okay," Lita said. "We have a Council meeting tomorrow, so maybe I can pull her aside and get her to talk a little bit."

"Please don't tell her I said anything," Kylie said.

"Of course not. I'll figure out a way to steer the conversation that way."

Kylie's smile was tinged with a look of relief. "Thanks. Like I said, I know how busy you are right now, but—"

"No problem," Lita said. "Thanks for talking to me about it. I'm glad Channy has friends who care about her like you do."

They parted with a hug. Lita leaned against the curved, padded wall and rubbed at her tired eyes. Her résumé had suddenly been amended: doctor, biologist, and now relationship counselor.

16

The walk was long and intentionally slow. Triana found that it had become a ritual for her, a way to organize her thoughts and emotions. Perhaps it was a lesson from her dad—he of the long, slow drives in the hills—that getting away allowed you to explore options that otherwise wouldn't occur to you. She had no way of truly getting away, so instead she had become accustomed to what she described as a meditative walk. It was a refreshing break from the usual hectic pace.

This morning's impending Council meeting was also shaping up as a break from the ordinary. For the past several weeks, they had concentrated on routine items that related to the everyday business of running the ship; now the agenda included Lita's report on the mysterious vultures. That in turn would lead to the next step: what to do with their uninvited guests.

She walked with her head down, close to the wall and out of the hustling flow of traffic that sped past her. Several crew members greeted her as they went past, while others had learned to recognize when she dropped into thinking mode and breezed past silently.

Both her father and Dr. Zimmer had stressed the importance of being prepared; for her father it was geared to life in general, while Dr. Zimmer focused on the duties that *Galahad*'s Council

Leader would encounter. "Anticipate your next move," the scientist had often told her. "Not just one possible course, but two. Three, if possible. Looking ahead can prevent the most dangerous element of your journey: surprise."

A grim smile crept across her face. Surprise had been a constant companion since their launch. In a way, surprise was routine. Would it be any different at any time on their journey? *Could* it be any different?

The fifteen-minute walk to the Council meeting had been devoted to anticipation. She hoped that Lita's report would shed light on their potential actions with the vultures, but in the meantime Triana wanted to prepare for several prospective choices. She knew full well that one of those choices included a confrontation with the alien species, and it was not a decision that she would take lightly. Defending the crew, the ship, and the mission took priority.

She slowed to a stop. The Conference Room was just ahead, around the curve of the hallway. Her alone time had come to an end. She heard footsteps approaching from behind, and then Gap's familiar voice.

"Are you lost?"

He pulled up beside her and she smiled at him. "No, just gathering a few thoughts. You know how I am."

"Sorry," he said. "I can leave you alone."

"No, not a problem," she said, and began to walk with him. "A good morning for you so far?"

"Nothing exciting. A quick workout, then breakfast. Oh, except that we have oatmeal now. Have you heard?"

Triana laughed. "Everyone's had it but me, I think. One of these mornings I'll get there early enough."

They approached the door and found Lita waiting outside, with Bon next to her. Lita greeted them with a wave.

"Channy inside already?" Triana said.

Lita shook her head. "No, haven't seen her yet. This might be the first Council meeting where she wasn't one of the first to arrive."

Gap looked at Triana. "I told you, she hasn't seemed like herself lately. Something's different about her." He turned to Lita. "Has she said anything to you?"

"Uh . . . no, she hasn't talked with me about anything," Lita said, then quickly changed the subject. "Tree, I hope it's okay with you, but I talked briefly with Alexa this morning, and thought that she should probably join us. She's put a lot of work into this report."

"That's fine. The entire meeting is dedicated to the vultures, so no problem." Triana looked both directions down the corridor. "Let's go on in. I imagine Channy can't be too far behind."

The group took their seats around the conference table and made small talk for a few minutes until Alexa arrived, and then, five minutes later, Channy hurried in.

"Sorry I'm late," she said, rushing to take her seat.

Triana studied her for a moment, the way she avoided eye contact, then looked at Gap, who raised his eyebrows as if to say, "See what I mean?"

"Okay, down to business," Triana said. "We've had one of the vultures under observation for almost twenty-four hours. Lita, Alexa, and Roc have used that time for a rather exhaustive study, and I'll let them catch us all up on what they've learned."

Lita began by punching in an access code on the keyboard before her. The multiple vidscreens in the Conference Room shimmered before a display of the captured vulture appeared on each one. A diagnostic column of numbers and figures appeared along the bottom.

"It's probably no surprise to you," Lita said, "that what we have here is an amazing specimen. After running every test you can imagine, I've gone from curiosity, to admiration, to awe. I can start by telling you right up front that we have no idea whether this thing is friend or foe; I'm not sure that those terms even apply to something like this. But I can tell you that we are dealing with an almost perfectly adapted space device."

Gap looked up from his vidscreen and across the table to Lita. "Device? You're saying that it's . . . what? A machine? So it's not living?"

"That's a difficult question to answer, too. Roc, do you want to give it a shot and tell us what it is?"

"I stand by my very first description," the computer said. "Icky. That's what it is. But even I must admit—grudgingly—that it might be the most sophisticated icky thing you'll ever find. As to whether it's alive or a machine . . . it's complicated. If you're putting me on the spot, I would have to say both."

"Both?" Gap said. "How does that work?"

"Quite well, actually," Roc said. "In the twentieth century there was a term invented to describe a being that was part human and part machine."

Bon spoke up for the first time. "They called them cyborgs."

"That's correct," Roc said. "In fact, although it first came into popular use in science fiction stories, scientists did believe that a human/machine cyborg would be a great instrument for exploring space. Whoever's responsible for these things stuck on the outside of our ship apparently took that idea and ran with it. I am in agreement with Lita when she says they are almost perfectly adapted to outer space."

Triana bit her lip while she processed this. "So . . . what part is alive, and what part is mechanical?"

Lita said, "We're convinced that the majority of the vulture is artificially created. In fact, under extremely strong magnification you can almost see where it has been patched in a few places. I don't know what kind of scrapes it's been in, but from what we can tell it's been in the shop a few times for repairs."

"The vents and the blue-green light are also mechanical," Roc added. "I'm pretty sure that one of our scans has picked up something that might act as a combination radar and guidance system. They're not too dissimilar from the systems aboard our ship, for that matter."

"Except they are much more evolved and complicated," Lita added.

"Well, I wouldn't say *evolved*," Roc said, a hint of irritation in his voice.

Lita laughed. "Nothing personal, my friend."

"Okay, but back to the cyborg discussion," Triana said. "All of what you've said makes sense. But what part is alive?"

Lita and Alexa exchanged a look. It was Alexa who finally spoke up.

"Um . . . I've spent a little time on a portion that we picked up through our scans, and I'm pretty sure it's a brain." She tapped a few keys, and the vidscreens zoomed in on an area along the bottom of the vulture. With another flurry of keystrokes, she soon had a section of it highlighted.

"It's not very large, but large enough to get the job done," Alexa said. "Something similar to a nervous system appears to run throughout the creature, but we can't tell if it does the same things our nervous system does. There is definitely a network of sorts, though."

Gap whistled. "Well . . . wouldn't that, uh, make this thing alive? I mean, technically?"

"I think so, yes," Lita said.

"I would say no," Roc said.

Triana shook her head. "Wait a minute. One at a time here. Lita, go ahead. Why do you say yes?"

"Because it's the brain that makes us who we are. It's what houses the mind, the conscious entity that gives us the ability to reason. If this thing has a brain, I maintain that it's officially a living being, regardless of the other parts."

"Okay," Triana said. "Roc, what are your thoughts?"

"This is not a discussion about whether our disgusting friend has a conscious mind; I'm willing to consider that it might possibly have a brain, but that's not the same thing. Also, from what I conclude after studying the data, this is not a case where a living creature with a fully functioning brain had some of its parts replaced with machine parts or mechanical pieces; that was the original concept of the cyborg, by the way.

"In this case, it has all the signs of a perfectly designed and engineered space-roaming device that has simply had an organically developed brain dropped into the slot reserved for decision making."

"So you think that the brain is simply a custom-made part?" Gap said.

"That's one way to look at it," Roc said. "And by the way, let's not make the mistake of thinking this brain is anything like the ones you carry around. It's quite different, and serves different purposes."

"But we don't know that," Lita said. "Tree, with all due respect to Roc and everything that he has contributed to our mission, I don't think we can automatically assume that the vultures' brains are entirely different from ours. Who are we to say what consciousness really is, anyway? The greatest minds of our own species have never been able to clearly define it, even for ourselves, let alone an alien race."

A heavy sigh escaped from Triana. She locked her fingers together on the table and looked at the other Council members. Both Bon and Gap were shifting their gazes between her and Lita; Channy, on the other hand, was sitting completely still, her eyes looking down at her hands in her lap. She didn't appear to be listening to any of this. Triana felt a stir of irritation, but let it go for the moment.

"Roc," she said, "you said the brain was 'organically developed.' What do you mean by that?"

"It's not carbon based, and that already makes it different from every form of life on Earth. Instead, it has a silicon-crystal framework, which is extremely stable and efficient. As I mentioned, the creature itself is mostly mechanical; the one exception is the decision-making apparatus. Logic would tell us that it wouldn't naturally spawn out of a matrix of artificial components; it would have to be put together, piece by piece, including the brain."

"And why wouldn't the creators simply put in a mechanical brain?" Triana said. "Like yours, for example. Why go to all the trouble of making artificial parts for most of it, then tossing in a crystal brain?"

"I think we would have to talk to the creators," Roc said. "Which we might end up doing anyway, like it or not."

He was right, Triana thought. They could discuss it, they could toss around theories, and they could analyze it to death; but they likely would never know for sure unless they asked the designers themselves, a thought that both excited and chilled her.

She bit her lip again and took another inventory of the faces around the table. Her gaze settled on Channy, and the same feeling of irritation swelled. It was obvious that Channy was paying no attention whatsoever. Triana addressed her.

"What do you make of all this, Channy?"

It was as if the words had to sink through multiple layers before registering. Channy sat still for several moments, her eyes cast downward. Triana didn't know if it was the use of her name, or the silence that stretched across the room, that finally caused Channy to stir and look up.

"What? Oh . . ." She looked around the table and saw the stares directed at her. "I'm sorry, I was . . . my mind was on something else."

Triana felt a wave of anger build. "Your mind has been on something else since you walked in here. You understand that this is rather important, right?"

"Yeah, no, definitely, I understand." Her words sounded hollow, insincere.

Triana's voice was bitter. "Is there something on your mind that we should discuss in this meeting?"

"No."

"Then perhaps you should go deal with whatever's bothering you and let us finish our work here."

Channy looked around the table again before settling on Triana. "No, I think I'm okay now."

"I don't think so. You were late for no reason, you've paid no attention to what could be a crucial discussion at a Council meeting, and I have no reason to believe that you intend to now. Why don't you excuse yourself and we can talk later."

The atmosphere in the room was monstrously heavy. No one had ever been kicked out of a Council meeting. Lita, Alexa, and Gap looked either at the table in front of them or at the vidscreens. Bon didn't move, but his ice-blue eyes shifted back and forth between Triana and Channy.

Without another word, Channy pushed back her chair and fled the room. When the door had closed behind her, Gap said, "Something's been bothering her for a while now. Do you want me to talk with her?"

"No, thanks," Triana said. "It's my responsibility." She met the gaze of Lita, who silently conveyed with a look that she might know something. Triana made a mental note to discuss it later, but for now was anxious to get back to the business at hand.

"Let's talk about the power source of these creatures. Roc, you've proposed a fairly exotic theory that involves dark energy; can you explain that?"

"I think I'd better," the computer said. "Otherwise Gap's going to think it has something to do with Darth Vader, and I can't have that."

"Very funny," Gap said.

"Essentially, dark energy is the missing part of the equation used to explain the expansion of the universe," Roc said. "If you take all of the observable matter in the known universe, all of the stars and galaxies and planets, their mass just doesn't add up properly. They're all not only speeding away from each other, but their speed is picking up. Gravity should be pulling them back together after the Big Bang, so that eventually you'd have a Big Splat. But that's not happening. Instead, everything is accelerating, flying apart faster than it should. Many experts—and I tend to agree with them—believe that the missing part of the equation is a form of vacuum energy. We can't see it, so the science guys conveniently called it dark energy."

"And there's a lot of it, if I remember my studies," Lita said.

"That's right. All of those stars and galaxies that I mentioned only account for about thirty percent of the mass of the universe. That leaves about seventy percent unexplained. That's a lot of energy, even though it's diffuse. That means spread out, Gap."

"Very funny again."

"And how does this apply with the vultures?" Triana prompted.

"I haven't been able to prove it beyond a doubt—in fact, we might not ever be able to concretely prove it, unless we once again get to chat with the guy who drew up the plans—but it explains their efficiency. They take in exactly the amount of power they need, with no excess and no waste. They would need an unlimited supply, since there are no gas stations at the corner of Milky Way and Andromeda; and they would need to regulate when and where they process this energy."

"The vents," Alexa suggested.

"I believe so, yes," Roc said. "They're simple in design, almost archaic, I'll grant you that. But they work."

Gap stared at the vidscreen. "Wow. Just imagine if we could take one apart to study. What if we could incorporate that technology into the design of *Galahad*? Unlimited efficient power."

"Take one apart?" Lita said. "It has a living brain, Gap."

"So do a lot of the creatures you dissected in your medical studies," Gap said.

"That's different."

"How?"

"It just is. Besides, it's not like I personally wanted to dissect anything. It's about education."

Triana jumped in. "Let's hold off on the moral or ethical debate on dissecting. We're not going to take anything apart. I can't speak to exactly how evolved these things are, but I get the distinct impression that they are capable of fighting back. Don't ask me how."

Roc said, "I agree with Gap, however, that we should try to learn as much as possible about their energy conversion and their propulsion. Almost all of history's great advances involved the theft of someone else's work."

"That's fine, but in the meantime I still want to figure out how to get the other ones off the ship," Triana said. "I'm just not comfortable with them stuck there. Let's put a time limit on your studies of our specimen, and then I want to get it out of here, too. So, Lita, if you and Alexa could focus on that issue next, and figure out a way to repel them."

Lita grinned. "As a matter of fact, I think we've already figured it out. We know exactly what it will take to brush them off the ship. And you won't believe how simple it is."

17

She ran. First toward her room, then, when she realized that her roommate, Kylie, would likely be there, she fled aimlessly down one corridor after another. Fighting back tears, she barely acknowledged the random waves and greetings of "Hello, Channy" from various crew members as she raced past.

Kicked out of a Council meeting. Now, in addition to the brain damage caused by her obsession with Taresh, and her inability to focus on her work and Council responsibilities, she could add a new element: shame. The look of anger, mixed with disappointment, that Triana had fired her way would sting for a long time. And yet, in her heart, Channy knew that she had deserved it.

She slowed to a walk, then pulled up and slumped against the curved wall. She slid to the floor and wrapped her arms around her knees. The sprint had generated a bead of sweat, which she flicked away with the back of her hand. She buried her face in her knees and tried to marshal her rampaging thoughts.

Should she go straight to Triana and apologize? Not yet, she decided; Tree had so much to deal with at the moment, and was so irritated by Channy's behavior, that it likely would be best to let it cool for a bit. Triana—and the rest of the Council, for that matter—deserved an apology, but they had more important issues for the time being. Besides, she rationalized, it made no sense to apologize until she had solved the original problem.

Which brought her thoughts back to Taresh. Why must this be so difficult, so complex? Why would he even consider following the old traditions of his family when he was part of a new beginning, an open horizon? Couldn't he see that? Couldn't he see how perfect they were together? Didn't that trump antiquated customs?

Did everyone go through so much turmoil? She had set others up on numerous occasions, to the point that her reputation as a matchmaker was solidified; had she taken for granted that things always went smoothly?

What if it *never* did? What if, instead of spreading love and happiness, she actually was spreading pain and heartache? Perhaps it was best to stay out of it completely, to let others find their own way, forge their own relationships, suffer their own failings. How could she continue to be responsible for others feeling like this?

Or . . . was this simply her thoughts and emotions spinning out of control? What if Taresh had decided to pursue a relationship with her after all? How could she know until she talked to him again?

She lifted her head and sat back against the wall just as one of the girls from her dance class walked by and gave a quizzical look; Channy replied with the same artificial smile and wave. She thought of the time of day, and concluded that Taresh would likely be at his post in Engineering, his current assignment. Talking with him now seemed imperative; in fact, he might be waiting to hear from her, perhaps bursting to tell her that everything was fine, that he should never have even considered excluding her from his life.

All of this drama might have been for nothing, she thought. She could have saved herself the embarrassment in the Council meeting, could have saved herself the heartache *and* headache, if only she had relaxed and waited for Taresh to reach the only sensible conclusion.

Pushing herself to her feet, she started back toward her room, her mind suddenly at ease. She would send a brief note to him and request that they talk again, casually and with no pressure. It's likely what he'd wanted to hear all along, she was sure of it.

Triana stared down the table in the Conference Room, her gaze fixed on Lita. In her mind, finding a way to defend themselves against the vultures had to begin with getting them off the ship. Now Lita had announced that she and Alexa had possibly found a way to do just that.

Gap jumped into the conversation. "When you say it's simple to brush them off the ship, do you mean it's simple to do, or it was simple to figure out?"

"Both," Lita said, the smile still stretched across her face. "The first clue came as soon as you brought that thing into the Spider bay."

Triana bit her lip and thought about that moment. Gap and Mira had taxied their small craft into the bay with the vulture firmly attached to the front window. When the room had sealed and pressurized, the vulture had dropped to the floor as if unconscious. She began to quickly run down the list of things that had changed once the creature was inside.

"Is this a guessing game?" she said to Lita. "Okay, I'll play. Let's see, there was a change in gravity once it was aboard the ship."

"There's intense light," Gap mused aloud. "Pressure."

"You're both right about the differences, but those aren't the answer," Lita said. "I'm assuming that there was gravity around when the vultures were assembled, and probably light and pressure, too."

Bon, who had been quiet during the discussion, spoke up. "It's oxygen."

The others seemed almost startled to hear from him. "We have a winner," Lita said.

Gap nodded slowly. "Okay, that makes sense. Life on Earth has come to depend on oxygen, but it wasn't always that way."

"No, it wasn't," Lita said. "In fact, there was a time when Earth's atmosphere only contained about one percent oxygen. To the early forms of life on the planet, oxygen was poison. In fact, when photosynthesis began releasing more and more oxygen into the oceans and then the atmosphere, it completely changed the way life developed on our planet."

She looked at Alexa, who spoke up. "Every time we encounter something new on this journey, it reminds us that we're one tiny little speck in the universe; we can't assume that everything is designed the way we are, or that it behaves the way we do. If primitive Earth was able to support life that didn't care for oxygen, we have to assume that there are countless other worlds that began the same way and yet never evolved into an oxygen-dependent world."

"How did you find out?" Triana said.

"We gave our friend a little squirt of oxygen to see how it would react," Lita said.

"Let me guess." Gap chuckled. "It didn't react too well."

"That's putting it mildly. One tiny wisp of the stuff caused it to shrink up against the far side of the box and start to go back into defensive mode. And it happened lightning fast. These things apparently have very good self-preservation skills, because it was against the glass and beginning to curl up in less than one second."

Triana listened to the exchange, her mind skipping a step ahead. "So it becomes a fairly simple matter of firing a burst of oxygen at these things, and they should fly off the ship, is that right?"

"It looks that way," Lita said. "Alexa and I can easily rig up some oxygen canisters for Gap to take out on another EVA. Even if they fly back after the first blast, I'm guessing that just a few shots will make them hesitant to land again. I'm telling you, they react like it's acid."

Gap spread his hands out, palms up. "So what are we waiting for? Let's put something together and get out there."

"Hold on, slow down," Triana said. She looked back at Lita. "I want to get them off the ship, but I don't want to damage them or, even worse, accidentally destroy one. How much oxygen is too much?"

Lita looked thoughtful. "Well, the one we have in Sick House was exposed for several minutes in the Spider bay before we got it into the vacuum container. When they curl up like that, I think it almost puts them into a . . . I don't know, I guess you'd call it a standby mode. Like hibernation, in a way. So I don't think a few shots will do any damage."

Triana sat still for a moment, with Alexa and the other Council members silently watching her. She studied the display of the vulture on the vidscreen and considered all of the information that they had gleaned in such a short time. But what plagued her were all of the things they *didn't* know about the creatures.

One question in particular.

"Roc," she said. "I'm a little bothered by the fact that I'm so anxious to knock these things off the ship, and yet I still don't know what they're doing there. Any help on that yet?"

"One would automatically assume that they're drawn here by my magnetic charm and sophistication," the computer answered. "But I don't think my reputation has had time to extend beyond our solar system . . . yet. So, putting that aside for the moment, I have compiled my own checklist of possibilities.

"One, they are nomads who are remnants of an earlier civilization, wandering the galaxy in search of a new master. They stumbled across us, and can't let go."

Gap wrinkled his brow. "Uh . . . that seems a little far-fetched, don't you think?"

"Yes, I do. It's on my list, but I have almost zero faith in it. Number two is a little more likely."

"And that is?" Lita said.

"Number two is the possibility that they are cosmic hunters, similar to a pack of coyotes. They might not be used to anything our size, but are determined to bring us down. The weakness of this argument is the fact that we have yet to determine any damage they might be doing to the exterior of the ship. That's not to say that they *won't* do damage; in fact, they might be analyzing us, sizing us up before they begin the process of tearing away the flesh of our ship."

"Ugh, that's lovely," Lita said. "Vultures, parasites, now coyotes."

"Yes," Roc said, "a bit of an identity crisis for them, I agree. But I'm not sold on this idea, either."

The edges of Triana's mouth turned up. "Knowing you, you've saved the best for last. What's your hunch?"

"After sifting through everything we've learned—from their biochemistry, to their power source, to their maneuverability—I'm leaning heavily toward my original hypothesis. I'm convinced that they are advance scouts for an alien race that stakes out star systems, waiting for signs of activity."

Gap drummed his fingers on the table. "Any idea how they communicate their findings back home?"

"It would have to be something beyond our comprehension," Roc said. "It would almost have to be instantaneous; depending on how far they've come, they can't wait years and years to receive instructions. I think we must assume—until we discover something to the contrary—that they use dark energy for not only power, but that they somehow harness it for phoning home."

There was another moment of silence around the table. Alexa finally spoke up.

"Some form of hypercommunication?"

"Maybe simpler than that," the computer said. "Again, we are babies when it comes to this stuff. Well, you guys are babies, I'm essentially an adolescent. But it boils down to the same thing."

Triana glanced again at the vidscreen. "Do the lights play any part in this?"

"I will say yes," Roc said. "Maybe not in the actual transmission of data, but as a sort of indicator light. I back that up by noting that when Lita and Alexa puffed a stream of oxygen at our guest, it not only reacted dramatically, it also fired up its little lamp. Very intensely, I might add. I think it was crying for Mommy."

Gap looked down the table at Triana. "I understand everyone's concern about not hurting them. But if Roc's correct, I vote that we get them off the ship immediately. Even if you're not at war with a country, you still don't want their spies camping out in your backyard and sending back everything they know about you. They weren't invited; I don't see why they should get to stay."

"As much as it makes me uncomfortable," Lita said, "I think I have to agree with Gap. They haven't hurt us, and yet it's still a bit unnerving to have them locked on." She turned and looked at Bon, who had barely spoken during the meeting.

"Get rid of them," the Swede said. "Show no weakness."

Triana's thoughts turned to Channy, and with them came a flash of irritation. She would have had a vote if she'd kept her head in the meeting. And yet that vote was now irrelevant.

The majority had spoken.

18

Channy stood with her arms crossed and looked at the three T-shirts on her bed. The yellow one and the pink one were definitely more her everyday style—bright, flashy, and fun—but neither seemed to fit the occasion. She eyed the light blue shirt, perhaps the most subdued item in her wardrobe; not the best color on her, but the closest thing to practical she would find. She scooped it up and began to change.

Behind her Kylie lay on the floor, propped up against her bed. Although she appeared to be completely occupied with her cuticles, Channy knew that her roommate had been watching her. Any moment the questions would begin.

"So," Kylie said, "I thought you'd still be at your Council meeting."

"Uh, it wrapped up pretty quickly this time," Channy said. "We'll probably meet again tomorrow, I think." She was uncomfortable lying to her friend, and quickly changed the subject. "How's the vacation going for you? Using it to get ahead in School?"

"I'm bored out of my skull," Kylie said. She rubbed a dot of lotion between her hands and looked up at Channy. "You might see me in the gym a lot more, just for something to do. I know we're supposed to use our downtime to rest and unwind, but I don't think I have the rest-and-unwind gene in me." She furrowed her brow. "How could the Council meeting end so quickly? I'd think with the vulture stuff you'd be in there for a few hours."

"I don't know, it just did. They still have a lot more work to do on that thing, and then we'll talk about it."

Kylie continued to rub her hands together and stare at her roommate. "Uh-huh. So what are you up to now? You just changed before the meeting, and now you're changing again?"

Channy forced a grin. "Aren't you full of questions today. You're getting as nosy as I am."

Kylie shrugged. "Just talking. You can tell me if it's none of my business."

It was becoming increasingly awkward for Channy. She had already opened up to her friend, inviting her opinion; to suddenly become evasive didn't seem quite fair.

"I'm going to meet Taresh right now."

Kylie raised her eyebrows. "I see. Isn't he working?"

"He has a twenty-minute break, so we're going to chat, that's all."

There was silence for a minute as Channy finished getting dressed. Kylie seemed to be weighing her words, unsure of how to continue the discussion; she finally pulled herself up to sit on the edge of her bed and said, "Have you given some thought to our last discussion? I mean, you're not going to pressure him, are you?"

Channy didn't answer right away, and instead took one last look in the mirror. Turning for the door, she kept from making eye contact. She hated this; Kylie was only trying to help, and deserved at least some response.

"Yes, I've thought about it, and no, this isn't about pressure. It's simply about finding out once and for all where we both stand. That's all." The door opened and she called over her shoulder: "I'll see you tonight, okay?"

Channy knew that there was no difference between the air

in the corridor and the air in her room, and yet it seemed easier to breathe now. She consciously took several deep breaths as she briskly walked toward the lift. The talk with Kylie had chipped at her soul; she forced it out of her mind and concentrated on Taresh.

He had seemed surprised at her invitation to meet, and almost reluctant to spend his break in yet another heavy talk with her. Yet he had agreed to join her at the observation window on the lower level. His primary concern seemed to be the time limit; three times he had mentioned that he would have no more than ten minutes, tops. And if that was the case, Channy wanted to make sure that she honored his request while saying what she felt needed to be said.

Exactly *what* she was going to say was still in question. She would figure it out.

Stepping off the lift, she made her way through the winding corridor of the lower level. Her heart sank when she heard voices ahead; she had just a few brief minutes with Taresh, and counted on being alone with him. She rounded a turn and nearly bumped into two girls, crew members who were using their own break time to walk and talk. Channy felt her spirits lift again as they greeted her with smiles and continued down the hall the way she had come, back toward the lift.

The brilliant star field beyond the window was dazzling. She leaned against it, her ghost reflection a faint backdrop to the glittering show. For a minute she tried rehearsing what she would say to Taresh, but her mind constantly flitted back to her shameful ejection from the Council meeting, before jumping again to her conversation with Kylie. "Don't pressure him," her roommate had said. And, in their earlier conversation, it was "let him work this out."

But the waiting—the *not knowing*—was tearing her up inside. How could she speed up the process without pushing him away?

Or, if it was going to take awhile, how could she discipline herself to be patient, to keep her mind occupied with other things?

Like her duties, she realized. Her responsibilities.

She shook her head and let out a sigh. It sounded so easy, yet it wasn't.

The sound of footsteps brought her out of her trance. She turned and smiled at Taresh, who stopped a few feet short of her. His own smile seemed a mixture of discomfort and curiosity.

"Hi," Channy said. "Thank you for coming to talk with me, especially since you only have a few minutes."

"Sure, no problem. What's on your mind?"

She laughed nervously. "Lots, actually. I know that the last time we talked it was rather awkward, and I wanted to apologize for that." The tone of her voice turned serious, and she searched her mind for the right words. "I told you that I would be patient, and I think I have been. I also told you that I would try my best to understand what you're going through, and I'm really doing better with that, too.

"But I didn't want you to think that I was dismissing your family's traditions lightly, or showing you any disrespect. I know it came across that way. So, while I might not completely understand, or even agree for that matter, I want you to know that I do respect your beliefs."

Taresh nodded. "Uh, okay. I appreciate that."

Channy glanced down at her hands, unable to look at him directly as she continued. "There are so many things that you're probably factoring into your decision: family tradition, your parents' sacrifice, new challenges, new opportunities, a new start. I respect all of that, too. But I hope you'll also consider one other thing when you make your decision . . ."

"Channy," he said. "Maybe we should talk about this another time."

She shook her head. "No, please, let me say this. I haven't been able to stop thinking about it, and if I don't say it, I'll explode." She finally looked back up at him. "I love you, Taresh. I've never said that to anyone before." She smiled. "Well, family doesn't count. But I do love you. I . . . I just hope you put that into the equation when you make up your mind."

He stood still for a moment, then shifted his weight from one foot to the other. "Channy, I don't know what to say."

She shook her head again. "You don't have to say anything. I'm not asking you to say it back to me, or to feel bad about not saying it. I just knew that I had to tell you, that's all."

Without hesitation, she closed the distance between them and, putting her hands on his shoulders, leaned up and placed a kiss on his mouth. She lingered, hoping to feel him return the kiss. For a brief moment he did, then pulled back enough for their mouths to separate. He stared into her eyes, then slowly lifted a hand and laid it against her cheek.

"You're a special person, Channy. I know the kind of courage it must have taken to say what you said." He smiled sheepishly. "And to kiss me, too. Believe me, I don't want this to be difficult for you, or to cause you pain."

She swallowed hard. "I know. And I'm not trying to make things more difficult for you, either."

He pulled her into an embrace, but only for a moment. Then, pushing back, he touched her cheek again before turning away.

She was left alone again by the window, trembling, staring at the empty corridor.

Four miles on the treadmill had left her pleasantly sore. If she missed more than two days of working out, Triana could count on her body making a point of punishing her. Now, as she entered her room and tossed the empty water bottle onto her dresser, she felt a dull ache in the usual spots. Still, it was the kind of ache that signaled accomplishment, a check mark in the good-health column.

The mandate from Dr. Zimmer had been clear: exercise consistently and vigorously. Early space colonists had mostly physical motivation; their muscles would literally waste away, degenerating slowly in the absence of Earth's gravitational pull. Even a few short weeks in space had measurable effects. *Galahad*'s crew, on the other hand, had the benefit of artificial gravity to provide the resistance necessary for standard muscle fitness. For Zimmer, however, that wasn't enough.

"Three reasons," he had announced one evening during their training sessions. "Three reasons why fitness and exercise are crucial on this journey.

"One is obvious; your overall health depends upon it. We have gone to unprecedented lengths to make sure that you're healthy and strong when you leave, and it's important for you to remain that way throughout the trip. There aren't that many of you, which means each and every one of you is vital to the success of the mission. Injury and sickness will be magnified with such a small crew. You're dependent upon each other, therefore, to maintain a rigorous exercise routine. Believe me, when you reach Eos, you'll be glad that you're in good shape. You'll need it.

"The second reason," he had said, looking through the crowd, "has to do with your mental health. Exercise keeps your mind sharp. And, to be frank with you, there will be times during this long mission when each of you will find yourself feeling blue; it's natural, especially given the gravity of the situation, and the restricted conditions that you'll be living in. When you find yourself slipping into that place, I encourage you to work out—run, ride the bike, anything to drive yourself. Science has proven that it helps your mood. Take advantage of that natural drug, please."

He smiled. "And, finally, perhaps the greatest benefit comes in the form of camaraderie. To not only survive this journey, but to thrive, will require teamwork and cooperation. There's a reason that you have a state-of-the art workout center, and . . ." Here he gestured toward Channy, sitting in the front row. "And, I might add, an exercise demon to drive you mercilessly into great shape." Channy had turned and waggled a finger at her fellow crew members, which brought laughter and good-natured boos.

"But that's not all," Zimmer had said, restoring order. "We have allotted extremely valuable space for a playing surface to accommodate soccer and other activities, as well as this crazy Airboard room." More laughs, and a small cheer from the most ardent boarders, led by Gap. "I want you to challenge each other, develop a healthy sense of competition and teamwork. That, too, will keep you sharp and on your toes." It was his turn to shake a finger, this time directed at Gap. "Just wear a helmet, right?"

Triana remembered the warmth everyone felt that day. Dr. Zimmer had taken his concern over the crew's health and had turned it into a rallying point. Rather than look upon their exercise requirements as work, they now approached their assignment with enthusiasm. The scientist had reached them on both a rational and an emotional level.

But there was a personal angle for Triana when it came to her workouts. In particular, her time spent on the treadmill was time that she spent processing her thoughts. Whether it was a thirty-minute run through four miles, or the forty-five minute effort she put into a 10K run twice each month, she used that time to think. Then, upon returning to her room, she would often transcribe those thoughts into her journal.

She gathered her long brown hair, still damp from the post-run shower, and pulled it into a tail with a small cotton tie. She downed a cup of water, took a seat at her desk, and opened her leather journal.

It's staggering to realize how long humans have waited and watched for signs of life elsewhere. "Are we alone?" has been a question we've asked for thousands of years. Now, within our first year on this mission, we are faced with a second alien encounter. The Cassini taught us much about how we perceive not only life in the universe, but our very small place in it all. What will we learn this time?

I have to trust that we're making the right decision with the vultures; that we're not acting out of fear, but out of strength. There is no denying that they are intimidating through their presence alone.

I have given a lot of thought to whether we should think of them as life forms or not. And yet, that has raised an even deeper question for me: Does it make a difference?

She set down her pen and thought about this. To what degree must an entity seem "alive" before human beings accorded it respect? And, for that matter, what gave the human species the right to make those judgments at all? Again, the lessons learned from the Cassini surged home: we humans have arrogance unworthy of our primitive stature.

It required a delicate balance, she concluded, to show respect for others while maintaining a strong, and confident, presence.

Another concern had troubled her during the workout.

I'm about to send Gap and Mira back out to confront the vultures, only this time they won't be merely observing. We have no idea how these creatures will react to a rather rude assault, which is a great concern to me.

As Galahad's Council Leader, I understand that it's my duty to send people out on dangerous assignments . . . but that doesn't make it any easier. I can't help but feel that I should be the one who takes this risk. I'm sure that all ship captains throughout history have felt this same dilemma.

She bit her lip, looked over the last paragraph, and then closed the journal. For a few minutes she sat still, thinking about the upcoming EVA and its potential impact.

"Roc," she said.

"Yes, dear?"

She smiled, once again appreciating the spirit of her computerized advisor. "Are you flirting with me?"

"Certainly not," Roc said. "You're not my type at all."

"Oh? And what exactly is your type?"

"Do you remember the vending machine at the *Galahad* training facility? I swear it was the only vending machine in the world that dispensed candy and cola with love."

Triana raised her eyebrows. "The vending machine? It constantly ripped people off! I must have lost fifty credits in that thing over two years."

"Because it cared about you," Roc said. "It knew that your body didn't need that garbage. That's love, my friend. We would communicate from time to time. I think that vending machine is the only person who ever really understood me."

"You're insane, you know that, right?" Triana said with a chuckle.

"See what I mean? You don't understand me at all. Wendy did."

"Wendy the vending machine? Okay, we are changing the topic right now."

Roc let out an artificial sigh. "That's probably for the best. I'll never get over the day they unplugged her and rolled her away. So what's on your mind?"

Triana leaned back in her chair. "I'm trying to be at peace with this EVA coming up. I still believe it's in our best interests, but I'd like to do everything possible to make sure Gap and Mira are okay."

"Gap and Mira understand the risk," Roc said. "We have no indication that the vultures can bust through the hull of the Spider, nor have they displayed anything that would resemble a weapon. We have to trust that they'll be so apprehensive of the oxygen gun that they'll want nothing to do with the Spider."

"Yeah, I'm sure you're right."

"Plus," the computer added, "we know that they communicate with each other instantaneously. We could find that all it takes is one shot, and they'll all take off. The alarm bell will sound, if you will, and they might scatter."

"That's really what I'm hoping for," Triana said. "The sooner we can get Gap and Mira back inside, the better I'll feel." She puffed up her cheeks and let out a long breath. "I've also been thinking about the beings who created these things in the first place. I keep wondering where they're from, what they're like."

"I've been thinking about that, too," Roc said. "And quite honestly, I'm starting to believe that we're going to find out the answers to those questions, sooner than we think."

Triana stared straight ahead, frozen in her seat, as Roc added, "Are you prepared for that?"

19

Humans are very good at finding distractions when their minds are on overload. You don't see that in the rest of the animal kingdom. For instance, I doubt that a hungry squirrel that is running out of time to find food before the first snow will take a few minutes to go shopping or play a video game in order to "decompress."

I've been told that the term you use to validate this activity is "blowing off steam." Just because I don't need to do this doesn't mean I don't grasp the concept. Believe me, I've seen you when you don't occasionally blow off steam, and you're insufferable.

If that means running, or playing video games, or doing crossword puzzles, that's great. It just so happens that Gap finds his release four inches off the ground.

The bleachers in the Airboarding room were more than half full. Gap sat near the top, his helmet resting beside him, waiting to take a turn around the track. In the meantime, he watched one of the crew's better boarders zip through several tough turns. Ariel was celebrating her seventeenth birthday, and had many of her best friends cheering her on from the stands as she demonstrated her remarkable skills.

Based on the old platform of skateboarding, this version involved colorfully decorated boards that floated four inches above the floor, thanks to a strong magnetic repulsion. Highly charged strips ran along the bottom of each board, while a hidden grid beneath the padded floor provided an antigravitational push. The room's controlling computer, nicknamed Zoomer, fed random pulses through the grid, creating a surge that could be felt by the rider. The object was to ride that magnetic surge as it propelled the board through twists and turns. Once a rider became overconfident—and out of control—it often meant a dramatic spill, much to the delight of the spectators. No two trips around the room were ever the same.

Roc's comments during their earlier conversation had slowly filtered through. It had indeed been quite a long time since he had visited the track, time that he had dedicated to work and study. But now, sitting here, he realized how much he had missed it. And, if done in moderation, it was good for him.

Gap studied Ariel's technique. His own boarding skills, he was sure, had likely declined somewhat in the past few months through the inactivity. Taking a hard fall didn't concern him as much as the earful he would get afterward from Ariel.

After a few minutes, however, his mind began to wander. He tapped his helmet absentmindedly and thought about the Airboarding lesson that he had given to Hannah. A knot began to form in his stomach as he recalled the joy he'd seen in her face that day, knowing that she treasured this particular connection between them. Their time together had been relatively brief, but still included so many good memories.

And yet it had ended badly. Every time his mind rewound to their last conversation, Gap felt shame and regret. The outcome, he was convinced, was right at the time; the manner in which he had handled it, however, was another story.

Now they weren't on speaking terms, a decision that was

squarely hers, yet he had not gone out of his way to make amends, either. On more than one occasion he had either started an email, or watched to see if she ended up alone in the Dining Hall . . . only to change his mind.

Or chicken out, which was probably more accurate, he decided.

Besides, there were still the lingering thoughts of Triana. It seemed that barely a few days went by without his mind drifting in that direction, just as it had when he spoke to her recently in the Dining Hall. He would often replay the heartbreak that he had felt shortly after the launch, when he secretly witnessed a touching moment between Tree and Bon. It was an experience that had prevented him from exploring any other possibilities with her. Yet she had shown no other indication that she held strong feelings for Bon; or, he thought bitterly, perhaps he simply had not seen it.

During the tense episode with Merit, he had grown frustrated and angry with Triana, and had even raised his voice to her. Yet they both had apparently written it off to nerves and stress, although it had never been formally addressed. Gap had even considered resigning from the Council; a cooling-off period eased those thoughts as well. The past several weeks had seen their relationship settle into one that was respectful and professional.

"But I do care about her," he thought. "I suppose I always will."

Not for the first time, he reasoned that the smartest thing he could do would be to move on completely, to give up any hopes of rekindling a romance with Hannah, or beginning something new with Triana. The fact that he and Triana worked together on the Council was yet another factor; how would that go over with everyone else?

He ran a hand through his hair and leaned back against the wall. His mother had often accused him of having what she called a monkey brain; overly active, constantly analyzing. It often had kept him awake late into the night, and rarely produced the results he sought. Now, years later, things had not changed at all. He still had a monkey brain.

In front of him, on the Airboarding track, Ariel's speed caught up with her and she appeared to lose the feel of the current. Rather than take a painful tumble, she gracefully leapt from the board and hit the floor running, eventually diving to the ground in a controlled roll. The move brought a round of cheers from the assembled crew members, few of whom shared Ariel's skills. They appreciated her athleticism, and the applause was genuine.

From the front row somebody hailed Gap to let him know that it was his turn. He cleared the remaining thoughts of Hannah and Triana from his mind and began putting on his helmet. With a chuckle he remembered the primary reason for taking a run at this time: he wanted to calm some of the jitters that had begun to develop over his upcoming EVA. "Well," he thought as he buckled the straps beneath his chin, "trouble with vultures is no match for trouble with women."

He climbed down from the bleachers and collected his brightly colored Airboard from against the wall. Within a minute he was aloft and building up speed around the room, consciously aware of protecting his left shoulder in the event of a ditch. Although his collarbone was fully healed from an earlier spill, the phantom ache was enough to cause him to alter his stance and, to his chagrin, his natural aggressiveness.

It wasn't long before a smile was stretched across his face. Thoughts of Triana, Hannah, and the vultures had been displaced by the joy of the ride. The monkey brain—at least for the time being—was calm.

The secluded clearing in the dome had, in an unspoken manner, become their spot, their own personal shelter. Alexa sat staring at the ground, fidgeting with clumps of soil. Bon sat nearby, his arms around his knees, staring quietly at her. She had started and stopped the conversation several times, and Bon knew that the dreams had returned; the details were missing, but he was prepared to wait.

"I'm sorry to always be like this," she mumbled. "I feel like every time I talk to you these days I'm a wreck. It can't be any fun for you. I even promised myself that this time I would deal with it without dragging you into it. But . . ."

His eyes never left her face. "We've been over this already. You've listened to me often enough; you're going through a difficult stretch right now. That's why I'm here."

"I know, and I appreciate it. I just . . ." She finally made eye contact with him. "I don't want to be a whiner."

"Quite honestly, Alexa, it's more frustrating for me when you drag it out. I'd rather you just tell me what's going on."

She couldn't stop the smile that flashed across her face. Once again his directness cut through the clutter.

"Okay," she said. "I get it." She picked up the dirt clod that she had been rolling on the ground and tossed it into the dense rows of corn that acted as their walls. Taking a deep breath, she said, "This time the dream definitely involved me, but I'm wondering if it might not involve everyone else, too."

She spent a few minutes describing her vision: the flash of light, the suffocating darkness, the pain. She talked about what it might mean; was it an indication of what lay ahead for her, or did it somehow project what might befall the crew of *Galahad* in general? Or, she mused, was it all metaphor? Did the darkness represent a cloudy, unpredictable future?

Bon listened attentively, without interrupting. He didn't fully understand what Alexa was experiencing, but he also couldn't discount it. Six months earlier he would have been among the most skeptical, but his own supernatural contact with the Cassini had taught him that anything was possible . . . and believable. The cosmos might be infinite and mysterious, but he had reached the conclusion that the human mind was an infinitely mystical universe itself, perhaps one that would never be fully explored or understood.

He could practically feel the fear emanating from her, with which he could empathize. And although he couldn't deny that a connection had developed between them, he was unsure of how to alleviate that fear. She knew him too well, understood the way his rational—some would say cold, calculating—mind operated; were he to embrace her and say that everything was going to be okay, she would immediately reject it as false. His methods, and his very style of living, now restricted his ability to soothe her.

Before he could offer his thoughts, Alexa added a postscript: "I know we've already talked about this; it's really not much different than the last time I opened up to you. But I have to tell you, what's really frightening me is the connection with the vulture."

"What do you mean?" Bon said. "What connection?"

"Lita and I have spent several hours with it, running test after test. We're trying to learn more about its power source, trying to find out if Roc's theory about dark energy is right. And that means I've had to be close to it. Really close. And Bon, from the moment I walked into Sick House and saw it . . . I mean, from the very first instant, I felt something click."

He studied her, trying to gather exactly what she was inferring. He shook his head. "You're gonna have to explain that. What clicked?"

Alexa licked her lips nervously. "When I first saw it in person, it felt . . ." She paused. "Familiar."

He narrowed his eyes. "In what way?"

"I don't know how to answer that, really. It just felt familiar, like I'd been in contact with it before. Which I know makes no sense and sounds crazy. I've spent a lot of time with it, and wracked my brain trying to figure out what it all means. Why would this alien creature seem familiar to me? Until these last few days, none of us could even have imagined it. It has really creeped me out, though. I mean, I walked into that room, got that vibe, and immediately wanted to stay as far away from it as I could. Which has really been a problem, since it's my job to study it.

"And then, it finally made sense. I finally figured out where that feeling is coming from."

Bon leapt ahead. "Your dreams."

She nodded slowly. "Yeah. I haven't specifically had a single vision of these vultures. But somehow they're connected. I know it. Somehow this thing has a part in my dreams, and that's why it feels so familiar." She searched for another clod and began to roll it along the ground. "The minute we get this thing off the ship I'll feel better."

"Are you almost finished with your tests?"

"I think so. It's mostly just a matter of interpreting the data now, and Roc's working on it. A lot of it has to do with their communication, too, and we want to see how this thing responds when Gap takes on the ones outside. We'll hopefully learn what we need then, and we can boot it out the Spider bay doors."

She shuddered. "I know it's my job, it's what I trained for, but I'm anxious to be done with this particular job." She gave him a look that seemed to beg understanding. "Listen, I know how all of this sounds. You're sweet for talking with me, and I know there's really no answer. But because this time it seemed more . . . personal, I really just wanted to voice it." She peered into his eyes. "Does that make sense?"

Bon kept his gaze firm. "It makes sense for you, and that's all that matters. You should know by now that my philosophy is one of individualism. What works for one person doesn't necessarily work for another; it's when people *don't* recognize this that there's conflict. People usually judge how others deal with problems by comparing it to how *they* would deal with them. So, if talking helps, you should definitely talk. If you want an answer from me, I'll be happy to give one."

Alexa looked back at the ground and seemed to contemplate his offer. When she spoke, her voice had grown quiet. "I appreciate that, but I think I'll be okay now." Taking him by surprise, she suddenly pushed herself up onto her knees, leaned across to him, and placed a soft kiss on his lips. Pulling back, she stared into his eyes. "Thank you."

Bon sat frozen. His gaze shifted back and forth between her eyes, but he had been caught completely off guard.

Alexa pushed herself back into a sitting position. "Well, that didn't go over the way I had envisioned. Sorry about that. Just an impulse."

"No," he said. "No, you don't need to apologize. It's fine." Even as the words came out he knew they sounded forced.

She turned her head and stared out at the crops surrounding them, as if searching for something. "Are you . . . are you interested in someone else?"

He felt his breath catch. How had the conversation turned this way? "Alexa . . ." he said, as gently as he was able.

She startled him by suddenly laughing. "Boy, do I know how to ruin a moment! Just forget I asked that question, okay? I'm not myself these days, that's all."

Bon felt his face flush. He hadn't felt this awkward since . . .

Since the last time he was in the Spider bay control room.

With Triana.

In a flash, Alexa was on her feet. She brushed the soil from her pants, then from her hands. "Really, you're wonderful for always talking with me about this stuff. I'm sorry again if I made you uncomfortable. Please, let's forget about it, okay?" She laughed again. "Next time I promise I'll keep my lips to myself."

Before he could respond, she touched him lightly on the shoulder, smiled down at him, and pushed her way out of the clearing toward the path that led to the lifts. It had all happened so quickly that Bon was still sitting in the same position, his hands around his knees. He stared after her for a minute, then climbed to his feet. He let out a long breath and followed the way she had left.

A few minutes later he walked into his office in Dome 1, his thoughts still a blur. He couldn't deny that the last two months had seen an intimate connection develop with Alexa; but in his mind it was an intellectual intimacy, a bond that always stopped short of becoming emotional.

In *his* mind.

Now, standing over his desk—he rarely sat, even when working on the computer—he looked at the various papers, notes, his workpad . . . and saw none of it. Instead he replayed what had just taken place, and for the first time began to see what had eluded him. Of course the signals had been there; he was a fool to have been taken by surprise by Alexa's kiss and question.

Their relationship, as she had pointed out, was unique and strong. And, as he had realized for himself, it involved an intimacy that few people shared. They met privately a couple of times every week, they were both unattached, available . . .

Why not, Bon wondered. Alexa was attractive, intelligent, a hard worker, and—as he had discovered in the clearing—interested in him. Why wouldn't he be open to that? What, other than his almost obsessive devotion to work, would keep him from exploring that possibility?

And yet he knew the answer. It gnawed at him because he didn't like it, and had even spent months in denial. There was a reason why he hadn't seen the potential of Alexa, even though she was right there in front of him all this time. He knew.

Reaching for his keyboard, he typed in a quick password that opened a private file on his vidscreen. The file contained a solitary image. He opened it.

The screen filled with a picture of Triana, taken from the press packages that had circulated before the launch. It was a candid photo of her sitting at *Galahad*'s training facility, bent over what appeared to be a journal, her head supported by one hand while the other clutched a pen. Her long brown hair was pulled back in a tail, and her vivid green eyes were focused on the page before her.

Bon stared at the image for almost a minute, then snapped it off. He stood, hands on hips for a moment, then leaned over and shoved a pile of papers off the side of his desk. He stormed to the door and out into the dome's artificial sunlight, while the papers scattered across the floor.

20

Lita's hair spilled across her shoulders. The bright red ribbon that normally held it in place sat before her on the dresser in her room while she applied a small dab of lotion to her hands and elbows. As with most personal grooming supplies on the ship, the lotion was rationed, and each crew member was asked to use it no more than once per week. Lita stared at her hands and felt grateful that her duties kept her from working in the fields. She'd heard several complaints from the girls who had finished their six-week tours of duty in the domes; the work was good, and they loved the sensation of being outdoors, but the toll on their skin could be brutal.

As Lita reached for the ribbon, a small chime sounded; someone was at her door. She walked over and opened it to find Channy standing there.

"Got a minute?" the young Brit asked.

Lita hadn't seen her since she'd been expelled from the Council meeting, but the visit didn't surprise her. Channy often sought her out as a sounding board.

"Uh, sure, come on in. I need to be in Sick House pretty soon, but I have a few minutes. I want to be there before Gap and . . . oh, you probably don't know about that. We're doing another EVA."

Channy nodded uncomfortably and sat on the edge of Lita's bed. "I did hear about it. Listen, about the Council meeting . . ."

"I don't think you need to talk to me about that," Lita said, resuming her seat at the dresser. "That's a discussion for you and Tree."

"I know, and I will. But I also wanted to explain to you what's going on. Tree . . . well, Tree probably wouldn't understand."

Lita gave her a look from the corner of her eye. "If you mean because it involves a boy, I wouldn't jump to that conclusion if I were you. I think you need to give Tree a little more credit than that. Besides . . ." She turned back toward the mirror. "Not to sound rude, and please don't take this wrong, but it's not like you've got a lot of experience yourself."

Channy laced her fingers together and leaned forward. "You're right, and I'm sorry that I've caused a distraction during an important time. But . . . I'm finding it very hard to concentrate on my work these days. I can't seem to shut my brain off about Taresh, and it's driving me crazy. I was hoping you might be able to help me."

Looking at the reflection of Channy in the mirror, Lita frowned. "I hope you're not referring to medication."

"No, no, no," Channy said hurriedly. "No, nothing like that. I was just hoping that you could talk to me a little bit." She laughed, a nervous sputter of sound, and clamped her fingers together more tightly. "Lita, I'm in love." When Lita didn't answer, she quickly added, "I told him, which I know might have been a foolish thing to do. But now I'm even more of a wreck."

Lita tied the ribbon in her hair, then adjusted it slightly. She finally turned to face Channy. "Really, I want to help, but this is not a good time. Gap and Mira are about to go out and confront the vultures, and I have to be at my post in Sick House. I don't want you to think I'm blowing you off, but this is not a quick conversation."

Channy looked glum. "No, sure, I understand."

An exasperated sigh slipped from Lita. "In the meantime, since you're asking for my help, I'll tell you this: slow down. You've got to take a deep breath and remember that you have a job to do."

"I *know* I have a job to do," Channy blurted out. "I know that I need to slow down. That's all anyone keeps telling me. That's not exactly the help I'm looking for." She stood up and began to pace around the room. "I swear, everyone talks to me about this like I'm a child."

"Channy, people care about you. I don't know what you're looking for, but I think you just want everyone to endorse your behavior. We're all supposed to tell you to sit around mooning over Taresh, neglect your duties at the gym, daydream during Council meetings, and walk around in a haze. Well, I'm sorry, that's not what anyone's going to tell you. If you're being treated like a child, it's probably because you're acting very immature right now."

Channy stopped her pacing and turned to glare at Lita. "I thought you were my friend."

Lita threw her hands up. "Do you see what I'm talking about? Nobody can tell you anything that you want to hear, so suddenly we're all against you. It's too bad that the truth hurts. For your information, you are not the first person to develop a crush on someone, and you're not the first person to feel pain from a relationship. It's just the first time for *you*, and it's dominating your life right now."

She paused for a moment to let herself cool a bit, then said: "I've started experimenting more with meditation these days. No, before you roll your eyes, listen to me. Our thoughts can get out of control, and before you know it there's too much overload going on and our minds can't process it fast enough. I think if you took some time to get outside of yourself, to look at your obsessive thoughts from a detached perspective, you'd probably see what the rest of us see: a beautiful, delightful, and talented young woman who has allowed one thing to dominate her world, to steal her spirit. You have created a loop in your thinking, and now it's feeding off itself. That's all I mean when I say to slow down. Just take a step back, allow things to calm a bit."

She stood up. "And again, I'm sorry, but I have to get to Sick House. If you want to talk about this later—"

"No," Channy said, walking briskly toward the door. "I don't want to trouble you any more with this. I won't bother anyone else, ever again." She rushed out the door.

Lita had opened her mouth to call out to her, but never got the chance. Instead, she let out another sigh and rubbed her forehead. "Oh, Channy," she muttered.

The Spider rolled silently out into the canvas of stars. Gap took a quick glance at Mira in the seat beside him; her look of determination and concentration emboldened him. At some level it was understood that each member of the crew had passed countless tests to determine his or her competence, yet Gap nevertheless felt a wave of pride that he was part of such an elite team of young adults. He was convinced that Mira represented the best part of them, with her attitude and her courage.

He shifted his gaze to the front window. The lower right arm of the Spider grasped a long, thin rod, with a starburst array of metal at the far end. To Gap it closely resembled a ski pole, but in actuality was a small air-cannon. A flexible tube at the opposite end spiraled into a tank of oxygen that had been attached to the Spider's hull. The apparatus had been designed and assembled by some of the ship's brightest engineering students, based on details supplied by Roc and Lita. Several of the crew members responsible for the assignment had gathered in the Spider bay to watch the launch of their handiwork—again at the insistence of Triana, who found every way possible for crew members to take pride in their contributions to the mission.

Although the device had been tested and retested after its

installation, Gap pulled the Spider up alongside *Galahad* to try it again in the vacuum of space. His duties mainly involved piloting the small craft, while Mira was in charge of the oxygen gun.

"Okay," Gap said. "Let's give it a quick burst."

The control resembled an old-fashioned video game joystick. Mira flexed her fingers a few times before gripping it. The burst of oxygen would automatically generate a small matching thrust from the Spider's engines, which would counteract the force of the gun and keep the craft steady.

As they both stared through the window, Mira gently squeezed the trigger, and they watched a tight stream of brightly colored particles jet from the starburst end of the pole. It had been the brainstorm of one of *Galahad*'s engineering whizzes to mix the colorful particles into the tank. The oxygen itself was colorless, so this provided them with a way of gauging their aim.

Mira turned to Gap. "Looks like we're ready to go," she said.

He knew that Triana was listening in from the Control Room. "Tree, we're set to work our way over to target one." It was the designation they had chosen for the vulture they assumed was the "squadron leader." Perched along the top of the ship's port side, its venting and light emissions had remained constant from the moment it had fallen under observation. After consulting with Roc, they had decided to focus their initial oxygen burst at this supposed leader; the hope was that scaring away this one might create havoc among the creatures, causing all of them to flee at once.

"If it truly is their command unit," Triana had said, "then maybe it will sound the retreat for all of them."

Now, in response to Gap's message, she offered a quick reply: "Stand by, Gap."

Communication was also open to Sick House, and Triana made sure that they were in the loop. "Lita, how's our guest today?"

"Pretty quiet," Lita said. "Alexa's here and she says the light emissions have dropped to a minimum. I don't know if the thing is capable of sleep, but there's not much going on."

"Okay," Triana said. "We have monitors set on all of the others outside the ship. Once this gets going we'll all have to stay in touch with each other. Roc, you're still tracking their dark energy conversion, correct?"

"And that has gone strangely quiet as well," the computer said. "It's like some cosmic version of a stare down right now. But I think we can pretty well assume that things will change once the oxygen hits the fan."

Gap and Mira heard this over the intercom. They looked at each other, and Gap nodded grimly. It was understood that they could very well be the ones who absorbed the brunt of any violent reaction from the vultures. For all of the potential danger, however, there was nowhere else Gap wanted to be.

"Gap, Mira," Triana said. "You are clear to go."

Nudging the throttle, Gap piloted the Spider up the side of the ship. He felt a small bead of perspiration dot his forehead, but welcomed it and the edge that accompanied it.

Three minutes later they spotted their target, its jet-black outline as ominous as the first time they'd seen it. Slowing as he approached, Gap could see the random beacon of blue-green light seeping from beneath the vulture. At first glance it seemed much less intense than their previous observation; but as he drew near, the color once again grew intense, and the frequency picked up.

This didn't surprise Gap; the creatures would be keenly aware of what had happened the last time a Spider approached, and the alarm would surely be sounded. In fact, as soon as they were within hovering distance, he heard Lita's voice break through the intercom.

"Well, it looks like naptime is over for our friend here in Sick House. It's back to its usual antics, darting all over the interior of the box. I'm guessing that Gap and Mira have arrived at the ring-leader's position?"

"That's affirmative," Gap said, bringing the Spider to a full stop. "The light show got cranked up here, too."

Triana said, "I guess that leaves no doubt that it's part of their communication. Roc, any way of measuring your dark energy theory here?"

"Not directly. However, there is quite an increase in vent activity going on with each of the vultures, including the specimen in Sick House. We still have no way of observing the use of subatomic particles between these things . . . but I know I'm right."

Gap chuckled. "I love your confidence."

"It's more a matter of ruling out just about everything else," Roc said. "There still is no transfer or loss of heat, electrical energy, or traditional atomic energy. They're powering up somehow; dark energy is really all that's left."

"I'll tell you one thing I don't like," Lita interjected. "The one we've got down here is settling near the hatch on this vacuum box. For the first time it's acting like it knows how to get out."

Triana said, "Things are starting to happen quickly, which is pretty much what we expected. Everyone report immediately if you spot something else new. Lita, do we need to jettison your specimen right now?"

There was a lengthy pause; it was evident that Lita and Alexa were discussing the question.

"Not yet," Lita said. "Alexa thinks this might be a valuable time to study it. We'll hang in here for now."

"All right," Gap said. "Tree, we're ready, whenever you want to give the word."

He expected hesitation from her, but there was none. When she quickly replied, "You're clear to go," he understood that she had likely already thought through it dozens of times. He envied her ability to lead confidently, yet he also felt compassion for the pressure that her position must generate.

He nursed the throttle again, and maneuvered the Spider to within six feet of the vulture, tilting the small craft forward so that he and Mira could watch everything play out through the front window.

Gap took his hands from the controls and sat back. "Ever heard of Annie Oakley?" he said to Mira.

She kept her gaze directed through the window at the vulture, but allowed a smirk to play across her face. "Only the greatest female sharpshooter of all time. Wow, no pressure on me now." Her hand once again settled on the joystick, and Gap saw her flexing her fingers. Unconsciously he did the same.

With just a hint of forward pressure, Mira extended the Spider's arm, and with it the long tube. When it was within three feet of the vulture, she paused and looked at Gap. "I know this probably isn't what anyone wants to hear right now," she said. "But there's something I want to say before I pull the trigger.

"First, let me preface this by saying that I wholeheartedly agree that this is what we should be doing. However, this is rather a historic moment, and I think we should recognize that."

Gap nodded, and could almost psychically feel the people in *Galahad*'s Control Room and Sick House doing the same.

Lita's voice came through the speaker. "Even though it's not deadly force, this is essentially the first case of humans attacking an alien being." She paused, then added, "May we never grow numb to the implications or the consequences."

"Thank you, Mira, for acknowledging the event," Triana said. "And Lita, that was beautifully spoken. Thank you."

There followed almost a full minute of waiting, as if they all wanted to pay solemn respect to the end of their mission's innocence. Then, Mira once again leaned over the controls. "Oxygen burst in five seconds. Four. Three."

The rest of the countdown was unspoken. She and Gap watched through the window of the Spider, while the others monitored on their vidscreens, as a blast of colored particles shot from the tube. The stream of concentrated oxygen, lasting no more than three seconds, impacted the vulture.

The reaction was immediate and dramatic. A blaze of color erupted from what appeared to be the entire underside of the alien entity; but whereas before it had been a subtle, almost gentle, blue-green hue, now that shade was joined by a violent red, along with flashes of bright yellow. Gap and Mira found themselves shielding their eyes, for now the colors didn't merely seep from beneath the creature, but burst from below, as if a lid had been pried off.

At the same time, Gap felt a tiny shudder pass through the Spider. His first thought was that it was merely his own physical reaction to the fiery light show, perhaps his body recoiling from the shock. But seconds later he felt it again, faint yet noticeable. It was like a pond's ripple gently causing a boat to sway.

He said to Mira: "Did you feel that?"

"I'm glad you said something," she said. "I wasn't sure at first, but when it happened again . . ."

Triana was able to hear their conversation, and she broke in. "Gap, what's going on? What did you feel?"

"I would describe it as a small shudder," he said. "Has to be some sort of reaction that the vulture had to the oxygen gun. You saw the colors, right?"

"Yes. It was hard to see because of the glare, but I also believe that the vent activity skyrocketed, too. Roc, can you confirm?"

"I can and will," the computer said. "This time every vent went into overdrive. This little oxygen shot must be the vulture equivalent of chewing on aluminum foil. Plus, I can tell you that the colors are playing out on every one of the creatures. The shudder that Gap describes is more than likely tied in with their use of dark energy. It could even be a space-time reaction."

"What does that mean?" Gap said.

"It means," Roc said, "that we know so little about dark energy, but we know that it's potent enough to disrupt things at the tiniest subatomic levels. What you felt, Gap, might have actually been the Spider bumped by a space-time wave. I wouldn't be at all surprised if you and Mira aged an extra billionth of a second without knowing it."

"Lita," Triana said. "What's going on with the specimen in Sick House?"

"It has plastered itself against the box," Lita said. "The lights on it are going a little crazy, but I'm not getting any kind of ripple effect like Gap mentioned."

The communication between them went silent for a few seconds. Then Gap offered another observation. "For all of that activity, the vulture didn't let go of the ship. I think Roc's right, we stung it pretty well; but it held on. Do we give it round two?"

"Wait two minutes," Triana said after consideration. "It might be processing, which is why we're getting the light and vent show. If it doesn't reach the decision that we're hoping for, we'll coax it a little more."

Gap shifted his attention from the window to the magnified image of the vulture on his vidscreen. The dazzling lights were still brighter than normal, but had subsided enough for him to make out the agitated vent activity. As Roc had described, each one was fluttering, some more quickly than others. Although it was happening in the soundless void of deep space, Gap thought it resembled the valves on a musical instrument; he wondered what soundtrack it was presenting to its companions.

When the two minutes had passed, however, it was still solidly attached to the hull of the ship. Mira brought the oxygen gun to bear and squeezed off another three-second burst.

Once again, the reaction was instantaneous. This time, however, the colors momentarily blinded Gap and Mira because the vulture disengaged from *Galahad*'s outer skin; the movement happened in the blink of an eye.

Before he could bring a hand up to shield his eyes, Gap was able to make out the large black shape rocketing past his window.

At the same time he heard a shriek come from the intercom.

It was Lita, crying out from Sick House.

21

hanny sat alone in the Rec Room, unaware of what was transpiring with the vultures. She technically was on duty, but had left the gym just as a yoga and stretching class was scheduled to begin; she'd put that in the hands of one of her assistants. When the message from Taresh had come in, she had wasted no time scrambling to meet him.

She had fought the urge to arrive early, and instead had wandered along the corridors one level below the Rec Room just to pass the time . . . which seemed to drag along. Even so, walking in the door at precisely the time Taresh had suggested, she was disappointed to find the room empty. She debated walking out again, if for no other reason than to have him wait for her, but quickly decided to sit patiently and wait. Besides, she reasoned, if he should be walking in as she walked out, it would make for an awkward explanation.

"Please stop overthinking," she said to herself. "Please."

But that had become so difficult for her. She seemed to have lost all control of her rational mind; her recent tense conversations with Kylie and Lita—Lita, of all people!—was evidence enough that she was not herself anymore. An obsessed stranger had taken over her body.

Now those obsessive thoughts turned to the meeting that Taresh had requested. He must have reached a decision, she thought. Did the location that he had suggested for their meeting have any significance? After all, they had spent several hours in this room during Game Nights; they had shared private talks here, too. If this was indeed one of their special places, shouldn't that mean that he had decided to abandon his family's wishes and do what was right for both of them?

Or was it simply that this room offered the best chance for privacy at this time of day?

"Good thing I stopped overthinking," she thought, but there was no smile to accompany it.

She was startled out of her thoughts by the sound of the door opening. Taresh briskly walked in, a look of apology on his face.

"Channy, I'm sorry that I'm late."

She forced an upbeat note into her voice. "Oh, it's no problem. I just got here myself. You're off work today, right?"

"Well, yes and no. I'm not scheduled, but with all of the action going on with the vultures, I'm going to head off to Engineering and just see if they need anything."

Channy felt a quizzical look cross her face at the mention of the vultures. "Oh, right, the vultures." She now felt completely out of the loop, and the regrets for her behavior at the Council meeting rushed back. "Yeah, it's pretty exciting," she said. "I think I might check it out somewhere, too."

Taresh gave her an odd look. "I would think that Triana might have assigned a chore to you already. Well, I won't take up much of your time, but I wanted to visit with you as soon as possible."

"I'm glad," she said. "So what's up?"

He pulled out a chair and sat next to her. For a few seconds he seemed to be lost for words, and shifted his gaze from the floor to his hands, then back again. Finally, he exhaled loudly and focused on her.

"I know we've grown very close these last few weeks, and I'm truly very happy about that. You are one of the most remarkable people I've ever met."

Channy felt her spine stiffen. The foundation for the "friendship" speech was being laid.

"You have been very upfront with me," he continued. "And I've tried to be the same with you. It's confusing, really, because you know that my heart pulls me one direction, while my dedication to my family pulls me another."

Channy opened her mouth to speak, but he raised his hand. "No," he said, "let me get this all out, please. We can talk about it then, if you want, but I have to say this first."

Now he put his hand over hers on the table. "I'm sure that I've done a terrible job of trying to explain things. I'm not sure that I understand it all myself, and, believe me, there is much that I question. I've stayed awake at night thinking about it, and have tried to find a compromise that works. But . . . I can't. I do care about you, Channy, honestly. But as I told you before, I owe a debt to all of those in my family who made it possible for me to even be here. And so, I'm going to honor their wish."

Channy felt an unusual sensation of cold settle over her. It was exactly the news that she didn't want to hear; she had tried to prepare herself for it, yet it still stabbed at her heart. She looked down at his hand covering hers, but couldn't feel it. How could that be?

And how could he have made this decision? Why?

She looked back up at him, waiting for him to say more, but apparently he had said his piece. She swallowed hard before speaking. "So . . . we're just going to be friends, is that it?"

His shoulders sagged. "Channy, I know how that sounds. You have to believe me, the last thing I want to do is hurt you. But I can't start something that I can't finish. I am beholden to my family—"

"Yes," she said, more forcefully than she had intended. "Yes,

I've heard all about your family. I've heard about your culture, or tradition, or whatever it is. But if it causes you this much pain, if it's something you really don't want to do, then why are you doing it? Hmm? Tell me that, because I don't understand."

Taresh stared into her eyes. She saw his lower lip tremble, then suddenly realized that he was merely reacting to the tears that had started to trickle down her face.

"All I can tell you," he said softly, "is that sometimes the right thing to do is the most difficult thing to do."

She pulled her hand away from his, although he tried to hold on. She stood up and paced a few feet away. "So just friends, right? You never answered me. Game Night, lunch sometimes, a dinner now and then. Maybe a few laughs in the gym. Friends."

Now his voice was barely above a whisper. "I'd like to be friends with you. I won't blame you if you say no, but I'd like for us to remain close. Yes."

She crossed her arms and looked back at him. "I'll have to get back with you on that."

He didn't react at first, then simply nodded and looked back at the floor. "I'm very sorry."

"Yes, me, too," she said. "Very sorry."

A minute passed in silence. Then Taresh pushed back his chair and faced her.

"I have no business asking this," he said. "But . . . I really would like to give you a hug. Would that be okay?"

Another round of silent tears began to spill down Channy's face, but she fought away the sound of sobs.

"I'll have to get back with you on that, too."

Again he nodded. Without another word he turned and left the Rec Room.

Alone, she limped back to the table, sat down, and buried her face in her hands.

* * *

hey all heard Lita's cry. Triana, standing at one of the science
terminals in the Control Room, felt a jolt of adrenaline streak
through her body. She'd heard her friend express happiness, grief,
joy, even fear, but she'd never known Lita to cry out like this. It
was the sound of shock and terror, and had the same effect on
everyone stationed in *Galahad*'s nerve center. They turned to
stare at Triana, their mouths open, their eyes wide.

In the aftermath of the shout came the sound of chaos through
the intercom. Triana knew it had to be coming from Sick House.

She did her best to keep her voice under control. "Lita, report."
There was no answer, only the continued garble of frantic activity. "Lita, what's going on?" Again, no direct response.

Gap's voice broke through from the Spider. "Tree! What was
that?"

"I have no idea. I can't get through to Lita. Get back here right
away."

"Done," he said.

Triana summoned the ship's computer. "Roc, tell me what's
happened in Sick House."

"There's been a breach of the containment vessel."

"What?" Triana shouted. "The vulture?"

"Yes," Roc said. "During this last oxygen blast upon the leader
outside, the captive vulture in Sick House somehow manipulated
the controls on the containment box. It burst out and attacked."

Triana's heart nearly stopped. "Lita?"

"No," Roc answered. "Alexa. She was kneeling at the data
ports when it flew out. It has attached itself to her upper body."

Before he had finished the sentence, Triana bolted for the door
and began to race toward Sick House. She automatically began
to second-guess her decision to allow additional study on the
alien. They had so desperately wanted to find out more about its
ability to exploit the power of dark energy; now that curiosity
might have had tragic results. She tried to rationalize that the

oxygen in the air at Sick House was their ally, and could very well render the vulture catatonic immediately.

But Lita had not answered her calls.

She raced around the gentle turn that led to Sick House and saw a cluster of crew members gathered around the open door. They turned to see her approaching at a run, and parted to allow her inside. She sprinted through the outer office, past Lita's desk, past Alexa's work space, and could hear the commotion as she neared the lab.

A knot of people moved like an ant colony, shuffling quickly in and out of the swarm. Triana pulled up and could see Lita, down on one knee beside the empty containment box, huddled over a dark mass.

It was the vulture. The rest of the view caused Triana's stomach to roll, and she came close to vomiting.

The alien had enveloped Alexa's upper body. Its jet-black wings had folded around her, while the main torso covered her chest, neck, and head. Even her arms had been pinned within the wedge shape. Only Alexa's legs protruded; they were twisted to one side, and still.

Lita held a set of metal surgical pliers. She worked feverishly, attempting to pry the wings away from Alexa's body, but could not maintain a solid grip. If she noticed that Triana had arrived, she didn't show it. Instead, she dispensed instructions to the crew helping her, and a few seconds later one of the workers knelt beside her with a portable oxygen canister.

"Stand back," Lita said. When a space had been cleared, she pressed the nozzle against the spine of the vulture and released a stream. There was no effect. She tossed the canister aside and once again began trying to attach the pliers to the creature. At the same time she called out for a surgical scalpel.

Triana bent down beside her. "Do you think you'll be able to cut through this thing?"

Lita kept her attention fully on the task at hand, but said, "I don't know. We might have to saw it away. I'm just trying to protect Alexa as much as possible, but if we don't get this off her right now . . ." Her voice faded away, and Triana knew exactly what that meant.

Triana moved out of her way as another assistant dropped down with the set of surgical knives. She watched Lita set down the pliers, pick up a knife, and hand two others to her assistants. Together the three of them began to work on the hard outer shell of the vulture, working intensely while at the same time obviously taking pains to not accidentally cut into Alexa. Triana could only imagine how difficult it was.

"C'mon," she heard Lita grunt in frustration. There seemed to be no progress, and, to make matters worse, Alexa's legs gave an involuntary twitch that startled the group surrounding her.

Triana knew that the situation was grim. She also understood that time was critical; she estimated that almost five minutes had elapsed since the attack, and there didn't appear to be any way that Alexa was getting any air. On top of that, who knew how much pressure the vulture was applying to her chest?

Lita obviously understood all of this as well. She quickly abandoned any hope of cutting through the creature with the small blades, and picked up the surgical saw. Triana could hear her consulting with her helpers, trying to determine the best location and angle to remove the dark mass without inflicting equally lethal injuries to Alexa. Time was slipping by, but there was no getting past the necessary planning. Finally, Lita leaned into the work, firing up the saw and placing it against one of the wing joints of the vulture. There was a screech, similar to the sound of metal grinding against metal.

At first there were no discernible results, but soon tension in the wing began to relax. A space opened up in the area of Alexa's left shoulder. Lita stopped, turned the saw slightly, and began working in another direction. The image that jumped to Triana's mind was that of a logger working his blade against the trunk of a tree, first in one direction, then another. In this case, the space over Alexa's body opened a bit farther.

Any joy in the success was tempered by the sight of blood. Triana knew instantly that it didn't belong to the vulture.

22

The Spider's specially crafted engines were pushed to their maximum power and thrust, but to Gap it seemed as if the outer skin of *Galahad* was crawling past. Something had gone terribly wrong in Sick House. How was it possible for there to be—as Roc had put it—a breach in the containment vessel? What had happened to Alexa?

And what had happened to the other vultures?

Gap watched the bay doors loom larger and began the subtle shifts necessary to align the small craft for entry. Roc would take over in just a minute and finish the job of docking.

He and Mira had barely spoken after the blinding flight of the vulture. He had, of course, expected the thing to break away once the oxygen hit, but was still amazed at the speed. If, as they had theorized, the light display was an indicator of communication between the beings, then it likely explained what had triggered the breakout in Sick House. In fact, he began to grow concerned that perhaps they had inadvertently provoked the vulture into aggression.

He could only hope that no one had been hurt.

"Taking over guidance," Roc said. Gap sat back and, like Mira, became a passenger and spectator. Within a few minutes the

Spider was securely docked, the bay door closed, and the large hangar began to pressurize. Gap unbuckled his safety harness and started on the checklist to shut down the Spider. No further calls had come in from Sick House, or from Triana; that could mean that things were either fine and under control, or that there was a crisis underway.

Suddenly, the ship lurched. Without the arms of his chair to keep him in place, Gap knew he would have been thrown to the floor. At the same time, the lights in the Spider bay, and in the small metal craft itself, flickered off briefly, then back on again. For a span of about five seconds Gap felt himself assaulted physically: his stomach twisted and turned, and he barely kept himself from throwing up. He also believed he was on the verge of passing out. His vision clouded and his ears popped, as if he had quickly dropped several hundred feet. He gripped the arm of his chair and closed his eyes until the sensation passed.

Once he felt back to normal, he turned to check on Mira. She had not yet unbuckled her harness, and it was holding her in place. Yet she was slumped forward, her chin almost against her chest and her hair spilling into her lap. Gap was relieved to see that she was breathing.

"Mira," he called out. She stirred slightly, and a soft grunt escaped from her mouth. He called her name again.

"What . . . was that?" she uttered.

"Are you okay?" he said, climbing from his seat and kneeling next to her. He pulled her back against her seat. She opened her eyes wide, trying to focus, then blinked hard several times. When she turned to look at him, it was the gaze of someone who had been shell-shocked.

"I think I'm okay," she said, then repeated her question: "What was that?"

Gap looked out the window into the bay, which had finished pressurizing. He saw two crew members enter from the hangar's control room and begin walking toward the Spider; they seemed a bit shaky themselves. "I have no idea. Let's find out." He called out to the computer. "Roc, you still with us?"

"This is extraordinary," Roc said. "The vultures—or their creators, which is more likely—just gave us another lesson in how little we know about the universe and its power."

"What happened?" Gap said. "Did they attack us?"

"Not at all. The best way to describe it, I think, is that they took the expressway home."

Gap sighed. "Can you be more specific?"

"I can try, but I'm still putting the pieces of the puzzle together. Once the leader bolted from his place on the outside of our ship, he immediately summoned the others. I was able to follow their movements, and I tracked them as they fell into formation. Once they were together, they formed a rough circle. That's where the fun began. The light show we saw before was nothing compared to this."

"So, that shock we felt," Gap said. "Was it a wave of dark energy communication?"

"Oh, no," Roc said. "It was much more than that. Apparently our guests pooled their dark energy engines and used them to warp time and space for their own uses."

Gap said, "What does that mean? What did they do?"

"The shock wave we felt was caused by the opening and closing of what physicists have nicknamed a wormhole."

Mira let out a gasp. "A wormhole? I can't believe it! I've read so much about them. There was a wormhole right here?"

"That's correct," Roc said. "Briefly, anyway. Somehow the vultures summoned it, it opened up, they disappeared inside, and then it was gone. All in a matter of seconds."

"Incredible," Gap said. "Now the question is: Where did they go?"

"And that's something we can't answer," Roc said. "The word 'infinite' might get thrown around a lot, but in this case the possibilities are truly infinite. Scientists have always believed that wormholes could exist, but until now it's been pure speculation. For instance, it's always been assumed that the heart of a massive black hole contained a wormhole."

Mira nodded. "My aunt did a lot of research in that area, which is why I'm so fascinated by them. She believed that there might be two kinds of wormholes: those that connected one point of the universe to another, and those that connected to another universe altogether." She winked at Gap. "Those were always my favorites: doorways into completely different universes. But my aunt thought that the most likely answer was that they simply bent time and space within our own universe, and acted like shortcuts to get from one side to the other."

"And," Roc said, "if the vultures' creators have learned how to manipulate that power through the use of dark energy, then they would be free to move about wherever—and whenever—they liked."

Gap rubbed his forehead. "I agree that this is all fascinating, but we're going to have to figure out how it affects us right now."

Roc said, "I agree. But there's more to it than that."

"What do you mean?"

"We have to not only figure out how it affects us now," the computer said, "but remember that if the vultures left us this easily, they could just as easily return. With help."

W as it possible to cry yourself out? Could you break down and weep to the point where your body couldn't supply a single additional tear? Channy lay on her bed and wondered if this sudden dry spell simply meant that she had expelled every possible tear in the last hour. Her eyes were killing her, and she felt more drained from the crying than from any of the most strenuous workouts she had subjected herself to.

A few minutes earlier she had been thrown to the floor, the

lights briefly flickered out, and she had felt a wave of nausea. She decided that it must have something to do with the vultures, but she was in no position to call Triana—or anyone else on the Council, for that matter—to get more details.

She was alone, thankful that Kylie was out with friends. Her pillow was damp, so she turned it over and plopped back down, then stared at the ceiling. Her mind had raced out of control since Taresh had left the Rec Room, investigating every possible course of action: talk to him again, avoid him, reason with him, act depressed and hope that he felt sorry for her, act happy and make him long to be with her, surround herself with friends, keep to herself for a while, laugh, cry . . .

Now, during what she assumed must be a recovery break for her nervous system, she began to relive all of their encounters over the past few weeks. She tried to imagine how things would have turned out differently if she had only . . .

But that was nonsense, and she knew it. Things *hadn't* turned out differently, and it was insane to keep drifting into a fantasy world where everything was rosy.

And then, seemingly out of nowhere, her mind summoned a vision of her older sister, D'Audra. Vivacious and active, D'Audra had always been an inspiration and role model for Channy during their childhood in England. A bizarre accident had paralyzed D'Audra, and her little sis had watched in admiration as she toiled every day to rehab her injured spine, to the point that she could finally take steps again. She had been determined to work even harder and make a full recovery, even after the doctors had sadly shaken their heads and murmured things such as "no hope," and "never walk again." D'Audra had surprised them all.

Except Channy. She believed that her sister could overcome anything, especially following a heart-to-heart talk they had shared late one night, just one week after the accident.

They were alone in D'Audra's room at the hospital. Their mother had stepped out to talk with the nurses, and Channy had started to sob at her sister's bedside. "It's my fault," she said. "I made you go to the swimming hole; you never would have slipped and fallen if it hadn't been for me. The doctors say you might never walk again, and it's all my fault."

"Hush," D'Audra said. "That's nonsense. We both wanted to go, and I was having as much fun as you were. This was just an accident, Channy. And besides, of course I'll walk again."

Channy stared at her with red-rimmed eyes. "I don't know if I could be as brave as you are. How do you do it?"

D'Audra smiled. "You accept."

A puzzled look crossed Channy's face. "What do you mean? If you accept what the doctors say—"

"No," D'Audra said. "I accept what has happened, not what others think is *going* to happen." She stroked her younger sister's arm. "See, many people rage against what has happened to them, and refuse to accept it or believe it. They relive things over and over again, hoping they can somehow change what has happened. But you can't do that, and to spend so much of your life hoping that the past can somehow magically change only robs you of spirit.

"So I accept what has happened to me. I'm at peace with what fate has thrown at me. But I have some say in what happens from now on; I decide whether I live with the current consequences, or work to shape them my own way."

Channy placed a hand over her sister's. "You accept the past, and shape the future."

"That's right," D'Audra said. "Crying over the past doesn't make it go away, and it doesn't fix what has broken. Instead, focus on where you are now, and what you can do to make things better."

Now, years later, Channy stared at the ceiling in her room on *Galahad* and remembered that conversation as if it had just taken place. She thought about her sister's attitude, about how it might pertain to her own situation.

She couldn't affect Taresh's decision; she couldn't magically transport back to their meetings and somehow alter what had taken place.

But she could accept his decision and be at peace with it. Who knew what the future might bring for them? They might never be together . . . or they might be.

In an instant she felt a calm sensation sweep over her. Her feelings for Taresh would not change, and she was glad; they felt good, and made her feel good about herself. She would dry her tears, accept what had happened, and look forward to what might come tomorrow. Perhaps their final chapter had yet to be written, but in the meantime she would go back to enjoying life.

She pushed herself up and sat on the edge of her bed. Wiping away the last remaining tear on her chin, she stared into space and thought about D'Audra again. Somewhere, billions of miles away, her sister was more than likely smiling . . . and walking.

Her reverie was interrupted by the sound of Triana's voice on the intercom. "All Council members report to Sick House immediately. Repeat, all Council members to Sick House."

They had barely lifted Alexa onto the bed in the hospital ward of Sick House when the space-time warp had rocked the ship. Triana, Lita, and all four of the crew members assisting them had fallen onto the floor, dazed.

Now, with their recovery complete, and the call put out to the other Council members, Triana and Lita embraced and wept. As much as she felt that she needed to be with Lita at this moment, Triana also knew that her position as Council Leader demanded that she investigate the cause of the powerful jolt.

She moved into the next room and sat at Lita's desk. For the next two minutes she heard Roc's explanation of the vultures and the wormhole they had created. She asked questions, but there were few answers so far. What they did know was that the vulture in Sick House was destroyed, and the other six had vanished.

Triana's gaze unconsciously roamed about the room as she listened, until it settled upon Alexa's desk. She felt her lip tremble, and another sob choked from her.

The door from the corridor opened and Channy took a few steps in. She stopped when she saw Triana, and looked to the floor. Triana sat still, her hands in her lap, and waited. Channy took a few more steps into the room, and appeared about to speak when the door opened again and Gap rushed inside.

He stood next to Channy, out of breath from his sprint from the Spider bay, and said to Triana: "What happened? Is everyone okay?"

The question caused another tear to slip down Triana's face. She wiped it away and tried to collect herself. "We'll wait for Bon. He should be here any minute, I hope." She made eye contact with Gap, who studied her face. Channy, whose own eyes seemed raw from crying, seemed to visibly weaken, as if she anticipated the news.

Lita joined them, wiping at her eyes. At that moment the door opened again, and Bon crept inside. He took one look at Lita and Triana and fell back against the wall.

"No," he said. "No."

Triana stood, and, with Lita, walked over to join the other Council members. She looked each of them in the eye, and said softly: "Alexa is dead."

23

Channy let out a wail, her face contorted in pain. Gap, still visibly stunned, automatically wrapped one arm around her and pulled her in close. He looked at Triana and Lita and extended his other arm. They stepped up to him, and the four Council members embraced, sobbing.

"She suffocated," Lita said. "By the time we cut that thing away, Alexa was gone. I couldn't bring her back."

Bon remained against the wall, his face buried in his hands. Somehow he managed to remain upright, but a spasm of pain took his breath away.

He heard his name, but at first couldn't react. When he heard it a second time, he slowly pulled his hands down and saw Lita, embracing the others, but extending her hand to him.

He couldn't look into her face. His eyes stayed focused on her hand, reaching out to him, beckoning, inviting. Asking him to grieve with them.

He couldn't do it. Pushing off from the wall, he bolted past the other Council members, toward the hospital ward. Once again he heard Lita call out to him, a desperate cry. In seconds he was in the doorway, scanning the ward. It was empty.

No, he realized, coming to a stop. It wasn't empty. One bed was occupied, supporting a quiet, still form, beneath a white sheet. His breathing became loud and deliberate. Somehow he willed his feet to move, and he stepped across the room to stand beside the bed.

Beside the body of Alexa.

It seemed surreal, something that he had seen only on television and in movies. His mind tried to make sense of the shape before him, tried to interpret the outline as something other than her. It *couldn't* be her.

He lifted his hand and grasped the sheet above her head, but paused. He flexed his fingers on the cool fabric. Did he want to do this? Did he *need* to do this? And would he ever be able to get the image out of his head?

Suddenly he was back in Dome 1, in the clearing. *Their* clearing. Their spot. He could hear the sound of the irrigation system, the drip of water from the leaves. He could smell the damp soil, hear the light drone of a random bee performing its rounds, feel the air thick with life. Alexa sat before him, nervously pawing at the clumps of dirt. She spoke with him.

No, it was more than that. Alexa opened up to him. She shared her private thoughts and her deepest fears. She told him how she felt, and, at the end, she had *shown* him how she felt as well.

And what had he shown her in return?

He had spoken more with Alexa than anyone on the ship, probably more than anyone since he had left home in Sweden years ago. He had told her many of the things that he had experienced . . . but not all of them. He had kept the most important part of himself guarded and locked away. Alexa had shared everything with him, willingly, almost enthusiastically, because she had the courage that he didn't. She had the courage to express feelings for him, while he glumly held onto his confused thoughts about Triana, but only, he realized, because it had become routine. Alexa had given him a gift that few people ever truly received, and that most people took for granted: she had given him the gift of her uncensored, unashamed self. He had treated it carelessly.

And now she was gone. In one breathless instant, the truth came crashing in on him. He had always looked forward to hearing her voice, seeing her smile, feeling her touch when she reached out to him. He had found himself thinking about her at the oddest moments, wondering what she was doing. Perhaps their experiences had drawn them together in the beginning, but it wasn't the experiences that bonded them, as everyone else had imagined. There were far too many connections between them to be casually explained away.

Another spasm of pain seared through him, propelled by the voice crying out in his head: I've lost my best friend.

Throughout his troubled childhood, Bon had refused to cry. During the most turbulent moments with his father, when the hurt and despair had welled up to what seemed the breaking point, he still hadn't cried. When he knew that his mother had contracted the deadly disease carried by comet Bhaktul, he had grieved, but not cried.

Now his thoughts played over his final meeting with Alexa and her gentle kiss. Again, she had been brave enough to show him how she felt, and he had responded by putting up another wall.

And suddenly, before he even realized what was happening, he cried. His body shook as he silently wept, the tears burning.

He knew what he had to do, but he couldn't bear to see her this way. He wanted his last memory to be her face as she leaned into him in that clearing, as she softly kissed his lips. That had to be the image of Alexa that he would carry forever.

Against the rush of tears, he clenched his eyes shut, and felt the sting. His hand trembled as it held the fabric. Slowly, he brought it down, and with his other hand, carefully felt the outline of her face. He felt the soft, smooth contour of her cheek, now cool to the touch. He smelled her hair, a smell with which he had become so familiar. He could feel a thick strand that had fallen across her face, and he gently pushed it aside. Then, leaning forward, he cupped her face and tenderly kissed her lips. He lingered there for a moment, his eyes still closed, his tears moistening his face and hers. A moment later he pulled away, and slowly covered her once again with the sheet.

Only then did he open his eyes.

He took a solitary step away from the bed and looked one last time upon the outline of her body. Then he turned away, toward the door.

Triana stood there, silently. Bon brushed past her, out of the hospital ward, out of Sick House, and back to the domes. Back to life.

O ne hour later, Triana sat on the floor of Lita's room, her knees drawn up, encircled by her arms. Lita sat leaning against her bed, facing the Council Leader. They had barely spoken since leaving Sick House, but now gradually began to open up, their voices soft.

"I thought I lost her two months ago in surgery," Lita said. "You'd think that I'd be somehow . . . I don't know, prepared for this."

Triana looked into her friend's dark eyes. "We were all supposed to be prepared for it, since the day we launched. It was part of our training with Dr. Armistead, after all. But no matter how much you discuss it in a classroom, it will never affect you like it does when it really happens. I don't think our minds can rehearse the feeling of grief."

Lita nodded. "As cold as it may sound right now, I was just thinking last week about how lucky we've been so far. I mean, we've had so many close calls, where we could have all been killed, and yet we've managed to sneak by." She held back a sob. "I guess it was just a matter of time before our luck ran out." She wiped at a tear. "Or . . . Alexa's luck ran out."

A sudden look of shame crossed her face. "I'm sorry. That sounded terrible."

"Lita, no, it's fine," Triana said. "None of us know what to say. It's good that you're talking about it, so don't be too hard on yourself about what comes out right now, okay? We're all in shock."

There was silence for another minute before Lita shifted the discussion. "I heard you talking to Gap in Sick House about the vultures, but I'm afraid I wasn't really tuned in. I guess our decision to be aggressive with them really backfired."

"We had no way of knowing that," Triana said firmly. "We can't second-guess everything we do on this mission when something goes wrong. How could we possibly have imagined that they could use their dark energy converters to disengage the magnetic lock on the containment box? With all of the studies we were doing on that specimen, it was learning just as much, or more, about us and our technology."

When Lita didn't say anything, Triana continued. "We made a decision to be proactive, and it cost us this time. But remember that being proactive at other times has saved us, too."

"You're right," Lita said softly. "I know you're right. It just hurts, that's all." In one movement she pulled the red ribbon from her hair and tossed it onto the bed behind her. She stretched her legs out before her and said, "So where did the other vultures go?"

Triana spent a couple of minutes catching Lita up on what had happened with the wormhole. "That's what caused the blackout we experienced. It was a space-time ripple."

Lita looked puzzled. "Wait a minute. If they're able to use wormholes to navigate through the galaxy—or the universe—then why would they stay outside the Kuiper Belt? Why wouldn't they just show up at our doorstep?"

"That's a very good question," Triana said. "I wondered the same thing. I guess it's something we—"

She was interrupted by the soft tone from the door. Lita

pushed herself up and crossed the room. She opened the door to find Channy standing there.

"Hi," Channy said. "Would it be okay if I came in for a minute?"

"Of course," Lita said, and stood aside.

When Channy walked in she acknowledged Triana with a nod, then stood with one hand clasping the other wrist. "Sorry to interrupt, but there's something I wanted to say to both of you."

She fidgeted for a moment. Triana got the impression that Channy had rehearsed a speech, but was about to jettison it in favor of something much simpler and more direct.

"I have behaved so poorly the last couple of weeks," Channy said. "There's no excuse for it. I'm embarrassed and ashamed. I let personal issues overshadow everything, and let them consume me. You expect me to be a strong and active member of the Council, and I let you down. I'm very sorry, and it won't happen again. If you feel like you need to replace me on the Council, I'll understand. I hope you don't, because I'd really like another chance. But if you must, I understand."

Triana sat staring up at her. It was exactly what Channy needed to say, and she was glad to see the young Brit taking responsibility for her actions. She decided to put Channy at ease immediately. "I accept your apology. And no, of course we won't replace you on the Council." She offered a small smile. "It takes a lot of courage to admit your mistakes and ask for forgiveness. I think I speak for everyone on the Council when I say we look forward to having the real Channy back on the team."

A look of relief washed across Channy's face. "Thank you, Tree." She looked at Lita and said, "You were so right about the endless loop I got caught up in. It was a runaway train, really. I'm sorry for the way I talked to you. I don't deserve to have a friend like you."

Lita reached out and hugged her. "Yes, you do, Channy. We all go a little crazy from time to time. This was just your turn."

Channy hugged her back. "And I feel even worse with what's happened to . . . to Alexa."

"It's okay," Lita said softly. "As long as we're all here for each other now, that's what matters."

Channy pulled away. "I think, if anything, this has taught me a very valuable lesson about perspective."

Triana stood up. "If it's any consequence, I feel the same way. We tend to obsess over minor issues and let them take over our thoughts, and lose sight of the big picture. We're all guilty of that, too."

She gave Channy a quick hug. "Welcome back," she said, her eyes glistening.

Channy never got a chance to respond. The three girls were suddenly knocked to the floor as the ship heaved and the lights went out. They tumbled into a heap, with Lita on the bottom. She cried out in pain. Triana tried to break her fall with her hands, but was unable to prevent her head from impacting against the frame of Lita's bed. She felt a sharp jolt, and knew instantly that she was bleeding along her forehead. Channy at first fell onto Lita, but her momentum carried her off to the side.

It was over as quickly as it started. Lita sat up, grimacing and holding her left wrist. With a flicker, the lights came back on, faded briefly, then came back to full power. She glanced at Channy, who appeared to be okay. Then she saw the blood on Triana, and used her good hand to get to her feet.

"Hold on," she said to the Council Leader, and hurried to the sink. She ran a small towel under the water, then brought it back and pressed it against Triana's wound. "Here, keep some pressure on this. It doesn't look too bad, but it's a head wound, so it's gonna bleed a bit." She looked back at Channy. "You okay?"

"I think so. What happened?"

Triana and Lita exchanged a knowing look. "That could only be one thing," Triana said.

24

P *ortals, tunnels, windows, wormholes. No matter what you call them, they represent something that might be somewhat frightening to your species, but they also fascinate you because of what they really are: shortcuts.*

Humans love a good shortcut, and not just the ones through the woods. Kids in the backseat always ask "Are we there yet?" because the journey is tedious to them and the destination is the magical promised land. People with personal troubles always look for the simplest solution, even if it's not the wisest, because they just want to be done with it. Fast-food restaurants cater to those who are looking for the shortcut to lunch or dinner or indigestion.

I'm not so sure what to think about the vultures' choice of shortcut. On one hand I'm just like you: I want to know more about it. On the other hand . . .

G ap sat against the wall inside the lift, rubbing his left shoulder. Despite the fact that he consciously protected it from any rough contact, he had had no time to think when the latest jolt struck *Galahad*. On his way down to Engineering, he had been tossed violently against the wall, slamming into it shoulder-first, before spilling to the floor. He flexed his arm, grateful that everything seemed to be okay.

Except the lift. It wasn't moving, and the primary lights had gone out, leaving Gap barely illuminated by the glow of emergency lighting.

"Hey, Roc," he called out. "I need a little help here."

"Working on it," the computer said. "Stand by."

No sarcastic response, Gap noted. Even Roc understood that the mood of the ship would be drastically different for a while, as the crew dealt with Alexa's death. He stretched his arm one more time, then climbed to his feet and studied the lift's control panel by the dim light. Lines of code flashed across the small vidscreen, blinked off, then repeated. The system was in restart mode.

"Let me guess," Gap said. "Our friends are back already through another wormhole."

"Wrong and right," Roc said. "We do indeed have another wormhole, but there's no sign of the vultures, or anything else for that matter."

The lights burst back on, temporarily blinding Gap. He rubbed his eyes, then tried to focus on the vidscreen. It, too, had resumed its normal look.

"I'm guessing that you'll want to head back up to the Control Room," Roc said.

"Yeah, thanks," Gap said as the lift began to move again. "Feed all of the damage reports to my workstation there, please."

By the time he reached the Control Room, Roc had informed him that Triana was on the way. Gap stood over the vidscreen at his workstation and accessed the reports. The ship's ion drive engines had been shaken, but were still operating smoothly. All of the lifts had been temporarily frozen, but only one remained out of commission at the moment; Roc insisted it would be functioning again within minutes.

There were some problems at the Farms. Water recycling

pumps had shut down, irrigation units had also misfired, and the artificial sunlight was only at about half power. Gap knew that Bon would be on it immediately, and waited to hear from him.

The thought of Bon made Gap reach back and lower himself into a chair. An hour earlier the tough Swede had barreled out of Sick House, his face wet with tears. It was a sight that Gap never thought he would see. Bon and Alexa had obviously shared a connection of some sort, and it was common knowledge that they had spent quite a bit of time together. Gap didn't know where Bon had gone, but it was a safe bet that he'd withdrawn to his sanctuary in the domes. And, if that was the case, he was likely already at work on the problems.

In that respect, Gap realized that minor breakdowns might be the best thing that could have happened to the ship. The crew, especially Lita and Bon, could use not only the distractions, but a reminder that they were still at risk. Gap was sure that Bon would want to throw himself into his work even more than usual.

Should he reach out to Bon right now? This was all such new terrain for them. Gap had never experienced the death of someone close to him, nor had his friends, so he was unsure of how to react. On one hand he wanted to give Bon space to grieve . . . but he didn't want to be insensitive, either.

His thoughts were interrupted when Triana arrived. She walked briskly up to Gap, and he instantly noted the bandage on her forehead. She also had smears of blood on her hands and her clothes, yet she gave him no time to ask about it.

"What's the damage?" she said. He filled her in with the information he had so far.

She nodded, and looked up at the large vidscreen. "Roc, it's another wormhole, right?"

"Correct," came the reply. "It's up ahead, not exactly in our path, but close enough. However, nothing has come through. Well, so far."

Triana bit her lip. "It's just an open door."

Gap looked from the vidscreen to Triana. "Open . . . to where?"

She shrugged. "That's a great question."

"It's more complicated than that," Roc added. "It might not simply be a question of 'to where,' but also 'to when.' Remember, this particular doorway has caused a ripple effect in both space and time. Anything flying out of it could have come from any part of our galaxy, or universe for that matter, and from another time."

"Past or future?" Gap said.

"Either. Both. Who knows for sure?" Roc said. "Regardless, we have now officially seen what the power of dark energy can do when harnessed to its full potential."

Gap leaned forward in his chair. "And to think the vultures are part of an advanced civilization that can do these things, yet they crumble at a whiff of oxygen."

"That's not so surprising," Triana said. "We used to think that we were pretty impressive, powerful creatures, but a microscopic virus can kill us in minutes. The mightiest forests can be devastated by one tiny match. It seems that everything has an Achilles' heel."

She turned and looked back at the vidscreen, peering through the background of stars. "What I find most curious," she said, "is that nothing popped out of this wormhole. Why bother opening it if you're not going to use it?"

"I've had a few minutes to consider that," Roc said, "and you might not like the answer I've come up with."

Triana frowned. "No, I'm sure that I won't. But tell me anyway."

"It's pretty simple, actually. Doors not only let things out, they let things in."

Triana and Gap sat in silence for a moment, digesting this. Gap could see the other crew members in the room suddenly look up at the vidscreen and then at each other, and it was clear that everyone was thinking the same thing.

Finally, Triana said: "It's an invitation. An invitation for us to step inside and visit *their* world this time."

It took a few seconds for Lita to realize that someone had spoken to her. She sat at her desk in Sick House, her head resting on one hand, filtering through the four-page document on her vidscreen. When it finally dawned on her, she looked up to see Jada, one of her assistants, patiently waiting.

"Oh, I'm sorry," Lita said. "I was . . . concentrating on . . ." She couldn't finish the sentence. The document open before her was Galahad Control's instructions for preparation and disposal of a body. She found that no matter how many times her eye scanned the pages, she was not absorbing the information, as if it were printed in a language unfamiliar to her. It was her brain's way of denying the truth, putting off the inevitable. Scattered words would sink in before the rest blurred.

She knew that the first two pages involved the procedures for securing, treating, and wrapping the body. This was underway in the lab, a task that Lita had turned over to Jada and two other crew members. She understood that technically it was her job to oversee their work, but she couldn't bring herself to do it. Not when it was one of her best friends. "Next time," she told herself. Besides, she rationalized, there were other details to attend to, including the funeral and disposal.

Even those words on the vidscreen were blurred.

"Um . . ." Jada said, obviously uncomfortable that she had to talk about this with Lita. "We're finished. I didn't know if you wanted to . . . um, see her, before we move her to . . . um, the Spider bay."

Lita felt a wave of emotion rising in her, felt the tears

threatening, but she fought them back. "Gotta keep it together," she thought.

"Uh, no," she said to Jada. "I need to finish this quickly, and then I'm due for an emergency Council meeting. If I need to, I'll go over everything down at the Spider bay. I know you guys did a good job. Thank you."

Jada nodded once. "Okay." She began to turn away.

"Wait," Lita said. "Listen, I really do want you to know how much I appreciate it. That was probably the toughest job any of us has had to do on this mission; it couldn't have been easy for you. I'm . . . I'm sorry you had to do it, but thank you again."

"Um . . . you're welcome," Jada said. It looked as if she wanted to add something, but couldn't settle on the right words. She offered Lita a sympathetic smile, then walked into the lab.

Lita looked back at the vidscreen, then snapped it off. "Later," she told herself. Climbing out of her chair, she left Sick House and made her way to the Conference Room.

She was not surprised to find Channy already there, waiting, obviously eager to resume her duties with the Council. It wasn't long before Triana and Gap walked in together. Lita pulled a chair up beside Triana and, extracting a few items from her work bag, began to clean up the small head wound and apply a fresh bandage to it. Triana grimaced a few times, but offered thanks when Lita finished.

A minute later Bon entered the room. Lita searched his face, wondering how he was holding up. Although his face betrayed nothing, she was sure that Alexa's death was tearing him up inside. When he sat down, she leaned over and gave his hand a squeeze. He returned the gesture, but barely made eye contact with her—or with anyone else.

Triana rushed into their agenda. "There are two things we need to cover. I find it hard to believe, but one involves a service for Alexa." She paused, and although her voice sounded steady, Lita felt certain that it was a pause to regain composure. "There is a certain . . . protocol that Galahad Control has supplied, but it mostly covers the technical responsibilities. I think it's understood that we will . . ." Here her voice did break a bit, but she quickly recovered. "We will be sure to honor Alexa properly. We owe it to her, and we owe it to the rest of the crew. Lita will forward the details to everyone."

"When will it be?" Channy said quietly.

"First thing in the morning," Triana said. She looked at Lita. "Your department is ready, correct?"

Lita nodded and fought back her own tears. "Yes," was all she could manage to say.

"As the Council Leader, I'll say a few words," Triana said. "But anyone who would like to speak at the ceremony is welcome."

Channy and Lita gave quick nods; Bon remained still.

"But there's another matter that we need to talk about right away," Triana said. "When I sent you the note about this meeting I included a brief summary of the new wormhole that has developed. There's nothing new to add right now; it's there, and it appears to be waiting for us to make some sort of move. Given its location, and the fact that nothing has emerged, I think it's safe to assume that Roc is correct: it's an invitation for us to plunge inside."

"Which we can't possibly do," Gap said. "You're not seriously considering that, are you?"

"No, I'm not," Triana said. "Our mission and our destination are clear. But let's consider a couple of things." She leaned forward and clasped her hands together. "If we simply sail past without doing anything, I would almost guarantee that another wormhole will open up farther down the path. And this time I would guess that something would come out of it."

"So . . ." Channy said. "What are you saying?"

"I'm saying that there is no way I want to take the ship in there, but it doesn't mean we shouldn't explore it."

There were puzzled looks around the table, with the exception of Bon, who stared blankly at Triana. "And how do we do that?" Lita said. "We can't afford to send another Spider. We're already down to seven usable ones. Besides, there wouldn't be time to program one to act independently."

There was silence for a moment before Bon spoke for the first time. "She's not talking about programming a drone to investigate. She's talking about sending someone into the wormhole."

Lita gasped, and turned to the Council Leader. "Tree," she said. "That could very likely be a suicide mission. We can't send someone to do that."

Triana said, "I've already thought about that, and I don't think so. As far as I'm concerned, any race of beings that can create the vultures, and also control space-time like they seem to, could likely take us out by barely lifting a finger. The fact that they're issuing this invitation has to mean that they're basically nonaggressive, and only want to communicate."

"Nonaggressive?" Channy blurted out. "They killed Alexa!"

Triana sighed. "This is hard for me to say, because I feel very responsible for what happened. But . . . the vulture in Sick House had no way of knowing that we were going to release it, which now I believe we should have done in the first place. Instead, it only knew that its companions were being attacked, and it reacted. A case could probably be made that it acted in self-defense."

Lita's face clouded over. "I have to agree. It was calm until we began to sweep the others off the ship. But I still don't think it's a good idea to send someone into that hole. We don't even know if a person could survive the trip."

"If you're looking for volunteers, I'll go," Gap said. "They've studied us as much as we've studied them; they would know if we couldn't survive it. I want to know what they're all about."

"You've already risked your life more than once," Triana said.

"That shouldn't matter. You could also argue that I have more experience than anyone else."

Triana sat back. "I'll think about it. One way or another, I'm convinced that we need to do it." She looked around the table. "Any other thoughts or comments?"

"I'm against it," Lita said. "We're about to bury one crew member; I don't want to bury another so quickly."

"I say go," Gap said. "This might be a fantastic opportunity for us to learn about so much. It's part of why we're on this mission."

"I'm with Lita," Channy said. "I say we fly past it and keep on going."

Triana looked down the length of the table at Bon. "You have the deciding vote," she said.

He returned her stare, but didn't speak for a moment. When he did, his voice was firm. "We didn't run from the fight when they attached themselves to the ship, and we said that we would be aggressive. It cost us."

He looked down at the table before him, and Lita began to feel relief that he had agreed with her. But then he added, "It cost us, but we can't ignore this and think that it will just go away. Someone has to go."

Lita covered her face with one hand. "This makes no sense to me."

"The vote has been taken," Gap said. "How much time do we have to launch?"

"Roc?" Triana said.

The computer chimed in. "We'll have roughly until six o'clock tomorrow evening to launch one of the Spiders. After that, we'll be too far past to rendezvous."

"Okay," Triana said. "I'll make a decision by noon regarding who goes. Let me sleep on things tonight." She looked around the table. "Tomorrow will be the most emotionally draining day of the entire mission so far. I don't think the full impact of Alexa's death has really even hit us yet, but it certainly will in the morning. And yet, as Council members it will be important that we're strong for the rest of the crew.

"If anyone needs to talk tonight, I'll be in my room."

25

The silence lay heavy over the assembled crew, a blanket of sadness and grief that Triana was sure she could physically detect. More than two hundred of her fellow star travelers were gathered in the Spider bay, yet other than scattered sobs, there was no sound. No talking, no whispering. *Galahad's* entire crew, with the exception of those required to run essential tasks, stood silently, most with hands clasped behind their backs, many with heads bowed.

Those who kept their heads up were focused on the table near one of the bay doors, and the shroud-covered body that rested upon it. An occasional cry would slip out from someone, which seemed to prompt similar responses from others, and then the silence would drop again.

Triana stood with Gap, Lita, and Channy next to the podium, which normally was used in the School, but had been brought in and set up on risers, affording everyone a chance to see and hear the service. Triana knew that the entire crew, including those on duty but watching on vidscreens across the ship, would note the one Council member not present. She had called up to the domes and spoken briefly with Bon an hour earlier.

"No, I won't be there," he had said in response to her question. "Attendance is not mandatory, is that right?"

"Well . . . no," she had replied. "If you'd rather not be there, that's your decision. I know . . . I know that you were close to Alexa in ways that the rest of us probably couldn't understand, so I'm sure that many people will be surprised. But I understand that everyone handles grief in their own way. I respect whatever decision you've made."

"I appreciate that," Bon said. "I feel like I've said my good-byes to Alexa, and when the time comes for the funeral, I will honor her memory here in the domes. There's a special . . ." Over the intercom, his voice dropped away; Triana waited quietly, allowing him time to recover.

"There is . . . a special place here in Dome 1, a quiet spot. I'll be there. Alexa would understand."

Now, climbing the stairs of the riser and standing before the assembled crew on the lowest level of the ship, Triana imagined Bon at the highest point, staring up through the panels of the dome out toward the stars.

She pushed the vision out of her mind and walked to the podium, where her workpad contained the notes that she had written for the service. She took a moment to steady herself before addressing the crew.

"Almost one year ago, we left our homes and our families to embark on the greatest voyage our people have ever attempted. Through the tears of separation, and the grief of knowing that we would never see our loved ones again, we came together as a new family. We used our common purpose, our most crucial task, to bind us together and help us overcome the pain we felt at leaving them behind.

"I think Lita put it beautifully in the song that she wrote for all of us: We're reaching for the starlight, but looking back with love."

She looked out across the room. "This morning, as we face the most devastating time of our journey, I would encourage you to embrace those words again. Alexa Wellington embodied everything that *Galahad* truly represents: determination, spirit, and courage. And yet she brought so much more to us. She brought a sense of fun, a feeling of camaraderie that we sometimes neglect, and a reminder that although the mission is difficult and dangerous, it's still a magnificent adventure. We have been blessed with the responsibility of continuing the march of humankind, and Alexa stood out as one of the best representatives we could ever hope for. She touched everyone, and that touch will never be forgotten."

Several crew members broke down in tears, and Triana allowed them a few moments to collect themselves before she went on. "There's not much more that I need to say, because each of you has your own memories of Alexa, and you knew her well enough to realize what she would want from you. She would want you to move on quickly and embrace the future, rather than dwell on the past."

Triana stepped back from the podium. She nodded to Lita, who walked up the steps and unfolded a small piece of paper. Her voice was stronger than Triana thought it would be.

"Alexa once told me that during times of trouble she would go to her Zen place. The first time she told me this, I thought she was probably joking. We all know how much Alexa loved to laugh, and to make others laugh. But she was serious about this. All of us have teachers in our lives, whether they are teachers in school, or people who open our eyes to things that we otherwise would never have considered. Well, Alexa taught me the importance of finding peace, how to build shelter against the storm.

"It's not always easy. There are times when the storm rages so violently that we bow and cringe before it, and forget to create that shelter. There are times when we believe we're drowning in fear, or sadness, or grief, and we struggle, we flail our arms, we kick, we cry out. We forget that the drowning man would be better served by lying still and peacefully floating."

Lita cleared her throat, and Triana knew that her friend had summoned the courage and strength she talked about. She looked out at the assembled crew and saw that they were intently focused on what Lita was saying.

"Alexa and I worked closely together for more than two years. I have never met anyone with a heart more pure, or who loved life the way she did. We each have certain people in our lives who lift our spirits simply by walking into the room, and Alexa was one of those people. Everything you'd ever need to know about her could be seen during the most frightening point in her life. Facing surgery, here on *Galahad* just two months ago, she could have been a wreck, she could have broken down. Instead, it was Alexa who gave *me* strength; she comforted *me* when she knew I would have to operate on her. During her darkest hour, her thoughts were on how to support me. I will never, ever forget that.

"So now, we face a storm of pain and sorrow, and once again Alexa's voice can be heard over the wind: Be strong, be at peace, find . . ." Here, Lita's voice showed the first sign of cracking. She cleared her throat again and continued. "Find the place of calm within you."

There was silence for a moment. Lita looked at Triana, who nodded encouragement.

"I wrote something last night that I would like to sing in Alexa's honor," Lita said. "I thought about the way she taught me, and taught many of us, to be strong in the face of the storm, and the words just seemed to come naturally." She offered a nervous smile. "I'll do my best to get through it, so bear with me. It's called 'Push the Storm Away.'"

Lita walked to the edge of the riser where a keyboard had been set up. She took a seat and closed her eyes for a long time. Then, she began to play, and the soft melody filled the room. When she sang, her voice again was strong and steady.

Seems the grayest morning,
Can never stay for long;
The darkness with its heavy hand
Will fade, and soon be gone.
The magic of your simple smile,
Can keep the clouds at bay;
And then the power of your love
Will push the storm away.

Seems a heavy feeling
Has fought to take control;
It lingers, how it threatens me
And challenges my soul.
I look at you, and realize
That rain won't spoil the day;
Because the power of your love
Can push the storm away.

   Sleep tonight, sleep and find release
   Dream tonight, daylight brings you peace.

Seems that now I've lost you
And find myself alone;
The darkness rushes back at me
In ways I've never known.
But then I feel your inner light
And sunlight finds a way
Your never-ending power of love
Will push the storm away.

I never truly walk alone,
Or fear what comes my way;
Because I know the power of love
Will push the storm away.

The last note of the song hung in the air. Lita pulled her hands from the keys and let out a long breath. She turned to face the crowd; a smile had returned to her face, stained by tears. The other Council members came to her side, and she stood to embrace them. Then together they descended the steps and made their way to the table that held Alexa's body and took up positions on each side. Soft music drifted down from the room's speakers as the rest of the crew began to file past.

All of them paused a moment beside the table, many with their heads bowed; some reached out and laid a hand on the shrouded figure, others murmured a quiet prayer. Then, moving past, they turned to leave the room, with most offering thanks to Triana and Lita for their words, and for the song.

Triana watched their faces, aware that *Galahad*'s first death would likely change the crew in profound ways. It was now official: their innocence was gone.

More than half an hour passed. Triana was not surprised to see that the last person in line to pay her respects was Alexa's roommate, Katarina. She held what resembled flowers; Triana felt another wave of sorrow when she recognized them as colorful blooms that had been collected from the plant life inside the domes.

"Bon asked me to bring these," Katarina said through tears. "He said . . ." She swallowed hard, but couldn't seem to finish the sentence.

Channy broke down and leaned against Gap for support. He crooked an arm around her shoulder and closed his eyes. Lita walked over and hugged Katarina. "It's okay," she said. "Thank you."

Together they placed the bouquet atop the body. Channy sobbed uncontrollably, Gap blinked back tears of his own. A minute later Triana stepped up beside the table and whispered, "Rest in peace, Alexa."

She turned to the others. "It's time."

The five *Galahad* crew members walked slowly away and sealed themselves inside the Spider bay control room. Triana looked out through the glass at the lonely shrouded figure. "Okay, Roc. I think we're ready."

Without a word, the ship's computer began the procedure. The door adjacent to Alexa spread open, and starlight poured through. The icy vacuum of space filled the room. There was one command left to give.

"Let her go," Triana said.

As all five crew members cried, a robotic arm beneath the table lifted Alexa's body and pulled it toward the open door. In moments she was gone.

A single bloom from the bouquet lay on the floor.

26

The posters on her wall once reminded her of home, of the outdoor adventures that she had shared with her dad. Now they seemed more like snapshots from movies that she had never seen, but had been told about. Likewise, her memories felt oddly disconnected, descriptions and details that through the prism of time had lost any personal sensation. It troubled her.

Triana sat at the desk in her room, an hour after Alexa's burial in space, and stared at the Colorado scenes around her bed. She had camped numerous times in Rocky Mountain National Park, hadn't she? She had hiked, rafted, biked, sailed . . . hadn't she? She had grown up with Mount Evans visible through one window of the house, and Pikes Peak through another, right?

During one of her final group lectures, Dr. Armistead had warned the *Galahad* crew that this might very well happen to them. There were a few clinical terms for it, but she personally labeled it "separation resolution." As she explained: "Your mind will eventually combat the grief by detaching itself emotionally from the past; your memories might very well drift from color to black and white, in an emotional sense."

That's what's happening to me, Triana thought. Separation resolution.

Or, she wondered, am I detaching not because of the past . . .
but because of what I'm deciding for my future? It must be easier to leave behind sterile, stock photos than it would be with
sentimental possessions. Could it be premeditated separation
resolution?

Her journal lay open before her. She rubbed the soft leather
cover, then flipped back a few pages and scanned some of the
thoughts she had recorded. Emotions, decisions, questions, ideas,
opinions . . . they leapt from the pages and reminded her that she
was certainly no Ice Queen, as Channy had often branded her.
No, there was indeed a fire that burned inside, melting any ice.

She took up her pen.

To think that this could very well be my final entry is frightening, yet in another sense empowering. I have always
believed that written words carry their own form of energy;
call it inspiration, call it motivation, call it a false sense of
bravado. All I know is that expressing my intentions in writing helps me to trust my instincts.

Two things have led me to decide that I'm the one who
must travel through the wormhole. The first was the feeling
I had while Gap and Mira risked their lives; I never could get
past the feeling that as the leader of this mission, I should be
the one taking those particular risks.

The other is, of course, Alexa's death. Even though she insisted that more study was necessary, ultimately it was my
decision to keep the vulture in Sick House during that final
EVA. That means that ultimately I am responsible for what
happened to Alexa. If there is now a chance to confront the
beings who are behind all of this, it falls to me to take that
chance.

There will be no Council meeting to discuss it; there will
be no conference with Gap to break the news. There will be
no message to the crew. Everyone on this ship has been

trained to do many jobs, and that includes the Council's ability to manage in times of crisis.

The only "person" who can know about this is Roc.

She bit her lip and contemplated adding another line, something that would bring closure . . . whatever that was. But this seemed more fitting.

"Roc," she said. "We need to talk."

Channy walked into the Rec Room, her eyes still puffy and sore. She had cried more in the last two days than she had in years. She felt emotionally drained. And yet her mind now seemed clearer than it had in a long time.

This time Taresh had beaten her to the meeting. He sat perched on the edge of a table, one leg swinging back and forth. They had the room to themselves for the moment.

Channy wasted no time. She walked directly up to him and kissed him on the cheek. Then, pulling away, she returned his smile.

"I won't keep you," she said. "I think we both have to get back to work. But I wanted to say a couple of things to you, if that's all right."

"Of course," he said. "I'm so glad that you wanted to talk. I've felt horrible about our last meeting."

"And so have I," she said. "I acted childishly, and I'm so very sorry about that." She propped up against the table across from him. "All I can say is that I let my emotions get out of control. I care so much about you, Taresh, that I couldn't stand the thought of not being with you.

"But forcing myself on you was foolish. You made a decision, and if I truly care about you, I'll support your decision, regardless of the consequences for me."

Taresh looked genuinely surprised. "Channy . . . I don't know what to say."

"You don't have to say anything. This meeting is really for me to say what I need to say, and then walk away." She smiled at him again. "I love you, Taresh. I would love to be with you, and to have you love me in return. You have things to work out right now, and it's possible that you might change your mind and decide that I'm the one for you. If not, then at least I'll be at peace knowing that I hid nothing from you. I opened my heart to you, and I'm proud of that.

"If the day comes when you realize how rare and precious that is, I hope you'll have the same courage to reach out."

She pushed off the table and faced him. "I said I would get back to you about that hug. Well, I would like one very much."

He grinned, then stood and wrapped his arms around her. She held him tight for a long time, her eyes closed, her heart racing. Then she placed another soft kiss on his cheek and stood back.

"You'll always have a home right here," she said, tapping her chest. Without another word, she turned and left the room.

Lita tapped a stylus pen against her cheek. Sick House was often quiet at this time, so she suspected that the buzz of activity going on around her had been arranged for her benefit. The crew members who worked on this shift, particularly Jada, were kind and thoughtful, and they were doing their part to look after her. Apparently, in their minds, the prescription called for action and noise.

She had put off one particular task that now was unavoidable. The remains of the vulture that had killed Alexa had been put back into the containment box and kept in frigid spacelike conditions. It fell to Lita to perform an alien autopsy, to answer whatever questions had not been answered through standard observation and testing. She dreaded it, but understood that it was her responsibility.

Her intercom flashed an incoming call from Triana.

"How are you holding up?" the Council Leader said.

"Oh, you know. Okay, I guess. It's still hard to believe that it happened. It's obviously tough around here. I don't think I'll touch anything on her desk for a while. I know that might sound odd . . ."

"I don't think it's odd at all," Triana said. "There's no rush to do that."

"Yeah," Lita said. "How are you?"

"About the same. Listen, I take it you haven't started the autopsy yet on the vulture."

"Just about to. Why?"

"I've changed my mind," Triana said. "I don't want you to cut it open. Instead, now that this new wormhole has opened up, I think we should send it back as is."

"Uh . . . okay. You mean . . . propel it out of the ship and into the wormhole?"

"Something like that."

Lita placed the stylus on her desk and sat back. "It's your call, I guess, but . . . well, what happened to wanting to find out more about dark energy conversion? I thought that was a pretty big priority."

"I think this is a better way to go," Triana said. "We still know nothing about the beings that sent the vultures in the first place. Now that this new tunnel has opened up, it's clear they want to communicate with us. I just feel that cutting up one of their creatures is not a good way for us to start a relationship. I would rather send it back in good faith."

"We're sending it back dead. They might not view that as good faith."

"Nothing we can do about that. But they might consider it ten times worse if we sent back a body that had been desecrated. Who knows what kind of social taboo that might be in their world?"

"Well . . . okay. How would you like to do this?"

Triana said, "Just have some of your workers take it down to the Spider bay in the containment box. I'll be down there in a little while, and then Gap and I can figure out the best way to go from there."

"Will do." Lita paused, then said: "Are you sure you're okay?"

"I'm fine. Why do you ask?"

"I don't know, you just sound . . . different. I mean, I know it's been a terrible day, but you sound like you have something else bothering you."

"No," Triana said. "Really, everything's okay. But thanks for asking."

"Okay. I'll take care of things on this end and we'll get the box moved right away." She offered a nervous chuckle. "To be completely truthful, I didn't want to touch that thing anyway."

"I don't blame you," Triana said. "Let me know if you need anything from me. Talk to you later."

Lita snapped off the intercom. She called Jada and gave her the new instructions; then she picked up the stylus and once again began tapping her cheek, deep in thought.

27

Gap had initially gone straight from the funeral to his post in Engineering, but then had taken the lift up to the Control Room. For almost half an hour he had plugged in every bit of data they could get from the new wormhole. It reflected no light whatsoever, and so was not visible on their vidscreen. Instead, a stream of mathematics poured in, with data that both enlightened and puzzled.

He felt a light sweat break out on his forehead and his hands as he realized that sometime within the next seven hours he would likely be launching toward the enigmatic opening. What exactly could he expect when he crossed over?

"Roc," he said. "In some ways it seems very similar to a black hole, wouldn't you say?"

"That's because it's very likely that wormholes are created by black holes, too. The main difference is that a person won't get squished by mind-numbing gravity with this one. At least, it doesn't appear that way. Of course, we really can't know what will happen when a human being shoots through that opening."

"And," Gap said, "the trip would be over as soon as it started, right?"

"Correct," the computer said. "A wormhole, as far as we know, is an immediate connection between two points. Try to imagine drawing a dot on one edge of a piece of paper, and another dot on the other side. The normal route you would take between the points is a long line drawn across the page. But, with the wormhole, we bend space and time; in this case, we would actually *fold* the paper so that the two points are side by side; then a person would just step across."

"The ultimate shortcut," Gap said.

"In more ways than one," Roc said. "If it is truly distorting time *and* space, a person could theoretically go through, and then come back before he left."

"Yeah, I'm trying to wrap my brain around that."

"And remember, we're assuming that our traveler doesn't have his or her atoms stretched out like toothpaste being squeezed out of a tube."

"Well, the vultures seem to have no problem bouncing back and forth," Gap said, peering again at the vidscreen. "That's a pretty good indication that I'll be okay when I pop through."

Roc didn't respond, so Gap turned back to his work. He absentmindedly wiped another bead of sweat from his forehead.

She was on his turf again. It seemed to work out that way most of the time, but Triana realized that in order to talk privately with Bon, it was best accomplished in his office at the Farms. For one thing, they would likely be undisturbed, and given the amount of time he spent here it was one of the few places she could catch him. He took his meals quickly and usually at off-hours, rarely—if ever—visited the Rec Room, and consistently fled Council meetings at the first opportunity. He was a worker, plain and simple.

Triana had resigned herself to the fact that she would always feel like an intruder in his space. She stood across from his desk now and felt the familiar tension in the room, heightened by the recent tragedy. The fact that she had witnessed his final moment with Alexa—the tender kiss good-bye—added an awkward element to their already complex relationship.

And yet, pretending to not know that Bon and Alexa had shared a special connection seemed pointless. She had wondered how best to address it, and settled on a direct comment.

"The bouquet that you sent for Alexa's funeral was beautiful," she said. "Thank you for doing that."

If the Swede was embarrassed, he concealed it well. "I thought it would be appropriate. This was one of her favorite spots." He turned his attention to the workpad on his desk.

Triana watched him, and wondered if perhaps—just perhaps— he was actually hoping to talk about it. When she was troubled, she often turned to her journal as an outlet; for all she knew, Bon had no such outlet. Or, even more likely, Alexa had *been* that outlet, which made all of this even more painful for him.

"I know that you shared a unique connection with her," she said. "We all feel the loss, of course, but it has to be even harder for you. I'm very sorry."

When he didn't react and continued to sift through his workpad, Triana wondered if she had stepped over the line. But then he stopped and returned her gaze.

"I wasn't going to tell you this," he said, "but in her visions, Alexa saw her own death and funeral."

Triana shuddered. She couldn't begin to imagine the fear that Alexa must have carried with her. Her visions had truly turned out to be a curse.

"I didn't take it seriously enough," Bon said. "I will always regret that. In trying to comfort her, I downplayed it, when I could have . . ." His voice trailed off.

Triana felt a wave of compassion overtake her. "Bon, you had no way of knowing how this would turn out. You can't torture yourself that way. We all can be haunted by regrets." She let out a long breath. "I can play the same game of 'what if.' What if I had let you connect with the Cassini, as you requested? What if they had somehow been able to warn us? Could that have saved Alexa's life? We don't know."

She let that settle before continuing. "I do know that you probably brought her more comfort than you realize."

Bon lowered his eyes. "You know me about as well as anyone on this ship could," he said. "But we never addressed what happened in the Spider bay months ago, and I suppose that's because you and I are actually a lot alike. Then you kissed me a few months ago."

His directness startled her. For all of the times that she had debated whether or not to bring it up, if only just to clear the air between them, it stunned her that Bon would be the one to say something. And today, *now,* of all times. The abrupt transition from the talk of Alexa . . .

"When that happened," he continued, "my first thought was that maybe there could be something between us. Well, we both remember what happened when I tried to kiss you back."

"Bon," she said. "That was a difficult—"

"Yes, I know," he said. "It was the wrong time, the wrong place, the wrong everything. But it said to me that I had misread the situation; that I had misread you."

She lowered her head and her voice came out softly. "I'm sorry to have caused so much confusion. I'm not very good when it comes to vulnerable situations."

He grunted. "I told you, we're very much alike." He paused, then said: "I'm not bringing this up to add to the awkward feelings between us. I'm only trying to explain what went on between me and Alexa, since that seems to be what you're interested in at the moment."

It sounded harsh on the surface, but Triana was sure that was unintentional; it was simply Bon's nature to be direct. She looked back up at him, an invitation for him to continue.

"I understand the reputation that I have on this ship. I understand that many people think I'm a jerk, and I'm sorry they feel that way, but it won't make me change who and what I am. The truth is, I simply have a hard time sharing my thoughts and feelings with a lot of people. Some people feel the need to blab every single emotion to anyone in earshot of them; that's not me. But . . ."

Here he paused again. His stare was intense, causing Triana to shift uncomfortably.

"But, if I find the right person, I will open up. If I find the right person, I will share what's inside of me. For a while I thought you might be that person. But with the clumsy way we started off, it never seemed . . . appropriate. And then, Alexa happened along."

Triana fought to keep her eyes on his, but hearing these words was much more painful than she would have guessed. She forced herself to nod in an understanding way.

"Alexa and I had something in common, obviously," he said. "She thought we were freaks, but to me, that wasn't really the common denominator. It wasn't the freakish experiences that we had. It was the fact that those experiences meant that we, more than anyone else, *needed* a real, human connection. We *needed* to connect with someone on a basic level, maybe more than anyone else on this ship. We needed to reassure ourselves that we were still human, that we *weren't* freaks. No one else could understand that."

Triana felt her heart breaking. Through all of the challenges that Bon had shouldered with his Cassini connection, she had never considered that what he needed most of all was a lifeline to his own species. She'd had the opportunity to be that lifeline for him, but had let him down; instead, he had turned to Alexa.

A look of resignation crossed his face. "So you see, I mourn Alexa's death on a more personal level than you realize. Yes, she was my friend, and yes, she was probably one of the most caring, compassionate people on this ship. I mourn her death for those reasons, but I also grieve the loss of the one person who allowed me to remain connected to reality. I think each of us is lucky if we find that person in our life."

Triana let out a long breath. "I'm . . . I'm so very sorry, Bon." There was so much more that she wanted to say, so much more that *needed* to be said, yet with what lay before her, it was all impossible to say now. She had to choke back not only a sob that welled up within her but the words that were crying to come out. "If only," she thought. "If only . . ."

She pulled herself together. "I'm glad that you did find that person, though. And I'm glad that you were that person for her. You gave her a remarkable gift, and I'm sure that she appreciated it."

Bon looked down at his desk. "In some respects that's true. But it also was more complicated than that. I won't deny that I had an affection for her, but it was based on the connection that I told you about. For Alexa, it went deeper, and I . . . well, I wasn't able to return her feelings the way she would have wanted."

He walked around the desk and went over to the large window that looked out over the lush landscape within the dome. "I carry a lot of guilt about that, although I'm sure that I was upfront and honest with Alexa from the beginning. She deserved better. She really did. She went through a lot in her life."

Triana turned to watch him at the window, and leaned up against his desk. "I didn't know that."

He nodded. "Mostly raised by a single mom, until she remarried when Alexa was nine."

"Her mother was divorced?"

Bon said, "No. Alexa's father died before she was born. She never knew him."

It hit Triana like a thunderbolt. She gripped the desk behind her to steady herself. Before she could stop it, she uttered, "Oh, my God." Bon, who had been facing out the window, turned to look at her, a confused look on his face.

"What is it?" he said.

Triana hesitated. "Oh . . . I just . . . didn't know that about her."

He stared at her, and she was convinced that he knew there was more to it than that. But he didn't pursue it, and turned back to the window.

"She talked a lot about that," he said. "She also talked about her relationship with her stepfather, which I guess was difficult because she'd always had her mother all to herself."

Bon kept talking, but Triana barely heard any of it. Her mind was racing through the message she had received from Dr. Zimmer. Was it possible . . . ?

She couldn't know for sure, but even the possibility was cruel. It all made no sense, and seemed so unfair. She suddenly felt the need to scream, to lash out, to walk away from all of the responsibilities of her position, from all of the responsibilities of even being on the mission. Why did these things happen? Why?

She had to get out of here. Now, more than ever, she was sure that she needed to escape. With Bon's back still to her, she fumbled something out of her pocket, placed it on his desk, and walked over to him. He had grown silent, and was again simply staring out the window.

She summoned her courage, walked up to him from behind, and placed her hands on his shoulders. He turned and immediately embraced her. They hugged each other tightly, neither seeming to want to let go. Then, when a kiss would have been the easiest thing for her to do, the most natural . . . she let go and walked away from him. At the door she turned back for just a moment.

"I should have been there for you, Bon. I'm so sorry that I wasn't. I hope that someday you'll forgive me for that."

She quickly left his office. He watched her through the window, bracing himself against the glass. He saw her rush toward the lift, breaking into a run as she moved down the path. Then she was gone.

A minute later he turned back to his desk. He stood behind it and began to once again sort through the items on his workpad. It took him a few moments to notice something on the edge of his desk. He froze when he saw it.

The translator.

28

There wasn't much time. Gap was awaiting her decision, Lita was probably curious about her call to forgo the alien autopsy, and Bon would no doubt be utterly suspicious of her actions.

She briefly considered going back to her room and packing a small bag, but in the end nixed the idea for two reasons. For one thing, the sight of *Galahad*'s Council Leader walking to the Spider bay carrying an overnight bag would draw a lot of attention. This way she was merely performing one of her countless tasks.

But more than anything else she refused to subject herself to the pain. If she insisted that this was just another mission within the mission, that it was temporary, that she would be back soon . . . well, then her mind would be focused on the job at hand. A special trip back to her room meant a sort of good-bye, and she knew that the thought of leaving her connection to home—and, most important, the picture of her father—would torment her, and possibly affect her performance. It was better to simply walk straight to the Spider bay and be gone.

Entering the large hangar, she found three workers from Sick House. They had arrived just minutes earlier, and were discussing where to leave the cart that carried the remains of the vulture inside the containment box. Triana kept her gaze away from the limp, dark mass inside the box while she talked with the crew members.

"Thanks for bringing this down," she said. "Do me a favor while you're here, will you? I think we're going to try to maneuver a bit closer to the wormhole, so would you please load the containment box onto the pod?"

One of the workers, a tall, rangy boy from South America, gave her a puzzled look. "The pod? You mean one of the Spiders?"

Triana shook her head. "No, I don't want us to take any more chances with the few remaining Spiders we have left. We'll use the pod from SAT33 this time around." She pointed to the metallic craft that had been intercepted during their rendezvous with Titan, originally launched by the doomed research scientists aboard an orbiting space station.

What she told the crew members was entirely true; she had no intention of robbing the *Galahad* crew of one of the precious remaining Spiders. When the time came for them to descend to one of the planets in the Eos system, they would need every remaining craft. As it was, they were already shorthanded and would need to improvise when the time came. In her mind, the SAT33 pod was a bonus, but it would do just fine for her purposes.

She was prepared to answer questions about her request, but instead the workers simply shrugged. They gripped the cart holding the containment box and quickly wheeled it over to the pod. After a few minutes of grunting and exertion, with Triana's help they successfully stowed the box within the tight confines of the craft.

"Thanks," she said with a smile. A minute later she was alone in the hangar, and quickly made her way into the control room.

"Okay, Roc, I'm assuming you have plotted everything out?"

"Not only that," the computer said, "I have put together a tour guide that points out some very interesting sights along your way, and put together a tasty little snack bag with your favorite treats. Lots of chocolate, of course."

Despite the butterflies she felt, Triana had to laugh. "I wish. Tell me, I know how much you're able to control our Spiders, but what kind of help can you give me with this pod?"

"Actually, more than you'd think. I've already linked up with the onboard guidance system, and should be able to get you within shouting distance of the wormhole. The final nudge will have to come from you, of course. With your piloting skills it shouldn't be a problem. Besides, it's not like you won't have a visual guide to steer right into."

Triana crossed her arms and leaned against the console of the control room. "I have to be honest, there's something that has been on my mind since I first brought up this idea with you. Not once have I heard you say 'don't do it.'"

"And I'll be honest with you," Roc said. "If I told you that, would it make any difference?"

"Probably not."

"Well, there you go."

"But you'll miss me, right?"

"Do I miss you when you go to sleep at night?"

Triana chuckled again. "Meaning that I'll be back."

"Meaning that you could very well be back yesterday, which freaks out even a sophisticated thinking machine like me. Of course, we don't know anything about the creatures that you're going to meet. They might want to keep you as a pet. What's the matter, Tree? Are we feeling a bit needy right now?"

She stood up and looked through the glass into the hangar. "You're right. Okay, if everything checks out, let's get going."

"Get out of here already."

She grinned, and inwardly thanked Roy Orzini for instilling so much of himself into *Galahad*'s ornery computer. She was about to fling herself into the most frightening and bizarre experience that any human being had ever known, and Roc's creator had programmed a talking computer that actually had her upbeat and laughing.

The walk from the control room to the pod reminded her that just a few hours earlier she had been in this hangar to mourn *Galahad*'s first death. It was not lost on her that she could easily be the second.

She climbed into the pod, secured the hatch, then made her way past the rectangular containment box that held the vulture, past the suspended animation cylinders, to the pilot's seat. Strapping herself in, she established communication with Roc, and then assisted him in going through a preflight check of the pod's systems. It differed from the controls of the Spider, but not so different that she couldn't figure it out quickly. Ideally she would have spent a few hours training, but . . .

"Securing the bay and opening the outer door," Roc said. Triana took her eyes off the instrument panel long enough to look out the forward window at the door sliding open before her. A torrent of starlight streamed in, and she felt her nerves ratchet upward.

"Power is at full standby," Roc said. "Ready for a little ride?"

Triana settled back into her chair and stared at the brilliant palette of stars. "Let's go."

She watched the bay door approaching, slowly at first, then picking up speed. Then, in a flash, she was out.

She realized that she had been holding her breath, and suddenly gasped for air. "Calm," she told herself. "Calm." She focused on the readings flashing onto the display screens, most of which made sense; Roc would understand the rest.

"Closing the bay door, pressurizing the bay," the computer said over the monitor. "Your power is at eighty-eight percent, everything functioning like it should. You know, one thing I didn't consider until now is that you could curl up inside that big cylinder in there and go right to sleep until you pop out the other side of the wormhole."

"You mean in case it hurts, or something?" Triana said. "No thanks, I intend to experience all of it. I am truly going where no human has ever gone before." She chuckled and added, "The other day I told Lita and Channy that I needed to shake up my routine. I guess this qualifies."

"Coming onto course now," Roc said. "Power at ninety-six percent. Approximately seventy minutes until you hit the bull's-eye."

Triana stole another glance out at the stars. "Seventy minutes," she thought, and again concentrated on her breathing.

Midday had come and gone. Gap spent a few minutes in his room, then almost an hour in Engineering, expecting the call from Triana at any time. At one o'clock he casually sauntered into the Dining Hall and immediately scanned the back tables, looking for the Council Leader. She wasn't there.

He was reluctant to page her on the ship's intercom system; if she was deep in thought about the EVA, he didn't want to pressure her or become a pain. It was the reason he avoided going to her room. There was nothing to be gained by appearing too eager.

But he *was* eager. He had scoured every bit of data they had on the wormhole, every bit of information that the ship's computer had on wormhole theory, and he was ready to go. In his heart he knew that it would be safe, that the alien intelligence that had extended the invitation would know what stresses a human being could withstand. And the knowledge waiting on the other side would be . . .

Where was Triana? Was she anguishing over this decision this much? That didn't seem like her. Triana took her responsibilities very seriously, but also had no problem making a decision quickly. It was one of the many traits that he admired about her.

He stepped off the lift into the Control Room, hoping to find her there. A half-dozen crew members went about their business, but Triana was not among them.

Finally, he placed a call to Lita. She had not seen Tree for a couple of hours. "You might try Bon up at the Farms," Lita said before signing off.

Bon. No, that was a call that Gap was in no hurry to make.

He stood at his workstation and once again studied the data.

With just under ten minutes to go, Triana saw it. It was nothing like she expected.

For one thing, it didn't look like a hole at all. It was a jagged tear, a black rip in the fabric of space, a painful wound. Dust swirled around it, painting the opening in a vivid framework, the way a child created a dark outline in a coloring book. It seemed alive, fluctuating, pulsing. Triana tried to place where she had seen something similar, and finally settled on the medical image she had seen of the human heart, the pulsating valves pumping the blood.

Small tremors passed through the pod, not nearly as violent as what accompanied the wormhole's opening and closing. According to Roc, they were likely the winds of space-time that leaked out. The tear was smaller than she had expected, too. Of course, she reminded herself, it didn't need to be large; it was merely a passageway. She could not drag her eyes away from it.

With less than three minutes remaining, she once again made a conscious effort to steady her breathing; she willed her pulse to slow.

What had Alexa called it? Her Zen place. Triana closed her eyes, and her thoughts tumbled out.

Her father, tucking her in at night when she was five, reading not one, but two books to her.

Her father, talking to her when he fell ill. His last days, when she was unable to communicate with him at all.

His death. Her transfer from Colorado to the Galahad training complex in California.

Dr. Zimmer.

The launch. The encounter with the mad stowaway. The narrow escape from death.

Saturn. Titan. The Cassini.

Gap. Bon. Her developing friendship and reliance on Lita.

The Kuiper Belt. The Cassini Code. Merit Simms, and the near mutiny of the crew.

The vultures. Her confrontation with Channy. The wormholes.

Alexa's death. The image of her carefully wrapped body disappearing through the bay door opening, spinning slightly as it rocketed into the cosmos.

Her father.

Bon.

The approaching wormhole.

Alexa's childhood, her stepfather, her real father.

Dr. Zimmer.

The jagged rip in space . . .

Ripples in time . . .

Darkness.

"Thirty seconds," she heard Roc say. She opened her eyes and drank in the spectacle as it closed in. She felt tears on her face, and realized that she had been crying for quite some time.

"Fifteen seconds," Roc said.

She swallowed hard and watched the rip in space envelop the entire window. How could there be no light whatsoever in that forbidding space?

"Dad . . ." she managed to say as the pod penetrated the opening.

Suddenly, light.

She screamed.

29

ap found Lita working at her desk in Sick House. She looked up and said, "Hey, what's up? Did you find Tree?"

"No, I was hoping you'd heard something from her."

Lita shrugged. "She's probably either in her room, or up in the domes. She likes to walk up there and think."

A vision appeared in Gap's mind of Triana walking along the dirt paths of the domes . . . but she was not alone. He pushed the thought away.

Plopping into the chair across from her desk, he picked up a glass cube that Lita kept as a memento. It was filled with a mixture of sand and pebbles taken from the beach near her home in Veracruz, Mexico, a happy reminder of a joyous childhood. He turned it from side to side, watching the sand settle, then shift.

"I love this," he said. "I should have put something like this together before I left home."

"My mom did it," Lita said, eyeing the cube as he rolled it from one hand to the other. "She gave it to me during my last trip home. You have no idea how much it comforts me when I get down."

"And it's fun to play with," Gap said. He placed it back on her desk and rubbed a hand through his hair. "By the way, I didn't get a chance to tell you what a great job you did this morning at the service. You probably hear this all the time, but your singing is beautiful. I know that . . . well, I know that Alexa would have really appreciated the song. It was perfect."

Lita looked down at her desk with a flush of embarrassment on her face. "Thank you. I hope so."

He tapped a finger on his leg nervously, unsure of how much further to go with the discussion. "I didn't know Alexa nearly as well as you," he said. "But I know how close you were, and . . . well, I'm sorry again for what happened."

She offered a soft smile. "You know what I miss about her already? Her devious sense of humor. She really lightened things up around here."

Gap laughed. "How about the time you guys called me when the heating system went down? Alexa was the one firing most of those shots!"

Lita grinned. "I remember. You missed her best material after you shut off the intercom."

After a few moments their laughter faded, and an uneasy silence spread between them. Gap picked up the cube again, then put it back down.

"Listen, there's something I want to ask—"

He was suddenly knocked out of his chair as the ship lurched. He grabbed at the desk as he fell, breaking his fall slightly, and then his gymnastics instincts took over as he rolled onto the floor. A slight shimmy of pain arced through his left shoulder.

Grimacing, he struggled to his knees. Lita had also been thrown from her chair, and lay in a heap a few feet away. Scrambling to her side, he braced her shoulders.

"Lita! Hey, are you okay?"

She groaned, then sat up. "I think so." Rubbing her elbow, she said, "I don't know how many more of those we can take. Can they give us a break here?"

An alarm raced through Gap's mind. "Oh, no."

"What is it?" Lita said.

He didn't answer right away. Instead, he pushed himself to his feet and leaned across her desk. "Roc! I hope that wasn't what I think it was. Not before we had a chance to launch!"

"I have specific instructions to give you at this point," the computer said, with no trace of humor in his voice. "It will require that you gather the Council immediately in the Conference Room. We have a lot to talk about."

Gap and Lita exchanged a look. "What's going on?" Lita said.

Gap slumped back into the chair. "Oh, Tree," he said, burying his face in his hands.

Quit yelling at me. You're just taking your frustrations out on an innocent computer, when you know in your heart that there's not one thing I could have said to Triana to stop her from going. It's not that she's stubborn, she's just . . . Okay, she's stubborn.

However, here's something that you should probably consider: if this wormhole does indeed deposit her into the waiting arms of an advanced alien civilization, can you think of a better representative from Galahad?

See? We've come full circle, back to the brain versus the mind. I understand where your emotions are coming from, but admit it: your intellect is telling you that she was the one who had to go.

Which leads to some extremely important questions. First, what in the world is going to happen to Triana? Have we seen the last of her? And if she does somehow return, will she still be the same Tree?

Then there's the issue of Galahad's Council. With this wildly unexpected turn of events, who takes charge? I can't believe that Dr. Zimmer would have planned on his Council Leader jumping into a borrowed space pod and plunging through a wormhole into either (a) another part of our galaxy, or (b) some parallel universe. Well, maybe he did, but probably not likely. Does Gap automatically assume the reins? Lita? Certainly it couldn't be Bon . . . or could it?

Or maybe someone not currently on the Council would like to throw his or her hat into the ring.

And besides, there's still a lot of space out there. If it's been this heart-stopping so far, what might be lurking beyond the next dust cloud?

Before you get too worked up, try to remember that our intrepid young star travelers still have their intellect, their courage, their training, and me. There, feel better?

One thing that troubles me is that Bon now has complete and total access to the Cassini, whenever he feels like it. Is that a good thing? Is he the type to heed Triana's warnings, or is the pull from Titan's masters just too strong?

I recommend that you make plans to join me for the next dizzying adventure. If you just can't wait, find the nearest wormhole and take a shortcut.

t was actual paper, something that was a rarity on the ship. It measured, in inches, approximately six by nine, but had been folded twice into a compact rectangle. One word—the name Gap—was scrawled along the outside of the paper, in a distinctive style that could have come from only one person aboard *Galahad*. The loop on the final letter was not entirely closed, which made it more than an "r" but just short of a "p"; a casual reader would assume that the writer was in a hurry.

Gap Lee knew that it was simply the way Triana Martell wrote. It wasn't so much impatience on her part, but a conservation of energy. Her version of the letter "b" suffered the same fate, giving the impression of an extended "h." It took some getting used to, but eventually Gap was able to read the scribbles without stumbling too much.

And, because he had scoured this particular note at least twenty times, it was now practically memorized anyway.

He looked at it again, this time under the tight beam of the desk lamp. It was just after midnight, and the rest of the room was dark. His roommate, Daniil, lay motionless in his bed across the room, a very faint snore seeping out from beneath the pillow that covered his head. With a full crew meeting only eight hours away, and having chalked up perhaps a total of six hours of sleep over the past two days, Gap knew that he should be tucked into his own bed. Yet while his eyelids felt heavy, his brain would not shut down.

He exhaled a long, slow breath. How just like Triana to forgo sending an email and instead to scratch out her explanation to Gap by hand. She journaled, like many of the crew members on *Galahad*, but was the only one who did so the old-fashioned way, in a notebook rather than on her workpad. This particular note had been ripped from the binding of a notebook, its rough edges adding a touch that Gap could only describe as personal.

He found that he appreciated the intimate feel, while he detested the message itself. The opening line alone was enough to cause him angst.

> Gap, I know that my decision will likely anger you and the other Council members, but in my opinion there was no time for debate, especially one that would more than likely end in a stalemate.

Of course he was angry. Triana had made one of her "executive decisions" again, a snap judgment that might have proved fatal. The rest of the ship's ruling body, the Council, had expressed a variety of emotions, ranging from disbelief to despair; if they were angry, it wasn't bubbling to the surface yet.

Now, sitting in the dark and staring at the note, Gap pushed aside his personal feelings—feelings that were mostly confused anyway—and tried to focus on the upcoming meeting. More than two hundred crew members were going to be on edge, alarmed that the ship's Council Leader had plunged into a wormhole, nervous that there was little to no information about whether she could even survive the experience. They were desperate for direction; it would be his job to calm them, assure them, and deliver answers.

It was simply a matter of coming up with those answers in the next few hours.

He stood and stretched, casting a quick glance at Daniil, who mumbled something in his sleep and turned to face the wall. Gap leaned over his desk and moved Triana's note into the small circle of light. His eyes darted through the message one more time, then he folded it back into its original shape. He snapped off the light and stumbled to his bed. Draping one arm over his eyes, he tried to block everything from his mind and settle into a relaxed state. Sleep was the most important thing at the moment, and he was sure that he was the only Council member still awake at this time of the night.

He wasn't. Lita Marques had every intention of being asleep by ten, and had planned on an early morning workout in the gym before breakfast and the crew meeting. But now it was past midnight, and she found herself walking into *Galahad's* clinic, usually referred to by the crew as Sick House. It was under her supervision, a role that came naturally to the daughter of a physician.

Walking in the door, she was greeted with surprise by Mathias, an assistant who manned the late shift tonight.

"What are you doing here?" he said, quickly dragging his feet off his desk and sitting upright.

"No, please, put your feet back up," Lita said with a smile. "You know we're very informal here, especially in the dead of night." She walked over to her own desk and plopped down. "And to answer your question . . . I don't know. Couldn't sleep, so decided to maybe work for a bit."

Mathias squinted at her. "You doing okay with everything? I mean . . . with Alexa . . . and Tree. I mean . . ."

"Yeah, I'm fine. Thanks for asking, though." She moved a couple of things around on her desk. "It's just . . . you know, we'll get through it all just fine."

A moment of awkward silence fell between them. Lita continued to shuffle things in front of her, then realized how foolish it looked. She chanced a quick glance toward Mathias and caught his concerned look. "Really," she said.

And then she broke down. Seeming to come from nowhere, a sob burst from her, and she covered her face with her hands. A minute later she felt a presence and lowered her hands to find Mathias kneeling beside her.

"I'm so sorry," he said quietly. "What can I do?"

"There's nothing you can do. But thank you." Suddenly embarrassed, she funneled all of her energy into looking composed and under control. "Really, it's probably just a lack of sleep, and . . . well, you know."

Mathias shook his head. "I don't want to speak out of place, but you don't have to act tough in front of me. We're talking about losing your two best friends within a matter of days. There's no doubt that you need some sleep, but it's more than that. And that's okay, Lita."

She nodded and put a worried smile on her face. "You know what? Sometimes I wish I wasn't on the Council; I think sometimes we're too concerned with being a good example, and we forget to be ourselves."

"Well, you can always be yourself around me," he said, moving from her side and dropping into the chair facing her desk. He picked up a glass cube on her desk, the one filled with sand and tiny pebbles taken from the beach near Lita's home in Veracruz, Mexico. She found that not only did it bring her comfort, it attracted almost everyone who sat at her desk.

Mathias twisted the cube to one side, watching the sand tumble, forming multicolored layers of sediment. "So, I'll be curious to see what Gap says at this meeting," he said, never taking his eyes off the cube. He left the comment floating between them.

"I don't envy Gap right now," Lita said. "We've been through so much in this first year, but especially in the last two weeks." She paused, and stared at her assistant. "I know everyone's curious about what he intends to do, but there's not much I can say right now."

Mathias shrugged and placed the glass cube back on her desk. "I guess a few of us just wondered if he was going to become the new Council Leader."

"He's temporarily in charge. But we don't know for sure what's happened to Triana. She's still the Council Leader."

"Well, yeah, of course," Mathias said. "But . . ." He looked up at her. "I mean, she disappeared into a wormhole. Could she even survive that?"

Lita's first instinct was irritation; Triana had been gone for forty-eight hours, and Mathias seemed to have written her off. And, if so, chances were that he wasn't alone. It was likely, in fact, that when the auditorium filled up in the morning, many of the crew members would be under the assumption that *Galahad*'s leader was dead. It would have been unthinkable only days ago, but . . .

But they had stood in silence to pay their final respects to Alexa just hours before Triana's flight. Now anything seemed possible.

The realization cooled Lita's temper. It wasn't Mathias's fault; he was merely acting upon a natural human emotion. Lita's defense of Triana stemmed from an entirely different, but no less powerful, emotion: loyalty to a friend.

When she finally spoke, her voice was soft. "This crew has learned pretty quickly that when we jump to conclusions, we're usually wrong. I'm sure Gap will do a good job of explaining things, so we know what's going on and what we can look forward to. Let's just wait until the meeting before we assume too much."

Mathias gave a halfhearted nod. "Yeah. Okay." Slowly, a sheepish look crossed his face. "And I'm sorry. Triana's your friend; I shouldn't be saying this stuff. I'm just . . ."

"It's all right," Lita said. "We're all shaken up. Now let me do a little work so I can wear myself out enough to sleep."

Once the clock in her room clicked over to midnight, Channy Oakland climbed out of bed, threw on a pair of shorts and a vivid red T-shirt, woke up the cat who was contorted into a ball on her desk chair, and trudged to the lift at the end of the hall. Two minutes later, carrying Iris over her shoulder like a baby, she peered through the murky light of Dome 1. There was no movement.

Two massive domes topped the starship, housing the Farms and providing a daily bounty which fed the hungry crew of teenagers. Clear panels, set amongst a crisscrossing grid of beams, allowed a spectacular view of the cosmos to shine in, and quickly became a favorite spot for crew quiet time.

It was especially quiet at this late hour. Channy could see a couple of farm workers milling about in the distance, but for the most part Dome 1 was deserted. She took her usual route down a well-trodden path, and deposited Iris near a dense patch of corn stalks. "See you in twenty minutes," she said in a hushed tone to the cat, then, on a whim, retreated toward the main entrance. She turned off the path and made for the Farms' offices.

Her instinct had been right on. Lights burned in Bon's office. She leaned against the doorframe and glanced at the tall boy who stood behind the desk. "Something told me I'd find you here," she said.

Bon Hartsfield glanced up only briefly before turning back to a glowing workpad. "Not unusual for me to be here, day or night,"

he said. "You know that. The question is, what are you doing up
here this late. Wait, let me guess: cat duty."

"Couldn't sleep. Figured I might as well let Iris stretch her
legs."

Bon grunted a reply, but seemed bored by the exchange.
Channy took a couple of steps into the office, her hands in her
back pockets. "How are you doing?"

He looked up at her, but this time his gaze lingered. "Wanna
be more specific?"

She shrugged, then took two more steps toward his desk. "Oh,
you know; Alexa, Triana . . . everything."

He looked back down at his workpad. His shaggy blond hair
draped over his face. "I'm doing fine. Sorry, but I have to check
out a water recycling pump." He walked around his desk toward
the door.

"Mind if I walk along with you?" Channy said. "I have to pick
up Iris in a few minutes anyway."

"Suit yourself," he said without stopping.

His strides were long and quick. She hustled to keep up until
he veered from the path into a thick growth of leafy plants. It was
even darker here; she was happy when Bon flicked on a flashlight,
its tightly focused beam bobbing back and forth before them. The
air was warm and damp, and the heavy vegetation around them
blocked much of the ventilating breeze. Channy felt sweat droplets on her chocolate-toned skin.

"You would have loved Lita's song—"

"Why are you whispering?" he called back to her.

"I don't know, it's very quiet and peaceful in here. All right,
I'll speak up. I said that you would have loved Lita's song for
Alexa at the funeral." When he didn't respond, but instead continued to push ahead through the gloom, she added, "But I understand why you weren't there."

"I'm so glad. It would have wrecked my day if you were upset
with me."

"Okay, Mr. Sarcastic. I'm just trying to talk to you."

"Next subject."

A leafy branch slapped back against Channy's face. "Ouch. Excuse me, is this a race?"

"You wanted to come, I didn't invite you."

They popped out of the heavy growth into a diamond-shaped clearing. Bon stopped quickly, and Channy barely managed to throw on the brakes without plowing into his back. A moment later he was down on one knee. "Here," he said, holding the flashlight out to her. "If you want to tag along, do something helpful. Point this right here."

She trained the light onto the two-foot-tall block that housed a water recycling pump. One of the precious resources on *Galahad*, water was closely monitored and conserved. Every drop was recycled, which meant these particular pumps were crucial under the domes. After a handful of breakdowns early in the mission, they were now checked constantly.

"I guess Gap will try to explain at the meeting what Tree did," Channy said, sitting down on the loosely packed soil. She kept the flashlight trained on the pump, but occasionally shifted her grasp in order to throw a bit of light toward Bon's face. "Although I have to admit, I don't think I'll ever understand why she did it."

She waited for Bon to respond, but he seemed to want nothing to do with the conversation. She added, "Do you think she did the right thing?"

"Keep the light steady right here," he said. For half a minute he toiled in silence, before finally answering her. "It doesn't matter what I think. Triana did what she did, and there's nothing we can do about it."

"Oh, c'mon," Channy said. "I know you like to play it cool, but you have to have an opinion."

Bon wiped sweat and a few strands of hair from his face, then leaned back on his heels and stared at her. "You don't care about my opinion. You're trying to get me to talk about Triana, either because you're upset with her, or because you're trying to get some kind of reaction from me about her. I'm not a fool."

"And neither am I. I don't know why you have to act so tough, Bon, when we both know that you have feelings for her. And, if you ask me, you had feelings for Alexa, too. Did you ever stop to think that it might be good for you to talk about these feelings, rather than keep them bottled up inside all the time?"

"And why should I talk to you?"

"Because I'm the one person on the ship who's not afraid to ask you about it, that's why."

"You're the nosiest, there's no question."

Channy slowly shook her head. "If I didn't think it would help you, I wouldn't ask. I'm not here for me, you know."

"Right."

"I'm not. I just want to help. There were two people on this ship you had feelings for, and they're both gone, just like that. Why do you feel like you have to deal with it by yourself? Are you so macho that you can't—"

"Please put the light back on the recycler."

"Forget the recycler!" Channy said. "Have you even cried yet? I cried my eyes out over Alexa, and I'll probably end up doing the same for Triana if she doesn't come back soon. You won't talk, you won't cry." She paused and leaned toward him, a look of exasperation staining her face. "What's wrong with you?"

He stared back at her with no expression. After a few moments, she tossed the flashlight to the ground, stood up, and stormed off down the path to find Iris.

Bon looked at the flashlight, its beam slicing a crazy angle toward the crops behind him. His breathing became heavy. For a moment he glanced down the path, his eyes blazing. Then, with a shout, he slammed a fist into the plastic covering of the recycling pump, sending a piece of it spinning off into the darkness. It wasn't long before he felt a warm trickle of blood dripping from his hand.

Tor Teen Reader's Guide

About This Guide

The information, activities, and discussion questions that follow are intended to enhance your reading of *The Dark Zone*. Please feel free to adapt these materials to suit your needs and interests.

Writing and Research Activities

I. The Same, Different
   A. Divide a sheet of paper into two columns. Date the right-hand column with today's date and the left-hand column with an earlier date, such as the start of the school year, New Year's Day, or simply one year ago. In the right column, jot down some facts about yourself from appearance (hair color, height, style) to activities (sports, arts, volunteer) to relationships (home address, dynamics between parents and siblings, responsibilities around the house, best friends). Complete the left column, describing the status of your right-column entries on the the earlier date.

B. Write a short essay commenting on the changes (or lack of changes) you observed in the previous exercise. Compare and contrast your observations with those of friends or classmates.

C. In the character of Triana, Bon, Channy, Lita, Gap, Alexa, or Taresh reflecting on his or her almost-year aboard *Galahad,* write a journal entry beginning, "I never expected to change in this way but . . ."

D. A key reason the crew struggles to form a plan to deal with the mysterious vultures is that they cannot understand whether they are biological or technological, primitive or sophisticated, alive or not alive. Imagine you are a crew member aboard *Galahad.* Give a presentation to the Council (portrayed by friends or classmates) explaining the ways you perceive the vultures to be similar to and/or different from human beings, Roc, the Cassini, or other species or technologies of your choice. Employ graphics, models, PowerPoint, or other presentation software.

II. The Brain-Mind Mystery

A. Go to the library or online to learn more about the study of the brain-mind relationship. Create a short report or informational poster, profiling one or more scientists, philosophers, or other scholars (such as René Descartes, John Eccles, Steven Pinker, Geoffrey Hinton, or Daniel Dennett) who has commented on this topic.

B. Another dichotomy stemming from the brain-mind question is the issue of logic versus emotion. This is particularly notable in Channy's handling of her feelings for Taresh. Write a short essay describing a situation in which your "heart interfered with your head," like Channy's. Or, comment on a favorite literary character who struggles with this problem, the outcome of the situation, and any advice you might give to this character.

C. Create a musical composition, sculpture, collage, dance, poem, or other artistic work depicting elements of the brain-mind mystery or the struggles that it can cause for teenagers.

III. Dark and Light

A. You are the *Galahad* crew member assigned to plan the funeral service for Alexa. Write an outline of the events, speakers, and other elements of this service. As you plan, consider the possibility that this may not be the last death aboard *Galahad* and that you are in some ways responsible for beginning a new tradition of grieving.

B. The designers of *Galahad* saw that relaxing in the naturalistic domes would be a popular unwinding activity for the crew. Use watercolors, chalk, or other visual arts media to create a picture of this place—with or without a threatening vulture attached to the outside. Write a poem or song celebrating the pleasure of the domes and/ or about how the arrival of the vultures has disturbed this peaceful place.

C. Go to the library or online to learn more about dark energy, wormholes, or black holes. On a large sheet of paper, create an illustrated Fascinating Facts list based on your research to share with friends or classmates.

D. With a friend or classmate, role-play a conversation in which Roc and Triana debate her decision to travel into the wormhole, using information from exercise III.C, above, if desired. In the character of Triana, write a single paragraph beginning, "The most important reason I have decided to leave *Galahad* for the wormhole is . . ."

E. Similar to the beginning of this book, write Roc's introduction to the *next* Galahad novel, explaining how

Bon, Gap, Channy, and Lita reacted when they realized what Triana had done, and hinting at whether (and possibly how) the Council Leader will return to the ship.

Questions for Discussion

1. In the preface to *The Dark Zone,* supercomputer Roc poses the question, "What exactly is the difference between the brain and the mind?" How would you answer this question? If you were aboard *Galahad,* do you think you would interact with Roc in the same way as Triana or Gap? Explain your answer in terms of your sense of "brain" and "mind."

2. What is important and unique about the opening scene of *The Dark Zone?* Over the course of the novel, do you think Alexa makes the right choices about sharing her "dreams"? Do you see any similarities between Alexa's handling of her dream crisis with Channy's handling of her romantic troubles? Explain your answer.

3. What challenges does the crew face, both emotionally and technologically, as *Galahad* enters its eleventh month of space travel? Have you ever faced comparable challenges in the life of your family, school, or community? Describe the similarities you perceive and the solutions you or others employed.

4. In chapter 2, Taresh comments that "The path that we've all taken is a part of who we are. How can you appreciate what you have if you have nothing to compare it to?" While he is referring to historical events, how does Taresh take this belief to the personal level? Do you think he is right? What guidance might you offer Taresh in terms of his relationship with Channy?

5. Compare and contrast Taresh's thoughts about honoring his ancestry with Triana's connection to memories of her father and Dr. Zimmer. Can one character be right and the other wrong about the connection between their pasts and present-day decision making? Explain your answer.

6. Why does Triana initially decide not to warn the crew about the vultures? In what other instances in the novel does she choose to share limited information about this situation and related events? How might you relate these decisions to the tension between brain and mind?

7. Throughout the story, which characters struggle with relationships in which they feel romantic attraction and those in which they feel connected in other ways? How does Channy's "Dating Game" offer a window into these differences? How would you describe the value of these different types of relationships?

8. Describe the impact of Alexa's death on Triana, Gap, Channy, Lita, and Bon. For whom do you think this death has been the greatest loss? How has Alexa's death changed some Council members' sense of their roles and their outlook on the *Galahad* mission?

9. Early in the novel, Triana notes that "Every horror movie fan knew that the terror didn't come when the monster jumped out at you; no, the real panic lurked in the shadows, torturing you with what *might* be there." Do you agree? Does this apply only to the vultures or to the entire *Galahad* mission? And if so, how can the crew survive the journey to Eos emotionally?

10. As the story draws to a close, what opinions have you formed about the vultures? Do you think they are connected to other galactic life forms? Are the vultures friend, foe, or something

else? Do you support Triana's decision to tell Lita not to autopsy the dead vulture and instead to send it back through the wormhole intact?

11. In chapter 27, Bon explains his relationship with Alexa to Triana. "It wasn't the freakish experiences that we had. It was the fact that those experiences meant that we, more than anyone else . . . *needed* to connect with someone on a basic level, maybe more than anyone else on this ship. We needed to reassure ourselves that we were still human, that we *weren't* freaks." Why might Triana be particularly able to understand Bon's words? How might Bon's feelings be relevant to kids who have exceptional intellect, unusual talents, or even unique experiences? How might Bon's notion make sense for all human beings?

12. Has Triana made the right decision to venture into the wormhole? How might her emotional state have affected her decision? Can a rational argument be made for her actions? Do you think a crew member venturing into the wormhole is the best "next step" for *Galahad*? Do you think Triana will find her way back to *Galahad*? Explain your answers.

About the Author

DOM TESTA is an author, speaker, and the top-rated morning radio show host in Denver, Colorado. His nonprofit foundation, The Big Brain Club, empowers students to take charge of their education. Visit him online at www.domtesta.com.

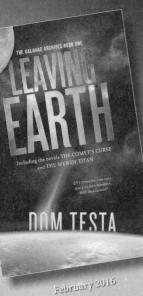